Waking Raphael

By the same author

Bombay Ice
Fish, Blood and Bone
A Table in Tuscany
A Table in Provence
Remarkable Feasts
The Indian Spice Trail

Waking Raphael

Leslie Forbes

WEIDENFELD & NICOLSON
LONDON

First published in Great Britain in 2003
by Weidenfeld & Nicolson

A CIP catalogue record for this book
is available from the British Library.

ISBN 0 297 82984 X

Typeset by Deltatype Ltd, Birkenhead, Merseyside

Printed in Great Britain by Clays Ltd, St Ives plc

Weidenfeld & Nicolson

The Orion Publishing Group Ltd
Orion House
5 Upper Saint Martin's Lane
London, WC2H 9EA

To Andrew, as always,
for giving me a wider sense of perspective,
and to Maya, the oracle.

Several months ago in a Warsaw gallery, two Polish politicians vandalised Maurizio Cattelan's life-size wax artwork of the Pope pole-axed by a meteorite, which they took to be anti-Catholic art. Even though they were restrained by attendants, it was too late to save the Pope from losing the bottom half of his leg.

Tate magazine, Autumn 2001

No., was the answer, after some little hesitation, no, I did not know what the poor man was required to say, in order to be pardoned, but would have recognised it at once, yes, at a glance, if I had seen it.

As the Story was Told, Samuel Beckett

MIRACLE NUMBER 1

A Galilean Transformation

'You see how he glances furtively over one shoulder, as if . . . as if he were escaping from the scene of a crime.' It was Charlotte's first rehearsal to camera, and the unforgiving television lights revealed her to be more nervous than the young man in the portrait she was describing. 'But is he the perpetrator of the crime or just a witness?' she went on. 'I believe the artist wants us to ask such questions, feel ourselves part of the plot. The picture, you see, represents a window into another space and time – in this case the fifteenth century. Everything in the painting is designed to reinforce the fiction that this young man, with one hand apparently on the picture frame, is about to vault from his world into ours.'

'To me he looks like Paolo,' said Donna. 'The same sexy mouth.'

Ignoring the girl, Charlotte continued, 'Another example of this arresting device is Raphael's portrait of *La Muta*, the "silent" or "mute" woman, a title acknowledging that she could, if she wished, speak to us of what she has seen, cross the boundary of the picture plane and – '

'Give each of us fair warning when our time is up,' finished one of the Italians on the film crew, tapping his watch. 'Lunchtime, in *this* case!'

For Muta, the first warning came in the shape of a wolf. The mute woman was near the ruined bell tower picking dandelion leaves for her lunch when an old thin wolf loped into San Rocco, a wolf who must be desperate or sick to come so close in broad daylight. Years ago Muta had seen wolves dancing together like gawky young partners at their first country fair, but this wolf was long past dancing. The animal stopped in the shade of the tower only metres from her, its tongue lolling dry between black stretched lips. The weary eyes cleared and widened as they caught sight of Muta and she saw the tongue curl back like a chameleon's and the jaws snap shut in a spray of bloody froth.

So they took each other in, the last survivors of what the world had been. Muta was close enough to see the clawmarks raked across the wolf's hindquarters and the ragged furrow ploughed by a bullet down its flank. One ear was ripped almost in half and flapped like the sail of a broken windmill with every heave of the creature's lungs. When some distant sound brought what was left of its torn ears to attention, Muta followed the old wolf's gaze and saw a pack of dogs appear on the horizon from the direction of the Villa Rosa. Too worn out to run far, the wolf swung its wedge of grizzled head, scanning the ruined hamlet for shelter, and before she could do anything it had made a dash for the bell tower, passing not more than an arm's length from where Muta stood.

She had to watch its fall. One of the weak places in her cellar's roof gave way and she stood to watch the wolf falling, kicking, scratching, its black-rimmed yellow eyes fixed on her, neither asking for help nor expecting it. Muta knew how that was.

The pack was closer now. In the lead was a long-legged veteran who had lost an eye and half his jaw three winters back defending his master from a wounded boar. Muta had seen that same dog take on a viper as thick in the middle as the dog's own head and grip that snake and shake it straight as a walking-stick. That dog would track the devil into Hades and back, Muta knew, and she knew too that the pack it led didn't hunt alone; the men must be close.

She turned to run for her cellar, but the wolf was there,

wounded or dead, and even a dead wolf could give away her secrets, and so as the pack of baying dogs streamed over the ruined vineyards towards San Rocco she acted against her instinct to hide, and ran not away from the pack but towards it, back and forth across the wolf's trail, her own rank underground smell disguising the wolf's as she waved her arms in their flapping dead men's clothes at the half-wild dogs, some of them even wilder from an earlier kill. When that failed to scatter them she threw stones, handfuls of turf, firewood. As the old one-eyed boarhound leapt up and caught a branch mid-air, snapping it in two with his misshapen jaws, Muta saw the hunters not far behind, approaching on foot. Her need to escape grew desperate. She kicked dirt in the dogs' faces, raged silently at them, turning her own face into a snarl and her hands into claws. Offended by the strange half-human's unwarranted attack, the dogs split from a pack into individuals and, wagging their tails in puzzlement, drew away from the mixed-up smell of woman and wolf to flow together on the far side of San Rocco.

Their masters were still some way off when Muta identified the man in front, a face she recognised, even now. She thought: Will he know me? Why has he come back after so long? Then she bolted, up towards the old road and all the other walking ghosts.

'Did you see that?' one of the hunters said.

The older man in the lead, closely watching the woman's progress up the steep hill, replied, 'You think she's living at San Rocco, Lorenzi?' The interrogator was a big, beefy animal in his early seventies, but fit, buffed up, expensively maintained, with a tone of voice that implied an infestation of vermin on his private property, vermin he had paid heavily to be rid of. He looked like someone who expected value for his money and had plenty of people willing to beat it out of you.

'I doubt it,' answered Lorenzi. 'She's more likely got a den up there where she joined the old German road. Those hills are riddled with caves, as you know.'

The older man leaned over to peer at something. 'She's lost a shoe.'

'Looks like a museum piece, something left over from the war.'

'Something left over from the War . . .' He picked up the shoe by its laces and shifted his pouchy, well-fed eyes to the hill where the running figure had disappeared. 'What's that scar-faced dog of Procopio's called? Baldassare? You told me he'd track anything?'

'Almost anything . . .'

But when they tried to catch Baldassare he refused to be caught. He stood back and looked at them and pulled the unscarred side of his face into a snarl to match the one given by the boar, then lit out on his own towards home.

'There goes our best dog,' said Lorenzi. 'Now what?'

Charlotte Penton, walking alone on one of the unmade-up tracks that circled and criss-crossed this tightly folded part of Italy like interlaced cobwebs, was contemplating the view from the crest of the hill back towards the Villa Rosa, the idyllic hotel where two hours earlier she had treated herself to a solitary and very expensive lunch. It was her first proper day off in six weeks, and with her restoration of the Raphael portrait nearing completion, Charlotte had vowed to allow herself a few treats before returning to London. There, as the result of her recent divorce, the solitude would be of a different, less voluntary kind.

She took a deep breath, enjoying the warm, sweet, afternoon air. Off to her right was a scene possessing all the orderly grace of a Raphael. In the foreground a corridor of painterly trees, groomed and plumed as feather dusters, led in a direct line of perspective up the hard white drive to the hotel gates, and beyond that to the spires and pantiled roofs of Urbino, rose-pink against the mauve of even more distant hill-towns. The light – that splendid, golden Italian light which softened the edges of objects while at the same time mysteriously making them clearer and more resonant – filled Charlotte up like a rich, heavy wine. She thought: I will always know this place; I have *already* known it. For as a student in Florence she had admired these same hills and castles in a portrait of Urbino's greatest ruler, Federigo da Montefeltro, so that even before coming here she had known this as a landscape she could love.

To her left was an equally familiar but altogether wilder view, of foothills rising steeply into the Apennines, only the odd ruined building holding back the encroaching woods and brush. It resembled the more grisly paintings she restored, early Flemish and German works of martyrs and crucifixions devoid of human optimism, their plunging chasms and savage torrents coded warnings for a violent or tragic life.

She thought of the hill she was traversing as the spine of a decision neatly splitting the country into before and after, either-or. As she mentally tossed a coin (ruins or civilisation: which should she choose?), her attention was drawn to the only movement in that divided landscape, a raggedy flapping figure running fast out of thick woods on the uncultivated side of the hill. About two kilometres away, perhaps less, the figure was barely identifiable as human, and what humanity it had was contradicted by the pack of dogs that appeared out of the same woods a few moments later. Straining against long leads, they dragged behind them five hunters with guns protruding stiffly from their silhouettes like the broomstick arms of scarecrows.

The baying of the dogs carried across the valley on an updraught of wind, so faintly that it seemed unconnected to the scene below. Charlotte at first imagined she was watching an Italian version of the mock hunts that took place near her parents' home in England, where the trail for the pack was laid by a sprinting man rather than a fox. But as the gap between the hunters and their prey closed, she saw the runner's movements become jerky, more inhuman; they conveyed a sense of urgency that negated any suggestion of play. The wedge of russet-coloured dogs and the hunters in loden green and brown were moving forward relentlessly, like part of the forest shifting itself, or a natural upheaval of the unforgiving earth.

Was it human or not, that solitary runner? Late afternoon sun flared in Charlotte's eyes, reducing the figures below to inksplashes drawn across a canvas landscape.

Were there still such things as manhunts with dogs? It didn't seem possible, not in 1993. Charlotte, accustomed to viewing herself as a spectator with little influence (except *after* the fact, where the damage was already done – a restorer, a patcher-up), took several minutes to react. Even as she began to push her way downhill through the rough brush, and then, absurdly, to run, she had no faith in what she was seeing or doing. She was too far away to make any difference, and with her ungainly progress matched as if in a mirror by the awkward gait of the other runner, Charlotte felt she was watching herself lose a race that had been lost already, an artist's painted drama in which the lucid geometry was fixed, pre-ordained.

The figure stumbled and rolled over the edge of a steep incline, momentarily out of sight. Three of the hunters broke into a run and, urging their animals on, the men mingled their own cries with the dogs' baying until it was hard to tell the difference between man and beast. Charlotte was spurred to call out – '*Stop! Basta! Enough!*' – words tossed back to her by the wind as if to emphasise the futility of her protest.

The pack reached the steep slope where the runner had fallen and pulled up sharply at the edge of the drop. Silent now, the dogs cast back and forth, tangling their leads into spaghetti. Two of them leapt off the bluff to be hung up yelping on the underbrush as the men tried with difficulty to unleash them.

Then all five hunters and their dogs scrambled over the edge and disappeared into the scrub.

Charlotte slowed to a walk and stared down into the valley, blinking her eyes rapidly as she waited for the hunters to reappear. She noticed the liquid sparkle of what might be a stream among the looming rocks and brush into which the hunt had vanished.

Five minutes passed. Ten. Her distance from whatever

narrative had taken place below reduced it to a nagging memory, remote as childhood. She thought of her soldier-father's delight in hunting. How she'd hated being sent to fetch something from their freezer, a frozen zoo of hooves and beaks!

Another minute and Charlotte made up her mind that her first impression of the hunt must have been mistaken. What I saw, she insisted to her inner jury, what I saw was no more than another group of Italians after a boar or stag. Easy to attribute her blurred 'vision' to all the close, precise work she'd been doing on the Raphael portrait, especially as in these last weeks her eyesight had been playing tricks on her. Late at night she would imagine the painted woman's finger tapping, the stubbornly mute mouth trembling with an urge to speak.

Then there was the weather, unusually hot for October. I should have brought water, Charlotte thought, turning back towards the safety of the Villa Rosa, I probably had too much wine at lunch.

On the same ridge about a kilometre further down the path from Charlotte was a scientist, home for a short visit after many years away. Professor Serafini of the Italian Committee for Investigation of Claims of the Paranormal had a viewpoint almost identical to hers, he was looking at the same field – yet saw nothing. Neither the hunters, nor their prey. Hearing Charlotte's story some weeks later, he would inform her that it was mathematically impossible to see what she claimed to have seen from her position at that time of day. On the back of an envelope he drew a diagram of the two hillsides, the angle of the sun's rays in relation to the deep valley and the fields between the San Rocco ridge and hers. Very precise, with dotted lines and angles marked a, b, c, etc. He said something like, 'With *origin* (you, Charlotte) at O and coordinates x, y, z,' and mentioned the Lorentz transformations, a set of equations for transforming the position and motion parameters from a frame of reference, 'which replaced the Galilean transformations'.

Charlotte didn't really understand the finer details of Serafini's explanation, but by then it didn't matter to her; she didn't need mathematical proof of what she had seen and turned away from in favour of the Villa Rosa. Nevertheless, she kept Serafini's envelope as a reminder of the limits of science, tucked into her old Raphael notebook next to the postcard of a cartoon by Goya whose caption seemed to sum up her experience: *The Sleep of Reason Produces Monsters.*

MIRACLE NUMBER 2

To See the Wolf

Muta waited until sunset to ensure that the hunters hadn't followed her upstream, then made a long detour, miles out of her way, before doubling back towards San Rocco hours later. She felt safe enough, despite the sullen glow from a huge red hunter's moon, until she was passing the concrete pens where the pigs were slaughtered. Then less safe. An itch started between her shoulderblades, a cold bristling up her neck, and about the same time she noticed the lights on, shining yellow when by this hour the only lights should be a pale fluorescent blue. The slaughter should be over for today. She crept forward into the scrubby cover above a pen where the pigs were massed in one corner, pressed closely together away from another slab of squealing raw pink flesh that seemed to spread or to *be* spread over their gate.

Silhouetted against the yellow light that should not have been on, there were men, shadowy and unrecognisable except for one, much older than the others, who stood apart and watched while the others stretched out something naked and boneless as a flayed hide not yet stripped.

Muta had time to recognise again this *thing* of her dark imaginings and as she saw the big skinning knife come out she knew it was all starting again and she began to back away on hands and knees through the broom and spiky juniper and over the tough cushions of wild thyme. Her palms were bleeding when she stood up at last, but the image of his face was still clear, confirming her suspicions that the killers were gathering again the way crows had been lately over Urbino's double hills (double-crossing hills, the mayor would say).

She made her way home on the old goat track through the scarecrow trees. At San Rocco she lit a branch of firewood, its flickering light guiding her over the fallen rooftiles of what had once been a kitchen into the shadows where the trap-door to her cellar was concealed. Twice she pushed her fingers under the moss that screened its door, her heart beating hard, and pulled them back, recalling the danger of a sick or cornered wolf, lessons taught by her father in the years when these mountains were full of wolves. She touched the knife in her belt, and, taking strength from the torch and the blade, finally heaved the door open and stood back.

When nothing happened, Muta cautiously moved round to where the ladder from below met the upper ground, inhaling the powerful smell of blood and wild animal urine. A real wolf, this time, although her inner demons often hit her with such force that she would drop unconscious and wake with a bruised skull, a twisted shoulder. She pulled the knife out and held the torch well in front. Pine resin caught in the flaming branch and for an instant a pair of yellow circles pierced the darkness at the base of the ladder like sparks cast from the resinous flames. Then the eyes flew towards Muta and the bloodied bristles on the wolf's jaws pumiced her face as it knocked her to the ground. She lunged out with the knife and the wolf grabbed her wrist the way the scarred old boarhound had grabbed the firewood, and she dropped the knife, waiting for the shake that would snap her wrist. The wolf's teeth pierced her skin, she felt its erring spirit pass into her, over her. Then she was free. The wolf was gone.

She picked up the knife again and climbed down the ladder into her cellar. The newspapers lining her walls from floor to ceiling were hanging in strips of half-words and fractured sentences where the wolf had torn its paws open scratching to escape. Blood had soaked into a rug, there was a new fall of earth from the ceiling, a toppled cupboard. None of her food was gone, though, not even the trout hanging up to smoke, and the water barrel hadn't been touched. Maybe the wolf was too frightened to eat and drink, or too sick. A fear of water, Muta remembered, was a sign of raging sickness.

MIRACLE NUMBER 3

A Doubting Finger

'Hey Primo, you ever tell anybody what you think happened at San Rocco?' asked the bartender at Urbino's Bar Raffaello. He poured a second grappa for his friend Primo the mayor, who had come in to buy a weekly lottery ticket, one of his few nods in the direction of improbable faith. A former Communist converted to cynicism by his old party's failure to ignite the Italian workers, the mayor had been even more cynical since 1991, when the Italian Communist party split in two and he was persuaded to join the non-Communist-but-still-vaguely-leftish half, the PDS or Partito Democratico della Sinistra. 'A better balanced party,' his wife had consoled him, to which he'd responded, 'Better balanced, certainly, with a testicle on each side of the fence.'

'Why, what happened at San Rocco, Franco?' he asked now.

'Ah, Primo, don't be like that. You can trust me.'

'You mean what happened a week ago at the pig farm?'

'Nah, everyone can figure that. Guy like Domenico Montagna who works for the consortium, guy with a past who drinks too much, talks too much – an accident's bound to happen upon him sooner or later. I'm talking about, you know, what happened *years* ago.'

'My wife. I told my wife.'

'Sure, your *wife*, everybody tells his wife . . . nobody else?'

'You know anyone who likes people who speak up, Franco, who *make a fuss*? The meek shall inherit the earth, after all, isn't that enough for them?' Primo, who knew the perpendicular nature of this region, how barren some of the dirt was around here, saw this promised inheritance as the Old Man having the last laugh: Here you go, you meek and mild, the dust and stones are all *yours*! 'Judgement Day may be a long time coming, they're gonna to have to wait,' Primo added, 'but what *more* could they possibly want?'

Franco poured them each another grappa. 'You think maybe it's different anywhere else?'

'What do I know, a guy who's never been out of Italy.'

'Me neither, except that one visit I made to Lourdes with my dead wife, may she rest in peace like she never did in life. But my brother Beppo who moved to Chicago, he's always saying – '

'Don't give me one of Beppo's Great Sayings, Franco. It's too early.'

'All I'm saying – '

'Now it's *you* who's saying?'

'All I'm saying is things can change, can't they, Primo? Like the Renaissance, for instance? I mean, when you – '

'Like the *Renaissance*, he says. For *instance*, he says. You think the likes of you and me can change the world, Franco?'

'Maybe not the world, but – '

'Why, you've barely changed this *bar* since you took it over thirty years ago from your late not-so-lamented wife's widowed aunt. God help us if you ever change a thing barring the radio station! Anyway, some things are best left alone, things you can't change, like what happened at San Rocco. You think about San Rocco too much, Franco, and you'll think yourself into a state of disillusioment with the whole human race.'

Charlotte Penton, trying and failing to concentrate on a letter to her ex-husband, felt no guilt about eavesdropping on the two Italians. These days she seemed to live most of her life through other people's eyes and ears. And if few people in Urbino realised how well she understood their language, even after six weeks of hearing her speak it, whose fault was that?

Perhaps I have become inaudible, she thought, invisible, at least to men, pruned and thinned out by my divorce from John to the twigginess desirable only in very young women. She'd like to be different. Just for a day she'd like to be the kind of person who could lie easily; she'd like to write, 'Italy has done wonders for my love life, John! I never realised sex could be like this!' More exclamation marks in her life, that's what she needed, but she contented herself with scribbling a few bland words about her progress in restoring the Raphael portrait and a brief commendation of her young assistants, Paolo and Anna, the local restorers who had already been working on the painting before her arrival.

'Paolo is a sweet boy who has a deep knowledge of the latest scientific developments in our field,' she wrote. Then added, with a sense of mischief: 'He is also very attractive and quite a rake – like Piero di Cosimo's wistful young satyr in the National Gallery.' Although she had no hope of inspiring jealousy in John these days, she was proud of herself for that last sentence. Perhaps its teasing spirit was the influence of this café next to the house where Raphael was born. She often came to read or write here in the Bar Raffaello, appreciating it for everything that in England would have made her hate it: the radio permanently tuned to Italian sports, the framed football shirts and ancient banners on the walls, the old ladies in blue-flowered housecoats who pushed through the beaded curtains every morning to read the local papers and exclaim with pleasurable dismay over the obituaries of friends and rivals.

The raffish little place was empty now apart from the bartender and his friend the mayor, which might be why their discussion kept breaking through her concentration, the words 'San Rocco' tolling in her ears with the insistence of a distant church bell. She'd heard of San Rocco before, Charlotte was thinking, as she collected her things to go; but where? Why did the name make her feel uneasy?

Primo watched the English woman leave, admiring her tall, slender figure – maybe a little bony for his taste, but he liked those startled blue eyes of hers that made you want to protect her. He liked, as well, her wide mouth and the milk-and-roses complexion that no Italian woman of her age would have. Then again, most Italian women of her age and class would dress sexier, make more of their looks.

'I tell you about that wolf at San Rocco last week?' asked Franco, not leaving the subject well enough alone. 'Wolf just vanished into thin air and left a woman in its place.'

'Another one of your miracles?'

'It's the truth I'm telling you! Guy I know took some hunters up that valley, told me this crazy gypsy woman sprang up out of nowhere, even scared that one-eyed boarhound of Procopio's – '

'Procopio was there?'

'He loaned them the dog – '

'Never! That old one-eyed dog? Procopio wouldn't loan Baldassarre out to *anyone*! That dog is the greatest all-round hunter and truffler he's ever owned! Why, that dog saved his life!'

'I know that, Primo, you think I don't know that? But one of these hunters was some big VIP Procopio owed a favour or something . . .'

'Oh, a *favour*.' Years in politics had given Primo a precise notion of where favours could land you. 'Must've been some *big* favour he owed . . .'

'You know Procopio's history.' From the shelf above his bar Franco took down one of the cups his local football team had won over the years. Polishing the electroplated gold with his cuff, he read his brother's name again. Maybe he should've followed Beppo to Chicago, like Beppo was always saying. Get away from this country to where the problems didn't smell so old and rotten when you turned them over. 'Anyway,' Franco said, 'makes you think, right?'

'Only thing it makes me think is these hunters made a mistake. No one except ghosts hangs around San Rocco. Not even gypsies. Why would they? Sure, the map still reads Località San Rocco, but you know – *everyone* knows – there's no real locality there any more, not since the war.' No location there, Primo thought, only *dis*location. Even here in Urbino there were no straight roads to the truth, while out there in the foothills beyond the city it was all ups and downs and dead ends and dying, dead mountain settlements, a home for wolves and vipers – and porcupines, decimators of the native iris rhizomes, which those spiky dinosaurs dug up with their leathery mitts like the hands of ancient *plongeurs*. As for the wild boar, they were always rootling out truffles and other mouldering, underground things. Primo had seen a few of those things himself, some he never wanted to see again, and these days he preferred to widen his horizons beyond places like San Rocco. He had a line worked out at various bars round Urbino, about Italy's long-standing political rot being just part and parcel of an inexorable cycle of ruin, renaissance and risorgimento: 'Reborn in the fifteenth century, resurrected from the ashes of the nineteenth and in a state of restoration ever since.' Catch him on his fourth grappa and he'd joke about how this phoenix nation he loved contained within its narrow boot such miraculous relics as the incorruptible tongue of Saint Anthony, the last breath of Saint Agatha, the gridiron on which St Lawrence was barbecued over a slow fire, the finger that Doubting Thomas poked into the side of the living Jesus after His Resurrection. ('It's true,' Franco had claimed last year. 'I saw it with my own eyes! The very finger! At Sante Croce in Rome!') And enough Feathers from the Wings of the Archangel Gabriel to make you awestruck by the sheer *scale* of angels.

'Yes,' said Primo, 'when Lucifer was hurled from Paradise and stood, a stranger in this breathing world, there must've been a helluva crash, Franco. He must have left his mark.'

'And you know where he left it, right, Primo?'

What Primo knew was that to reveal the truth about San Rocco now would take a miracle and a miracle-worker – and he didn't believe in miracles any more, not even economic miracles.

MIRACLE NUMBER 4

A Dream Recovered

'*Madonna!*'

Count Malaspino was speaking more to himself than to the girl who stood perfectly naked in front of him. Perfect in every detail she seemed, yet to look at them (the older man fully clothed, the girl balancing on a footstool while he squeezed and moulded her flesh with his hands), you'd think he was sculpting her out of clay, altering her silhouette to suit a more stringent concept of perfection.

Then again, maybe he'd said, 'Ma donna!' thought the young Canadian, or 'ma Donna'. Three generations removed from her Italian roots, Donna Ricco's grasp of the language didn't extend much beyond knowing that her Christian name meant 'lady' or 'woman'.

'The face of a Caravaggio,' murmured the Count, 'no, a Raphael.'

'Ava Gardner, my dad says.'

Count Malaspino frowned slightly at her comment and pressed close behind to slip his right hand under her left breast, as if he were about to lift her by it from the footstool to another, more stable pedestal. 'Do this,' he said, and dutifully she cupped her breast, keeping her hand there while he stepped aside to examine his arrangement. 'What – ' she started, but he pushed his finger against her mouth to silence her, then inside, and she closed her lips around it. 'The hand . . . further up,' he said, 'your finger caressing the nipple . . . '

Shifting her weight from haunch to haunch, Donna tried not to giggle – or to talk, which was more difficult. Who was it told her she couldn't shut up to save her life? A high-school jock called Mike Bradshaw, that's who. Back in the days when Donna was a fat kid with braces and a Roman nose that hadn't yet been brought in line with current TV standards of beauty. Well, getta load of *this*, Mikey-boy!

'And your left hand down . . . further down, hiding your sex but still suggesting it at the same time . . . That's it. Yes . . . you have her expression almost exactly. La Fornarina by Raphael. Or . . . '

Donna might not get all his allusions, but she was a quick study, she caught his general drift, and she didn't mind being saddled with the role of silent muse because she felt . . . what? Outside herself, that was it! On the verge of getting behind the Mona Lisa to discover what Mona was so damned smug about. How had Charlotte put it last week? Something about stepping over the frame into a familiar landscape, 'immediately recognisable, *as of a dream recovered*'. That's what Donna was looking for in Italy. Not money, but something . . . *lost*, never found. Something seen in the background to paintings and the dream landscape of old movies like *The Barefoot Contessa*, her dad's favourite Ava Gardner film.

Twenty-one years old and not particularly well educated, OK, but foxy, smart, dead set on improving herself, Donna saw this Count as a guy who could teach her things, tell her things, *wonderful* things that no one else knew or could tell her. He was part of her Big Chance, the one her dad was always going on at her not to miss. 'Don't marry for money,' says Dad, paying for the nose job, 'but go where money is.' He'd be pleased to know that the Count's title wasn't just one of those social lubricants used by Italians to make life's bitter pills slip down more easily (no plain misters in Italy: everyone she met was a '*professore*', a '*dottore*'). Count Malaspino was the Real Thing. The one hundred percent Genuine Article.

Donna had recognised his authenticity long before she'd climbed the steps outside to reach a loggia about as long as a city block. *Loggia*, she thought, a posh word for veranda she'd learned in her crash course on art history in Rome – where she'd also learned to appreciate this kind of apartment, full of marble torsos and broken terracotta pots and limbless clay statues and odd bits of armour. No glitzy *new* antiques like her own folks had. Nothing *shiny* here, nothing whole. Donna could imagine herself in this place – you bet! The kind of castle on a hill you saw from a distance, or inside from behind red ropes. *La Contessa*. Envious whispers: she was born in Canada, can you believe it? But from a Roman family . . . An *old* Roman family, Donna amended for the benefit of her imaginary audience, remembering how important it was in Europe not just to have come from a place, but to have stayed there a very long time *and have the paperwork to prove it*. Provenance: that was a word Charlotte Penton used a lot.

It was Charlotte's admiring comment about this hotel, coupled with the description in a guidebook, that had convinced Donna to blow her budget and take the twenty-minute taxi ride from Urbino to eat here: 'The Villa Rosa, which time seems to have forgotten, was built in the 1500s as a hunting palace for the Malaspino family. Converted to a hotel in the 1950s, it still retains many of the original palatial features, including the Malaspino coat-of-arms engraved over entrances to the public rooms. The hotel restaurant, furnished in Belle Epoque style, is among the region's finest, and historically minded visitors can request the hotel suite rumoured to have been favoured by Mussolini and his mistress.'

Count Malaspino's ancient record player trailed off now in a series of scratchy sighs. 'Marvellous, wasn't it?' he said. 'Alessandro Moreschi, the last great Marchesine castrato – '

'Castrato?'

'One of our musici evirati . . . A man who sacrificed everything to gain the voice of an angel . . . '

A man perhaps no more dispossessed than I am, thought the Count, and what have I gained? I have become a hotelier, a PR man. Acre by acre, friend by friend, everything I was has vanished since the War to be colonised by foreigners like this girl who come to Italy hoping to buy into a history and a way of life that barely exist any more. Even the Villa Rosa, his uncle's favourite, had had to be turned into a hotel, while his own childhood home had been sold off years ago and was followed soon after by the rest of his grandmother's estate. Apart from the few broken remnants in this apartment, all that was left of his old life could be seen through the windows facing the steep, rough hills above San Rocco. Contour lines once clearly drawn in whitestone terracing were smudged now with bramble or erased entirely by decades of earthfall and spreading couchgrass, so that only a ragged shadow showed where the farm walls had stood.

Yet when I was young, he thought, those man-made terraces seemed no less secure than any other natural geological outcrop. Before the War, his father's property had seemed to be a living manifestation of the painting cycle 'Good and Bad Government', Lorenzetti's gentle allegory on virtue, which portrayed the 'well-governed' countryside as a theatre of culture, trade and hunting – beautiful *because* cultivated, in sharp contrast to the violent, savage chaos pictured under a diabolic tyrant.

The tyrant my father chose to follow, thought the Count.

He looked back at the naked girl and saw that she had transferred her gaze to a wine bottle on the table, a reflected Italy where all signs of pastoral neglect were reduced to a tidy miniature, with pairs of crows circling above postage-stamp villas like roving quotation marks around an idea that remained inexpressible – or irrecoverable, anyway, out of reach.

He poured them both some more wine, dipping his finger in it to trace a series of fluid red contour lines round the girl's breasts. Affluent breasts, he thought, from a new and affluent country. A place for clean slates, for fresh starts.

Had Donna been more analytical, she might have found unpleasant parallels in his lines of dissection. Here was a girl who'd perused a few meat markets in the last few years, chewed her fair share of tenderloin. She'd seen those charts with the rump steak, filet mignon and stewing chuck mapped out for consummation. Yet the red boundary lines Count Malaspino had marked out gave her the sense of each breast being precious, as had the way he'd whispered, 'I want to make love to you' when they'd met in his restaurant across the courtyard. OK, it was a line like any other line, but nobody said 'make love' to her any more, not one of the football stars and tennis coaches and cocky television directors who'd been her general experience of men. They said, 'You really turn me on' or 'You're so fuckable' or 'Wanna go to bed? Wanna fuck? Wanna do the dirty?' Or they just did it. Unzipped and did it, no prelims.

'Is it not to your liking, my dear?'

'What?'

'This wine . . .' He nodded at her glass, barely touched. 'The very last bottle of an exceptional vintage from my grandmother's vines.'

'No, it's . . . ah . . . great. But I usually drink white wine – Chardonnay, I love Chardonnay. Really cold. Napa Valley, that's *great* for wine.'

'We must educate your palate, my dear . . .' His fingers trailed down her spine and between her buttocks. 'You see, a wine may be stiff-backed, unyielding in its youth, but when ready . . .' The fingers slipped inside to explore. 'It loosens its reserve, there is an exciting mix of tar, flowers, jam and *fur*.'

After a few minutes he asked, 'You enjoyed that, cara?'

'Yeah, sure!' Donna tried to keep the disappointment from her voice. If only he would take his clothes off, so it didn't feel so much like a doctor's examination, standing naked on a stool while he poked around down there with skinny fingers. Any minute now he'd get out his stethoscope. Or his *corkscrew*! She stifled a giggle. As long as he didn't turn into one of those men who made animal noises while they were fucking her, pretended to be lions or big hairy bears. Or that Frenchman last month in Paris who had toot-tooted, 'Je viens, je viens, je viens, je viens!' for several minutes before his climactic: 'J'arrive!' What was she, a train station? Last week, James, her director, had asked to pour cold Heinz beans over her bare bum! Not partial to baked beans, even on toast, Donna had refused, guessing they were a precursor to something much less edible. Now James has cooled things off and he has this warning look in his eye like there's trouble choo choo chooing towards her down the track.

The Count cupped his palms under her breasts, weighing them, pressing them closer together, then slid his hands across her belly, still brown from the summer, and down the inside of her long muscular legs.

Donna noticed the coin of bald tan scalp circled by his thinning hair and thought of an uncle who'd had hair like that. Dead now. Uncle *Pietro*, that was it. Pete, they called him when he came to the States for a visit. She was fourteen, fat, and grateful for his gentle gallantry. Had a thing for Uncle Petes ever since. And this one, this Count, was really handsome, but in a sad kind of blurred Gregory Peckish way that must make him older than anyone she'd ever dated. Then again, a *Count*!

He was whispering something she couldn't hear. 'Pardon?'

'Etruscans,' he answered. 'Athletes like you, who cultivated vines here three thousand years ago among the wild olives and myrtle.'

Donna thought she had an Aunt Myrtle, maybe a cousin.

'The Romans called them savages, vicious even, and trampled over that subtle, sensuous culture with their broad conquerors' feet. But just because a fool kills a nightingale with a stone, is he greater than the nightingale?' D. H. Lawrence wrote that, the Count remembered, and Dieter taught it to me. Kneeling at the girl's feet, he ran his fingers across Donna's high instep.

'My great-grandad was from Rome,' the girl said.

He wasn't really listening. Kneeling aggravated his joints, and the pain reminded him of those other old men who had bound him by his past actions into their own vicious circle. Only a few days in Urbino after years away and already the memories were troubling him. He was thinking how girls like this one – most people – lived their whole lives without discovering what they were made of, whereas he had learned (had been taught) the bitter, ugly truth at the age of twelve. Had those other old men confessed their sins? Was there a priest anywhere who could forgive them for what the Count preferred to call, even in English, the *incidente*? A crime that should earn all of them a place in the clamorous circlings of Hell, he thought, a crime for which he'd spent his life in expiation. An unspeakable crime in every sense . . . yet how did men calibrate what could be spoken in these days when newspapers were sold on the back of atrocities, one ever more obscene than another?

How much could he speak of to this girl? What he needed from her he now doubted she could supply.

Rising stiffly to his feet, he took a restorative mouthful of wine. Perhaps it was the pain in his knees from the hard tiled floor that made him feel so sad, perhaps it was regret at how little he had left to offer this or any other young woman. Putting down his wine, he crossed the room and returned with a small clay figure, cradling it in his hands. The last memory still undamaged. 'This vessel is a relic of my grandmother's estate,' he said. 'A small Etruscan lady from perhaps the third century BC, found near here during the War in a mound of broken pantiles – by one of my dearest childhood friends, a German archaeology student.' This wasn't quite true, but it was how he preferred to remember the past. 'She was discovered in the hollow grassy tumuli where my grandmother's contadini used to store their wine. No one had believed until then that the Etruscans came this far east, but my friend was certain of it when I showed him those tumuli. Typical of Etruscan tombs, Dieter told me: one hill for their living and a second for their dead.'

He stroked the long eyes and legs and the ambiguous, half-smiling mouth, then ran his fingers across the coiled hair to slip them inside the cavity of her head with the same instinct he had slipped them inside the girl's mouth. 'Would you like to hold her for a moment?'

'No, that's OK, thanks. It looks kinda fragile.'

Donna wasn't sure she liked the statue, a sort of vase with exaggerated hips and raised arms forming handles. A *vessel* he'd called it. She had a sudden flash of herself as a cheap imitation, lit up like one of those plastic Madonnas that had started to weep real tears. Except real Madonnas were never naked. 'Can I put my clothes on now? I'm kinda cold.'

'Oh my dear, how thoughtless of me!' He removed his jacket and placed it over her shoulders. 'Come upstairs where it's warmer.'

He knew it would be wise to send her away before things got messy. With age and indulgence his small perversities had been magnified, moved onto another plane until he couldn't be certain that even a young girl like this one (especially a young girl like this one) could guarantee success. Yet he chose to forget the risks. He hated to be alone.

In his bedroom, the Count sat down and began slowly to unknot his tie.

'She is my most precious possession, that little statue,' he said, stalling the girl, postponing the moment when he would remove his shirt and let her see the ugly tracing of scar tissue across his back. Would the scars make her understand, or would he have to explain? He was so weary of explanations, and he found that English, a language useful for business, was too precise in these circumstances; it didn't roll off the tongue with the slippery 'ohs' and 'ahs' of Italian. 'The single thing I would save in a fire . . . Does that strike you as strange? No doubt you would choose a photograph of your parents or your brothers and sisters. But for me it is this statue, this priceless vessel made for a dead Etruscan and hidden away in caves filled with the shadows of lost lives.' A reminder of Dieter.

'The shadows of lost lives,' she repeated softly. 'I'd like to see those caves. Where are they?'

'Oh, they don't exist any more. The village was destroyed during the War. It's a ruin now, nothing but a bell tower left.'

'What was it called?' She liked to put a name on things, a brand.

'San Rocco.' He was pleased to have caught her imagination, and the pleasure combined with the memory of the friend he had once loved stirred him. He put his hands between his legs and felt it. 'But for the grenades we would never have found her . . .' A miracle, he thought and, prolonging the sensation, he closed his eyes and whispered – not to the girl beside him, but to the silent terracotta woman, 'Beneath those caves where she had slept for centuries, secretly smiling up through the rubble, slowly working her way to the surface.'

Donna wasn't superstitious, she didn't even read her daily horoscope, but she felt a shiver inside her then like a premonition, something to do with the landscape this man was describing, a place where white boulders pushed up through a pelt of scrappy green like kneecaps or ribcages buckling the grass in a giant cemetery. She could almost *hear* the wind shuddering around the buried statue and the imagined sound moved her and made her ache in a way the Count's fingers had failed to, the way certain notes had in the strange music he'd played, the way Europe did. Like . . . the end of summer- . . . or . . . She couldn't put it into words exactly, her desire to be part of something old and fine and even more beautiful for being nearly used up. Leaning down, she wrapped her arms around the man at her feet and pressed her lips and then her cheek into his neck. She felt a kind of love, the beginnings of it. 'Let me – ' *make love to you*, she would have finished (however corny and old-fashioned it sounded), but his eyes flew open and he broke free of her and stood up, his face very pale.

'What is it?' she said.

He moved to the bedroom door and waved his hand at her in a peremptory demand for silence.

MIRACLE NUMBER 5

An Etruscan Eye

'My wife.' Count Malaspino did no more than mouth the words, and once again his furious hand movement demanded silence from Donna, like a man signalling a dog in obedience class.

A woman's voice called up the stairs, her accent American to Donna's ears, 'This consortium is such a bore!'

'I thought you would be later, my darling,' replied the Count, with the same pliant, practised tenderness he had used earlier. He left the room and pulled the door almost shut, unaware of Donna slipping behind him to listen.

'It's not good enough for them, the word of a Munich banker's daughter,' she heard the woman say. 'So I am afraid you must come down to the conference room and flaunt your pedigree yet again.'

'I'm sure you can manage these people, my dear.' The Count added something in Italian, to which his wife responded in English, 'Pig-farmers and gangsters and chicken-breeders – '

'It was your idea to come back here,' he said gently.

'I wanted roots again, Dado. You can't keep running away for ever.'

'And your brothers can't keep bailing us out for ever.'

'But these people they've found – you have no idea! Perhaps my brothers were ill advised. Apart from Lorenzi, who is – '

'Lorenzi?'

'Salvatore Lorenzi, who – '

'Not . . . the former police chief?'

'Is that what he was? I have no idea, but at least he's a gentleman – '

'You didn't tell me Lorenzi was in on this . . . this . . . consortium . . . '

'I gave you the list of names, but perhaps you have been too busy to read them, too busy promoting the theatre – or was it the ballet, I forget. A ballerina, wasn't it, the last time?'

Donna moved out onto the landing, where she could see and be seen by the Count, whose eyes never wavered. 'Let me find a suitable jacket, my darling, and I'll be right with you,' he told his wife and quickly moved back down the hall, ushering Donna into the bedroom.

'I'm so sorry, my beautiful girl,' he said. 'I must leave you now, and you must get dressed and let yourself out once I've gone.' He removed his jacket from her shoulders and donned it himself. 'I'll send my assistant in a few minutes to collect you and see that you get a reliable taxi. Or there's a back way out – that might be better.' He nodded at a door in the corner and from his wallet took a generous handful of lire, tucking it into her hand.

'What's this?' She had to force the words out.

'To cover your journey back to . . . wherever you came from.'

Donna couldn't speak. For a moment after she heard his footsteps on the stairs she stood as he had left her, trying not to cry, her hand clutching the money. Then she walked naked to the head of the stairs and stopped with her back to the huge mirror on the landing, studying the woman below, who was listening to her husband in the living-room. A profile sleek as a cat's, Donna saw, blonde hair swept into an elaborate coil, clothes in shades of cream and ivory: *La Contessa*. So that's what it took. All the colour bleached out.

The Count reappeared, briefcase in hand. 'Very businesslike, Dado,' said his wife. 'You should impress the pig-farmers downstairs. By the way, my brother tells me two of them are being investigated by these intrepid "Clean Hands" magistrates in Milan. Should that worry us? At the very least they are suspected of offering bribes to obtain public contracts.'

'So was Carlo De Benedetti, the owner of our two biggest newspapers, and it hasn't stopped sales of *La Repubblica* and *L'Espresso*. If the magistrates continue to prosecute everyone in Italy who is guilty of such minor forms of bribery, as they have been doing for almost two years, the courts will be tied up until kingdom come.'

'I suppose you are counting on your friend Carlo Seguita – '

'He's not my friend!' the Count snapped. 'I wish your brothers had approached any banker in London other than him.'

'So you keep insisting, my darling, but if that's the case, why did you invite Seguita to use these apartments last week? Why did you – '

'I didn't invite him. He asked. Demanded, really. He was here on *our* business, remember. And . . . he's not a man I like to offend.'

'Business? Wolf-hunting or boar-hunting or some such baroque idea? Is there something you are not telling me about this Seguita, Dado?'

'There's nothing to tell,' the Count said.

'Well, for all his Savile Row suits, he strikes me as no more than mafioso mutton dressed as Mayfair lamb. I too wish my brothers had chosen another – '

'I think we should discuss these details another time, my dear.'

'I've been trying for months to discuss these *details*, as you call them.'

A flicker of light off the mirror behind Donna must have caught the Countess's eye at that moment, and for the first time she glanced up the stairs. With practised timing, Donna waited for the older woman to take her in. She watched the Countess's smooth face shift into an expression of tight fatigue, then Donna forced a smile, held her arm out stiffly and let go of the Count's money.

Gay as wedding confetti, the notes fluttered downward. The

Count's head, following their trail, twisted up to Donna as if his neck joints needed oiling, the lines on his face deepening until they could have gathered dust.

'Are you planning to leave your young visitor in this state of undress?' his wife remarked. 'Or have you made other arrangements?'

The Count laid his hand heavily on his wife's shoulder. He looked suddenly older, antique, a brittle porcelain statuette in need of support. 'Other arrangements have been made,' he said. His hand slipped down to take her arm and together they moved along the hall and out the door.

Donna felt her chest being squeezed in a vice. It hurt her to breathe. She turned and caught sight of herself in the mirror, exposed as the fat kid again, the last one picked for the team, the last one asked to dance. Collecting her clothes from the bedroom, she crept down the marble stairs to the living-room to retrieve the centurion-style sandals that had made such a dent in her first pay cheque.

The Count's statue was standing where he'd left it on the table next to the wine bottle. Maybe it was thunder coming, raising this hot pounding in Donna's head, but she felt a kind of . . . *summons* from that little earth-brown woman with her long narrow feet and eyes and strangely curving mouth. Squatting on bare haunches to study the statue, Donna saw how the figure's hefty buttocks were reflected in the wine bottle (still half full, the *very last* bottle from his grandmother's estate) and she dropped her sandals to place her hand against the green glass, covering up that reminder of her own double-exposure upstairs.

Impulsively she gave the bottle a gentle push. Back and forth, back and forth it rocked before toppling slowly slowly slowly to the floor, shattering glass and red wine across the old tiles.

It wasn't enough. Not satisfied with the broken glass and the stain of red (a *permanent* stain, Donna suspected, with the perception of a girl whose father had made a lot of money installing terrazzo flooring), she let anger flood through her – boiling oil, no prisoners, burn and pillage and nuke the bastards. She picked up the little statue, her fingers sensing the fragility in its old, brittle clay (what was her dad always telling her? 'Babe, you've got a real *eye* for good things!'), and snapped the feet off easily, moving her hands up to spread them across the muscular red-brown legs, which didn't put up much resistance either. And to break the hollow torso took only one light smack against the table – although the head, surprisingly, remained intact, if not for long. Raising her arm in an overhead tennis serve, Donna threw it as hard as she could against the far wall, where its enigmatic expression shattered instantly.

Priceless, he'd said. His priceless *vessel*. Well, now it was worthless. A conqueror, she marched barefoot to the door, oblivious to the pain in her foot until she saw the bloody prints left behind. The small piece of red clay she had to extract from her sole left a deep cut; there would certainly be a scar. But Donna flung away that last remaining shard of history with a careless volley.

Exorcism took rather longer for Count Malaspino. Returning after several hours, he heard from his assistant of Donna's hasty departure. 'The young . . . *lady* you were . . . interviewing . . . the television presenter . . . '

'*Television* presenter!'

'Yes, sir. From a series being made about the Renaissance. She's presenting the programme on the Raphael restoration you are sponsoring.'

'*That* girl?' Preposterous! 'Why, she doesn't even speak Italian!' He tried to remember the conversation with his wife: how much had been in English? Would it matter? Cursing himself for a susceptible old fool, Count Malaspino imagined what the girl might have overheard. He had to assume, to hope for both their sakes, that the names and associations would mean nothing to her.

'She went past me, sir, without a word!' Right past the windows where the Count and Countess stood with their backs to her, talking smoothly to all the local bigwigs. The Count's assistant thought it tactful not to mention her bare feet – in October! And that red dress she was wearing, *almost* wearing! So form-fitting (and on such a form) it was clear she'd had nothing under it. The boss was a lucky bastard!

'She didn't steal anything?' the Count asked. It had happened before, but he thought he'd become a better judge of character.

'I don't think so, sir. She left not long after you, and she had only a small purse with her. But . . . there seems to have been . . . an accident . . .'

The Count entered the apartment alone and followed Donna's bloody footprints into the living-room, where he stopped short at the sight of her Roman sandals among the broken glass and the terracotta remains of his grandmother's statue. Vicious little savage! So completely had the statue been destroyed that only a concerted effort brought to light the last piece of any size, a shard of blood-stained terracotta eye in which he wanted to believe there was still the suggestion of an Etruscan smile. Kneeling to retrieve it, he found his own eyes filling with easy tears.

He heard the outside door open then and his wife's warning: 'I've brought Dottore Lorenzi, Dado! He has been speaking with fondness of your uncle and father, whom he knew during the War – '

'And of the marvellous views we used to enjoy from these windows – '

The Count turned awkwardly towards the voice, one of the voices he had tried for years to wipe from his memory. Because of the glass and clay around him, he was still struggling to his feet when a tall, elegant old man of military bearing appeared, framed in the living-room doorway. 'The hills above San Rocco,' finished the old man, looking with interest at the debris and the half-kneeling Malaspino, who held in one wine-stained hand the broken piece of statue and in the other Donna's Roman sandals. 'They bring back such memories, do they not, Count? I'm sure your father, were he still alive, would be pleased to know you were re-establishing old connections.'

Paolo saw Donna later, striding barefoot through Urbino as if she owned the streets, her red dress an Amazon's warning flag. 'Donna!' he called out from the café where he was sitting with friends. 'Donna!' But she didn't hear him, or pretended not to.

'You read this announcement?' asked his friend Fabio. 'They finally released details about that old man, Domenico Montagna, the guy who died last week in the pig farm out by San Rocco . . .' He rattled the newspaper impatiently. 'Paolo, are you *listening* to me or mourning the passing of that witch in red?'

'I'm listening, I'm listening.' Paolo sighed, and through his stiff black hair he ran a hand still freckled with paint from the day before. His failure to make progress with Donna worried him almost as much as did the slow progress on the Raphael restoration, which had taken longer than predicted thanks to the city council's vacillation over how to deal with a flaw in the portrait, a concealed correction or 'pentimento' that his cleaning of the portrait had uncovered. He felt guilty that Charlotte, whose skill and dedication he greatly admired, was putting in longer hours than he was. In fact she seemed obsessed with the Raphael. Watching Charlotte stroke the painting with her fine brushes (as if it were skin, not canvas), Paolo decided that this was one way she expressed the sensuous side of her nature – perhaps the only way, since her divorce. But he also had a sensuous, passionate nature, and how was he to prove it to the beautiful Donna if he was working all the time? In a few days her filming here would be finished and she would be on her way to make the next programme in the next city. He sighed again and glanced across the piazza in the direction where the girl had disappeared.

Fabio was still engrossed in the newspaper report. 'They say Montagna must have stayed behind with a bottle after the factory closed. He shouldn't even have been there at that time of night. Apparently he had a lot of alcohol in his blood and fell by mistake into one of the chemical baths they use to strip the hides.'

'They wrote that – "by mistake"? Who's the reporter?' Paolo snatched the paper away to read the credit. 'I thought so! Stefano Craxi is such a fool! What, he thinks anybody would do it deliberately, throw themselves in an acid bath?'

'Only reason he had any blood left to check was because his fall set the alarms off and the custodian managed to pull out what was left of the guy with one of the big meathooks.'

Paolo grimaced with distaste at the pizza on his plate.

'You believe that story?' asked Fabio.

'Who believes anything they read in the papers? You can bet this is a story like any other "news" story, a story that suits somebody.'

'Especially the Nerruzzi consortium.'

MIRACLE NUMBER 6

Donna's Breasts

Paolo told himself that he wasn't attracted simply to Donna's beauty. He knew lots of equally beautiful girls. It's her openness I admire, he decided, her spirit, her willingness to try new things. Or if it *is* her beauty, what is it about her combination of breasts and lips and thighs that I find so appealing? So far as he could tell, Donna's breasts, for example, while large, were no rounder or firmer, the nipples no more prominent than his friend Flavia's (who had the advantage of being a petite, blue-eyed blonde, the type he generally preferred). Though Donna's legs were certainly longer, in that special North American way, leggy like a colt's.

At university he had believed that beauty could be analysed, broken down into an alignment of spheres, angles and pyramidal compositions. A scientist at heart, he had tried in his art history thesis to establish a precise mathematical formula for various artists' preferences and presentations of beauty. This way, he hoped, their work could be more easily understood. His hero was the great Italian architect and theorist Ernesto Rogers, whose dream – a Renaissance man's dream – was to use industry in the interests of a more humane society. 'From the spoon to the city' had been Rogers' design ideal, and Paolo had wanted to come up with a similar manifesto, at the very least the kind of convincing answers offered by art historians like E. H. Gombrich, who had argued that the Mona Lisa's greatest significance did not lie in her famous not-quite-smile, but rather in da Vinci's use of *sfumato*, the blurred outline and mellow colours that allow one form to merge with another and always leave something to our imagination.

'The technique of the mystery thus established, while the mystery itself remains,' had been Charlotte's dry comment on Gombrich's theory.

Paolo's efforts to impose logic on beauty were eventually frustrated by randomness, by *random* attractions. Why, for example, were some seashells beautiful? For what purpose? If form followed function, as his professors taught him, why were beautiful women no better at producing children than ugly ones?

He had begun with an examination of *La Fornarina*, the portrait of a half-naked woman who had probably been Raphael's mistress, a darkly sensual, very *real* beauty quite dissimilar to the angelic blondes generally associated with Raphael. Failing to establish any definitive measurements that would differentiate La Fornarina's famous left breast, say, from a Pintoricchio breast, the young restorer had still managed to discover something he found rather interesting. His X-ray examination had shown how the artist had initially painted an extensive and detailed landscape behind his sitter, then replaced it with an intimate background of bristling dark foliage. Myrtle, quince and laurel, the dark bushy *hairy* leaves closely enfolded the cream and dusky rose of La Fornarina's exposed breasts and belly in a deliberately suggestive manner. They kept her secret from the world, made her a creature to be handled privately, probed, investigated, as well as displayed for others' admiration. Why this alteration? Paolo, diverted from the course of his mathematical proof by his interest in the couple's sex life, had wondered: was Raphael's relationship consummated with La Fornarina during the course of the painting? Is that why he had sacrificed the broader horizon, to indicate the couple's new intimacy?

That's what love can do to you, he thought now. Love can make you lose sight of the wider picture. Only half-listening to his friend's plans for what he called their 'mutual performance art', Paolo asked him, 'What'd you say, Fabio? Oh yes, sure, another miracle, why not.'

MIRACLE NUMBER 7

The Dynamics of a Composition

On the same day, a Sunday, many valley people claimed to have heard the cracked bell of San Rocco ring true for the first time since the tragedy fifty years earlier. 'A miracle!' some insisted. 'A bad omen!' said others.

Although the unlikelihood of such an occurrence was later established by the Italian Committee to Assist Victims of Charlatans and Gurus, it seems that the bell was also heard by the art restorer, Charlotte Penton. Very English she looked that afternoon, all her bony edges blurred in woolly shades of grey and beige and sensible navy, a foggy cloud of London weather moving briskly through the highly coloured autumn woods southwest of Urbino and the Villa Rosa. Like a misplaced watercolour in an exhibition of Titian oils, she thought, and just as lost.

Middle-aged, in mid-life crisis, Charlotte was no believer in miracles; she knew that clocks can't be turned back. Listening to the distant peal, she considered how each bell had its own voice: some chimed gaily, some rang a brassy note, while others, tolling with funereal resonance, cost us; they levied a fee. This bell did not strike her as a toll-taker, not yet, although it did make her glance up at what could be seen of the sky through the dense canopy of leaves, and that bright ceramic blue, now softening to mauve, led her to conclude that here under the trees it would be dark soon.

The bell faded away into a loamy stillness. Oppressed by the deepening silence, Charlotte deliberately kicked the leaves, crunching them with her walking boots, but the sound of her own footsteps, over-amplified in the mute woods, made her wonder if it was time to give up on the 'Pleasant Hill Ramble' described by her guidebook, *Short Walks in Urbino's Environs*, a book she had followed conscientiously, despite its early evidence of unreliability. None of the promised 'sights' had been forthcoming. No 'View of Villas framed by Mountains, a Suggestive Mix of Nature and Architecture'. No 'Ruined Medieval Hamlet of San Rocco with its Romanesque Bell Tower Suggestive of Untouched Old Italia'.

Still, Charlotte was reluctant to abandon such a suggestive region, particularly as San Rocco was the object of her hike. Triggered by the mayor's conversation in the Bar Raffaello earlier this morning, her mind's fickle catalogue had recovered a lost memory probably responsible for her 'vision' on the hill above the Villa Rosa. The painting of a wolf hunt, that's what she'd remembered; a minor painting – late eighteenth-century, perhaps – that she and Paolo must have seen at least a month ago, soon after she'd arrived from London. Yet it came back to her clearly now: the running figure of the wolf, the spiralling cycle of violent activity directing your eye past the hunters in the foreground towards an idyllic hill village in the middle distance where the words 'San Rocco' were lettered in gold – and beyond that towards the Villa Rosa, also identified in gold.

Why had that landscape, one of the unimportant paintings displayed in the Ducal Palace's dim upper rooms, made such an impression on her? Charlotte could only surmise that its significance must lie in Paolo's comment at that time. 'This is the only record of San Rocco,' he'd said. 'It doesn't exist any more. Something terrible happened there, years ago.'

And considering how elusive San Rocco has proved today, she thought, perhaps he was right. Checking her watch, she decided to continue along the path she was following for no more than another fifteen minutes. She was always doing this, setting limitations, trying to restore order to an unruly world.

Ten minutes later the path had vanished into a fretwork of animal tracks. The clear, lively bells Charlotte heard then (from cows? goats?) were one more reminder of the late hour, and, admitting defeat, she turned to retrace her steps. For as much as she loved the picture of herself strolling without fear through the bosky Italian twilight, she had little desire to explore the reality.

Escaping reality, along with the satisfaction of actually feeling *needed* for the first time in a long time, had drawn her to Italy, a place where she remembered being happy before her marriage. She had arrived six weeks ago in the small and perfect Renaissance city of Urbino to help Paolo and Anna complete the final restoration of various minor Raphaels, the most important of which was *La Muta*, one of a handful of his works still remaining here in the artist's birthplace.

Restoration had become Charlotte's entire world ever since her perfectly amicable divorce from her perfectly amicable husband. John, on the other hand, a successful art critic, had let their twelve years together slip from his fingers as easily as he did old editions of the Royal Academy's journal. After a 'decent' interval, he had married his much younger, somewhat overweight but keenly reproductive assistant (one of many who had 'assisted' him over the years, Charlotte had learned), and fathered a child. Named Hypermnestra or Cloacina or some such thing, thought Charlotte acidly, remembering the aversion to having children that her ex-husband had once professed to share with her. The responsibility of bringing yet more children into such an unloving world was too great, they'd agreed.

Both in their late forties, she and John were 'still good friends' after the divorce, there were 'no hard feelings', they still 'saw each other from time to time' (only two times in the last year, if Charlotte were honest). At least, that was the story she handed out like a reliably unread church bulletin to their mutual friends. How mutual were those friends these days? Not very, it transpired. More his than hers.

Unlike the dissolution of her marriage, the restoration of Raphael's *Mute Woman* had been less than smooth. Most of the conflict had arisen because Charlotte, against her better judgement, had become an advisor on a television film about Raphael's brief time in Urbino, part of a series being made about the Italian Renaissance. She was reminded suddenly of a nickname given her by the crew. *Sister* Charlotte: not austerely elegant (as she had once imagined herself), but prim and narrow. A pencil of a woman, full of lead. Was she always so dull?

More bells, closer now, and violent, jolted Charlotte out of her thoughts. She heard branches breaking, a shout. The ground was vibrating through her shoes. This was an earthquake zone, but –

The mules came out of nowhere, a roiling dark cloud bursting through the beech-woods and plunging towards her, huge and black and shaggy, ripping up the ground and smashing undergrowth in their way. Charlotte threw herself against a tree and felt them pass so close to her that she could smell the grassy steam from their nostrils. One of the logs bouncing off their harnessed backs hit her leg hard and tore a long rent in her trousers. Almost obscured by the clouds of dust thrown up behind the animals was a giant of a man waving an axe in one hand and a coiled leather bullwhip in the other and singing or shouting something Charlotte didn't understand. Tripping over the logs his panicky mules had dropped in their flight, he savagely cursed the mother, the sister, *all* the relations of God and disappeared downhill, swallowed up as quickly as he'd appeared.

DOO dah DOO dah . . . The words of his song drifted back to her, the harsh voice trailing away indecipherably . . . *Bedma monay onna bo'taidmare, sumuddybedon da bay* . . . only the tune and the chorus implausibly familiar: 'Camptown Race-track' . . . *oh duh DOO dah DAY.*

In two minutes it was over. The woods had resumed their silence. Charlotte, wiping her wet face with her hand, noticed that her palm came away smeared with blood – mules' blood, not her own: she felt no pain. It amazed her, even pleased her, to think that so close to Urbino there would still be men using mules to collect firewood. In her imagination (more romantic than her exterior sobriety suggested) she saw the animals as stampeding phantoms of all the earth's lost herds, returning for one last rampage across the planet. She felt caught up in the kind of wild landscape in which da Vinci had placed his *Virgin of the Rocks*, the dynamics of the composition inseparable from its dramatic content.

Her anxiety returned when she patted her pockets for the guidebook and realised that she must have dropped it in the muddy battlefield left by the mules' passing. But it was, after all, an unreliable book, thought Charlotte, and, convinced that she knew which direction to take, she set off for Urbino.

The new path Charlotte followed for some twenty minutes must once have been a stream-bed, perhaps still *was* a stream in spring, for her feet kept sinking into the fudgy ground and she almost lost a shoe in the mud. She was very hot, but couldn't afford to carry her jacket because she needed to keep her hands free on the incline. Time and again she slipped in the mud and only saved herself from sliding down the hill by grabbing at the tangle of thorny brush, piercing her hands on brambles.

Finally brought up short in a snarl of nettles, Charlotte had to admit that she was hopelessly lost. The woods were quite dark. No birds called, no breath of wind stirred. If not for another resonant peal from the bell she had heard earlier, her situation would have felt even more desperate. But where there was a church bell ringing, there must be people. Head up, she listened carefully, then followed the sound, struggling over branches and thrusting undergrowth. When eventually she emerged onto a track that led across open woods and down a steep hill, she was limping badly from where she'd been bruised by the log off the mules.

The hill's contours were delineated by overgrown grapevines, and from the vines' liver-spotted condition it was clear that no one had farmed here for a long time. Tattered leaves were strung like dirty washing along the broken wires, as uncared-for as the tumbled, mossy stones from the hill's terracing. Thankfully, though, a small settlement was visible in a valley half a mile or so below, and a bell tower (possibly belonging to the 'Ruined Medieval Hamlet of San Rocco'?), source of the ringing bell.

A rough track led down to the hamlet; she could see it clearly, but what at first appeared to be paths to the road kept rising again or ending in steep walls and tangles of rusting barbed wire, a wandering maze. At last Charlotte was convinced she had found a safe route and confidently moved forward. At that moment the wolf rose up from behind a wall.

Charlotte stopped dead in her tracks. Her small cry of distress brought the creature's ragged ears forward and it lowered its narrow head, growling. Old fears filled Charlotte. *Was* it a wolf? Perhaps she was imagining . . . perhaps it was a lost dog. But why didn't it bark, surely a dog would bark? It looked famished, ribs bony as knuckles, its coat dull, matted, worn to scabbed skin in patches. Was it sick? There was a restless energy about it that suggested rabies . . . and wolves were pack animals: why was it here alone? Or *was* it alone? Charlotte's eyes were drawn over her shoulder. When her gaze returned to the wolf it had advanced a few paces. No more than ten metres separated them now, and from this distance she could see the open wounds ploughed along the bony shoulder and across its ribcage to its flanks.

The animal took two more steps and lowered its shoulders. Its jaws parted and snapped shut. Charlotte wanted to shout, but her voice failed. She saw the muscular haunches flex and crouch to spring. Three strides and it would be on her. Slowly, trying not to limp heavily, Charlotte moved step by step backwards up the hill.

And step by step the wolf followed. Every time Charlotte hesitated, it lowered its head again and growled deep in its throat. She became aware that it was herding her quite deliberately back to the edge of the woods. She remembered television programmes, old films of deer being driven to where the pack waited. The hamlet with its reassuring bell vanished again behind a curve in the hill. They had almost reached the woods, the pursuer and the prey, and if they reached the woods . . . as the implications of that thought registered, Charlotte stepped back awkwardly and felt her bad ankle give way.

MIRACLE NUMBER 8

Inferno

Charlotte closed her eyes and gave in, only to find herself stumbling out onto a broad clear track, unpaved but well used. By some miracle the wolf hesitated at the edge, it pulled back, and she watched with amazement as the raggedy-pelted creature wheeled round and loped off.

For a few moments Charlotte couldn't move. Not until her legs had stopped trembling and her heart had approached its normal beat did she begin to make her way down the road. If Geoffrey could see her now! She managed a weak smile at the idea, convinced that her superior at the gallery she worked for in London viewed her as a bookish figure incapable of finding her way around anything more primitive than a museum lavatory. It was he who had rung not long after she'd arrived in Italy and suggested heavily that it would be a 'good thing' for her to be part of this Anglo-American TV production. 'The series will be broadcast worldwide, you know,' Geoffrey had said, emphasising the significance of potential sponsors, international acclaim, etc., etc.

Two days ago, when she'd complained to him that her script's historical accuracy was being sacrificed on the altar of the presenter's 'lively' personality, he had stressed how much he was counting on her to keep the gallery's name 'right there at the forefront'. Charlotte had tried to explain that this TV series he'd supported wasn't quite the serious reassessment of the Renaissance its producer had led Geoffrey to believe. 'It's cable TV, you know, highly superficial. More like a . . . a pop band doing Bach.'

'A cover version?' Geoffrey sounded amused. 'Well, that could be interesting. We're always looking for new markets ...'

'The presenter is a child, Geoffrey! She has only the barest grasp of art history ... She ... she can't even pronounce the painters' names!'

Charlotte couldn't imagine how the girl got the job. Looks, she supposed. Sex appeal.

'This production is turning the Renaissance into a soundbite, Geoffrey, no more than another ... another ... a fashionable logo!' Charlotte was bad at expressing things she cared about. Often she would find herself stammering, when her emotions rose too close to the surface, if not resorting to complete silence.

'Now, don't be a snob, Charlotte. Nothing wrong with encouraging a younger audience!' Geoffrey at his bureaucratic best. 'You know we're trying to broaden the gallery's appeal. If you think changes are needed, speak up, Charlotte! Don't hang back!'

She hadn't had the courage to confess to the changes already made. How would it sound? Basically, Geoffrey, all I do now is make additions to the director's script which he and his lovely presenter then take out again. Originally Charlotte had been pencilled in as one of the talking heads to be interviewed by Donna, the presenter (who wouldn't know a Raphael from a Renault), but faced with a camera, Charlotte's shyness had come across as arrogance, her cool English reserve had proved impossible to melt and her role had slipped into an advisory capacity.

Reserve: this was Charlotte's problem in everything. Not like their lovely presenter, oh no! The closest she got to any kind of reservation was in booking a table for lunch. Lovely Donna simply opened her mouth and talked and talked and talked, never worried for a minute that what she had to say was not the wittiest, the most profound insight into anything and everything that anyone and everyone has ever had. Charlotte had seldom heard anyone who could talk so much and say so little. The camera didn't stop Donna, the legion of historical experts and admiring lesser Italian aristocracy (all men) didn't stop her. Only one thing stopped her: any script changes suggested by Charlotte.

'The *historicity* of a *pentimento*!' Donna had moaned yesterday. 'Who ever heard people talk like that?'

Hurd peepol tok. In her head Charlotte had mimicked the accent, before answering mildly, 'I have.' Hear that, Geoffrey? I spoke up!

'But you're so . . . *clever*, Charlotte.' Donna had slid her luscious dark gaze across to the director. 'I mean ordinary people. *Pentimento*: it sounds like some kinda mint chocolate! I mean, if you want to *restore* this painting, why *preserve* one of Raphael's mistakes?'

'Surely, even . . .' Charlotte stopped. Surely even *you*, she'd wanted to say, even *you*, a badly educated representative of a barbarian race like *you*, must see how important it is to establish whether a pentimento is the work of a restorer or implies repentance on the part of an artist! Of course Charlotte had said nothing of the sort; instead she'd gently appealed to the director, 'Don't you agree, James, that this pentimento is historically interesting to a painting like La Muta?'

'The reference is a little . . . uh, *oblique*,' said James, at the mercy, no doubt, of Donna's big breasts and tiny skirt, her lithe, curvy hips and long, slender thighs and those high heels she tottered around in. Ri*di*culous shoes! How could women expect to be taken seriously if they wore such shoes! 'Maybe Donna has a point?' he added.

Donna always did, thought Charlotte, who agreed to drop the reference. As *she* always did. Tuesday morning the finished painting was to be returned to the city's Ducal Palace. And then, thought Charlotte with relief, I'll be finished with these television people for good.

She felt more comfortable when the path she was following reached a broader dirt road along the valley floor. It was good to be able to stretch the backs of her legs, aching from the long descent on uneven ground. By now she was persuaded that the wolf was not a wolf at all but a stray hunting dog. Still, she was comforted to see the stripes of a ploughed field in the distance and a small tractor with caterpillar treads of the kind needed for this steep terrain, although she felt less easy upon reaching the settlement first glimpsed from above; for if there was a bell-ringer here, it was no more than a ghost raised by the brisk and chilly wind blowing off the Apennines. The tiny hamlet, or what must once have been a hamlet, was now just a hollow shell, the only sign of life a posy of wild flowers laid at the base of the chapel's roofless bell tower. Charlotte, moving closer to see how fresh they were, noticed that the heavy wooden door was pock-marked and splintered by old bullet-holes. She became aware of being watched, and looking over her shoulder saw the wolf, the dog, not twenty feet away, lying across the road she had intended to take, with its head up and alert and its long legs stretched out in the position of Anubis, the jackal god associated with burial grounds and the dead. As if expecting her. Waiting for her.

With her back against the stones Muta crouched in the cold chamber at the base of the tower and felt the bell's vibration run over her skin like a jet of water. She threw her head back to let the tower draw her up into the sky past the herbs and weeds thrusting their fibrous roots into the mortar. Wild mallow, leeks and clary, and the pretty *salvastrella* without which no salad is beautiful, and hyssop to cleanse men's souls of sin that they may be purified and their souls made whiter than snow . . . all Mama's lessons and the priest's lessons, plants that give gut-ache or cure it, those that lose their bitterness when stewed up with bacon fat and onions, and those to stop bleeding, some bleeding . . . *other old lessons coming back since that day, that face, a week ago* . . . never had there been such bleeding, blood with a light of its own, black in the moonlight and only red where their torches shone. She saw the knife go in quick enough, although to the inexpert butcher wielding the blade it must have felt like pushing through the layers of a hard black cabbage, not easy to manoeuvre the way he'd seen others do. In the end they threw the knife away and blew up all the words that might ever be spoken, and all the blue shades scattered, and bones and broken words falling back to mark the place where the serpent had fallen and risen up again.

With difficulty Muta pulled herself out of her mixed-up visions – a week ago, a year ago, fifty years – to scan the other woman through a crack in the tower's loose stones. She saw the gaunt wolf as well and knew it for a wolf, *her* wolf. It didn't frighten her any more. Like the wolf, she had for years consumed so little, taken up so small a space on earth, that she felt sure of being safe, as long as silence was preserved.

She was mistaken. Still, every miracle has its price. She had found the knife, she had dug it up, she had the knife at least. Another relic among the bones and bullets and eight odd gloves and boots and teeth missing their gums that she kept in the basket next to the ladder in her cellar of memory.

Backing slowly away from the wolf, Charlotte once again found the safety of the gravel road before she felt confident enough to break contact with those yellow eyes and to stride on quickly, her back tenderly exposed. She was headed away from the direction she imagined would lead eventually to Urbino, but towards that distant tractor, an indication of human presence which seemed preferable to the risk of passing the wolf again.

With the exception of the tractor, she was walking through a medieval almanac come to life. A Book of Hours, she thought, aware more than ever of the fading light. The spectral hides of oxen shone whiter now against the dark hills, and the sky had taken on that luminous quality employed by painters of the Quattrocento to give their Transfigurations and Annunciations a prescient, surreal quality. Expecting angels and doves, Charlotte heard the squeak of bats, then the leathery rustle as their broken umbrella silhouettes swooped out of prehistory to catch insects brought by the dusk. She passed one empty farmhouse after another. Occasionally she glanced over her shoulder to see if the wolf was following. But the creature kept to the shadows, out of sight.

Fattoria Procopio read the hand-painted sign on the first set of inhabited buildings she came to, another mile down the road. While faded and pock-marked with hunters' bullet-holes, the name was still clear, the same as the café Charlotte frequented in Urbino. About the only clear thing in this muddied landscape, she decided. A Bosch scene, a Breughel farm stretched beyond the tangle of broken and rusted equipment and the cages packed too closely with rabbits and chickens. Yes, Charlotte decided, young 'Hell' Breughel had been at work here with his diabolical brush, transforming what might have been an idyllic Italian farmhouse into a place fit only for browbeaten peasants. This part of Untouched Old Italia could *do* with having its roots touched up. Admittedly, six mules stampeding through it hadn't helped the farm's appearance. Tied by rope now to rings in the stable wall, those once frantic beasts had been reduced to docility with the help of six identical piles of hay. Any logs they hadn't managed to buck and strew across the hillside had been piled randomly outside the stable door. From somewhere inside this stable or perhaps in a yard beyond it Charlotte could hear men's voices accompanied by a strange chorus . . . '*DOO dah DOO dah*.' The contented snorts and whinnies of the mules made the direction unclear.

'Hello?' she called out. 'Um . . . *c'è qualcuno*?'

A dog appeared out of nowhere howling and Charlotte stepped sharply back as it ran at her, only pulled up short by its chain. Unable to tell if the one-eyed creature was vicious or not, for its face was already distorted into a snarl by a terrible scar that ran from nose to left ear, she made her way cautiously between the dog and the mules, wading through the batter of mud, urine and manure they had churned up. Eyes rolled, a couple of the animals lashed out with their feet or snapped at her with yellow teeth. Charlotte was wondering if it would be ridiculous to knock on the stable door, when it flew open and she was faced with the muleteer she had last seen in the woods, his face now splattered with blood.

'*Madr' Dio!*' he swore, stepping back a pace, as if she were the more monstrous figure. The scummy, soap-rinsed eyes seemed too far apart to focus. 'I'm sorry . . . um, mi dispiace,' she stammered. He bent to collect two logs the size of grown men, tossing them onto his shoulder with no more difficulty than he would a coat. His free paw gestured for her to follow him into the stable, and after a brief hesitation she did, although the set of his unfocused eyes and his thick voice made her uneasy.

Inside it was too dark to do more than smell the cows and hear their gentle snuffles. She had to feel her way forward along the wooden wall of what she assumed were animal stalls, using as a guide the only light, a wedge of flickering reddish-yellow from a door left slightly ajar on the far side of the barn. Her chaperon shouted, '*Venga! Venga!*' Hurrying to catch up, she was just behind him when he hauled the door open onto a concrete pen and exposed the origins of that flickering light.

Fire, she noticed first, trying to concentrate on its acrid smoke as she was hit by the stench of sweat and urine and excrement and the sweetish smell of blood. A scene she was not meant to witness. She saw three big men stripped to the waist. Bloody skin, trousers, shoes. Blood on the walls and knives and splashed over the fired-up cauldron. Buckets heaving with bloody intestines. Fresh guts on the concrete floor and a poor bloody squealing creature hoisted up by a rope round its heels.

Charlotte stepped back and the man beside her roared, 'EVVIVA IL COLTELLO!' Two of the other men repeated his cry, 'EVVIVA IL COLTELLO!' The meaning of that phrase – Long live the knife! – struck her as a scream came from the creature twisting on the rope and Charlotte felt the same sound shamefully well up in her own throat.

'*Doo dah, doo dah*,' hummed the muleteer.

The man holding the knife was silent. His eyes, in a mask of dirt and blood, were ringed with white, his huge torso naked under a floor-length leather apron and shining slickly red, a savage god. Barely hesitating at Charlotte's cry, he raised his arm with its red knife and plunged it into the pig's throat, grunting with the effort of the blow and stepping back quickly, his face averted, though not quickly enough to avoid the jet of blood spewing out of the neck wound, the arterial blood with a dark light of its own, and pumping in irregular jets as the pig's heart beat and beat and slowed and finally stopped.

It seemed to go on for a very long time. Red red red red red.

And then black.

MIRACLE NUMBER 9

Lucifer's Gate

When Charlotte came to, she was sitting (*sprawling*, she worried, straightening up) on a bench in a neat walled courtyard. Facing her was a thick-necked, fleshy-faced man, one huge hand gripping a cigar broad and long enough to cudgel tough prisoners into confession. He seemed much too large for the chair he had turned back to front to straddle like a horse, and his position on the chair, combined with his rough sunburned features and marble-tight curls of greying auburn hair, gave him the look of a terracotta maquette. A centaur, Charlotte thought immediately. Unfinished, but a centaur, nonetheless, the artist's intention quite clear.

She was disconcerted both by the man's unashamed, faintly amused gaze and by his immaculate clothes. Spotless brogues and a white silk shirt held by silver cufflinks were hardly what one expected from a farmer. Who was he? Where had he come from? 'I'm sorry,' she began. 'I mean, mi dispiace.' Her Italian deserted her. She wished there was a woman around, the farmer's wife. But the neatness here – bootscrapers by the farmhouse door instead of geraniums, scrubbed bricks instead of a lawn – appeared to be purely functional, not feminine.

'It is for me to apologise,' answered the man in correct, if heavily accented English. 'My . . .' He searched for a word, shook his big head in evident frustration and continued. 'Angelino, that . . . *castrato stupido*, whose family connection to me I cannot remember how to say in English any more – he should not have brought you . . . He should have warned the butcher he had a visitor . . . a *sensitive*, visitor.'

'It was dreadful, appalling!' she whispered, relieved to find herself in civilised company. 'I never imagined, I never . . . '

'I am sorry you were a witness, signora, but it was a pig killing, you know, not a murder. This kind of dreadful atrocity is performed every autumn, so that people like you may enjoy their prosciutto and their lardo and their speck. There are much worse ways to die . . . or to live, for that matter. I assure you, so far as I can, never having been in its precise place,' he conceded, with a slight smile, 'the pig feels no pain after the initial cut, provided one finds the artery quickly.'

'They could have used a gun! In England we . . . and that . . . that man . . . '

He let her stutter into silence before responding, 'That man?'

'The butcher,' she whispered. 'Terrible . . . he seemed to . . . *enjoy* it. And the screams . . . ' Almost human, she thought.

'Ah. Him. Well, you can't expect poetry from a butcher. Still, there are ways of being a good butcher just like there are ways of being a good poet. As for the pig's screams – like you, it is not fond of the smell of blood. Especially its own . . . and perhaps the blood of its friends and relations, if it is capable of such distinctions. In this way, with the knife, the pig dies slowly, it's true, but the blood may be used in sausages. With a gun, the pig is no less dead, but its blood remains in the flesh, making the meat very flabby.'

Every good butcher keeps them bleeding long: Charlotte retrieved the buried quote, soothing herself with a reference to the past, where she was more comfortable. Never a great meat-eater, she thought now of Leonardo da Vinci's prediction that a time would come when men looked on the murder of animals as they looked upon the murder of men. Leonardo the vegetarian, who had called the human mouth 'a sepulchre for all animals'.

'It's late,' the big man announced abruptly, consulting his watch. 'We must see about getting you back to civilisation, Signora Penton.'

She registered his use of her name with a mild frisson of dismay. 'How do you know my name, signor . . . '

'Could I fail to? Urbino's newspaper is full of the scandalous restoration of Raffaello, and of this international television company who have come to celebrate the restoration of La Muta to her rightful place. You are the clever restorer, and there is also the other one, the one . . . who is so . . . lively.'

The one who *never bloody shuts up*, thought Charlotte. 'And *you* are?' The question came out more frostily than she'd intended.

'Procopio, Francesco Procopio. This is my fattoria, my farm in which you have chosen to faint.'

Charlotte had quite forgotten the sign on the farm gate. 'Procopio? Like the café in Urbino?'

'Procopio, like the man who invented ice-cream. I only make it.'

'Then . . . is it *your* café?' Despite his smart clothes, she found it difficult to picture this wide, slab-sided Goliath in the café's pristine interior.

'And my cooking.'

Charlotte studied the massive senatorial head, the hands like meat platters. She couldn't imagine those wrestler's mitts gripping the cup of jasmine flowers that Procopio's menu advertised was needed for each serving of its special ice-cream. This was a man who still smacked of the mountain and the hard rock, as Dante put it. Even if his mountainous muscle had softened with age (was he fifty? sixty?), neither Procopio's physique nor his clothes fitted his claim to be Urbino's Michelangelo of marzipan, its Brunelleschi of spun sugar. Charlotte, with a trained eye for the subtle evidence of forgers and restorers, assessed the silk shirt he wore, its long double cuffs (impractical for a cook), and would have placed him as a croupier – no, a nightclub bouncer, a circus strongman, with a fat lady in a tutu balanced on each hand.

Procopio smiled and stood up. 'I make ice-cream – that is, when I am not murdering innocent pigs.'

'That . . . that . . . it was . . . *you*?' For an instant she closed her eyes against the image and when she opened them again she saw that her host's smile had vanished. He looked tired, worn out (that weary grunt as the knife went in).

'So, signora, after receiving my confession, do you consider it safe for me to drop you at the Pensione Raffaello, where I believe you are staying?'

'Thank you, you're too kind. I can walk . . . if you will show me the right path.' This response sounded so ungracious that, forgetting the wolf, she quickly added, 'It is too far for you to drive me back to town . . .' But Procopio frowned and insisted there was no easy path, the road was rough.

Limping to the man's jeep, Charlotte managed with difficulty to avoid glancing in the direction of the stable yard. Procopio made no effort to relieve her discomfort. Fortunately, the noise as he started up his vehicle covered their silence, and the long driveway out of the farm was so rough, the jeep so loud, that no conversation was possible until they reached a smoother track where her chauffeur was able to shift up a gear.

Charlotte was aware of having caused offence, and a very English desire to paper over the cracks in her good manners made her unusually voluble. 'I've never fainted in my life,' she began. 'It was silly of me to . . . You must think me very naive to have reacted so . . . melodramatically . . . to what is part of . . . life here.' She wanted to show this man that she was not unversed in Italian culture (although why should his opinion matter?). 'Tell me, Signor Procopio, the men helping you with . . . Your assistants – they shouted a phrase just before you . . . Was it "Evviva il coltello"?'

He nodded.

'Which means, I believe, "Long live the knife"?'

'It does.'

'An old saying?' she asked brightly.

'Mm.'

'With local butchers?'

'Not exactly . . .' Procopio made great play of changing gears, checking his rear-view mirror, all the tasks he had performed automatically until then. 'Look, signora, if you must know ... if you want the whole story ...' Now it was the café-owner who was at a loss for the right words.

'I'm sorry – ' she began.

'You should be sorry for the poor bastards who ...' He lifted one hand from the wheel and slapped it down again like a man smacking the rear of a reluctant donkey. 'Look, you must know that here in Le Marche we are famous for more than Raphael and Rossini and the Duke of Montefeltro!'

She had a feeling that he had been about to say something entirely different, but he continued, warming to his theme, 'Take Norcia, my mother's town in Umbria – '

'Oh yes,' she said. 'Well known for salami, isn't it?'

'And other exports besides salami – although it is through their skill at pig slaughtering and boar gelding that the itinerant Norcini achieved a certain notoriety around here ... '

She smiled and nodded, encouraging him to continue.

'You see, fame also came to Le Marche from the abundance of its ... its musici evirati ... Voices of angels, they had! The toast of Europe's concert halls in the Ottocento and Novecento!'

'I don't quite understand the connection – ' She stopped abruptly as the ugly picture became clear.

'The connection between gelding boars and gelding men?' he asked. 'Well, signora, to put it bluntly, for those peasants who were poor but ambitious in the last centuries, there remained always this opportunity to send any spare offspring to a Norcino, a butcher, where a coltello Norcino waited to turn Marchigiani boys into angels. So it became the custom for the audience at concerts here to salute a castrato of singular brilliance with the cry, "Evviva il coltello!" And now when the *pig* sings, signora, my men salute. That is what you heard.'

'I understand. Yes.' She turned her eyes away and stared out the jeep window. It was fully dark now. Superimposed on what she could see of the steep valley through which they drove was the reflection of her own bony face, all angles with exhaustion, her eyes enormous with fatigue, her mousy blonde hair matted on one side from the mud where she'd fallen. Pointlessly she scraped her fingers through it. A dandruff of mud (and blood?) settled slowly onto her trousers. She wanted to mention the wolf, but the more she thought about it, the more unlikely a wolf seemed. 'On my walk to your farm I passed a ruined bell tower, Signor Procopio,' she began, trying for the sound of mildly interested tourist.

He didn't take his eyes from the road.

'Was that by any chance San Rocco?'

'Used to be. Around here you will more often hear it called La porta di Lucifero or sometimes L'aeroporto di Lucifero.'

'Lucifer's Gate? His *airport*?' Her thoughts were diverted from the wolf. 'Whyever for?'

'Bad things happened there. In the War. A grenade or a mine destroyed most of the village, made a crater big enough for Lucifer to have landed when he was turned out of Heaven, so say the people who believe in such things.' He smiled a little, not one of the people who believe in such things.

'Is that why it was abandoned?'

'Not entirely abandoned. A friendly ghost occasionally leaves offerings.'

'You are the ghost?'

'Not me! A mute woman who works as a cleaner at the Ducal Palace.'

'A *mute* woman.'

Reluctantly he added, 'They say in this valley that she saw the wolf for the first time, years ago, and it's been shadowing her ever since.'

'I don't understand. I . . .'

'You never heard this saying? Everyone round here will tell you straight: if a man sees a wolf before the wolf sees him, he will lose his voice from fright, he'll be struck dumb.' His heavy-lidded eyes flicked towards her. 'I'm only repeating a story told to outsiders.'

'Like me, you mean.'

He grinned. 'Like anybody – from Carpegna, even, which is maybe fifteen kilometres away, maybe less. People in this valley know how to stop tongues wagging, they know that muteness is no bad thing. Give the devil a name and you let loose whatever demons you fear the most.'

'This mute woman . . . is she . . . was she from one of the families who used to live at San Rocco?'

'The families who lived there are all gone,' he replied quickly. 'Nobody knows why she comes. She's a little *pazza* – a little crazy.'

Her next question was cut off as he wrenched the jeep around and up an even narrower track. Charlotte grabbed for a strap hanging from the roof.

'Now I show you something *really* crazy.'

He sounded angry. What had she said to offend him this time? 'This is a short cut to Urbino, Signor Procopio?'

'If you like. A short *cut*, certo.'

His retort summoned an image of the row of knives lined up in his concrete yard. 'It seems unused, this road,' she said nervously. 'Very bumpy.'

'But straight. The Germans always built straight roads. Their network skirted these hills in 1944. All round here you find stretches of cobbled road laid by the Germans to facilitate transport.'

Charlotte's thoughts ran: He could take me anywhere . . . and with these sudden tempers . . . Who knows where I am now, apart from his fellow butchers, that half-wit . . . This is wild country . . . But surely there are other farms . . . although I have seen no houses for quite some time. Her agitated inner dialogue slowly wound down as the jeep topped another hill and she saw in the distance the lights of Urbino, with the city's glory, the Facciata dei Torricini, its western façade of slender, spired towers, rising five storeys high out of the hillside. The walls were floodlit silvery mauve against the indigo of the Montefeltro range, giving Urbino the ethereal quality of an Arthur Rackham watercolour in a book of fairy tales. To believe that nothing terrible could happen within sight of Urbino's towers was as romantic as those old stories, Charlotte knew. Nevertheless, the small hopeful part of her left behind after John's desertion did cling to just such a belief.

Procopio parked the jeep and lit a cigar. Down to their right lay a factory, brilliantly illuminated, and from it the unmistakable odour of pig slurry rose to fill Charlotte's nose. Nervously she glanced at the man beside her. 'Have a look!' he said, gesturing with the cigar. 'Have a good long look down there!' She stretched her neck to peer out the window and had a view into a heaving mass of muddied pink flesh closely confined within high concrete cubes. 'This is your modern way of breeding pigs,' he said.

The animals stood up to their bellies in mud, jammed in so closely that none could turn except with the agreement of all. Only by standing on each other would the low-slung beasts have been able to view a patch of sky. Charlotte looked away again.

'Me, I kill only three, four pigs a day in season, signora, but this factory, they slaughter fifteen hundred a week. It is piece-rate pay for the workers, so speed is of the essence: fifteen minutes per animal for electrocution, stabbing, degutting and dispatch to the chillers.'

'Yes, I take your point, Signor Procopio.' Her voice was shaking. 'There is no need for you to keep me here any longer.'

Ignoring her protest, he continued, punctuating his next words with stabs of the cigar, 'How do I know this? I worked here when I started as a butcher . . . Uncle Tito got me the job. Good old Tito. Never let me forget the *big* favour he did me . . .'

As he began to paint a vivid picture of his first hideously botched attempts to slaughter animals, Charlotte flinched away. It was like being stoned, this pummelling, insistent description. The pig's shrill screams going on and on, higher and higher, its blood coming from twenty different wounds as Procopio stabbed and hacked and failed to find the artery. 'My loyal workmates refused to jeopardise their own wages by stopping to help.' The stabbing, the flaps of skin, the other men's eyes turned away. On and on and on. 'Dangerous place, signora.

Not only for pigs. A man was killed there last week. Off duty, had no business being there at that time. They say he was drunk, but who knows? Maybe he was working overtime . . . maybe he was just in the wrong place at the wrong time . . . as you were today . . .'

Was the man *threatening* her now? Was this some kind of oblique *threat*? Was he getting a kick out of frightening her?

'That is the problem of piece-rate butchery, signora. Not only animal rights but people rights go out the window if men can't get a living wage.'

'I'd like to go home now please, Signor Procopio. Or if you wish, I can get out here.'

He started up the jeep without a word, racing the motor as he did a sharp U-turn back the way they had come. He threw the half-finished cigar out the window. After a few minutes he apologised, 'I am sorry, that was wrong of me.' He ran one big hand through his wiry, bullish curls. 'I am sorry,' he repeated, his voice contrite. 'My only excuse – '

'There is no need.' You *bastard*!

'Yes, please, there is. Every need. I should not have brought you to this place. But I see you come into my café every day to eat and although you never see me, I am honoured you choose my café and now when we meet at last you are so contemptuous of . . . You see, my poor pigs, they get fat on corn and acorns and table scraps, yet these factory pigs are deemed much tastier on their diet of antibiotics and steroids. The EC has given the consortium who owns this pig farm a licence to sell meat. Not me, though! My methods are not clean enough. A group of English food journalists was flown here to sample the consortium's product. They were wined and dined in the original Nerruzzi family villa and shown the original Nerruzzi family-run side of the business, very rustic and charming . . . Of course, they never went near this place or near the chemical company that makes the Nerruzzi consortium's pig-feed or the petrochemical company that runs its trans-European lorries! And now, with the help of EC money and new building technology supplied by our friends in the south, the consortium is able to expand further – '

'Our friends in the south?' she asked, to stem the tide of words.

He gave her a strange look, as if he thought she was trying to trick him. 'Our friends who are such experts on cement,' he said after a minute. 'They provide the consortium with cheap housing units, automatic feeders, concrete stalls where sows may be tethered so they don't roll on their offspring . . .'

They had reached the paved road leading to Urbino. With relief, Charlotte turned her thoughts away from the man's words, up towards the Ducal Palace's high battlements.

' . . . if there is *room* for the sows to roll,' the voice beside her persisted.

Camelot, thought Charlotte. It was a title Urbino had almost deserved, certainly between 1450 and 1508, when the mountainous duchy was ruled by its own Arthur, the warrior-prince Federigo da Montefeltro. What had Raphael's friend Baldassare Castiglione said of the prince? . . . That among his other commendable enterprises he had built on the rugged site of Urbino 'a palace which many believe to be the most beautiful in Italy; furnishing it so well and appropriately that it seemed more like a city than a mere palace.' Certainly at this distance it was impossible to tell where castle stopped and city began, while during Federigo's time Urbino had outshone every European city in art, courtly life and devotion to the New Learning. In his library he had collected every text of the classical world, and in his court the most urbane of poets, scholars and courtiers, both male and female . . .

'More likely they sit on the young out of exhaustion,' Procopio said.

Yes, Charlotte decided, resisting the man's efforts to drag her back down to his level, yes, Urbino represents the true spirit of Renaissance, more so even than Florence, a city she found to be a muscular, austere, unpretty sort of place, a bachelor's town. Florence had always stood for commerce and the Pope, its people less interested in princes than in football and banking, whereas Urbino, like Siena, was feudal, pro-Emperor, a city of aristocrats lit by the Age of Chivalry's dying fires. 'Burnt Sienna', the colour of its bricks. In Florence painters discovered volume and, with brawling Masaccio, gave Adam the muscles of a Tuscan labourer.

And Urbino? Urbino had gentle Raphael.

There was a loud thump. Briefly pressed like a medieval peeping tom's against the car windshield appeared the startled golden eye and heraldic crest of a cock pheasant. As the big man slammed his foot on the brakes, the bird slid off, leaving a smear of blood on the driver's side. Procopio got out and walked back down the road. Charlotte, unable to remove her eyes from the rear-view mirror, watched him, lit in red by the car's back lights, pick up the bird and snap its neck efficiently between his meaty fingers, then stride back to the car, all in the space of two minutes.

He opened the back door. The car reverberated as the heavy bird landed inside. When the man got in next to her he was still wiping his bloodied hands on a cloth, which he tossed over his shoulder. His hands left a dark, sticky mark on the gear-shift and the steering-wheel and a few bright drops of red were soaking into one of his white, softly-folded double cuffs. He switched on the windshield wipers and the blood was smeared back and forth across the window. '*Che cazzata!*' he swore. 'Sorry, I forgot to refill the what-you-call, the window-cleaning bottle.' He picked up the cloth from behind him and got out to wipe the windshield by hand. There were still red smears around the edges when he got back in.

What am I doing here with this awful man? She despised everything about him: his fleshy face, his manicured butcher's hands with the faint line – of grime? blood? – still under the nails, his pretentious clothes, so unsuited to his position. Although not, perhaps, to his ambition.

'Meanwhile the government earns the liberal votes by saying they are going to put an end to hunting small birds!' said Procopio, as if he hadn't been interrupted. 'Easier than dealing with factory farming, because birds are prettier than pigs and chickens, they sing such nice songs.'

She found her voice at last. 'There must be EC regu—'

'This consortium is not to be bothered by regulations. This consortium has its fingers in a lot more than pork pies . . . Even Count Malaspino won't complain, although his pretty hotel, the Villa Rosa, it is on the Urbino side of this pig farm, and when the wind is in the wrong direction he gets a bad smell his hotel guests are not so fond of. Of course, Malaspino is used to the smell. He is very – I don't know how you say . . . *spregiudicato*.'

'Unprejudiced,' Charlotte responded sharply. 'Isn't that a good thing?'

'Unprejudiced,' said Procopio, drawing the word out so that it sounded like a doubtful virtue. 'That is one translation, yes. Also broad-minded, free and easy. But always here we have more than one meaning, so you might say that this Count is broad-minded about who he does business with, as well as what he smells. Very *unprejudiced* about bad smells.'

MIRACLE NUMBER 10

The Grave Stillness of Angels

'Signora Tommaso's widowed sister has been miraculously cured of the gout, did you hear, Primo?' In the Bar Raffaello Franco was giving his regular report to the mayor.

It was later that Sunday evening. After Charlotte's eventful drive back with Procopio she'd needed a reassuring shot of grappa, one of her preferred sedatives, along with Campari or sometimes a carafe of the region's hard white wine – even two carafes. Here the restorer felt safe, unobserved by her colleagues and secure in the knowledge that the Bar Raffaello was too far from the 'centre' of things to attract anyone under forty.

'Her sister took her to see the mummies in Urbania,' Franco went on. 'You hear? The congealed blood of Urbania's mummified saint was seen to liquefy inside its container.'

'Unseasonally,' his friend grinned. 'It usually happens in August.'

'This was different, Primo: next day, the gout was gone and Signora Tommaso's sister could walk.'

'Why did it have to happen in Urbania?' complained the mayor, who was always jealous of any threat to his own city's reputation as cultural capital of the Marches. 'We've just as good a mummy collection – like that one all the women love, the lady who died of a Caesarian! And why should we have only one miracle this year, when every little pissant place that can muster up the cost of a plaster virgin is running with bloody miracles!'

Franco shook his head. No church-goer since his wife died, he still felt uneasy about the mayor's vocal contempt for religion. Looking away, he scanned a row of unnaturally coloured imported liqueurs that nobody would choose willingly unless it was the odd tourist who stumbled in. Why keep them? They came with the bar, that's why, inherited from his dead wife's widowed aunt, a dragon who turned up twice weekly to check on the new custodian. *Still* new after thirty years.

'What's that one?' Primo asked.

'Which one?'

'The pink stuff in the bottle shaped like a violin.'

Franco took the bottle down and read its label. 'It's in Portugese. Fatima something. The old lady bought it years ago at Lourdes.'

'Why d'you keep it, if you don't know what it is?'

'Good luck, I guess.'

'Superstition, you mean.' Primo stirred his finger to indicate a shot of the unidentified pink liqueur. 'Maybe I can get Professor Serafini to set up one of his public performances, a scientific investigation.'

'I thought he only looked at fake miracles.'

'You want me to believe this miracle of the gouty leg was genuine?'

His friend swiped a cloth several times over the already gleaming Formica bar. 'No, no, I suppose not. I'm only telling you what Signora Tommaso told me. You know she donated a substantial amount to the guild who maintain that church?'

'Now there's a *true* miracle! Mean as a Tuscan with her money, La Tommaso is! She'll have every weak-bladdered widow and pilgrim with a limp taking themselves off there, and Urbania will be raking in the loot.'

'It's starting already. Signora Tommaso mentioned the miracle to her friend at the Pensione of Our Holy Mother and four of the guests checked out that afternoon, heading for Urbania.'

'Bastards! You know, it's all these *miracles* got Serafini down here from Milan. I'm thinking maybe he could prove this blood wasn't blood . . . show people it wasn't magic after all! Like I'm always telling you, Franco: if people want answers to their problems, then molecules, not miracles, are the way forward! Atoms, not angels!'

'Well, atoms and molecules are a little impersonal, Primo. It's hard for a person to get attached to a molecule. Maybe in cases like Signora Tommaso's sister molecules just aren't enough – you ever consider that? And what can Serafini do about her leg? Everyone has seen the evidence.'

'Evidence? *What* evidence? You can't use the leg of Signora Tommaso's widowed sister as evidence of miracles!'

'OK, not evidence . . . But she's walking again and the swelling has gone down on her leg. Remember the one she always has a woollen sock on?'

The mayor was muttering to himself, 'Of course, we'd have to move fast. Serafini was planning to leave tomorrow . . .'

'Signora Tommaso says her sister went out yesterday and bought three pairs of sheer black stockings. Very expensive, very sexy.' He swiped the bar again. 'How old you think she is? Younger than me . . . fifty, maybe?'

'Sixty, if she's a day, the old hag . . .'

The bartender smiled and nodded. 'Not so old, not so old . . . Sheer black stockings – imagine! She hasn't worn stockings in twenty years.'

'How many years is it since those bastards started running that cemetery of the mummies as a tourist concession? Twenty years, you say?'

'More like ten . . . You think they still make such things as real *silk* stockings, Primo? They used to feel so nice. My wife (may she rest in peace), she used to wear them for me when she was feeling frisky. And her legs were not as good as Signora Tommaso's sister's.'

'Barrago the magician's in town as well,' the mayor argued, 'and he often works with Serafini. Together they would make a good show.'

'I think she would too, Primo! A good show! She had beautiful legs as a girl, didn't she?' With as much care as he had polished the Formica he smoothed his hand over the few remaining hairs on his head. 'You know, I might just call in on my day off, see how her cure is going.'

'It was obviously a hoax, this blood, not a cure.'

'Yes, yes, I'm sure you are right, Primo. You're a smart man, educated, but what I want to know is: does this hoax . . . well, does it make Signora Tommaso's sister's black silk stockings any less of a miracle?'

On the other side of Urbino, in a sparc and beautiful Renaissance room lit only by the moon, two men are rhythmically beating a third. They have stripped him half-naked and bound him to a graceful column supporting a small gold statue of some classical god or other, perhaps Apollo, as oblivious as most gods to entreaties from humans. The men wielding whips have bare arms to allow for easy movement, and the moonlight marbleises their skin, as it does the skin of their victim, turning it pale and cold as the white stone motifs in the floor's complex geometry.

There are two onlookers, venerable old men, both bored. They've heard it all before. The pleas for Mama, God, mercy. Father, why hast thou forsaken me? And sure enough, after his initial struggles, after making promises he can't keep, the beaten man has slipped beyond consciousness. The only sound disturbing the night is the spongy slap slap of the whips.

Outside the room are three other distinguished men in conversation, apparently unconcerned, although one of them – golden-haired, angelic – seems more distracted than his two companions. His gaze fixed in the distance, he listens with a grave stillness, perhaps to a sound from inside. Very faint, owing to the thickness of the building's old walls, it might be bats or the slap of bare feet on a wet marble floor; it might be the sound of a butcher tenderising a thick steak.

The man's screams, of course, had been louder. But those people who pass the building, observing the three men conversing calmly outside, think it best to follow their example and remain deaf to the muted screams. It's not our business, passers-by say. If such distinguished men do not feel the need to interfere, why should we? The screams they can attribute to many causes: nightmares, a domestic quarrel, the rehearsal of a play. And in one way the passing spectators are right, the scene *is* a rehearsal, the first of many, the re-enactment of an old nightmare.

Donna flung open the shutters of her room on Monday morning and came face to face with a Madonna whose expression of saccharine melancholy, only slightly chipped, glowed even more sweetly in the mellow October sun. For a moment the two Donnas confronted each other (all kinds of signs, warnings, *portents*, for those who are looking). One at least twelve feet high, no hint of Jewish blood in her glassy cornflower-blue eyes, golden curls and salmon pink plaster cheeks. The other, a formidable rival with a stubborn pagan face still powerfully Etruscan or Roman, despite the nose job. Only the living woman looked bold enough to press claims of virgin motherhood, and the Holy Mother, conceding defeat, sank from view and was carried off bobbing and swaying to the university, her fluorescent polychrome due for restoration by students on the course, 'Conservation of Cultural Goods'. And there in the studio, within hours, she began to weep salt tears.

To Donna it seemed that everything in Europe was being restored, the past re-invented with better plumbing. A never-ending process, she figured, considering how overcrowded the country was with old stuff. Nowhere in Italy could you go without tripping over a Roman column.

This was her second day alone in Urbino. 'Take some time off!' James had said, as he and the crew disappeared to do linking shots around the countryside. She wasn't needed until tomorrow, when Raphael's Mute would be returned to the Ducal Palace. Charlotte and her two assistants, Anna and Paolo, were putting the finishing touches to the painting, and

Donna, free as a bird, was suffering pangs of anxiety. She'd slept in late, dawdled over breakfast, and still found herself with empty hours to fill.

Donna told herself, I must get out of this room, I must *do* something. Go for a walk in the park and read over my lines. Visit those paintings I'm supposed to have studied. The idea immediately made her more depressed. She thought of the endless Annunciations and Transfigurations she'd had to describe since getting this job, all the saints and battle scenes in Urbino. Most of them just so much struggling muscle to Donna. San Sebastian, with maybe fifteen arrows sticking out of him, was it likely he'd wear that simpering expression?

The portraits, though, Donna liked them, especially the one of Duke Federigo reading, an unlikely occupation for a guy with that old boxer's mug, but kinda sexy. 'Always painted in profile from his left side,' Paolo had told her. He often took the time to explain things if he saw she didn't understand. 'It's said the Duke had a tryst with a young woman in an oak wood, and on seeing her again at a joust, he put a sprig of oak leaves in his visor which prevented it closing properly, allowing his opponent's lance to pierce the helmet and destroy his eye.'

Paolo had a crush on her, Donna was pretty sure, but she couldn't take him seriously. She didn't dare: she was already twenty-*one*! She'd got off to a bad start because she was lazy and fell in love too easily, but now she had this great opportunity, like her dad kept reminding her, maybe because he'd paid for her year of European Film Studies at a Canadian college and the short course in Rome on Renaissance art (which she'd pretended was a Bachelors in Art History to get this job). Now even more aware of her own rough edges, she was determined to *do* something with her life, *be* somebody. Paolo was too similar to boys she knew in Toronto, boys who, after high school, made it an inch further up the ladder than their folks and then settled for a small house and a big mortgage. Before you know it, three screaming kids, their wife's left them, alimony, bumpety bump and down the rungs they slide.

Today, though, Donna was depressed by her humiliation at

the Count's (and the broken statue, she shouldn't have done that, but she was trying not to think about it); she'd like Paolo to give her a boost of confidence. What she'd do: buy some postcards and write them in the Caffè Repubblica, where everybody in Urbino hung out. She could have one of those pastries the place baked twice daily. Maybe not. All this pasta: she was *definitely* gaining weight. James had mentioned it, teasing her in his sneaky English way that made you look dumb if you got hurt or angry.

Donna's route to the café took her past Raphael's house, now a museum, where she was surprised to see a bronze statue of the artist, bluey-green with verdigris, obviously transferred here from its customary position in the piazza at the top of the Via Raffaello. Moving statues: it disoriented her for a minute. She thought it was a funny position to choose, given that this street was one of the town's few through routes for cars. And whoever was responsible for the move hadn't even bothered to clean off the pigeon shit. Splattered as usual, Raphael stood with palette and brushes held aloft, confidently awaiting divine inspiration. The movers had also forgotten to bring the nineteenth-century figure 'Spirit of Renaissance' which usually reclined at Raphael's feet, a beautiful half-naked girl waking as if from a long sleep.

'An old fat philosopher in a toga would be more symbolic of the Renaissance spirit than a pretty girl,' Paolo had said of this allegorical figure. Donna hadn't really understood what he meant, but she'd laughed along with everyone else. *Ha ha ha.* Half the time she didn't know what the *fuck* they were all talking about. Another thing she couldn't tell Dad.

What had Donna learned about the Renaissance after six weeks' study and another six weeks reading scripts? Whole *libraries* devoted to the subject and no one could agree on a date, that's what! Which in her view made the Renaissance less of a rebirth and more of a slow wake-up, or a long voyage back to a place you loved. Catholic Donna had seen her share of births, one sister already on her fifth baby, and if she knew *anything*, it was that being born was no slow fucking journey, it was a sudden, painful and bloody *arrival*. Unless maybe rebirth, second time round, wasn't so bad.

At that moment Raphael winked at her with a verdigris eyelid and the astonished Donna nearly fell off her high heels. She noticed the coins in an upturned beret at the statue's dead-still feet. Un*fucking*believable! She'd never seen such a realistic living statue. Smiling broadly, she added some change to the hat, a gesture Raphael greeted by gravely placing a verdigris hand against his verdigris chest and feigning an expression of love-struck bronze, slightly smearing the greasepaint he'd used to achieve his convincing metallic skin.

On the marble table next to her hot chocolate and pile of postcards Donna laid a book, title up: *The Book of the Courtier* by Baldassare Castiglione, a guy from Urbino who had been painted by Raphael. The book was one she'd heard Paolo discussing with Charlotte. It seemed pretty slow to her, but buying it was part of Donna's ongoing transformation of herself into the kind of person who might like such a book, or at least read it. Anything could happen on a day when Raphael winked at you!

Suddenly Donna liked everything about Italy – the old grand-dads in the café next to her, looking like they'd always been there, the sense of *their* grand-dads doing the same thing, and grand-dads before them. She couldn't understand what the old guys were saying, but she could hear their sentences folding in and out of each other, something to do with the way all Italian words finished in vowels, everything connected, ways of connecting she couldn't even imagine. Nothing ever ended, there was just that sexy slide into the next word, the next possibility. You could feel it in the air, a place alive with the texture of possibilities.

The three old men who were sitting in the sunshine near Donna were reminiscing: 'That's another squealer won't mess up any more careers.'

'Two down.'

'Best way to deal with squealers. Always has been, always will be.'

'What was the song the American was singing that night?' asked an old man with the upright bearing of a retired military officer, who until then had been quietly admiring the beautiful young foreigner writing postcards, a girl he had last seen walking barefoot across the courtyard from Dado's apartments. 'He was a squealer . . .'

His friend softly hummed a plantation melody.

'That's it! "Camtan Reztrak"!'

'I come down dah wid my head caved in, *doo* dah, *doo* dah,' whispered the eldest of the three, whose English was more fluent.

'Hat, not *head* caved in!' corrected the military man, a stickler for facts. Then, noticing the sardonic expression on the singer's face, he laughed.

'I never understood all that "doo dah, doo dah" business,' said the first. 'What's it mean?'

'Means nothing at all, means pointless nonsense.' His military friend hummed the chorus to himself, 'Doo dah . . . makes you think of Dado, doesn't it? Bit of a liability these days, our Dado.'

MIRACLE NUMBER 11

Pentimento

Had Donna passed the Casa Raffaello a few minutes later, she would have witnessed the arrival of Count Malaspino, one of several contributors to the Raphael restoration. James had persuaded him to be filmed at the opening ceremony, a fact that the television director failed to mention to Donna. Charlotte and her two assistants, however, had been aware of the Count's proposed contribution, as they had been of his reputation (hotelier, socialite, celebrated benefactor of the arts). They knew, as well, that he hadn't lived in Urbino since his youth and had returned from Paris only this weekend for the first time in many years.

He arrived alone, with none of the fanfare Charlotte had come to expect from Italian bureaucrats, and took her hand on their introduction, dipping his head as if he were about to kiss it. A tall, thin man with longish grey hair brushed back from a high brow, he was dressed in silky tweeds of the kind Italians imagine to be typical of an English 'country' look (and are far too new and supple to be so) and a fine white cashmere turtleneck that gave him a faintly ecclesiastical air.

'I have seen his picture in Vogue Italia,' Anna had said excitedly, before the Count's arrival. 'So *noble* looking – exactly how one imagines a Count.'

'Almost *too* exactly!' Paolo mocked. 'I suspect retouching. A little gesso maybe overflowed the cracks and blurred the original, the canvas has been re-stretched just here?' With his fingers Paolo tightened the skin over his own almost Slavic cheekbones, further enhancing his resemblance to a young satyr. Or to Puck, Charlotte thought. Already he had the requisite moustache, and the goatee sharp and spiky as his black hair. He lacked only horns and a pair of pointed ears to complete the satirical impression. Paolo's appearance, she decided, perfectly suited the Casa Raffaello, where Raphael was born and remained for his early years. The house had belonged to Raphael's father, Giovanni Santi, a successful painter in his own right, and it retained a cosy feel of domesticity that Charlotte loved, just as she loved the story (however apocryphal) of the young Raphael first learning to grind pigments in the open courtyard that led off the kitchen.

Some mornings she would bring a flask of tea and drink it in this courtyard, where she could smell woodsmoke drifting over the rooftops from the first cooking fires of the day. On cold days she would curl up inside on one of the second storey's window seats facing the Via Raffaello, primitive stone benches carved out of the building's immensely thick exterior walls and worn away by centuries of dreamers like herself to a concave surface as slippery as bars of soap. Sitting on these benches, working in this house, gave Charlotte a certain frisson, a sense of intimate contact with Raphael. From her perspective in the window little had changed in Urbino. Oh, the stone touched by the artist had long since become part of the city's dust, but she liked to imagine a young Raphael just here, studying the same steeply angled view of the street two floors below and the same large windows in the houses opposite, almost close enough to touch. So close, that she had been startled this morning to look across and see an old man – tall, severely handsome and with an upright, military bearing – staring straight into the room where she sat. He seemed to be measuring the distance between them, and she had a disturbing flashback to the wolf or wild dog she'd seen yesterday. Yet this man's face, though predatory, was not at all wolfish. More beaky. A hawk, a crow.

'Paolo,' she said now, 'you don't by any chance know who lives in the house opposite this one, two floors up?'

'Maybe – what's he look like?'

She gave him a rough description.

'Sounds like Lorenzi, the father of our police chief. Used to be Chief himself. A real old Fascist, my grandfather says, but a great collector, a patron of the arts now. Why?'

'Oh, nothing.' She found it difficult to come to terms with the idea of the country she loved harbouring the old guard from a war that had cost Europe so much. One simply had to accept that beauty and ugliness often went hand in hand, she told herself, and turned her attention back to the printed 'Object Report Form' she made for each stage of a restoration. It listed the painting's original condition first (including damage inflicted by earlier repairs), followed by a treatment record of chemicals and paints used and the type of lining or patching linen required.

Watching Charlotte, Paolo was impressed as always by the meticulous care she took, even when working on the minor pictures they were restoring along with Raphael's mute woman. Although he and Anna had done a lot of preparatory cleaning before Charlotte's arrival six weeks ago, they had not been as diligent about materials as she had since taught them to be. He still worried that they hadn't done enough research on the synthetic varnish used to protect *La Muta*'s cleaned surface.

'We were advised . . . we *hope* this varnish will not discolour in future . . .' Paolo had said nervously, a week after meeting his more conscientious English colleague.

'I have complete faith in you,' Charlotte had responded, earning his instant loyalty. Since then he had been responsible for documenting her daily progress in photographs. The first weeks she had spent infilling any losses in *La Muta*'s paint with a water-based putty, texturing it to conform to the original surface, then retouching these areas using pigments she had chosen for their reversibility and stability. He saw immediately how adept she was at matching the colours, texture and missing elements of the original composition, so sensitive to the artist's intentions that Paolo would have sworn Raffaello himself was whispering in her ear. 'She has his eyes at the end of her paintbrush,' said Anna.

When it came to the final inpainting, they were intrigued that

Charlotte always removed the magnifying goggles she wore for the earlier, more technical side of her restoration. She would become even quieter than usual, very still. Paolo was aware of her steadying herself at her easel like a monk preparing to meditate before a holy mountain.

Both of the young restorers loved the sense of almost Buddhist calm Charlotte brought to the chaos of their studio, the way she arranged the diverse shapes of her brushes and putty knives and pots of paint in a pleasing, orderly pattern. 'Making a picture herself,' Anna said. Aware of doing the reverse, Paolo made a conscious effort not to let his messier work habits interfere with his English colleague's space, and was ashamed one day when he came in earlier than usual to find that Charlotte had had to tidy up after him before starting her own work.

Their workspace was in the former studio of Raphael's father, normally reserved for exhibits sponsored by the Accademia Raffaello. For the last six weeks this whitewashed room had been partly cordoned off so that Urbino's citizens and visitors might observe the restoration, an aspect to the commission that Charlotte hated. She disliked being 'on show', especially while working, and often came to Raphael's house very early in the morning to explore undisturbed the small, safe world of the canvas.

Creating a mental picture was easier with Raphael, Charlotte found, than with less documented painters. For reference she had his self-portrait as a dreamy young poet, she had various academic theses, she had the biography by Vasari, who, for all his errors, was at least born while his subject was alive. Vasari too had been a painter, from a neighbouring province, therefore he could be said to speak with Raphael's accent. 'Raphael was always indulging his sexual appetites,' Vasari wrote, 'and in this matter his friends were probably more indulgent and tolerant than they should have been.' Reading Vasari, Charlotte could begin to 'hear' Raphael, as she could see what kind of women he admired from studying the faces he gave his Madonnas and Magdalenes.

'Other artists could paint a saintly face,' Anna mused dreamily, 'but Raphael could paint the saint's very thoughts.'

'He makes you see the sinner behind all saints,' the irreverent Paolo amended, to the distress of Anna, a devoutly Catholic young woman.

And this was Raphael's genius, thought Charlotte, to transform his Virgins and Christ Childs and aged Josephs into a sensuous, fleshy Italian family, for all their angelic expressions. Not that the sponsors of this restoration had allowed her to state such thoughts in the exhibition catalogue. They had edited from the text any mention of Raphael's sex life (let alone the Holy Family's), abhorring Charlotte's suggestion that their 'divine painter' had had a famously lustful appetite for women, dozens of mistresses, and in the end married one of them – possibly this woman, in fact: *La Muta*, who was not an aristocrat but a peasant, the baker's daughter. Was that her secret, the motive for her sealed lips? Raphael himself had certainly kept her background well hidden.

The sponsors' revised version read, 'Raphael embodied the attitudes of Renaissance humanists, men who accepted that the study of science and of pagan scholars like Plato and Cicero could lead mankind away from the idea of inborn sinfulness towards a growing faith in human potential.'

Suitably anodyne. But it was their catalogue, their painting, not hers, thought Charlotte, who attempted in her work to suppress all evidence of her own identity. Lately, perhaps because she was painting in Raphael's house, she had found herself talking to him in her dreams. And although she woke with no memory of the actual words spoken, there remained in her mind a sense of the elegant shape and flow of that language from another century. I am an interpreter, Charlotte thought, an archaeologist digging through the layers of other restorers' paint to unearth the truth; or, as she sometimes saw herself, a translator. Like translation, restoration inevitably reflected its era's fashions and prejudices and politics; each translator cast the shadow of his or her own light source. *La Muta*, for example, cloistered by her frame, had become to Charlotte a symbol of all the silent women in the world who had no one to speak for them, women invisible within the purdah of silence.

Every day when she finished work at the palace Muta came to watch the kind, blue-eyed foreigner nursing the other mute back to life, making her young again with her careful fingers. She stared into the painted face (a window in the wall, another watcher in the night) and silently told her, *I know what you have witnessed, I see the wolf in your eyes. You can keep a secret as well as I.* Today, observing how the fine wrinkles had vanished and the yellow painted skin freshened and bloomed again, Muta felt both envious and resentful of the nurse's touch. Why should the other mute be restored and not *her*, she wondered, then was suddenly transfixed as the crowd parted to let a tall man through, the shade of someone half-remembered, half-imagined. She waited for him to recognise her, watching his eyes pass over the faces and never come to rest on hers, as if she had no more living substance than the painted woman on the wall. Was it him? Two of them returned?

'She certainly seems younger than I remember,' the Count was saying. 'Like a childhood friend who has mysteriously remained the same age while I myself have grown old.'

Charlotte was unhappily aware that he probably expected from her the kind of compliments offered with easy profligacy by Italians. Hopeless at small talk, she became even stiffer. 'Have you noticed how the cleaning reveals the *sfumato* technique learned by Raphael in Florence?'

'That is what makes his colours blend into one another so imperceptibly,' he said. 'Like smoke . . . vanishing in the air.'

'Charlotte is responsible for the subtlety,' Paolo interjected. 'She is a real artist.'

Charlotte flushed with embarrassment. 'I'm a craftsman, no

more than that. Retouching – inpainting – is my only real forte.' She wasn't being falsely modest. Oils, acrylics, watercolours; figurative, expressionist, surrealist: at one time she'd tried them all. Her trouble was that she lacked a subject, couldn't see the point of adding one more mediocre artist to the pool screaming 'Me! Me! Me! Look at Me! See how original I am, how unique!' With no creative spark of her own (as John had never hesitated to point out to her), she preferred to repair what existed already rather than add to the clutter. Still, she was pleased that her work had brought *La Muta*'s creamy skin back to life, even if the emerald-and-rose velvet gown now shone so lusciously that one critic had mocked the restoration as a 'Benetton Raphael', much the same words he had used earlier to deride the revived ceiling of the Sistine Chapel.

'Paolo and Anna are far more up to date on scientific practice than I am,' said Charlotte, who was grateful that neither of her two assistants had ever shown the slightest resentment at her promotion over their heads. Anna, with moderate talent but a prodigious capacity for taking pains, seemed content to lay in the backgrounds, while Paolo took care of most of the chemical analyses. 'When I started my career, conservation was less of an exact science,' Charlotte admitted.

Count Malaspino turned back to *La Muta*, who stared out of the canvas at him with her strange, unbalanced eyes. 'This is the shadow of the pentimento?' he asked, stretching out one long thin finger. 'Here across the woman's eyebrow?' He was referring to the scar revealed after the old retouching had been removed by Paolo and Anna. This blemish had run from the right side of *La Muta*'s forehead, through her eyebrow and into the socket, possibly accounting for her stubborn, slightly cross-eyed stare, which gave the portrait an underlying feeling of tension that had led Paolo to nickname it *L'Ammutinata*, 'the mutinous woman'. 'I see you have not entirely painted the scar out again,' said the Count.

'It is *largely* concealed,' Paolo said. 'The city council decided that the people of Urbino were not yet ready to see their lady with such an unsightly blemish.' A sore point with Charlotte, who saw it as a betrayal of Raphael's wishes. 'The decision was . . . controversial,' she said, putting the case mildly as usual. 'Our tests revealed the old over-painting to have been done at a later period – and not by Raphael.'

'Really?' said the Count. 'What proof do you have that the scar wasn't covered by the older Raphael?'

'It's more of a . . . feeling.' The word embarrassed Charlotte, these days wary of emotions, but she could hardly say, I *know* this artist, he was too fond of humanity, warts and all, to have covered up this scar. Didn't Raphael, in his portrait of the wall-eyed Tommaso Inghiriami, have his sitter look away from us, so that Tommaso's skewed eye, while less disturbing, was still honestly portrayed? And in the painting of his friend, Baldassare Castiglione, although Raphael concealed with a velvet hat the writer's baldness (of which Castiglione was greatly ashamed) and focused on his clear blue eyes, he certainly did not add a hair to the shiny scalp.

But none of this was *scientific* proof, Charlotte knew. Struggling for words, she was pleased to hear Paolo speak up, 'For early paintings like this one Raphael used thin paint for his flesh tones, Count, which makes it hard to disguise another artist's additions – and the area around the scar was very thick, the brushwork far less sure than Raphael's.'

Paolo hated having to justify their theories to this Count and all the other rich men and ministers of culture and town councillors who kept him in work. And whose reputations, in turn, I consolidate, he thought, although my work isn't good enough for them. He should've been further up the ladder by now. *Would've* been, with better family connections. His Marxist grandfather derided him for being akin to a TV make-up artist, 'Covering up the blemishes instead of exposing the truth. Papering over the cracks in this rotten edifice of a country!'

'I'm depressed enough about my work without you on my back!' Paolo had told him.

'If you are depressed,' said his grandfather, 'it is because you try to be a servant of the ruling classes and they reject you.'

Only for the moment, thought Paolo, giving the Count a courtier's smile. He had plans. A way of using his skills to more spectacular effect. Encouraged by this knowledge, he kept his resentment to himself and offered up his skills like any other merchant laying out his wares. 'Oils tend to darken dramatically over the first years, Count Malaspino, and later painting soon fails to match the original.'

'I see . . . The causes of decay are inherent in the materials of painting . . . as they are in us, as they are in us . . .'

'Yes, well . . .' said Charlotte. 'If it interests you, the palace is displaying several photographs Paolo has taken of La Muta before and after we retouched the scar.'

'For the council to consider the error of their cover-up?' Malaspino suggested with a smile.

Muta felt her anger, unexpressed for decades, still intact and potent. She was a concealed mine, a fuse that, if lit with a voice, could explode and blast everyone, *everything*. Sick and cold from remembering, a roaring in her head, she felt herself rising into the silence, above the crowd, through the ceiling, the roof, up with the circling pairs of black crows until she could see the whole of Urbino province stretched out far below, the ruins of San Rocco in the distance – except now it was not ruined, it was whole again and she was falling, she was no longer soaring but sinking towards the lake of ice where she was frozen again, at their mercy. She could feel the rage filling her until, just when she thought it could not be contained, the two guards began to move the crowd out. Visiting hours over.

She pushed her way through the same old faces, coming and going and never changing, into the open air where she could breathe again and think about what she had seen and what she must now do.

MIRACLE NUMBER 12

The Helicoidal Ramp

Since the day when her particular wolf loped into San Rocco looking for sanctuary, Muta had known it was watching. Her *particular*. On her long walks into the city she felt this dogged wolf, this *Canis lupus* dogging her footsteps, always there – reminding her, stalking her, *led* by her – as far as the paved road beyond the San Rocco valley, where it would fade away at last as the palace city came into view.

Today, the warm October sun turned Urbino's domes and conical spires and hanging gardens into a shimmering promise of escape. A fragile promise (you could crack that eggshell-blue sky with a teaspoon), still the mute woman believed in it. She took a deep breath and stretched every bone in her spare ribcage, raising her eyes towards the confetti battle of doves and crows above Duke Federigo's palace, searching for some good omen to be read in that daily conflict of black and white. The crows looked too black against the light, hurling themselves up from the balconies between the twin turrets like bird-shaped bullet-holes rapidly tearing through a painting of blue sky to the darkness beyond. No difference today that Muta could detect, except perhaps for an increase in their numbers, a gathering of crows. Yet as she approached the Mercatale square she felt able to claw and bite her way out of this furred silence she was trapped in. She felt . . . *alive*! A living, breathing witness. *Alive*, when she shouldn't be.

From the broad Mercatale square to the foot of the Ducal Palace's twin turrets, an enclosed passageway of shallow steps spirals upwards in great curling sweeps designed originally to accommodate the strides of horses climbing into the Duke's stables. Think of this helicoidal ramp as an ear, the city's whispering inner ear, which it almost resembles, if an ear were to be constructed entirely in those narrow, shell-pink bricks common to medieval Italian buildings. The ramp's auditory ability is certainly recognised by its ancient caretaker, who regularly curses it (as if the ramp could indeed hear). 'Auricula!' he spits, a vulgar sexual reference to the Virgin Mary's ear, through which she was said to have been impregnated by God. 'Ragazzi sporcano per tutto!' he grumbles at anyone who will listen to his complaints about the scrawled graffiti. Privately he dirties the ramp himself with his malevolent contempt for all things feminine, cursing it with the selection of juicy obscenities he reserves for women's sexual organs.

Graffiti on the ramp's walls can be traced back five hundred years, code for the city's comings and goings, a silent record of gossip and tragedy. Take 'Cesare', for instance, who, ten years after he scratched his name in a rough heart with his girl, 'Angela', soon to be his wife, beat her to death with a carjack. Just a foot away is a much earlier signature, 'Francesco', who went on to build Urbino's first permanent theatre and sire thirty grandchildren and God alone knows how many great-grandchildren and great-great and great-great-great, their signatures carved near his. As is Carla Gentili's, age sixteen, a partisan of ferocious courage, two years before she met her German lover Franz, who would be strung up beside her by the Nazis for refusing to mine the walls of Urbino. Next to Carla's name you will find the words SEMPRE VIVA, carved in the early 1960s by her illegitimate son (of Franz, everyone suspects), at the time a science student at Urbino's university. His careful incision gives some hint of the later success he would have as a surgeon, the profession of Franz's grandfather in Munich, which gives credibility to the town gossip. Fascists and football players, painters and decorators: they're all here.

Including another Francesco, Francesco Mazzini, when he still had hopes and illusions, before he became a gambler, a drunkard, a cop who took bribes. Before he changed his name and his profession and discovered the restorative powers of Sicilian ice-cream.

Each day on her way to work the mute woman has climbed these wheeling auricular stairs, sixteen years now, since their restoration in 1977, sharing her route with countless tour groups, historians and architectural students. She never takes the new mechanical lift. Nor does she stop, as others do, to admire the ramp's ingenious design, conceived by the brilliant Sienese, Francesco di Giorgio Martini, who in the closing decades of the fifteenth century contributed so much of Tuscany's Renaissance purity to the medieval complexities of the Ducal Palace.

The mute woman, aware only of the living history of individual bricks, climbs for the sheer pleasure of being enclosed within this curving, airy tunnel whose rosy whorls and coils remind her of an enormous snail shell. Wanting to put its hollow chambers to her ear and listen, she runs her hands along the shell-pink brick, feels all the lost and present voices under her fingers, offering consolation. She hears them whispering in her head, lovers obliterated by newer lovers, stories worn away into dust like hers.

Meeting her on these stairs, other palace staff give her a wide berth, avoiding her unconsciously, the way they avoid walking under ladders. In a country where noise and bustle and crowds are valued, where every car and moped is in a hurry to overtake, this solitary woman is an oddity, her silence an accusation.

The caretaker doesn't like her either. Illogically, for the mute is said not to be able to read or write, he consigns her to the group of hooligans who wantonly carve and spray their names across the bricks in his custody. He says she has *il malocchio*, the evil eye. He says she looks too young for her age. *His* age – and look at *him*! Tall as a man and straight-backed, Muta and her stubborn witchy survival make other superstitious people wonder: what contract has she made – and with whom? Uncomfortable, those mirrored eyes of hers; you can see the wolf behind the cage. If she is not the devil's offspring, then she is certainly *trouble*. A troubling reminder of how miracles can waylay the natural course of things, upset the best-laid plans.

MIRACLE NUMBER 13

The Fallibility of Perspective

Entering the Ducal Palace on the morning that Raphael's painting was to be returned to its old position in the Duchess Salon, Charlotte passed under the palace's covered gateway into the Courtyard of Honour, a serene quadrangle to which the repeating patterns of Corinthian columns and lofty arches gave an extraordinary feeling of lightness. The perfect proportions were emphasised by fine criss-crossing lines of white marble laid in the red-brick herringbone floor, as if the marks chalked up by the original architect had been set permanently in stone.

Charlotte barely noticed the tall woman with a broom who stood sweeping the bricks at the epicentre of these crossing lines. A lesson in perspective. Another warning missed. As usual, Charlotte was more concerned with the past. She was thinking about what the French philosopher Jean Starobinski had called '*architecture parlante*', architecture that speaks to us, buildings that proclaim both their goals and their meaning, the way this perfect courtyard did. She had the sense of stepping onto a platform only recently vacated by some great orator of the Classical Age. A spectral Plato might be awaiting his cue behind one of the graceful columns, the shade of Socrates behind another. Or she had shrunk like Alice (a childhood fantasy) and wandered into *The Ideal City*. One of her favourite paintings in the palace's collection, it offered a Utopian view into a perfect Renaissance square which was, apart from two nesting pigeons, curiously devoid of life. Even the octagonal fountains were 'quiet'. The lack of people in the empty square and the rigorous perspective employed on the imaginary buildings (also empty) had led Charlotte to believe that its mysteriously anonymous artist might have been an architect active in Urbino in the fifteenth century – perhaps Laurano himself, Architect-in-Chief of this very palace. Her reasoning was that many architects disliked the disorder people introduced to their buildings, whereas painters, involved in a messy business themselves, were more tolerant of human noise and mess.

Charlotte didn't take in the woman on those converging lines of perspective, but she did notice the courtyard's curiously steely light. An identical dawn clarity pervades *The Ideal City*, she decided, and this, combined with the picture's (and today's) emphatic, almost *expectant* silence, contributes to its sense of suspended animation. A stage set waiting for the actors to enter so that the Renaissance might begin. Let the fountains play, the strolling musicians sing, strike up the band!

'Raphael's Portrait of a Gentlewoman, or *La Muta*, may translate as either "the mute woman" or "the silent woman" –' Donna recited, and was immediately reduced to giggles by the Italian sound man's whisper, 'A *silent* woman – what a rare and precious concept!'

'Take two!' called James, and Donna began again. More relaxed this time, she managed without the quiver of an eyelash to mention the generous financial assistence from Count Malaspino (she'd nearly shit a *brick* when she read the revised script this morning!) and the painting's return after months to its rightful place here in Urbino's Palazzo Ducale.

So far, so good. The next paragraph was awkward, an even more wordy version of the script Charlotte had tried and failed to present a week ago. Charlotte wouldn't be so quick to include all this *vocabulary*, thought Donna, not if she'd had to continue reciting the damned sentences herself. Taking a deep breath and remembering to smile, she pressed on: 'With this portrait Raphael adopted a convention from earlier Flemish works, a ledge painted at the bottom of the picture, apparently supporting the woman's forearm. But La Muta actually extends her finger and appears to press it against the picture frame as if to open it,' Donna tried desperately to catch her breath without breaking the rhythm, 'this hand with its extending finger reinforcing the friction – '

'The *fiction*,' said the script girl.

'The *fiction* of the painting as an extension of the space occupied by the beholder.' *Beholder*! Donna thought. Who the *fuck* says 'beholder'!

'That was great, Donna,' said James, 'but I wonder- ... mmm ... could you just take it from the top again?'

Donna did as she was told, then moved on: 'The pressing finger as much as her sealed lips hints that far from being locked in the past, she may have a secret that she could, if she wished, impart to us; yet she chooses to remain silent ... Hey, James? Why can't I just say: If this painting could talk it could tell us a few things?'

'Because – ' Charlotte burst out, and stopped abruptly when James fixed his ironic gaze on her.

'Charlotte? You don't find that acceptable?'

'No,' she said, less vehemently. 'No, I don't, because ... one of the interesting things about the painting is ... is the *mystery* of this woman's silence. It's her *silence* that speaks ... to a different side of us ... It makes us doubt our own answers, even destroys belief ... whereas ... whereas ... mediocre art simply makes a statement.'

The instant she had finished this impassioned speech, Charlotte regretted it, knowing how vulnerable it left her if the director did not accept her point of view. And sure enough, James remarked drily that in this particular case, given the audience, he agreed with Donna, whom he signalled to start again.

Donna caught the eyeroll he gave the cameraman and assumed James was making fun of her own inability to read the script, and she saw Charlotte do that disapproving thing with her lips, pursing them like a duck's ass, as if she were going to put her fingers there and hail a cab. Behind her, some old cleaning lady had joined the onlookers. *Jesus*, Donna thought, why don't they just let the whole *world* in to watch me fuck up!

She soon ran into more difficulties: '... just as in the Vatican, Raphael used architectural elephants – *shit*!'

'Take five.'

A deep breath, a bright smile, breathe in, out: '... Raphael used architectural *elements* to disguise the inclusion of a – '

'The intrusion, not inclusion,' corrected the script girl.

'Take six.'

'... architectural estimates – ' She saw the Count's wife whisper in his ear and then in Anna's. All three nodding and smiling.

'Take seven.'

Donna could feel herself losing it even before the words tangled up in her mouth: '... architects to disguise the elephants – *fuck*!' The security guard, sensing tension in the air, looked up from *Visto*, the cheap TV magazine he was reading. The crew were grinning, but a tense James struck a line through a long paragraph and said bluntly, 'All right, Donna. We'll drop that line and take it from ... halfway down that page.'

Charlotte watched the complex ideas she had tried to express being lopped off, compressed in the name of simplicity. Did people have to be spoon-fed everything in this fast-food era? Was everything suspect that could not be acquired quickly, with a plastic surgeon's scalpel, a personal trainer or a handful of cash? Equality was the ambition, to be equally ignorant, to *celebrate* ignorance. A far cry from the Renaissance ideals of the Duke responsible for this palace. She tried to concentrate on the vast room's plaster ceiling frieze of cupids and rams' skulls, only to be distracted by a strong smell of aftershave emanating from a priest next to her. He wore a goatee and the latest in fashionable glasses, at odds with the antique origins of his black hooded cassock. Beside him, she noticed with a start, was the old gentleman of military aspect she had seen from Raphael's window yesterday morning, his gaze today fixed on the Count.

'Take eight.'

Paolo, noticing the strain on Donna's face and the dark circles under her arms, wished he could do something to help. Eyes lowered, fists clenched, he experienced all her mistakes as his own; he *willed* her to succeed. When James made a caustic remark about her to the cameraman, Paolo scowled, so deeply did he feel the comment to be directed at part of himself. He thought: she's too young for this, there will be nothing left of her when they've finished. He wanted to take her away now, before the damage was done.

'Take nine.'

Donna moving her hands and head as stiffly as a plastic doll's.

Ten. Eleven. Twelve.

Numbers and words pounding in her like the pulse of migraine. Her mouth almost incapable of forming sentences. Ordinary words like 'finger' and 'frame' sounded meaningless, a foreign language. Everyone was stifling smiles or yawns. Was the cleaning woman laughing too? She had moved closer, no doubt to get a better look at the dumb Canadian making a fool of herself.

Donna got to take fourteen before James asked if she needed a break.

'No, I'm OK. What I think is, what I think is . . .' Her voice was wobbling, on the brink of tears. Get a grip, kiddo. 'I think I'll just take that sentence to the end? Then retake from the top if necessary?' She looked down at her toes and whispered a prayer: Please God, if I get it right this time I promise never to say another bad word about that old bitch . . . about Charlotte, and I'll write a long letter home to Mom tonight, and . . .

She looked up and saw Paolo, a single friendly face. For Donna, who was conscious of her beauty in the way people are of new shoes, forever appraising it, checking in the mirrors of shop windows for scuffs, Paolo was confirmation that she wasn't a fat kid from Toronto any more. With his eyes willing her to succeed, she managed to steel herself and take the script from the beginning, not a fucking semi-colon out of place. Sweat pouring down inside her dress, pantyhose sticking to her crotch, God knows what she looked like as she got to the final lap . . .

Shit! She'd taken the last sentence too fast. She couldn't do it again . . . not with all these faces . . . the Count nodding and smiling, nodding and smiling . . .

When a wink from the cameraman reassured her, Donna's huge smile of relief, matched by Paolo's, lit up the television monitors. James was playing the tape back to check for level and lighting, but the crew, Charlotte, everyone, knew it was OK. In giving *La Muta* the tremulous voice of an involuntary witness, Donna had lent poignancy to a dry script, as if the perfectly beautiful living speaking girl had identified with the marred and silent image she described. Two women framed: one in canvas and wood, one on film.

Donna's refusal to give up had earned even Charlotte's grudging respect. I would *hate* it, she thought. I *did* hate it: everyone aware of your slightest mistake, thinking they could do your job better. She tried to consider the girl objectively. A face Raphael would have loved, certainly, but what would he have intended by this collection of features? Who does she remind me of . . . Another fatally attractive woman. Emma Hamilton, that's it, Romney's highly coloured rendition of Nelson's mistress, the voluptuous, full-lipped, rosy-cheeked triangular face with its dark brows and straight classical nose. Though Charlotte doubted that Donna, like Emma, was born to die tragically. If the Canadian girl was dumb, she was 'dumb like a fox', as one of the crew had put it, and with her undoubted gift for mimicry it was possible that new ideas and new vocabulary, sliding off at first, might eventually stick- . . . like *mud thrown at a wall*, thought Charlotte, momentarily abandoning her generous attitude.

'That's fine, Donna,' James called. 'Now could you introduce Count Malaspino, then step out of frame and we'll have him draw the curtain.'

Oh, the Count was a cool customer, all right, thought Donna, deciding that this ceremonial occasion fitted him like his tailored linen suit. Slippery with charm and practised at openings of all kinds (as she knew), he directed a politician's smile of professional insincerity at the camera, then launched into a speech about how delighted he and his wife were to have sponsored the restoration.

Blah-di-blah-di-blah . . . Donna gazed sweetly at him, her eyebrows raised in innocent concentration. She thought: I'd like to drive my five-inch spikeheels into his sleepy eyes. I'd like to stomp on his long nose. What did Charlotte call him? *Patrician.* I'd like to grab the long patrician dick that probably goes with the long patrician nose and slice them both off with a pair of common shears.

Count Malaspino extended his arm, never letting his eyes leave the camera lens for an instant, and drew back the velvet curtain concealing *La Muta*, 'To conclude – '

One moment the old cleaning lady was part of the audience, the next she had leapt – whether directly at the painting or at the Count or both, it was hard to say. Striking him a violent blow on the side of his face, drawing blood, the force of her spring carried her forward until she ripped through the creamy throat of Raphael's *La Muta*, tearing six inches of the canvas. She turned to face the audience, panting, blood on her hands, her caged eyes narrowed. There was a moment of fatally suspended animation, one of those moments that in retrospect stretchs to hours. Then the cleaning woman bolted.

The speed and silence of the attack made it all the more shocking.

'A knife! She had a knife!'

'No! It was her nails, I saw them – talons!'

Donna wasn't too shocked to be inwardly glad at the way Count Malaspino's speech had been cut off. Now Count Smoothy's just standing there, blood on his smooth chops, blood on his smooth suit, no more fucking speechifying today, no *sir*! The girl took in the excited faces all round her. Scandal! Violence! Everyone loving it, bored with all the talk talk talk, no one giving a good goddamn about the picture . . . except for Charlotte. Donna couldn't believe it. Miss Prissy Pants was staring at the Raphael with this *look*, this white, drained *look*! Anyone'd think it was a *kid* got stabbed!

The room was so silent you could hear the cleaning woman's footsteps echoing down the hallway. Suddenly everyone started shouting and pushing in different directions. Two guards ran after the woman. Charlotte saw Lorenzi speak to three beefy men in indistinguishable slate-grey suits and shortly after that the three moved off down the hall where the guards had disappeared. Donna was trying to make her way through the crowd towards Paolo, whose usually merry face had looked so drawn and worried while she was struggling with the script. To thank him for his support, that was all she intended. Or . . . maybe more. But people who wanted to see what had happened to the Count stopped in passing to shake her hand, kiss her cheeks, pat her hair and her shoulder and tell her she was a *brava ragazza*, a *bella ragazza*, as if the presence of a pretty girl were a talisman protecting the tall aristocrat from more serious harm.

Paolo wanted to hold Donna close in his arms and stroke her, take her to a room where they could be alone. He thought of licking the sweat off her, under her breasts, between her legs. He closed his eyes for an instant and tried to think about something else. Varnish. Gesso. When he opened them again, a wall of Urbino's VIPs had surged forward, pressing her back into the circle around the Count and his solicitous wife, marvelling at the blood on his jacket and congratulating Donna on her courage.

Muta stopped to catch her breath and felt the floor resonate under her feet. Men coming fast behind her. She turned and ran, leading them on through room after room, her flight observed by the walls of angels and saints and whispering courtiers whom she knew would never betray her. She had polished every smile and wound, every weary bone in every frame.

On this western side, furthest from the Court of Honour, the palace was constrained by the cliff out of which it grew like a great rocky outcrop. Rooms were compressed into odd shapes and stretched out to wrap around the edge and, even more awkwardly, around a second courtyard. Smaller and smaller the rooms got, a disorienting maze of dressing chambers and vestibules and miniature private chapels, linked by the spiralling stairs within the palace's twin towers. At the heart of the maze was one of the smallest rooms of all – the Duke's tiny study, in which all the symbols of the Renaissance culture had been condensed by some wizard of marquetry into a space the size of a cupboard. Empty of furniture, empty of everything except ideas, its walls were filled floor to ceiling with inlaid wooden scenes in a miraculous perspective that defied the flat surface. *Trompe l'oeil* cupboards with pierced screens appeared to open into the room, revealing shelves of *trompe l'oeil* mandolins and *trompe l'oeil* mathematical instruments. A *trompe l'oeil* squirrel ate a nut on a *trompe l'oeil* balcony, while beyond it stretched an entire *trompe l'oeil* world celebrating Federigo's conversion from man of war to man of peace. This was the centre, the heart of the palace. A room no bigger than a word.

Muta, behind one of the study's massive doors, watched the guards enter. Men new to the palace, she didn't recognise their faces. They stopped dead to stare around them. 'Look, Michele!' said the older man, pointing at the armour that appeared to hang from a hook by the door. His young friend was studying the 3-D light effects on a pile of flat marquetry books designed to look as if they had been strewn casually inside the cupboard. 'You seen this, Leo?'

They had to see her, there was nowhere to hide. Gripping the knife, Muta flattened herself against the wall and imagined herself as still and brown as the wooden books: *I have been in many shapes, before I attained a congenial form. I have been a narrow blade, I have been a painted smile, I have been a word in a book.*

The two guards moved off without a glance at the door that barely hid her, could not hide her, in fact. When the floor ceased vibrating underfoot she slipped out and down the tower's spiral stairs, in her pocket a key that opened the door to the palace's mirror world underground, vaulted brick chambers like chilly catacombs where Muta knew a place where no one would look for her – and if they did, would not find her.

With the palace closed today except to the staff and VIPs, all lamps except the emergency spots had been switched off. No electric light reached the small, dank space she'd entered. Her only guide was a saucer of clear blue sky suspended far overhead, the colour of the Madonna's robes.

Outside this room was the warning sign she did not or could not read:

PERICOLOSO! *Inside this room is the 'neviera', a deep conical well in which snow from the hanging garden above the basement was collected. Do not approach the mouth of the well, which has become dangerously worn and highly unstable over the centuries.*

MIRACLE NUMBER 14

Galileo's Law of Falling Bodies

The two security guards passed back through the Duke's Audience Chamber and found Lorenzi's men waiting for them in the room beyond. 'We've been through all this part of the palace,' Michele announced proudly to the other three.

'You checked the cellars, Leo?' one of Lorenzi's men asked the older guard, second cousin of his brother-in-law.

'There's no access from the tower entrance up here without a key.'

'You must have a key.'

Leo looked at Michele, who blushed and stammered, 'No, well, I – '

'He was dazzled by the beautiful TV star,' Leo said drily. 'He left them downstairs by mistake.'

'She would have keys, the cleaner, yes?'

'Well – '

'We have to check the cellars.'

Entering the ramped tunnel leading underground from the Courtyard of Honour, Leo zipped up the jacket of his thin uniform. He was in his mid-sixties, a tired, quiet, sharp-faced man who felt the damp chill long before the five men reached the signs directing visitors towards an ancient frigidarium. 'My brother works here regularly, that's how I got the job today,' said the chattier Michele to Lorenzi's men. 'I usually do heavy-duty security, know what I mean?' He winked broadly. 'My brother – he's not here today, he's sick, or he could tell you stuff about this place you wouldn't believe! He knows this place like the back of his hand and he says there are almost as many rooms down here as there are up there,' Michele continued, happy to be able to show off his own more limited knowledge. Ignoring him, the other four stopped in the vaulted brick corridor to study a plan of the *sotterranei.* 'That map shows only the rooms they've clearly identified,' Michele said, 'the kitchens and laundry and dyeing chambers and the Duchess's Turkish bath. There's also a stables and saddle-room.'

'Jesus, look at all these fucking wells!' said one of Lorenzi's three, paying no attention to this idiot who was no doubt hoping to impress them so they'd put in a good word for him with their boss. 'She could be anywhere!'

'Those are just the ones they've restored,' said Michele. 'There are more under these floors, along with sewers and chutes where the shit and piss of the horses used to be emptied.'

The man who clearly had seniority over Lorenzi's group wore the mildly irritated expression of someone bothered by a noisy fly. 'There, at the end of this corridor,' he said to Leo, 'is that the exit from the tower off the Duke's study?' At Leo's nod he said, 'Let's start there.'

Only a few metres down the corridor Leo pointed to a footprint outlined faintly on the damp herringbone bricks.

'She must be in the neviera,' he said. 'There's no way out of there.'

'I'll guard this doorway,' responded one of Lorenzi's men. 'In case she gets past you.' As soon as the museum's two security guards were out of sight he transferred his knife into a more accessible pocket.

Cautiously Muta climbed over the worn lip of the well and began to inch down a wall which sloped almost imperceptibly inwards. Below was sheer blackness. Cold air rising up from the bottom of the well hit her with the density of icy water. Catching her breath, she glanced up for consolation towards the clear moon of sky. A torch beam flashed across the small room above and she lost her grip and skidded a metre down the slope, braking herself against a tough fern. Her feet kept slipping on the well's mossy sides and she had to wedge her fingers between the bricks, scratching with her toes to find the weeds that would hold her weight.

'Don't go near the edge,' Leo warned Lorenzi's men. 'It's unstable.' He indicated the sign.

'I can read,' the leader said, stepping forward to shine a beam of light into the darkness.

Muta pressed herself into the wall as the finger of light felt its way towards her over the bricks. The cold worked its way into her ears and in her head she heard a voice leading her further into a frozen lake so bound with ice it did not look like water but like glass.

'It's a well,' said Michele. 'They used it to collect snow to preserve their food and drink. See that hole up there? That's the hanging garden where – '

'Shut the fuck up,' said the leader of Lorenzi's men. 'Fredo, shine your torch down here beside mine. I think I see something.'

Obediently Fredo moved forward.

'Over there, where the moss and ferns start.'

The two men leaned into the mouth of the well and aimed their torches at Muta's hand, mottled green and black from her descent over the bricks. She pushed her fingers further into the wall, felt the crumbling mortar work its way sharply under her nails. 'Look! Isn't that a – ' began Fredo. His next words were lost in a rumble of bricks and mortar and then a roar as the lip of the well collapsed inward after five hundred years of stability, carrying him with it. Fredo's jacket buttons raked Muta's back as he fell and the bricks bounced off her shoulders and tore her long hair free in whippy strands. Her head was dragged backwards, her throat uplifted like a deer's for slaughter. She felt the vibration as he hit the ground below, sending a shudder and another blast of cold air back up the well-shaft. Her fingers, icy cold, seemed unable to grip the stones any longer.

Upstairs the noise and chaos was still mounting, as increasingly inaccurate descriptions of the event were exchanged with the utmost conviction.

'Silent as a panther,' said one of the English crew. 'Eerie, that silence! And the strength of her! Like she was catapulted from a cannon!'

'Very cold,' said his friend. 'Nasty, she looked.'

'Une vraie louve!' agreed a French lighting man.

Louve, thought Charlotte: the old word for a she-wolf or lustful woman.

The cameraman explained to James that in all the chaos his lens must have been knocked to one side so that he'd managed to film only the patternless stampede of well-shod feet. Neither of the two security cameras focused on the painting had recorded anything except static.

Only Charlotte and the priest noticed what was happening to *La Muta*. The priest fell to his knees and crossed himself, bringing the crowd once more to silence. They watched a red stain welling up through the torn skin of the canvas and slowly spilling down it, much as it had down the Count's cheek and onto his admirably tailored jacket.

'*Miracolo!*' cried the priest, pointing with a trembling hand.

'Nonsense!' announced a male voice, and Charlotte saw that it came from a little man in the mayor's group who sported a gingery moustache that made him look ferrety, not entirely trustworthy. 'It's no miracle,' he insisted, and his thick glasses promptly slipped down his nose, to be pushed back by impatient fingers. 'Just some of the Count's blood – '

'No, Professor Serafini!' said one of the local sound men, a once devout but now lapsed Catholic. 'See: the blood is still running.'

At that moment Lorenzi's remaining two men, along with the two security guards, burst through the crowd shouting for help, but what with the miraculous blood and the younger security guard's loud complaints about blind corridors and transgressions of safety precautions, it was several minutes before they could get anyone to listen. Eventually an ambulance was called, as well as the police and the fire brigade, while Michele continued to complain, threatening a conferral with his union and arguing that his response to the attack had been delayed by the dignitaries surrounding the Count. He wondered if it was within their jurisdiction as security guards to arrest an armed and violent criminal. He mentioned a strike action. He was sure they deserved at least the minimum danger pay if such things were to become a regular occurrence. Leo sat down on a bench and searched for the place he'd left off in a story about this week's lotto winners in *Visto*. Amazing what mundane things people chose to spend their winnings on, he thought. When he won, he intended to get his mother's cataracts fixed so she could watch her favourite TV programmes again and then open a chain of pizza restaurants like they had in America.

To Charlotte, the Count appeared remarkably unmoved by the turn of events. His only response to the story of the fallen man in the well was to murmur, 'How tragic,' then begin a long description of his boyhood interest in Galileo. 'One day I convinced my tutor to help me carry an apple and a pumpkin to the top of the tower at San Rocco,' he said to the local dignitaries who were gathered around him. 'This was before the War, before it was ruined, of course. And from that tower we dropped those two unequal bodies, hoping to test Galileo's "Law of Fall". At the time I was fascinated by how Galileo had turned away from the medieval approach to science to search for natural or physical laws, which are revealed by *measuring*, as opposed to the philosophers' search for causes, revealed by *reasoning*.'

The men nodded and congratulated the Count on his precocity as a boy. 'How much faster did the pumpkin fall?' asked one of them, contractor for the shoddiest tourist chalets around Urbino.

'It didn't fall faster, you moron!' muttered the mayor. 'That's the point!'

The Count, overhearing Primo's comment, shook his head. How wrong the mayor was! The point, Malaspino thought, is how we measure evil, which is all about causes. We can measure the *results* of evil, certainly, but can we apply Galileo's 'Law of Falling Bodies' to man's fall from grace? Would a good man have fallen from that tower more slowly than an evil one, drifted gently to the ground, perhaps? The Count knew for a fact that he would not.

When the vibration had stopped, Muta continued her precarious descent of the well-shaft to the dry earth and weeds on the bottom where the man's body lay partially concealed by bricks. She squatted on her haunches to stare into his open, unblinking eyes. Although there was no blood, she was enough of a hunter to know that the soul had gone, and she closed the lids with her thumb before stepping over the body to climb through a gap in the wall and up another steep chute into the hanging garden above, where she made her way back to the main entrance gate without a soul taking notice. In the helicoidal ramp she started to run, round and round, dizzy within that circling auricular chamber, until finally she stumbled out into the Piazza Mercatale to catch her breath in the deep blue shade of the Sanzio Theatre. From here she would have taken a bus, as she did most days, but today she felt that all eyes were against her. So, head down, she tramped southwest along the winding mountain road to Urbania and Sansepolcro, then cut south beyond Montesoffio, where she felt safe. No one except hunters and fishermen and the last of the old partisans from the War knew these steep hills and river valleys as she did. Muta had fished streams as far as the steep limestone crevices of the Gola di Furlo, and if she had been able to speak, her knowledge of the secret places for white and black truffles could have made her fortune in the truffle market at Acqualagna.

In the dark, exhausted, she reached San Rocco and rested her hand on the tower to feel the bell welcoming her back. Ignoring the wolf's shadow, she slipped her fingers under the mossy skin and lifted the door and climbed down into the cellar full of stories and pictures that did not belong to her except by association. Among the bottles of fruit bleached to white after years in alcohol she lit a candle and held it up to read a label: *Susine damascena, raccolta '44*. Damask plums, picked in the late summer of 1944, when she was twelve. 'Plums from Damascus,' said a voice inside her. One of her own? A dead voice, anyway. All of them dead and only the damask plums preserved.

Rolling the words *susine damascena* silently over her tongue until she could almost taste the dusky fruit, Muta let the day's uproar slip away into the lost years. She skirted villages and stole from farms, shelled, shot at, people dying, bodies eaten by dogs, dogs eaten by people. She crept along roads curling like white snakes through the mountains. She built a fire with the only dry wood available, three wooden crosses on which names were written in a language not her own, while souls ranged thick as trees around her and the shades of people she had known or thought she had known regarded her with grave and tranquil eyes.

Usually it wasn't until the nights lengthened in late November that her family and the other families began gathering for *La Veglia* . . . except – *yes!* – she could close her eyes and *smell* the season . . . It was *October* that year, not November, because her mother had just picked the medlars. 'Medlars in the basket for San Francesco,' they said, 'ripe in time for San Simone': the strange fruit was not good if eaten before ageing and bletting, when its taste became like chocolate. Not that they'd had much chocolate, until the Chocolate Man came. That's what she called him: *the Chocolate Man*.

It was October, she remembered, because there were scarecrows in the fruit trees. That year the bad weather had come early, with dense mist hanging along the streams in the valley like swirling bonfire smoke . . . and the priest, who had taken time with her, taught her letters, words, phrases, the priest said the mist was from the shelling where her brothers should be but weren't, a secret to be kept at all costs. At all costs. If a person could be rich from all the words not spoken, all the secrets kept, then Poor Muta was rich, Muta who had hoarded speech as a miser hoards gold.

Her brothers had called her the Watcher – and she had watched all right! She used to fall asleep in the stables' prickly hay and wake early in the morning, cold and stiff but smelling sweetly of dried grass. Until that final night, the last watch of all, when a cold wind had blown through the valley after dark, sucking up the fog to leave a hard clear sky in which the moon hung white as the pillow-cases they used for the scarecrows' faces.

Doo dah, doo dah . . .

They had butchered a pig that night and the body was hung up spreadeagled to dry, although in her dreams Muta saw more than one silhouette against the light, red on the trees where they strung them up . . . on the blood-red scarecrow trees. Was that another place, when she was wandering, or maybe a more recent slaughter?

Now she had begun to pay them back. This was only the first bite.

MIRACLE NUMBER 15

The Restoration of Lost Summers

'To wake a dead man.' The voice came from behind Charlotte, who looked up from the local paper to find Francesco Procopio reading it over her shoulder, the first time she'd seen him working in his own café. Perhaps he didn't wait on tables; he made no move now to offer her a menu.

'Vegliare un morto . . . that's what it means,' he said. The ceiling fans beating overhead caused the newspaper to flutter feebly under her hand as if in protest at his translation. 'And Veglia funebre is a funeral, a wakening, a . . . what you call it – '

'A wake.'

'That's it.'

Charlotte couldn't be bothered explaining, yet again, that she did actually speak quite good Italian, but something in Procopio's face prompted her to ask, 'You knew him?'

'Who?'

'The dead man.'

'No . . . not well . . . He was the old man who died at that place I showed you, the pig farm . . . Anyway, that's what it means, the phrase, although in my heart I have to say that such a man has not earned any sort of miraculous awakening. One of the old Fascists who survived the War.'

'Still, an old man. He didn't deserve to die like – '

'You are naive, Signora Penton, if you think men improve with age like wine or cheese. They are just as vicious with grey hair. It was an old boar who attacked my dog Baldassarre and took off half his face. Without Baldassarre it would've been *my* face. If we are to wake up any old men, let us have your

Raphael. Apicius, too, I would like to pass the time with. He had some good recipes.'

There was little chance for Raphael, Charlotte thought, turning back to her paper. They might as well hold a funeral right now. Weeks, maybe months it would take to restore *La Muta*, and even then, given how much of the paint and canvas fibres had been destroyed, the painting would never be the same. Whatever the final result, *La Muta* would no longer be Raphael's. Charlotte felt depressed both by the picture's mutilation that morning and by the hours she'd spent in the police station answering questions. One at a time eye-witnesses had been grilled, then collectively, in various permutations: Italians together, English-speakers together, an Anglo-Italian mixture etc., etc.

'Why are you reading Italian obituaries?' asked Procopio.

Charlotte wished he would go away, or bring her a cup of tea, or *anything*. She couldn't bear to talk about the incident, not to this man, at least, who appeared to have all the sensitivity of a butcher's block. 'I was just . . . taking my mind off something . . . while waiting for my *tea*.'

The emphasis she put on the last word caused his eyebrows to lift in amusement. 'I heard of tea and sympathy, but tea and obituaries, this is a new one for me. Is it an English passatempo . . . ah, hobby?'

Procopio leaned rather closer than she would have wished and pressed a finger greasy from cooking onto her newspaper, smudging the newsprint. She was acutely aware of his savoury-sweet, oily smell of marzipan and chocolate.

'Here,' he said, 'where they say about holding a "Veglia" for the dead man . . . very antique phrase. Means the watches of the night, the waking time. Used to be a gathering during the winter months, farming families meeting to exchange gossip. I remember the Veglia from when I was a boy. Then during the War the Communists and the partisans used la Veglia as a disguise for their recruiting activities. Once you let politics into your fairy tales – pow! – you're finished! Politics was the death of la Veglia. Politics and TV.'

'How interesting . . . ' she said, leaning further away from him to stare fixedly at the newspaper. These days she was accustomed to sitting silently with a book or paper, transmitting the message: Feel no pity for *me*! I enjoy this, I'm alone by choice. Divorce had turned her at one stroke into the kind of woman who is largely ignored by waiters, then cursed by them for leaving too small a tip.

'Mmmm hmmm,' the big man said eventually, a very imprecise sound with a lot of cream in it. 'I suppose the signora would like her usual pot of lemon tea. No gelato, no granita, even on hot days.' This was a not very subtle reminder of his café's chief fame. 'But then the English take tea even in summer, I remember. Tea and . . . sandwiches with cucumber, which must make the bread very wet. Like the English summer.'

'Actually, I prefer shortbread or fruit tarts to ice-cream. I'm not that fond of ice-cream.' Loathe it, in fact. Its cloying, sickly *sameness*, its very *predictability* (unusually for Charlotte, who liked safe things, reliability). Her distaste she owed to her ex-husband, whose abstemious manner had disguised a prodigious appetite for rich, creamy food and strong drink – and other women, as it turned out.

To judge by Procopio's expression, she might as well have said she didn't like babies or Ferraris. 'In Italy, ice-cream has restored men to *life*!' he insisted.

'Surely not.' *Italietta*, she thought: Paolo's word for his nation's tendency towards trifling levity about serious issues.

'But yes!' the big man insisted. 'I know this to be true. Conservation and restoration are my specialities too! Just like you I am – ' he cast around for the word, 'a restaurateur. Yes?'

'A restaurateur does refer to someone who runs a restaurant, but – '

With both hands, he waved away any distinctions. 'We are both in the business of restoration, except I appreciate your work, as you do not mine.'

If she'd thought for one *second* that this man would understand or appreciate the difference, she'd explain to him that restoration, unlike ice-cream, was a long, slow process, even when the damage wasn't as bad as the madwoman today had caused. All the work Paolo had put in before she'd arrived in Urbino! *Weeks* he'd spent removing from *La Muta* the clumsy restoration efforts of previous centuries, carefully stripping back and analysing traces of old cleaning materials ranging from retsina to bread. Under his skilled hands the familiar, cracked umber varnish had been lifted, a delicate operation involving the painstaking testing of one solvent after another to ensure that the original paint remained intact.

All that work destroyed in a few seconds! Unrestored, Charlotte's eyes dropped again to her newspaper. She'd switched from *La Repubblica* to the local paper in an attempt to avoid the national's endless reportage of Milan's *Mani Pulite* or 'Clean Hands' trials. Before arriving in Italy she'd hardly been aware of this Pandora's box of political corruption, which had been thrown open in the spring of '92 by a small pool of Milanese investigative magistrates. They were determined to bring to light the system of *tangenti* or kickbacks operated by Italy's two main political parties and their partners in business (some clearly affiliated to the Mafia), and to crack open the barrier of 'honourable silence' that had surrounded the system and reinforced it for decades. The personal courage shown by these crusading magistrates, who daily risked their lives (and *lost* them, in some cases), must be without precedent in Europe, Charlotte thought. But with more than half the members of the Senate and Chamber of Deputies now served notice that they were under suspicion, the public were becoming sated, almost indifferent to the web of corruption which Italy's press had dubbed *Tangentopoli* – Bribesville, Kickback City.

No wonder Paolo and his young friends were so disenchanted, thought Charlotte. No wonder their vocabulary was so full of words deriding their own countrymen! 'Government *all'italiana*,' Paolo dismissively shrugged off the *Tangentopoli* scandal, and of the army of over-dressed officials attending *La Muta*'s elaborate opening ceremony this morning, he'd said contemptuously, 'Molto *italico*', a word from Italy's Fascist era that was now synonymous with any cynically bombastic posturing – while *italiota*, the oath merited by an unyielding cretin, Paolo had reserved for the security guard Michele who had threatened strike action.

'Lemon tea, as usual,' said Procopio.

Charlotte looked up to find him placing a tall frosted goblet in front of her, clearly not tea. 'No, I ordered – ' she began, noticing that the glass contained tea with a scoop of ice-cream. But she lacked the energy to send it back, and reluctantly pushing her spoon into the glass, she watched as a creamy globe, lunar in colour and texture, broke the surface. She scooped up a little, expecting the usual blast of sickly sweetness, only to be surprised as a flood of citrousy granules swept over her tongue, melted instantly and was gone, leaving in its wake a flavour neither sour nor sweet and not quite lemon, as if an exotic citrus fruit had released its sharp oil onto clean sugared snow. She closed her eyes. There was another taste, more complex and elusive, yet familiar. 'It's – ' she started. 'What *is* this?'

'*This*, signora, is how tea is served in the bars in Sicily. Poured over a scoop of granita just before it is brought to the table.' He tipped his magisterial forehead in the direction of her glass. 'My own speciality is made with bergamot from Calabria.'

'Bergamot! That's it! The taste of Earl Grey tea!'

'Very restoring, yes? And now I offer you a special treat . . .' He headed towards the kitchen again.

'No, signor . . . really, I don't want . . .' she called after him.

Deaf to her protest, he was back in minutes with three silver bowls containing frosty pastel crescents. 'In these, signora, you will find the entire history of Palermo, capital of ice-cream since its days as an Arab emirate, a place where men have lived – and died – for ice-cream.'

Without asking her permission, he seated himself opposite her at the table. 'Close your eyes.' He dipped a long spoon into the first bowl and held it out towards her mouth.

'No, Signor Procopio, I . . .' Leaning away, embarrassed, she glanced around the café to see if anyone had noticed his attentions. It was a cavernous room into which very little daylight penetrated, an old-fashioned interior, chiefly distinguished by faded photographs of Procopio's award-winning window displays for local celebrations, and by a collection of mirrors in which were reflected a hundred times over the doughy outlines of a few solitary women, women who looked as if they'd been born wearing fur coats, as serious about their afternoon pastries as they were about their gold jewellery, and not at all concerned with anything that didn't involve variations on the theme of sugar, chocolate and cream. Despite their evident lack of interest, Charlotte had no intention of allowing Procopio to feed her. Feeling ungracious, she shook her head, refusing to play the big man's foolish game.

He held the spoon close to her firmly sealed lips for a moment longer before blithely licking off the ice-cream himself, a gesture she found disturbingly intimate, as if the spoon had actually been inside her mouth. Pushing the bowl towards her with a fresh spoon, this time handle first, he said, 'You should stop thinking so much and start living more, signora. Get out and see wider horizons. I suspect you have been working too close to the canvas.'

The *cheek* of the man!

'But for the moment it is enough to close your eyes, please, and picture yourself a little girl, tightly laced into your pointed satin bodice and facing your black crow of a governess, the two of you eating large pink ices of this cinnamon concoction.'

Unwillingly she followed his instructions, taking a mouthful of what proved to be spicy, almost peppery granules that had melted by the time they reached her throat. She heard him say, 'Granita di cannella, the flavour of a forgotten Sicilian childhood.'

The next ice was milky white. 'Now *this*,' he said proudly, '*this* you will get only here, perhaps not even in Sicilia any more. Ice-cream the way my Sicilian grandmother once prepared it. She told me that the goatherds who drove their flocks through her town used to milk the nannies on the spot, then she would flavour the milk with almonds . . . *bitter* almonds, you must have, to achieve the proper taste of melancholia.'

'Why melancholy?' Charlotte asked, interested in spite of herself. 'Because bitter almonds are poisonous?'

'The flavour of a lost place, the melancholy taste of summers long ago, must always be a little bitter.'

Ridiculous man, she thought. Hopelessly romantic, his emotions slightly too sticky and sweet, like ice-cream. The idea didn't sit well in conjunction with her memories of him killing the pig. A sentimental butcher! She was inclined to pay her bill and leave, soak away this day in her bathtub. Yet once again Charlotte found herself tempted by the big man into slipping the silver spoon into her mouth.

'Bianca storia,' he whispered. 'A white paper on which to write a lost history.'

So it proceeded, bowl by bowl, flavour by flavour, as, with the gravity of a judge discussing arcane aspects of the law, Procopio unfolded to her the antique origins and alchemical powers of Sicilian ice-cream. Much later, when story and history, art and artist had merged and become indistinguishable, as they often do in Italy, Charlotte would recall that hour quite clearly, and retain in her memory the final and most haunting flavour of all. '*Gelsomino* . . . jasmine, the taste of all the loves we had and lost – or *might* have had . . . So many "o"s – you hear them?' Barely a whisper this time: '*Gelato di gelsomino*.' And down her throat passed a perfumed concentrate of the *Arabian Nights*. Intoxicating, a heady, bruised-flower fragrance carried on a hot summer wind.

Opening her eyes, Charlotte took in Procopio's fists lying on the white marble table like sledgehammers on a bedsheet, his lazy smile (no doubt flattered at the ease of her seduction). There was something so *childish* about all of this . . . so . . . It annoyed her to find that her shoulders were no longer hunched and tense, the brittle, fractured feeling in her head had smoothed away.

'So, what is the problem that you brought into my café tonight, signora? Has it faded from your mind?'

'Problem? I . . .'

'You were worried – up here.' He reached across to touch her forehead, but she jerked her head away before his hand could reach her.

'No . . . I . . . It's been a long day . . .' Her eyes dropped from his face to his huge, meaty hands with the thin black stain under the nails. Men's hands had always been important to her, perhaps because her profession made her so aware of their potential. She remembered the pig, the pheasant. A picture came into her head of these hands as disembodied props from a Buñuel film, dancing from the butcher's yard to the dainty candied landscapes in Procopio's windows, the muscular fingers paddling in chocolate lava squeezed from Etnas of sponge, the calloused palms curving lecherously over hillocks of quince jelly and quivering dunes of the deep-fried pistachio patties known as Chancellor's Buttocks.

'It's chocolate,' Procopio said.

Her cheeks slowly flushed. 'What?'

'Under my nails. Dark, bitter chocolate. The stain is hard to remove. In case you wondered.'

'No . . . of course not! I wasn't . . . no . . . I was . . . the painting . . . you must have heard . . .' To cover up her lie, Charlotte found herself nervously stammering out the events of her long, weary day.

'And believe it or not,' she finished, 'the woman reponsible for destroying the painting has been a cleaner at the palace for twenty years. Yet no one knows anything of her family or where she lives – nothing! Fingerprints were taken from the bucket and mop she used, proving only that she had no criminal record. Indeed, no record, no history of any kind! It's as if she didn't exist. Imagine letting her loose in such a place! Everyone agrees she has always been odd – pazza, you say?'

As soon as the word *pazza* left her mouth, Charlotte recalled Procopio's story of the crazy woman who left flowers at San Rocco. Hadn't he said she worked at the palace? But if there was a connection, why didn't Procopio mention it now? She began to describe the woman, giving him the opportunity to speak up. 'Deaf and dumb, the staff claim, although no one knows for sure. They say she's never spoken or seemed to hear, and she can't – or didn't – read or write . . . Muta, they called her, like Raphael's painting. She was said to be very fond of it.'

'How old is she, this mute?' This was the first question from Procopio, silent all through her story.

'In her late fifties, early sixties perhaps? With one of those timeless, iconic faces, like the Greek actress, Irene Papas.' Charlotte waited, but Procopio added nothing further. 'Imagine someone of her age not being able to read or write, even if totally mute . . . '

'If she is this age you say, then she was born at a time when the country people here were not so excited by education, especially of girls.'

'I wonder if . . . is it possible . . . she might be the same woman who leaves flowers at San Rocco . . . '

His eyes narrowed. 'What makes you think that?'

'You said that a – '

'I never said it was Muta – ' He made an irritable sound, aware of having revealed more than he'd meant to.

'The cleaning woman who did this,' Charlotte began cautiously, 'if she is . . . a little pazza, as they said, a little crazy, why give her a job in the – '

'It doesn't take much to clean a floor, signora. And if she has never shown anything but love for these precious things until now, what is the harm? Anyway, you don't seem so sure she attacked the painting deliberately.'

'Reports differ.' Most witnesses had insisted that she was aiming for the painting, a few thought her thrust had been meant for the Count, for Donna, even for the mayor of Urbino – whom 'everybody knew to be a Communist'. 'I had the impression . . . well, it was impossible to be sure, but it seemed to me that it was the Count she attacked. Might she have some grudge against him?'

'No! He has been here only four or five times since the War.' Procopio's voice was almost hostile.

'Do you think this has something to do with the War?'

'Of course not! I meant no such thing! Not at all!'

'It does seem . . . unlikely . . . but . . . you were telling me yesterday about the destruction of San Rocco during the War – '

'Ugly things happen, signora, and not only during the War. Maybe this poor mute's family was responsible for some of them.'

'Well, if these two mute women *are* the same one, at least we know where she can be found.' Ignoring the tight look he gave her, she finished, 'At the bell tower.'

But the big man no longer seemed to be listening. His eyes had flicked to a point beyond her and now he stood up and nodded his head at the new arrivals. In one of the antique convex mirrors which always gave Charlotte the impression she was looking at the whole world through the wrong end of the telescope she observed Procopio's cool gaze directed at three old men in camel-hair coats who were making a fuss over the ice-cream. They were very distinguished, their silver hair beautifully groomed. One of them, with the beaky profile of an eagle or hawk, gave her a slight bow of recognition. Lorenzi, the former Chief of Police. Paolo had confirmed his identity that morning in the palace. She wondered how well Lorenzi had known the man who'd been killed falling down the well. When she looked back at Procopio, his expression was even more stony, hacked out by a chisel.

'Just a little *restoratif*,' the military man had joked to Procopio, on the first occasion when he and the other two old men had come into the café. 'Just to restore his memory,' they'd said to each other, 'remind him who's who and what's what.' Or who *was* who and what *was* what, they'd added. If they had now become three of Procopio's most loyal customers, it wasn't because of that other business years ago; it was his ice-cream! 'Best in town!' they often congratulated him. As were his cakes, unusually elaborate for any café north of Naples. No one made cakes like Francesco. 'Inherited from the Sicilian side, from that aunt of his, Tito's widow,' said the one who often brought his grandchildren here. 'Good old Tito. Lousy butcher, but useful.'

So skilled was Francesco as a baker that the three old men had almost forgotten their original reason for coming. Almost, but not quite. 'She still around, the Sicilian?'

'His housekeeper now. Nice woman. Quiet.'

The military man made a gesture of zipping up his lips.

'Sure, sure,' agreed the one with a few dark streaks threading his hair. 'Those Sicilians know how to keep their mouths shut.'

'And Angelino's a half-wit, what could he say?'

The military man nodded in Charlotte's direction. 'Frankie's pretty friendly with her.'

The other took in Procopio's body language with a practised stare. 'He won't give us any problems. Long memory, our Frankie. It's business as usual for him.'

'You think he's fucking her, Lorenzi?'

'Not yet,' answered the military friend. 'But soon. He's a big man . . . for the *ladies*, anyway – and I mean *big*!' Under the table, hidden from everyone except his friends, he made an obscene gesture with his fist. 'Ladies like a bit of cream.'

'Such a hot shot, why pick old meat?' asked Grandad, his acquisitive eyes calculating to a gram the weight of Charlotte's breasts and buttocks.

'Old meat is easy meat. You just have to stew it longer.'

They all laughed. The military man was still smiling as he checked the menu. 'You having jasmine sorbet today or the Chancellor's Buttocks?'

Not until they had agreed on their choices did the old men raise the important issue of the day. 'So, this magistrate those bastards have found for the case in Milan against Seguita's men, you think he can be turned, Lorenzi?' asked Grandad.

'I haven't known many who couldn't.'

'And most of them are dead!'

They all smiled broadly again. 'You going to need any outside help, after this tragic loss of your man today?'

'Plenty more where he came from.'

'You did tell me she was mute,' Charlotte said rather briskly, 'the woman from Lucifer's airport, or whatever you called it?'

Procopio began to pick up the dishes, not meeting her eyes. This final question had brought the shutters down. She felt excluded as effectively as she did in the siesta hours when the whole of Urbino locked its doors.

'I have never heard her speak, signora,' he said very softly. 'But there are many reasons to keep silent. It's no bad thing, a reputation for silence, as I told you before.'

Leaving the café, Charlotte was conscious of the fans beating in the big dark room behind her like the wings of a large predatory bird about to take off.

MIRACLE NUMBER 16

Devil's Blood

Charlotte went directly from Procopio's to the Casa Raffaello, where the damaged masterpiece had been transferred in the early afternoon. There she learned from Anna, her assistant, that the painting was being kept in a small locked cupboard under armed guard. No one, not even those who would eventually be responsible for restoring it, was being allowed access until the painting had been photographed by a forensic team.

'They want to take samples of the blood,' explained Anna, 'to send to the Institute for Forensic Medicine at the University of Roma and also to the Vatican's Gemelli Hospital, where the blood type will be tested.'

'Why the Vatican?'

'In case it is holy blood.'

'What nonsense!'

The girl moved her head cautiously from side to side, unwilling to dismiss the suggestion of a miracle.

'You've seen such hoaxes often enough in your work, Anna!'

'How could a poor simple woman like the mute know about these things, Charlotte? What motive could she have for perpetrating a hoax?'

Anna's pious expression made Charlotte impatient. The girl had the milky, placid yet stubborn features of one of the local white oxen, and she grasped at religious enlightenment with the same unrelenting tenaciousness those medieval cattle practised when reaching for grass. Probably what makes her so patient at performing the often tedious and always painstaking part of this job, Charlotte conceded.

'Because you are not Catholic you have difficulty believing, signora.'

Charlotte had had a similar conversation with the Count while they were waiting to be questioned in the police station. To take her mind off the zoo smells of men's urine, she had been reduced to reading a notice in the bland waiting room: 'It has come to our attention that someone is making available the Padre Pio Centre's third-Class relics, advertising them as second Class, thus getting $50 for a $3 stipend request, whereas the decision as to when first- and second-Class relics of the Blessed Pio become available lies solely at the discretion of the Capuchin General in Rome.' The Count had inclined his long handsome head towards her with interest. 'You are a Catholic, signora?'

'Not even a Protestant, Count Malaspino . . .' She hesitated to expand on anything so nebulous as her religious beliefs, but he seemed to be waiting for an explanation. 'Though I was raised one . . . You might call me a lapsed atheist . . . travelling towards some general faith.'

'Then I hope your voyage is a successful one,' he said, smiling. 'So many people are only religious tourists these days. And what does a traveller like you feel about today's miracle? Perhaps you don't believe in miracles, Signora Penton?'

'Certain miracles: planes, electricity, the Berlin Wall coming down . . .'

'Not weeping Madonnas or paintings which bleed?'

'If it *is* blood on the Raphael . . . I believe it's more likely to be a drop or two of some colouring like devil's blood – '

'Devil's blood!'

'A romantic description of a rather mundane substance, I'm afraid, Count.'

'Really? Do go on, Signora Penton.' His eyes wandered over the yellowed walls with their distressing stains. 'I'm sure we won't be going anywhere in a hurry . . .'

'Well . . .' Charlotte didn't want to bore him with the

technical aspects of her work, although it was the mixture of art, science and history in restoration that she herself found most inspiring. 'Devil's blood, you see, is a fat-soluble resin familiar since the middle ages, Count. Mix it into some natural fats and waxes with a low melting-point that would be triggered by the heat of the television lights and – '

'A miracle. Is such a hoax likely?'

'Hoaxes are not unusual in my field, certainly not a new idea.' In the medieval period quite a profit had been made from the sale of spurious relics, Charlotte knew. Artists, constantly experimenting with pigments and gessos, were ideally placed to perpetrate such frauds. 'The Turin shroud, for instance,' she began.

'You think the shroud is also a fraud?'

She hesitated, not wanting to offend him. 'All I can say is that the shroud has been carbon-dated to the fourteenth century, a time when there was as keen a rivalry between religious centres as there is now between theme parks. If you add to this the medieval world's need to encourage believers . . .'

'Is encouraging people to hope for a better world such a bad thing?'

It is if you are making money out of the poor and the credulous, thought Charlotte, knowing that these were largely the people spending their money on relics. 'I'm sure you are aware, Count, that over the years even objects which have no more than *touched* the original relic have been accorded the same sanctity as the original . . .'

'If they truly give people some consolation, isn't their sanctity justified?'

'It would be a dangerous attitude in my profession! If *my* brushstrokes came to be valued more than the artist's . . . That's like . . . an art or theatre critic who begins to think he is more important than the artists he reviews.' Like John, in fact, who was more interested in ruining artistic reputations than in making them. His professional ego during their marriage had kept pace with his swelling paunch, while she, as if in protest, had become correspondingly thinner and more retiring. Perhaps their divorce had been all for the best. If she'd remained any longer in the shadow cast by his enormous physical and metaphysical presence, she'd have wound up no more than a brown leaf to sweep up with the cat hair. As it was, she'd developed few friends of her own, and those she had seemed preoccupied these days with their children, their elderly parents, other friends with children – like John, now.

'So if the Mona Lisa's enigmatic expression were to be attributed to a later restorer,' the Count pressed her, 'Caravaggio, let's say: would you choose to remove an old friend's smile just because Leonardo hadn't intended it?'

Charlotte suspected this of being an allusion to yesterday's discussion about *La Muta*'s scar, and feeling herself on dangerous ground, she replied cautiously, 'My job, Count, is to remain true to the original artist.'

'Truth, whatever the cost.' He shrugged. 'Well, when it comes to the miraculous you are not alone. The Vatican itself favours a sceptical attitude these days, especially in the case of inanimate objects. This century the Virgin Mary has made more visitations than in all of recorded history, yet the Vatican since 1830 has authenticated only fifteen of Her apparitions, and a single weeping Madonna.'

Even *one* seemed excessive to Charlotte, but she refrained from mentioning it. 'I hope . . . I hope you don't think I've been mocking your religious beliefs, Count Malaspino.'

'Not at all, Signora Penton. You are from a country and an age based on a religion of doubt, endless doubt. For a modern Protestant, bread always remains bread, I think you'll agree. Even during the Eucharist it is no more than a symbol. Whereas in a Catholic country like mine, bread and wine are regularly transmogrified into the actual flesh and blood of Christ. Nothing is ever simply *itself* in Italy. Always there is the possibility – and the *hope* – of becoming something else, something better.'

They were interrupted then by a senior police officer, who led Charlotte upstairs to a room on the top floor. Seating himself with his back to the single enormous window, his face shadowed, he indicated gruffly that she take the hard chair facing him, and in a bored voice proceeded to question her. The sun shone in her eyes with the intensity of a spotlight used to force confessions. It distracted Charlotte, as did a noisy row of pigeons shuffling along the outside window ledge like gossiping old women in a bus queue, from time to time peering keenly in. She had trouble hearing, so loud was the persistent cooing and scratching. 'Blasted pigeons!' the policeman said at last, when she asked him for the third time to repeat a question. 'Every morning they fight with the rooks above the palace and every morning the rooks chase them back here to the safety of our roof.'

Charlotte was surprised that the pigeons found any room to land, given the snarl of wires and antennae protecting the station.

'They're outsiders, these rooks,' complained the officer, as if that made all the difference. 'They came up here from the poorest parts of the South and little by little they become more populous and belligerent. Another indication that our country is becoming more . . . southern . . .'

She supposed he was implying that the Mafia's influence was spreading. 'About the Raphael attack . . .' she said.

'Please continue, signora. You seem to be implying that the miracle is a hoax.'

'Well . . .' Warily she expanded on the theme, offering him a few theories of how the hoax might have been perpetrated, while he linked his fingers over a belly as taut as a hard-boiled egg, remarking 'claro, claro' from time to time, although from what she could determine, her arguments did not seem at all 'clear' to him. Convinced that the chubby man behind the desk hadn't really listened to a word, Charlotte was surprised when he suddenly fixed her with a gaze as bright as the pigeons' outside.

'Our largest consumer protection group, CODACONS, takes such allegations very seriously, Signora Penton,' he said. 'Do you wish to lodge a formal complaint?'

'A complaint? No . . . Against whom? And on what charge?'

'For the moment we might issue it against "unknown persons", the charge being "abuso della credulità popolare".'

Abuse of the people's trust? Charlotte had never heard of such a thing. 'Fraud, you mean?'

He rearranged several pencils to frame more precisely the paper on his desk. 'Of a sort, yes: *pious* fraud, normally dealt with by the Church. The Vatican is highly sensitive to charges of superstition.'

'But the Raphael is a *secular* painting, not a religious relic . . .'

His fat chin moved up and down, acknowledging her point. 'One might still invoke a law introduced in the 1930s to deter magicians and hoaxers from hoodwinking the public with dubious miracles.'

She tried not to smile at his pronunciation of the word 'hoodwink', proudly drawn from a source of antiquated English vocabulary.

'However,' he went on, 'I ask you to consider carefully the consequences of making a formal charge, for under Italian law, once an accusation is made, the public prosecutor is obliged to open a full-scale criminal investigation.' The wizened eyes, embedded like raisins in his shiny bun of a face, peered out at her shrewdly. 'Such cases have been known to drag on for *years*, even when there was found to be insufficient evidence.'

'I'm not suggesting . . . I couldn't possibly be involved . . .'

The policeman ostentatiously ticked a box in the form before rewarding her with a satisfied smile. 'So we leave your testimony as is?'

The Chief studied her as she left – her crisp white blouse, her pleated skirt, her navy jacket buttoned just *so*. So *English*, so snooty and bony, so removed from real life. What could such a woman with her overriding concern for dead painters know about the kind of pressure a living cop endured – from the top, the middle, the press, the gutter? He had been advised to bury this story as best he could, and so he would. He doubted if she would give them any more trouble. People like her, they came to Italy for a few months with their pathetic vision of the way it could be run, if only some country like their own was in charge, and then they left with their bottles of extra-virgin olive oil and their organic pasta and their Antinori wines. *Pah!* Not one of them had ever stopped the Tiber from flowing. To *Hell* with her! He picked up the phone and dialled his mistress, a forty-something bottle blonde, big in all the right places. Melissa: even her name, with its sussurating hint of silky underwear fluttering off plump shoulders, put him in a good mood.

Charlotte felt nothing but scorn for people like the policeman who had interviewed her this morning, people who were content to be *seen* to do their job while in fact making little effort actually to do it. She hadn't liked his assessment of her as someone who would not dirty her hands, a justification for his own inaction. And yet he was right in a way, she thought, returning from the fruitless visit to Raphael's house; I *never* allow myself to get involved except with my work. Never *personally* involved. Even with Paolo she was aware of keeping a wary distance. Why? Is it the threat of mess, the loss of control? No doubt a psychologist would offer some tedious theory about my childhood as an army brat moving from post to post and never settling anywhere, or my fear of being hurt again, as I was by John. Yet other people have worse things happen to them and don't recoil from commitment as I do. Discouraged, she pushed open the *pensione* door.

'Count Malaspino has left several phone message for you!' said the concierge excitedly as soon as Charlotte crossed the threshold.

Returning the Count's call, Charlotte spoke to his wife: 'Has there been some breakthrough in the case since this morning, Countess? Have they found the woman from San Rocco?'

'San Rocco! Whatever made you – ' The Countess sounded uncharacteristically breathless. 'No . . . no . . . we . . . that is . . .' There was a pause, then she continued more calmly: 'My husband and I wanted to invite the film crew and all those involved in the Raphael restoration to a meeting at our hotel this Saturday. We would like the opportunity to discuss with all of you a matter of importance. But my husband would like to speak to you first alone, Signora Penton. Are you free for lunch, perhaps on Thursday?'

By noon the next day a crowd of pilgrims demanding to see the miraculous bleeding picture had gathered outside the Casa Raffaello, and although the pilgrims dispersed for several hours over the lunch period, they were back again in full force at four o'clock. Charlotte had to push through them to enter Raphael's house, her easy entrance earning several resentful shouts.

All three restorers had been rung as soon as the forensic team had finished with the painting. 'It's still weeping tears of blood!' Anna said, meeting Charlotte in the ground floor exhibition space of the house. 'The security guards told me the blood is still running!'

'Then it's the humidity . . . It has been hot and muggy for October.'

'Perhaps.' Anna was clearly unwilling to accept such a prosaic explanation. 'Members of the Accademia want La Muta moved from here to somewhere even more secure,' she said as the two women climbed the broad stone stairs to the top floor where, for security's sake, the painting was being held in the library of the Accademia Raffaello. 'They worry that the people outside may damage this museum if they are not allowed to see the painting's wounds.'

'They are not *wounds*, Anna!' Charlotte snapped, increasingly irritated by her colleague's religious sentiments. How could the girl maintain these superstitions while working in a scientific field?

'The only wounds are to the security firm's pride!' Paolo called across to them. He was looking more Puckish than usual, perched cross-legged on the brick cistern in the first-storey inner courtyard.

The security guards let the three restorers into the inner sanctum on the top floor, first checking their credentials with a thoroughness that Charlotte wished had been shown the previous day. They were warned that only photos and notes were allowed. 'No touching the painting and no interfering with the blood.' Anna immediately crossed herself at the sight of the red stain, which made Paolo grin. As he set up his camera Charlotte carefully began to examine the picture. She made as thorough notes as possible, although there was only so much she could do under the circumstances. Their usual routine would have been to remove the canvas from its frame and take samples of the stain so that it could be tested using what she considered to be the genuine 'miracle' of spectrum technology, but they had been advised by the police not to tamper with the blood until the Vatican had established its origins. Her protests that the longer the stain was left to soak into the canvas, the more damage it would do, were to no avail. And so far they had found no hidden secret behind the canvas, no clues to indicate how the hoax had been achieved. 'Although there was a small backing patch on the canvas when we delivered it to the palace,' Charlotte said, 'and that seems to have disappeared.'

'It may have been torn off in that madwoman's attack,' Anna suggested, 'or dropped off when the painting was being transported back here to Raphael's house.'

Paolo nodded. 'Our poor mutineer. Her pretty throat has been well and truly cut. A talented plastic surgeon will be needed to cover up that scar. And if the surgery is not careful she will look even more like a mutinous pirate!'

Anna burst into tears. 'How can you make fun! La *povera* donna!'

Paolo put his arm around his weeping colleague and gave her a hug. 'Calma, mia cara. Il Dottore arriva subito.' Then, letting his easy gigolo's charm slip for a moment, he lifted his eyes to Charlotte. 'You *will* stay, won't you, *cara*? See this through?'

'Well, I . . .'

'You must realise how much we need your English nature to curb our Latin tendency to frivolity and superstition.'

She was touched by the sincerity in his voice. 'I'm not sure, Paolo. This is such a mess. Who knows when we'll get permission to make the repairs that should be started now, not later?'

Charlotte stared at the painting lying in shreds and whispers on the table, only one eye still intact. She didn't know if she could face beginning the restoration all over again, living inside this painting again, as she did with all the paintings that moved her. She held inner conversations with their characters, gave the women jealous courtiers, loyal husbands, the passionate love life Charlotte herself lacked. John had mocked her for the lengths she went to research 'her' artists. 'You're as nosy as a maiden aunt!' he'd said, at first speaking affectionately about her obsessive attention to detail. In the end it was one of the 'personality disorders' he'd cited in their divorce. That and her refusal to have children. Yet despite his sarcasm, Charlotte had few qualms about her detective work. She took her cue from the fifteenth-century *Craftsman's Handbook* by Cennini. He had written that painters needed to discover things not seen, things hiding themselves under the shadow of natural objects, and to fix them with the hand, presenting to plain sight what does not actually exist.

Continuing her slow and careful examination of the ravaged picture, she felt a sense of defeat at how thoroughly the attack had undone their restoration work, tearing threads of canvas as well as paint away from the left side of the picture and once again revealing the scar on *La Muta*'s face. The pentimento. Charlotte had the uncanny impression that she was seeing the living muscles and veins under the painted woman's flesh, as well as something else she could not quite put her finger on.

MIRACLE NUMBER 17

Charlotte's Passeggiata

Donna had spent the morning going over the Raphael clips with James and the editor, trying to see if there was enough on film to make a programme. They had been advised by the police not to leave town until further notice, and when she'd asked James how this would affect their schedule for the Renaissance series, he'd been vaguer than usual. Towards the end of the day she'd had her anxieties confirmed that he had plans up his sleeve to cut her contribution. 'Anything I can do?' she'd asked him.

'Sure, get us some decent coffee.'

A week ago she would've snapped that it wasn't her fucking job to get the coffee, but things had changed, her confidence was being chipped away. She went to the café. Returning with the men's coffees a few minutes later, she heard them laughing about one of the rejected film clips, laughter that roused her suspicions when it stopped abruptly as she entered the room. 'What's that, you never showed me that,' she said, pointing at the screen.

The editor quickly spun the film past the frame she'd seen. 'Nothing, Donna.'

'Yes it is. Show me.'

'We have to get on with work,' said James. 'There's plenty to do.'

She slammed their coffees down hard enough to spill over his script.

'Steady on!' he said.

'*Show me the fucking shot!*'

James shrugged and they rewound the film to a shot where

the script girl had been reading the lines in a cruel imitation of Donna, moving her hands and legs stiffly up and down like a mechanical toy. The sound was fuzzy, but clear enough.

'We could do a Warhol on her,' said James off-screen. 'Use her face and lip-sync it to another voice. She's not much more than a ventriloquist's dummy anyway.'

'It's a joke, Donna, we were joking,' he said now, rolling his eyes at the editor (*Prima donnas, you have to humour them!*).

Donna stormed out of the room without another word and returned to her hotel, where she lay down on the bed and stared at what looked like an oil-stain in the shape of a woman's face on the ceiling. How could she feel lonely with so many people in the streets below, so much *noise*? She missed home, she missed her family, she missed thrashing her brother at tennis. What time was it back home? Her folks were early risers, she might catch her dad before he left for work if she phoned now.

'Just a sec', honey!' said her mom when Donna got through. 'Dad's taking the trash out and I know he wants to hear all your adventures.'

The phone line was a good one for a change. None of those disturbing time lapses that made you feel the other person was bored or not listening or dead. Donna could hear the coconut shell sound – clip *clop* clip *clop* – of her mother's wooden sandals retreating down the hall. She must be wearing her Scholl correctives. She heard Mom calling, 'Bob! Bob! It's Donna!' Doors slamming. Clip *clop*. Mom: 'Dad's coming, hon'!'

Minutes of expensive silence ticking away. James had told her she was spending too much on calls, but what the fuck. Then her dad on the extension saying how great it was to hear from her, what a *time* she must be having, seeing she phoned home so seldom, work must be going real good and it was a great opportunity for a gal like her.

Took five minutes before she managed to squeeze in a comment.

'Our friends can hardly wait to see you on the TV, honey!' interjected Mom before Donna could finish. 'Except Sheila –

was she *green*! Her daughter Casey – you remember Casey, *sure* you do, two years above you in high school? Anyway, Casey has been trying and *trying* to break into the news and getting nowhere!'

Had she met any nice guys over there, asked Dad, but watch yourself because you know those Italians!

And so on. Donna getting in maybe five words at the most. Nothing about being lonely, nothing about how insecure this great *opportunity* made her feel. How could she tell them when they were so *proud* of her, she was going to make them so *proud*.

What she said was, 'Yeah, it's great, Dad, Mom. Yeah, I'll be sure to keep in touch. No, I'm OK, it's the line.' She felt like crying when she got off the phone. At home there would've been someone to fill in the silence, give her a chore to do.

She had to get out of this fucking room.

In the streets again, Donna became one more face in the crowded Piazza San Francesco, where jugglers and a fire-eater were performing. The pyrotechnician's blazing torches and burning swords had carved him just enough room, with men, women and children pressing as close as they dared, *closer*, liking the hairbreadth distance from their own destruction, thinking: if anyone's going to get it, it's *him*, the repository of danger, the scapegoat, the pathetic bastard who has to make a living this way because he has no connections to get him the new Fiat dealership, the desk job selling Urbino as the European Dental Association's next conference destination. A small army of vendors with confectionery and tourist trinkets had acted quickly, anxious to take advantage of their unexpected customers. One man waved a copy of a paper bearing the headline in Italian, 'Raphael bleeds for us!' while another enterprising salesman boasted balloons printed with an image of *La Muta* weeping tears and a third, unaware of the reason for this gathering, sold feathery bird masks of a kind popular in Venice during Carnival. One comedian with his tray full of roasted nuts pushed through shouting 'Noci! Noci! Noci fresche: get them before the world ends!'

In the hour that Charlotte and her two assistants had been at work, the pilgrims around Raphael's house had been joined by dozens more supporters, who blocked the street as far downhill as the Piazza San Francesco. More pilgrims were arriving by every bus and three burly policemen had been recruited in an attempt to move people away from the museum's door and out of the Via Raffaello so that cars could get through.

'*Daccela! Daccela!*' people chanted. 'Give her to us! Give her to us!'

Beyond the breathing space cleared by the police, Charlotte was aware of an immovable crowd of hundreds, their faces gilded by the church candles each person held. An ecclesiastical aroma of incense and beeswax mixed with the smell of chestnuts that were burning on several small charcoal braziers, the smoky atmosphere sending whispering shadows up the tall buildings.

'Look, Anna – escaping souls!' Paolo teased.

'Why has this particular miracle caused such a storm and not the others?' Charlotte asked him, shouting to be heard over the noise.

'Maybe because that man died in the well, which some people are saying was an act of God – or because one of the guards who chased after the Raphael's mute attacker heard the mute speak . . . *claims* he did . . .' His next words were lost in another roar, '*Daccela! Daccela!*'

Between a gap in the buildings Charlotte could see straight through to the sweep of hills beyond Urbino's walls. The night sky above them was an intense mesmeric blue, not the nicotine yellow of London and other big cities. Then the blue slipped away as she watched and the sky was just dark, stars slowly burning through it like the flickering candles reflected in Paolo's eyes. Ahead she caught sight of James, filming the crowds with a small crew. The director's silhouette was unmistakable, an animated set of chopsticks on which his suede jacket ruckled as if a wire coat-hanger inside the jacket had been pulled down vertically, further compressing his already non-existent shoulders. 'Marvellous, isn't it!' James called as they drew nearer. He gestured excitedly around him. 'This crowd, the candles, the whole spectacle! And Serafini is staying on for a few weeks – '

An appreciative whistle issued from Paolo, who'd caught the end of this sentence. 'Serafini! That's – ' He linked his arm through Charlotte's to stop the tide of people pulling them apart.

The director, meanwhile, had spotted someone more interesting. Pressing the headphones to his ear, he called, 'Gotta run, Charlotte! Monsignor Segugio is just arriving.'

Segugio? Charlotte tried to imagine what he meant. Tracker? Sleuth? 'Bishop *Bloodhound*?' she said to Paolo. Was this another mix-up attributable to James's fractured Italian? Even in Italy, where slapstick was relished, such a name was farcical.

'Monsignor Seguita, the Vatican's miracle-chaser . . .' The director's voice, like the Cheshire Cat's equally smug leer, lingered briefly after he had vanished.

She turned to Paolo. 'What is he talking about?'

A pilgrim's shoulder buffeted them apart at that moment and she lost half of Paolo's answer: '. . . if Segugio has turned up as well, we are in for the full circus!' he finished.

More waves of people pummelled against her, washing her downhill. She lost sight of Anna, then Paolo, who bobbed up beside a man in a cape and a grotesque mask and gripped her arm more tightly, steering her out of the fastest human current. 'Paolo! Where's Anna gone?'

'To pray for our redemption.' His dark pupils were flaming with candles. 'Shall we drink to our lost souls in the Caffè Repubblica?'

'I should . . .' Ring Geoffrey, she thought.

'Should should should!' Paolo mocked. 'Join me, carissima Carlotta, per favore, my heart is sighing for your company. Let us watch the clowns and magicians begin to gather.' Smiling at his nonsense, Charlotte allowed him to guide her down the street to join the half of young Urbino who mysteriously preferred the Caffè Repubblica to any of the other indistinguishable cafés dotting the Piazza Repubblica. Preference was a question of the hour; at an imprecise time known only to the inner circle, these same beauties and their cavaliers would move a few metres further along to the Caffè Duomo, then off around the town and back again past the same cafés, the same people. Charlotte enjoyed this nightly *passeggiata*, an early evening fashion parade common to every town in Italy. She classified it neatly as an opportunity not only for Italians to look good, the all-important *fare bella figura*, but also for them to cement the kind of group loyalties which to Charlotte suggested a large extended family, with all the tensions and lack of independence such familial ties implied. *Campanilismo* the Italians called it, a bond that united a community born within sound of the city's bells.

In an almost identical café abutting the one where Charlotte and Paolo found a table, three old men were chatting quietly. 'San Rocco has been mentioned,' said the eldest, a man with the pouting lips and rosy cheeks of an ageing cherub. 'I don't like it.'

'Dado will never talk,' said the second. 'He wouldn't dare.'

'And Francesco?' asked the third, a military gentleman.

The other two shook their heads. 'It's true that Francesco has given us grief before,' the second man reminded them. His granddaughter, a barefoot angel who had been playing in the piazza with some of her friends, came running towards him to receive consolation for a bruised knee. 'There, there, my treasure,' he crooned, cuddling her for a moment before releasing her with a pat on her bottom to return to her friends. 'Then there's this English cunt,' her grandpapa said to the other two men. 'I heard she made a fuss at the station, but backed off quick.'

'She has the discretion of her race. I'm more worried about the American. She and the cops were getting very cosy.'

'For the sake of her tits, I bet, nothing more.'

'Nice tits,' said Grandpa, and the other two nodded appreciatively.

'She likes to show them off.'

'That could be arranged,' smiled the cherub.

'So, the Vatican has sent Segùgio, one of their big guns . . .' mused Paolo. He rattled the ice in a violent pink Campari soda.

'Who is he, exactly?'

'His real name is Seguita,' answered a blond boy who a minute earlier had been lounging artfully under the colonnaded shops opposite. Now he joined the crowd of young people next to their table, most of them students at the Accademia delle Belle Arti or on the university's degree course, Conservation of Cultural Goods. 'Seguita works in forensic pathology at the Vatican's Gemelli Hospital.'

'Ciao, Fabio,' said Paolo. 'You know Fabio Lorenzi, Charlotte? No? You must have seen him around town . . . He used to be a painter, until he discovered he had nothing to say, so now he confines his creativity to football and makes money as a living statue of Raphael. A disappointment to his father, our eminent police chief, but a real alchemist with paint. So good at imitating bronze, even the pigeons can't appreciate the difference. His head and shoulders are always covered in their appreciation.'

The blond acknowledged this double-edged compliment with an almost imperceptible dip of his head, still showing a trace of the greenish gel he used to simulate verdigris. 'The press nicknamed him Segugio – the Sleuth, the Tracker,' Fabio continued, 'after he uncovered the charlatan who faked the Lazarus miracle in Naples three years ago. Segugio disproved the reincarnation and since then he has become the Vatican's official miracle authenticator.'

'*Dis*proved a miracle?' said Charlotte. 'And he works for the Vatican?'

'The Vatican doesn't like to be seen to encourage dubious miracles,' Paolo said drily, 'or not *too* many, anyway.'

'Segugio is so handsome, *bellissimo*, so stern and fierce, yet gentle!' said a girl next to Fabio.

'Bellissimo, vero,' her girlfriend concurred.

'Ma *vecchio*, cara Flavia, he is very *old* . . . not like me!' Paolo, playing to his expanding audience with an actor's dramatic hand movements, took up the brief history of Monsignor Seguita's career. 'Any time there is a reported miracle that attracts press attention, Segugio's chief opponent, Andrea Serafini, comes to investigate. And where you find a case truly interesting to Serafini, there you most probably find Segugio soon after him, lined up against him like an opposing bishop in a chess match.'

'More like two figures on a carousel,' said Fabio, 'chasing each other round and round, never getting any closer. No loser, no winner.'

'James mentioned Serafini,' Charlotte said. 'Is he another Church man?'

'*Serafini?*' Paolo shared an amused look with Fabio. 'He's an old friend of our mayor. Can't stand the Church – *especially* Segugio!' Professor Andrea Serafini, he explained, was a local boy who had left Urbino to join the founders of CICAP, the Italian Committee for Investigation of Claims of the Paranormal. 'He is one of Italy's foremost investigator of miracles.'

'CICAP was founded four or five years ago, for investigations into psychic healing and ESP,' added Fabio, 'but now Serafini focuses more on pious frauds . . . even sometimes at the clergy's request.'

Paolo smiled sweetly at Charlotte. 'You know that over the last couple of months there have been several unexplained miracles in our region.'

'Where does Serafini get his expertise?' she asked.

'He has a day job as head of the department of organic chemistry at the University of Milan,' said Paolo.

Flavia twisted her pretty mouth into a pout. 'He is not so handsome as Segugio.' When her girlfriends agreed, the young men began to mock them for this crush on a man of the Church.

'Because you can't have him, you want him!' concluded Fabio.

Paolo got down on one knee before the pretty blonde. 'Have *me*, carissima Flavia! I offer you my heart, my soul! I long to give you a football team of fat bambini!'

The object of his declaration tried not to smile. 'Who is going to fatten these bambini – *me*, I suppose? While you flirt with Miss Canada?'

'Povero Paolo, he has eyes only for La Belladonna!' said Fabio.

Paolo's grin slipped for a moment before he managed to pin it back in place and embark on an elaborate tease regarding Fabio's supposed romance with one of the statues in the palace. 'Is it the terracotta cherub by della Robbia? Or perhaps Duccio's marble Madonna, she is very pretty . . . though I hear marble can be chilly in bed.'

'Better than Donna,' persisted Fabio. 'La femme fatale, who has eyes only for men who can help her up the ladder . . .'

MIRACLE NUMBER 18

Angels and Atoms

Charlotte was amusing herself by trying to picture a chess match between an organic chemist interested in disproving the paranormal and a clerical sleuth determined to find proof of the miraculous. Imagine their army of pawns: molecules on one side, angels on the other, visible to the naked eye only by their actions and reactions. Back and forth, round and round her mind the angels and molecules moved, while in front of her the citizens of Urbino strolled and stared and shopped and kissed or shook hands with friends they had seen only hours before – and every evening for the last eight hundred years – and sat to take a thimble of coffee and moved on to the next café for a brief *aperitivo* and moved on again, arm in arm, a slow and formal dance. From time to time a few of the Raphael pilgrims appeared, candles briefly extinguished, to refresh themselves with wine or coffee before resuming their vigil. It was a year when billowing velvet jackets were being worn with tight leggings in harlequin and paisley patterns the colours of autumn fruits, and these Renaissance silhouettes, endlessly repeated before Charlotte's dazzled eyes, made her see the boys and girls, men and women, as courtiers in Gozzoli's frescoes for the Medici in Florence, or as painted figures in an antique carousel.

Watching four, five generations pass each other, split and separate and regroup, each oval face showing traces of the next, she wondered how they could bear it, those beautiful madonnas nursing plump babes in arms, with their own ageing reflected in mother, grandmother, great-grandmother, a clear view into the future? The perfect, rose-flushed olive skin first losing its bloom, then yellowing, cracking, peeling away to the bone underneath. No restoration possible, thought childless, atheist Charlotte. Except in another life. What of the older generation, with a living portrait of Dorian Gray always before them, mirroring their own irrecoverable beauty? Yet people went on eating, drinking, putting one foot in front of the other, one baby after another, in the unconsidered certainty that reproduction was the answer. And perhaps they were right, perhaps the miracle lay in continuation. How would she know? Seldom had she felt more removed from the world's driving motivation than here at the centre of this swirling cavalcade circling and circling the narrowly proscribed piazzas and *strade* of the unwritten *passeggiata* route in a widening spiral until, one by one, they slipped away – for Campari, for dinner, for good.

Since her run-in with James that afternoon, Donna's anxiety had increased. She'd phoned one of the Italian runners and learned that the script had changed, the focus had moved elsewhere. 'James is working on a story about the growing cult around La Muta,' explained the Italian. So he was shooting a new film, Donna worried. *Without* her! Without even *telling* her! A news reporter is what he needed, not a pretty face to parrot his script – and not even *that* very well. And this was to be her Big Chance!

When she caught sight of Paolo in the café, she forgot all about discouraging him and beamed a smile that drew him to his feet and prompted predatory expressions on the faces of all the men in their vicinity. She didn't spot Charlotte, a wispy presence in shades of beige, until Paolo pulled a chair out for Donna to sit next to him. 'Oh . . . hi, Charlotte.'

'We are discussing outbreaks of dubious miracles,' Paolo said.

'And *genuine* miracles, of course!' added Fabio. 'The possibility that this crazy mute woman was or might be driven to speech.'

Donna was pleased to talk about anything, just to *talk*. 'Oh yeah? Well, there's this girl I knew? She didn't, like, speak at all

– not at *all* – until she was eight? Just wrote stuff in chalk on a blackboard thing her folks strung around her neck. And then – *bam!* – ' Donna snapped her fingers, 'she starts talking, all at once, but with a stutter.'

'It was a movie,' said Flavia, dismissively. '*The Piano*.'

'No, this was, like, years ago I heard it? From the girl herself?'

Proceeding to expand on her story, Donna could feel her audience's attention waning, with Paolo the only one really listening. The other boys were staring at her tits or flirting in Italian with Flavia and her friends, Charlotte off in her usual dream world. 'Anyway, this girl? She didn't start to speak until her parents sent her to a Jesuit school. The Jesuits taught her to breathe differently . . . and then she started to sing . . . Well, all I'm saying . . . that girl, like, what she had to say couldn't be expressed in words but only in music? I mean, it was kind of a miracle?'

Nervously she gulped some smoke and blew a perfect ring, her breasts rising with her inhalation and further threatening the skin-tight T-shirt. A walking advertisement for procreation, Charlotte thought. Even today, in running shoes and Lycra shorts, Donna radiated sex. It wasn't her fault, not when every magazine and newspaper sold women the idea that they could dress like prostitutes and still be taken seriously. Only gay men were quite so blatant, but at least they were less confused about the signals they transmitted. Sex was power, beauty was power. Even fat, middle-aged men like John could find young pretty girls to love them: the law held true now, just as it had in Raphael's time. But it's not so much Donna's youth and looks I envy, Charlotte argued to herself, it's her naive North American certainty that life can be changed so easily for the better: *People can learn to breathe and then to sing!*

And perhaps, Charlotte admitted, perhaps I'd like someone to look at me again – just once – in the way Paolo is looking at her.

Averting her eyes, she watched a young priest in a hooded black cassock enter the *tabacchi* opposite and emerge smoking a cigar and clutching a Lotto ticket. When he passed their table she recognised his fashionable glasses and the smell of his powerful aftershave. He'd been present at the attack on *La Muta* yesterday, as had the policeman sauntering by, one of the Polizia Municipale, flashy in matching white leather belt and holster, who gave Donna a long hungry stare. If I sit here long enough, thought Charlotte, every player from yesterday's tragedy will make an appearance, the same players taking turns in different roles. Idly she read the names on the war memorial next to her, Urbino men who had died in Africa: ARCANGELI Francesco, SANTINI Domenico, SPEZI Pietro, TORRI Domenico . . . The men who died for Mussolini no less mourned.

Charlotte became aware that Donna was explaining her experience at the police station. 'This cop, he told me the cleaning firm's been paying the mute a pittance for years – in cash, undeclared, so they never had to register her as an employee. Nobody knows where she lives. She's just there, all day, every day. They say she can't hear or speak or write – not so far as anyone knows. Nobody gets it, why she'd attack the Raphael.'

'You thought it was the painting she attacked, not the Count?' asked Charlotte.

The girl's eyes flicked towards her. 'That's only what it seemed like . . . to me, I mean.'

When Paolo went off to buy cigarettes, the conversation drifted back into Italian, leaving Donna increasingly isolated. Oh, the boys were happy enough to pay her compliments from time to time (while their girlfriends through narrowed eyes brooded on revenge), but even when they slipped into English she couldn't match their effortless command of art, architecture, film, politics. And when they deigned to address a question to her, it was to ask what she was doing now the Raphael installation was on hold. Did she like the Teatro this, the Santuario that?

I'm doing *nothing*, Donna wanted to shout. I've seen fuck all!

'Do you write your own scripts?' asked Flavia.

'Mostly James and Charlotte do that.'

Flavia's friend: 'Do you research them?'

'No, Charlotte does.' In other circumstances Donna would've lied, as she often did, in an attempt to fit in or to sound more interesting. But she couldn't lie now, not with Charlotte listening.

'Is Charlotte one of the presenters?'

'No.' But Donna bet she was just *loving* this ritual humiliation of the crass Canadian.

Donna could hear the question they didn't ask: So how did *you* get the job? She wanted to scream, *I slept with the fucking executive producer and then the fucking director*, is that *OK* with you guys? I mean, *can you handle it?*

Charlotte, highly sensitive to the feelings of other outsiders, observed that Donna's thin smile was as stretched to its limits as her T-shirt. She asked herself: Why on earth should I feel compelled to come to this wretched girl's rescue? Yet she did: 'Actually . . . actually, Donna puts the life into my . . . my rather *academic* words. She reminds me that Raphael was a man first of all, not an object of study.'

This minor act of charity was rewarded by Donna's surprised look of gratitude. 'That's nice of you to say, Charlotte! I only wish I had your . . . your, you know, *grasp* of the subject . . .'

Charlotte smiled, mildly surprised to be on the same side for a change, and Donna was quick to respond, fixing a good imitation of interest on her face and enquiring how the work on Raphael's painting was progressing. Charlotte tried not to give any answers above what she judged to be Donna's level of expertise, for although the girl's questions were fairly naive, she was obviously working hard to learn. Charlotte was amazed to remain her focus of attention even after Paolo returned.

When Charlotte eventually rose to leave, the moon was overhead, a ridiculously operatic full moon that silvered the young people's skin and filled her with nostalgia for her own student days in Florence.

'I'll walk with you,' Donna said.

'I'm going straight back to my pensione.' Charlotte didn't intend to sound so abrupt, but she was tired, she wanted a bath, she wanted to read over her notes and assess the Raphael's damage. In short, she'd had enough infusion of youthful energy for one day, enough talk. 'You must have other . . .' She glanced at Paolo, whose face had been stripped of its animation.

'No, really, I'd like the walk!'

Paolo started to speak, then caught Fabio's eyes and shut up again. Pointedly the boy turned his face away from Donna and began flirting in Italian with one of the other girls.

As they left the table, Charlotte noticed the old men at the next café for the first time, and nodded in acknowledgement.

Lorenzi's eyes, like Paolo's, followed Charlotte and Donna until the women disappeared into the crowd. The three old men agreed that they were right to have organised a fellow to keep an eye on things. 'In case something has to be done.'

'Nothing hasty, though.'

They had reached the age when a man is finally at peace with the world, if he is ever going to be. Why should their peace be disturbed by history? They were not without influence, after all. Phone-calls had been made, insurance against eventualities, and further strings could be pulled.

'Benny's a good man,' said the cherub. 'Never let me down yet, never does anything uncalled for.' And if something *was* called for . . . well, what was one more small tragedy when compared to the happiness of their large and influential and, after all, *innocent* families?

Almost immediately after leaving the café it became clear to Donna and Charlotte that both the Via Raffaello and the parallel streets on either side of it were impassable, blocked by pilgrims. 'We'll have to take a longer route to your pensione,' said Donna, 'the back way through the arcades below the palace and then cut across the Via Mazzini further down.'

'That's almost a complete circle.'

'Yeah well, this place – it's hard to get to grips with, right? Like there's no logic to the roads. I mean, there's no *centre* . . . I can't explain . . .'

'I know what you mean.'

'You *do*?'

'Yes.' Charlotte smiled at the girl's incredulity. 'No matter where you walk in Urbino, the centre is elusive.' Charlotte could understand how a Canadian could feel lost in this place, without the grid of streets that defined so many North American cities. In some of the bigger places like Rome and Milan you got those same long straight avenues, of course, clear lines of perspective, but towns like Urbino had been built as defendable positions, not celebrations of Empire, and soldiers built on hills, at the top of cliffs.

By rights the Piazza Repubblica should feel like Urbino's core, Charlotte knew, with its central position between the two hills that had given the city its ancient name of Urbs Bina or 'double town'; yet the piazza seemed more like a forgotten suburban square on the edge of a much greater city. Displaced, perhaps, because of the way in which geography had cut the piazza into a cheese wedge gnawed at the edges by traffic, or because of the more imposing Piazza Duca Federigo nearby, setting for the Ducal Palace, the Duomo and the church of San Domenico. Everywhere in Italy Charlotte had observed this tension between the modern republican state and a longer tradition of family ties, tribalism, religion. A *passeggiata* spiralling round and round a single idea: that's how she saw it. A city in the form of a labyrinthine palace focused on Duke Federigo's tiny study, and all merging into the character of the bookish warrior Federigo, who put his faith first in the sword and finally in the word.

'Ellooosive . . .' Donna unrolled the word as slowly as a carpet. 'Maybe. But I can't work out why I get disoriented when the place is so small. I mean, I grew up in Toronto. Anyway, wherever you go in Urbino you wind up circling round and round the palace. It's like there is no escape.'

'Yes, quite.'

'*Quite*: that's one of those words the English use to mean practically anything, right? You'd need, like, a whole dictionary to translate it?'

'Perhaps.'

Charlotte's soft assent whispered off the colonnade's arched roof, stretched like a taut brick marquee high over their heads. Soaring up to their left was the massive shoulder of the Ducal Palace, a sheer cliff from which two specks plummeted, swiftly becoming a crow in pursuit of a dove which for one heart-stopping moment seemed frozen in mid-air, a prophetic image, before swooping down into the tunnelling arcades and up again until they disappeared over the palace turrets.

Following the birds' dizzying passage, Charlotte glanced up some fifty feet of solid brick to where the windows of the *sotterranei* began. Only in these arcades would one guess that the palace's 'underground' actually rose several floors *above* this street's ground level. From inside and out the palace's edges were contradictory, she knew, and wondered what other lost, hidden things, what detritus, lay beneath those echoing cata-combs with their empty wells and cisterns and the chutes cleverly devised to eliminate waste.

She failed to notice the grey-haired, grey-suited man of ordinary, even anonymous appearance who was standing in the palace's shadow, almost part of it, his gaze closely tracking the two women's progress under the arcades. He was a grey man altogether, not the kind of man people remember. Up close you would see that his eyes too were grey, although without the sheen of his mohair suit. They had a curious flatness, like pewter or badly tarnished silver. He strolled off in the women's wake, easily keeping up with them but never overtaking, a man whose skin fit snugly over well-used muscles. If you didn't stare into his tarnished eyes for too long you'd take him for a harmless type, a salesman of sports equipment or insurance, maybe – door to door, something that kept him active. In fact, his work might be considered a form of insurance. *Life* insurance, he'd tell you (if you were foolish enough to probe), because once he'd entered your life it might need insuring.

MIRACLE NUMBER 19

A Double Town

'Raphael: you must really like his stuff, huh?' Donna asked.

'I certainly hold Raphael in high regard,' Charlotte began, 'although it's not really necessary for me to admire the work of an artist in order to restore one of his paintings.' She loved Raphael the man as much or more than Raphael the painter, because he had faith in people at a time far more corrupt and cruel and hopeless than her own cynical, secular century. Would this girl appreciate such distinctions? 'It's . . . how shall I put it, Donna? Think of icing a cake someone else made. If you have a trusted recipe to follow and a picture of what it should look like when finished, the result can be successful . . . even if you don't like that particular cake recipe yourself.' Oh dear, she thought, that sounded terribly patronising!

Fortunately the girl wasn't listening. She grabbed Charlotte's arm. 'Look! Over there!' They had crossed the Via Mazzini and were climbing into the maze of streets beyond. 'It's *her* – the old broad who attacked the Raphael! Behind the guy selling balloons with that weird face from the Turin shroud on them! Behind him – look!'

The balloons bobbed and swayed like masks, first revealing then concealing a woman whose thick dark brows and narrow-eyed Byzantine features were familiar to Charlotte from a thousand Middle Eastern icons. The mute woman had turned her head in their direction. Yellow and red lights from a fire-eater shot across her face, and Charlotte was reminded of an avenging archangel, an idol consumed by flames.

Suddenly, perhaps alerted by an instinct for self-preservation, the woman was gone, and the girl after her.

Donna hadn't stopped to consider what she would do if she caught up to Raphael's attacker. She was thinking: wait until James hears about this, he'll wish he'd filmed it, he'll see what I can do . . . Up one steep hill she gained on the mute, pausing only for an instant before leaping over the head of a small fierce dog that ran out of a lane barking and snapping. The old lady circled round to reach the Via Mazzini again and she *had* to give up soon, she *couldn't* outrun Donna on this main street. Yet she did, ignoring the traffic as if it didn't exist and vanishing into the medieval warren of lanes that rose up towards the palace's north wall. Donna, only seconds behind, chose a lane at random and raced up it only to find herself back near the empty dark arcades of the Corso Garibaldi by the helicoidal ramp.

The ramp's gates were open – unusual for this late at night, Donna knew. She stood by the entrance and listened carefully. Could she hear running footsteps? Or voices, whispers, a muffled, aching, irregular beat like waves heard from a distance. The sounds drew her a little way inside, where the dark slow downwards spiral was lit only by the moon. Inching her way a few steps forward, Donna put her hand for support against the bricks. She read the graffiti with her fingers: the elaborate script of earlier times, the crude scratchings of her own.

There they were again – whispers. Closer. Donna was paralysed, with the darkness reaching out from below and now, from behind her – footsteps.

Crack! The lights came on like a gunshot. A bellowed stream of Italian words was magnified, repeated and extended by the ramp's echoing tunnel of bricks: *Pezzo di merda! merda! Putta! Putta! Stronza! Stronza! Viperetta!* The old caretaker followed his own voice down and around the curving wall.

'I'm sorry, did you see a woman run – ' Donna's question was cut off as the old man raised his cane and shook it at her, prodding her and edging past like a defensive crab until he stood a cane's distance away below her on the shallow steps. Pushing and poking at her, he urged Donna backwards. She was forced to retreat up the ramp and onto the street, watching as he slammed the gate in her face and locked it, still muttering what she rightly took to be curses. But she was sure – almost sure – that there had been someone else ahead of her in the spiral before the caretaker appeared. If it *was* the mute woman, she might have had keys to the gate, in which case she would now be in the Mercatale square. Donna retraced her steps at a run, only hesitating in the city gate where cars and people and interurban buses kept stopping to discharge their passengers. More pilgrims were arriving daily, most of them women, short, fat and dark, dressed in widow's black. Black widows seeking salvation, inspiration, motivation, delaying Donna for several minutes before she could cross to the entrance of the helicoidal ramp. Its lower gate was now locked. Would the mute have hidden in the underground car-park? If so, she'd be cornered. Moving out of the way as a bus slowly pulled off to her right, Donna looked up to see Muta watching her from its window, her antique features out of place in the modern frame.

'Stop!' Donna shouted. 'Stop!' She ran after the bus, pounding on the rear of the vehicle with her fist until it picked up speed and pulled away.

'*Shit!*' Donna's fist hurt and the adrenaline rush had left her sick and weak. People were staring at her, the dumb foreigner. Slowly she retraced her steps back towards Charlotte's *pensione*. Aware of needing a cigarette, she stopped in the Via Mazzini to feel in her pocket for her lighter. It must have dropped out in the street. Shit shit *shit*!

From one of the crossing streets a thin man in a grey suit appeared and Donna called out, using two of the ten or twenty Italian words she knew, '*Permesso, signor!*' She held up a cigarette in appeal. As he lit it, she barely took him in, couldn't have told you what he looked like. She clocked a vague impression of general greyness, that was all, and maybe the muscular hands that cupped his lighter, an athletic spring in his step as he walked away. But lots of Italian men walked like that, making the most of their hips. Paolo had the moves down pat. The thought of Paolo made Donna smile and wiped from her mind all memory of the thin grey man who'd appeared out of nowhere to light her cigarette.

Charlotte had been waiting in the lobby for twenty minutes by the time Donna returned. 'Lost her . . . She grabbed a bus at the Borgo Mercatale.'

'Did you get the number?'

'I was trying to catch the driver's eye, make him stop.'

Trust the girl to imagine he would have stopped, Charlotte thought.

'It was heading southwest . . . any use?'

Towards Tufo and Montesoffio, then; the direction Charlotte had walked on the day she wound up at Procopio's farm.

'What is it, Charlotte? That mean something to you?'

In ordinary circumstances Charlotte played a close game, kept her cards to herself. But tonight she felt allied with the Canadian for a change, and so, with encouragement from a wide-eyed Donna, she proceeded to expand on her suspicions about the mute woman who left flowers by the bullet-ridden door of San Rocco.

'You think maybe she's the same woman, the one who attacked the Raphael!' Donna responded eagerly. 'Let's check her out! I'm sick of hanging around waiting for something to happen! How about tomorrow morning? C'm' on, Charlotte! It'll be fun!'

'In the morning I have to write up my notes on the damages to the Raphael and then fax my office,' said Charlotte, already regretting having confided in the girl. 'Then I'm having lunch with Count Malaspino.'

'Oh yeah? With the Count? Good luck.'

'Whatever do you mean?'

'Nothing . . . Hey, you know, if James doesn't need me

tomorrow, I might go and, like, check out this San Rocco place, get a head start on the cops!'

'The police? How would they . . . I haven't told anyone . . . except you . . .'

'Yeah, but they're bound to find out sooner or later, right?'

Against her better judgement Charlotte said, 'If you could wait a day . . . I might be free . . . the day after tomorrow, in the afternoon . . .'

Donna beamed one of her big Colgate smiles. 'Great! I'll see you at twelve-oh-one, day after tomorrow.'

'Until then . . . would you . . .' It was difficult for Charlotte to ask. 'Could you . . . keep this information a secret . . . just between us?'

'A secret? Why?'

'Oh, no reason . . . I just think . . . it's better if not too many people know.'

Charlotte let herself into her room on the top floor of the *pensione*, an attic she'd chosen for its view over the city's pantiled skyline. The first night in Urbino she'd watched with keen pleasure as swallows dived and squeaked at her eye-level, their silhouettes kite-sharp against a sliver of moon. But she'd lived here long enough to regret her choice of accommodation. Whatever the weather, the room remained hot and dark and airless, almost too sweetly scented with the herbal tea and apples she kept for her solitary breakfasts. Chamomile, the smell of cautious middle age, she thought, walking to the tiny window and throwing open the green wooden shutters, closed tightly by the concierge every morning.

Immediately a smoky aroma of roasting chestnuts drifted in from the stall below, dispelling her claustrophobia.

She made a mug of tea with her plug-in immersion heater and began to go over the notes collected in preparation for restoring *La Muta*, a thick file that had greatly amused Paolo, especially after he'd read the pages on mutism. 'What are we, Charlotte, picture *therapists*?'

'No,' she'd answered. 'No . . . but . . . I think Raphael's

intention was to show us what silence *feels* like, the way it spirals in on itself, either through a loss of language or . . . a failure to communicate. And if the scar over her eye was linked to her mutism, the cause of it, it might help us.'

'Mutism is like a sphinx,' Charlotte read now, the phrase she had copied from a book on the subject. 'Both captivating and disquieting, this silent riddle stares back at us defiantly, a mystery even language pathologists find difficult to solve.' She scanned the early photos Paolo had taken of Raphael's mute woman shortly after he'd stripped back the old layers of varnish and paint. The mouth even more mulishly pressed shut here, the scar quite disturbing. No wonder the town council had wanted it covered up again!

A few pages on in her file she found this note: 'Aggression may follow after treatment of the "hysterical" or functional mute. One patient indicated that she deliberately refused to speak in order to build up her interior feelings of resentment. If she had expressed herself vocally, formed that silent anger into words, her rage would have dissipated, lost its strength. When treatment of her mutism succeeded, the patient was exceedingly violent and full of hatred. She fought against being discharged from the hospital to her family's home because she was afraid of the savage crimes she might commit against those she held responsible for her speechlessness.'

At the bottom of her notes Charlotte now added: 'If a woman had to stop talking to save her life, what would it take to start her talking again?'

Then she wrote: 'A person with no voice has no more history than a stone does or a dog.'

The grey man had not forgotten Donna. He was enjoying thoughts about how he'd put those big tits of hers to use if the old men gave him the opportunity. If they didn't, well, he knew a whore in Rome, same long black hair, long legs. Get her to dress up in the same clothes, that skimpy red thing the

Canadian bitch wore, do some things to her, have some fun. That whore'd do most things. Smiling, he strolled on through the back streets of Urbino. 'Getting the lay of the land,' he called it. When he felt an unexpected tap on his shoulder, he whirled around with surprising speed, jamming one hand inside the left side of his jacket.

'Easy, easy,' said the other man softly. 'Just a joke, Benny.' His eyes narrowed with cautious amusement.

'Alberto. Will wonders never cease.' The grey man didn't appear overly pleased. 'Heard you died in that thing in Palermo. What a cock-up.'

'The operation was a failure but the patient lived.'

'Nice scar.'

The other man, younger, flashier, touched a livid furrow that ran from his right cheekbone into the hair above his ear. 'Oh this? Cheap tattoo. Suits me, don't it?'

'What you doing here?'

'Business. You?'

'Vacation.'

The younger man smiled broadly, lifting his chin slightly toward his colleague's left side. 'Good hunting round here, they say.'

'So I've heard.'

'Well, happy holidays!'

'Yeah, sure. See ya around.' The grey man walked off.

'I hope not, Benito,' whispered the other. 'I sure as hell hope not.'

MIRACLE NUMBER 20

A Raphael Cartoon

'It's only a phone-call,' said the voice at the other end of the telephone.

'You gave me your word I wouldn't have any more – '

'Words are for breaking, as none should know better than you. We don't want any more miracles, do we? No more death-bed confessions, that sort of thing? Too many people in confessional mode these days.'

'But I have no quarrel, no connection to – '

'That is the whole point, your lack of connection to this brave magistrate in Milan with the big flapping mouth and the passion for truth and retribution. The time you order the start of this . . . thing . . . with him is important. Should dates be checked or calls recorded, my associates and I will be seen to have been in business meetings or street cafés with hundreds of witnesses. You see, old friend, we haven't emerged unscathed from almost two years of trials in Milan without careful preparation. Now I am giving you the opportunity to help us in this . . . just as you helped us once before, remember? As we helped you recently . . .'

'I don't think' . . . He knew that this man and his consortium of 'associates' were perfectly capable of performing their unpleasant tasks without his assistance. The phone-call was unnecessary, just part of their game of cat and mouse with him. Forcing me another step into the past I left behind years ago, he thought. Daring me to make a bid for freedom. *At which point they can bat me back again.*

The man's voice warmed up a little, became positively

jocular, a pastiche of his adopted country. 'Come on, old boy! Buck up! One phone-call, that's all! Call it proof of your honourable intentions. You have an excellent alibi – lunch with an Englishwoman! Who would question such a perfect cover?'

Or *yours*, thought the other man. Or yours. 'There is nothing . . . *fatal* involved, is there?'

'Just a little warning, a little lesson, that's all.'

Hopelessly Charlotte dragged a comb through her lank blonde hair. 'Take a good look at yourself!' she said aloud. 'You might as well wear a wimple.' Yet even after glancing in the mirror to confirm the worst (thin, faded, flat-chested is what she saw), she failed to suppress a sense of anticipation about lunch with Count Malaspino. For the last few days she'd nourished a silly fantasy of him as a sort of modern-day Duke Federigo, a thought she put firmly out of her mind as she assembled her usual layers of separates, convent clothes in the shades of beige and navy with a touch of mud that said: 'I'm middle aged and English, so please don't look at me, I'd rather you didn't.'

When the concierge rang to say that a parcel for Signora Penton had been delivered by hand, the woman sounded almost conspiratorial, and looked it, holding up a small clear-sided box with a tangled knot of fresh jasmine inside. Opening the box, Charlotte breathed in the tiny white flower's heady perfume and eagerly read the attached card: 'Signora Penton, you must feel bad about your painting. Please accept this souvenir of our conversation about ice-cream. Looking forward to tea, 3.30 as usual. Francesco Procopio.' The signature gave her a sharp pang which she attributed to disappointment.

'You want me to put them in water in your room?' asked the concierge. 'Makes very nice smell!'

'Yes, thank you.' Charlotte handed her the devalued box of flowers and left the *pensione* before the old woman could ask any more questions.

Pigeons were queuing up to have a bath in the fountain of the

Piazza Repubblica, their squabbles adding to the noise of university students passing through on their way home to lunch. It was so warm that a pizza café up the road had thrown open its doors and the chef was sitting on a bench in his kitchen whites with his face turned up to catch the sun. Woodsmoke from his ovens drifted towards Charlotte. The bonfire smell, combined with the long blue shadows and the sand-coloured cobbles set in a wave pattern across the square, made her think of summer walks with John along windy pebbled beaches on the Norfolk coast.

She met the Count in an elegant little restaurant hidden away in a back-street cellar carved out of the hillside. With windows only at the front and the weight of a six-storey medieval building pressing down from above, daylight did not penetrate much further than a few steps beyond the doorway. The restaurant, lit only by candles, felt like a cave where the whole town kept its secrets, and Charlotte had difficulty seeing her way to the table after the brilliant October sun outside. Walking ahead of Count Malaspino, she stumbled, and he caught her arm to prevent her falling. 'I'm terribly sorry, Count!'

'Dado, please.'

'It's just . . . it was so bright outside . . .'

'Ah . . . well, you who come from a country with so little sun are always seeking it, whereas for us in Italy it is essential that one can completely shut out the light. Perhaps we have developed a different attitude to it, who knows?'

As her eyes slowly adjusted, Charlotte recognised several of the other diners: VIPs present at the Raphael attack, a senior policeman she'd seen in the station afterwards, two of the elegant old men who were friends of the ex-Chief of Police. All the men waved or nodded gravely at her escort. 'For someone who has been away such a long time you have retained many friends here, Count Malaspino,' she said.

'Call me Dado, please!' he answered. 'And most of these men are not my . . . they are – were – old friends of my father's.'

The maitre d' seated them at a table slightly too large for easy conversation. When Charlotte leaned forward to speak, the starched linen tablecloth rucked up and threatened to overturn her water glass. She grabbed the glass and took a sip and, replacing it, saw that her action had transferred butter from the silver butter dish to her sleeve. Long habituated to this conspiracy of small inanimate objects against her, she dabbed absently at the greasemark, noting the Count's effortless air of command. When he leaned towards her the linen offered no resistance, the glasses remained at stiff attention, as did the waiter who took the Count's order of dishes found nowhere on the menu.

'You must try these, Charlotte,' Count Malaspino said. 'Olive farcite with crema fritta, a speciality of Ascoli Piceno, home of Rossini's favourite cellist, who belonged to the noble Vitali family . . . allies with my family,' he added modestly. 'Rossini, you know, was a passionate gourmand.'

'Oh really?' Charlotte found the stuffed and deep-fried olives impressive less for their flavour than for the effort needed to prepare them.

'He is said to have wept only twice in his life – first when he heard Paganini play his violin and second on a boat when a truffle-stuffed turkey in front of him fell overboard.'

'How interesting.' Charlotte tried to make suitably encouraging noises, meanwhile struggling with a large bread roll which managed to be both rock hard and crumbly at the same time.

Eventually Count Malaspino got to the point. 'I wish to make you a proposition . . .'

Her bread roll shattered.

'A proposition of *work*,' the Count went on. 'For in English the word "proposition" has another meaning, no? Such a fascinating language . . . My wife, who is German, but raised in America, she speaks it infinitely better than I . . .' After an expectant pause in which Charlotte failed miserably to make adequate protests about his linguistic skills, the Count continued, 'A proposal to begin the restoration of various frescoes and family artwork at my home, the Villa Rosa, where you would, of course, be our guest.'

Charlotte brushed at the crumbs in her lap. 'Surely you . . . you would want . . . an Italian for such a enterprise?'

'Normally, yes. But my wife is most impressed by your reputation in England, signora – as am I. And your work here has been exemplary.' He elaborated on their reasons for deeming Charlotte the best person for this project, dropping, like maraschino cherries into the dryish fruit cake of her life, a generous sprinkling of the brightest names in Italian art collecting, the kind of people with whom, he hinted, she might soon become closely acquainted.

At Charlotte's muttered comment that she had to return to London as soon as the Raphael project was tied up, the Count briefly covered her hand with his, which trembled very slightly, the vibration one feels in a bell after it has stopped ringing. 'I hope you will forgive me,' he said, 'but in anticipation of this argument I have gone behind your back and spoken to dear Geoffrey, who is delighted by this opportunity for you . . .'

'Dear Geoffrey' mentioned no such connection to *me*, thought Charlotte, resentful but unsurprised. Geoffrey had been trying to encourage her to quit for months, no doubt because she didn't match the gallery's new upbeat youthful image (or Geoffrey's new upbeat youthful facelift). She noticed the Count glance at the clock on the restaurant wall. Five to two. 'I'm sure you must have more urgent – '

'No, no!' He smiled and touched her again with his trembling hand. 'A phone-call I promised to make. Will you excuse me for a moment?'

They began promptly at two. Because they were men of limited imagination, they thought it would be amusing to remind him of his famous art collection. Raphael he liked, so Raphael they gave him, one of his many Raphael cartoons pinned up opposite him for inspiration. Their crucifixion, however, was rather more accurate than Raphael's. Knowing how a man's own weight could be used against him, and that rich fat men die more quickly than poor thin ones, they didn't bother with nails and a cross. A tree on the flat Lombard plain sufficed instead, and a rope to lash the fat man's bare arms behind him – high up, his shoulder-blades wrenched at an impossible angle and the whole mass of his heavy body dragging him down. The tendons of his neck and shoulders ripped and frayed until he couldn't hold up his head any more, which was the whole point of the exercise, after all. Above his head they nailed the hand-painted sign they'd brought:

SPAVENTAPASSERI

Scarecrow. They took a few Polaroids and gave them to him as a souvenir when they cut him down. 'A warning to all the other squealers,' they told him. 'Pass the word round to your friends and colleagues.'

On a wave of white truffle aroma the next round of dishes arrived.

Charlotte the realist, Charlotte the pessimist, knew that people did not wave magic wands and change other people's lives. She had prepared sensible objections to the Count's proposal while he was making his phone-call, but on his return he dealt with them as effortlessly as he did the waiters and the parade of dishes and wines that kept appearing and disappearing in front of her. For a few minutes she resisted letting his persuasive arguments raise her hopes, but gradually he won her over. Her mind filled with pleasant possibilities. She could exchange her dark London flat for a villa in this light-filled country! She wouldn't have to grit her teeth through any further recitations from John about his precious little Cloaca's latest insight!

Only once was the Count's seamless composure at all ruffled, when, in the course of explaining the extent of the damages to *La Muta*, she asked if he had any idea why the cleaning woman had attacked him.

'Attacked *me*?'

'Oh, well, it seemed to me . . .' she floundered. 'At least, I thought . . . perhaps to do with the War . . . the Villa Rosa . . . not far from San Rocco . . .'

Abruptly he put down his knife and fork. 'The *War*? San Rocco? I'm afraid I can't see the connection!'

'I'm terribly sorry, I . . . You see . . . a man from Urbino, he said – '

'This man must be a trouble-maker of the worst sort!' The Count wiped his narrow mouth with the napkin and arranged the linen folds very precisely back on his lap.

'No! I mean to say . . . it wasn't him who . . . it was me . . .' She blushed deeply. 'He only mentioned that this mute woman may have . . . family connections to San Rocco . . . to whatever happened at San Rocco . . . and I . . .'

'Family connections?' He picked up his napkin and again wiped his mouth. 'From what little I know about the San Rocco incident, the hamlet was destroyed by German mines . . . or perhaps by partisans who suspected the people there of collaborating with the Germans. There were no witnesses, you see, only rumours. Germans or partisans, Italy is full of such stories.' He dropped the napkin on the table and brushed his hands together briskly.

Charlotte, still flushed a deep pink, apologised again.

'Of course you couldn't know any of this,' he said graciously.

'Please . . . I must . . . You see, Procopio told me that a mute woman leaves flowers there, on the site of – '

'Procopio? Not a local name. Sicilian. An immigrant from the South. A Communist, trying to make a name for himself.'

'Oh I don't think so! Not Procopio . . .'

'If you say so, signora, I believe it. Still, you must tell your friend to stop spreading such dangerous stories.'

'Procopio is not exactly a friend . . . He's just . . . I met him by . . . He's the owner of the café opposite Raphael's house.'

'Ah. That explains it. His real name is Francesco Mazzini. He changed it some years ago, I believe for good reasons, Signora Penton.' They were back on formal terms. 'A man of disagreeable reputation to whom you would be wise not to listen – and I would advise you not to discuss these allegations about San Rocco with anyone else. I know I can trust you. The English are so much . . . quieter, more discreet than we Italians. So much better at keeping secrets.' The Count picked up the menu produced by a silent waiter. 'Now, what shall we have for dessert? *Pudding*, I think you call it in England? Such a charming country. Is that where you studied, or did you have a year abroad, as so many English students do?'

With an effort she forced her attention back onto familiar ground. 'A year in Florence . . . studying the early Renaissance.'

'They tell me the term "Renaissance" has fallen into disfavour in critical circles, Signora Penton, that it is no longer modish to accept the idea of a cultural and spiritual rebirth ousting our paralysing medieval sense of human inadequacy. Yet we are fated always to dream of a time before we fell from grace, are we not? A Golden Age?'

Once again he turned his considerable charm on her, as if the incident about San Rocco had never been mentioned. Charlotte found herself describing a youthful passion for the fifteenth-century paintings of martyrs and saints and madonnas she had studied so long ago. The Count's interest made her feel as if that happy time in Florence had occurred quite recently – perhaps last year, the year before at the outside. She sipped the golden wine, her glass constantly refilled, and studied the strange face of the man opposite, wanting to like it. Individually his features were good – very good – without somehow being a good match. He was handsome, yet curiously sketchy, as if he had moved slightly at the crucial point when the photographer had clicked the shutter.

The Count placed his hand on hers, longer this time. Charlotte was surprised not to be disturbed by his intimacy, the way she was by Procopio's, whose sheer physical *presence* made her uneasy. Almost feminine in his grace, the Count's patrician dignity made the contact less personal, perhaps, whereas everything about Procopio was so concentrated that he gave the impression of forcibly restraining some violent action. Rooms felt too small when he walked into them, bones too brittle. A disagreeable reputation? He certainly seemed capable of more than cakes and bacon.

'I am most interested in the thoughts you expressed about della Francesca's Flagellation,' the Count said, several glasses of wine later.

'Oh . . . yes . . .' She recalled asserting a little drunkenly that the painting was remarkable for the way Piero della Francesca had used perspective to ensure the remote figure of the prisoner remained central, but even more so for its enigmatic allegory. 'Is the victim of the flagellation Christ? St Martin? St Jerome?' she had asked. 'Experts differ. What interests me is the stillness of the picture, the pearly interior of the courtyard in which the beating is taking place, and the ambiguity: a courtyard moonlit, while in the forefront of the picture three figures converse in a garden flooded by daylight, oblivious to the act behind them. One of the three is golden-haired, barefoot – perhaps an angel? – yet even more remote than his companions from the flagellation. If he *is* an angel, why doesn't he do something? That has always bothered me. What would it take to disturb the grave stillness of those three figures? It is as if they are deaf to the beaten man.'

'One section of the picture set in the past,' the Count concluded, 'and the other in the present.'

Or you could see it as an overlapping of past and present, Charlotte thought; della Francesca's illustration of the laws of perspective and their implications. 'And then there is the scourged figure's own strange serenity . . .' she said aloud, 'oblivious to the pain.'

'You find it strange?'

'I suppose one explanation is that the daylit scene represents what we *choose* to see, while the moonlit flagellation shows the darker side, the reality we turn away from.'

Smiling, the Count stood to pull out her chair, and said, 'Perhaps the figure is serene simply because his destiny has been fulfilled?'

There was no difficulty about the bill. Any question of the Count paying for lunch was dismissed by the restaurant padrone. So delightful to have Signor Conto and his charming guest here! More, an *honour* that they should stay so long, the man insisted as they were leaving the restaurant.

So *long*? With a shock Charlotte discovered that lunch had taken almost three hours. Already she was thirty minutes late for tea with Francesco Procopio. 'Oh dear!'

The Count understood perfectly. 'Such an important – and *charming* woman must, of course, have *many* engagements.'

He held charming Charlotte's arm just above the elbow as they negotiated the steps outside. She felt remarkably content, even more so when the Count continued to hold her arm all through the streets. Approaching Procopio's, the Count took her hands in both of his. 'You *will* remember my warning about this man? He is not a good person for someone like you to know.'

MIRACLE NUMBER 21

An Unsigned Pietà

Stumbling into the café, now more than an hour late, Charlotte nodded absent-mindedly at the living statue of Raphael, who held the door for her, leaving a smear of metallic green on the handle. She was slightly worried about her late arrival, but tea with Procopio had, after all, been a loose engagement. She put his gift of jasmine firmly out of her mind, and took a bar stool beside the mayor, for whom Procopio's was as regular a stop as the Bar Raffaello.

'This town is filling up with charlatans and gurus, Cosimo!' he was grumbling to the bartender. No doubt he would be making a similar complaint tonight at the Raffaello.

'Don't complain, Dottore,' the bartender grinned. 'It's very good for business – Francesco's, at least. And what's good for the town's business must be good for the town's mayor!'

The mayor tossed back his espresso, wiped his elaborate moustache free of coffee and sighed. 'You know who I have to entertain tonight? That bastard Cesare, who claims to be the only lawyer in history to set the Virgin Mary free . . .'

Charlotte waited while the two men discussed in some detail the extent to which Lawyer Cesare was a bastard. When the mayor left, she asked for Procopio, finding it quite difficult to pronounce his name with any clarity. In silent response to the question the bartender confirmed her late arrival on his watch. He checked his watch against the brass clock on the wall. He swiped the bar several times. Finally he answered in broken English, 'Boss he wait forty minutes, mebbe more, signora. Now he gone home.'

'I see . . . Could you give me his number?'

'No telefono at da fattoria, signora.' With a towel he flicked a speck of imaginary dust from the zinc counter.

'I expect I'll see him here tomorrow.' Why was she explaining herself?

'Not expec' him tomorrow. Ver' busy. Occupy himself wit' pigs.'

'Yes, well . . . do please convey my apologies when you see him . . .'

The man was making a pretence of not listening. Damn Procopio! thought Charlotte, her alcoholic elation ruined by a feeling of guilt and anticlimax and the beginning of a headache. What right had he . . .

'Ciao, Fabio!' Donna said, as she stopped in front of the statue of Raphael, now ensconced opposite the doorway of the bishop's house, a minor palace behind the main cathedral. Only by the flutter of a verdigris eyelid did the living bronze betray his awareness of her presence. The small crowd of tourists he'd attracted was admiring his green hands, his green ears, his startling ability to hold the green paintbrush aloft. So familiar a sight was Fabio around the streets of Urbino that the grey insurance man slid by without noticing him and hesitated opposite the doorway where Donna had entered. At that moment a policeman recently recruited from Rome happened to be passing. His alarm at seeing the thin grey man was briefly evident before both men looked the other way with studied non-recognition.

Donna was amazed by the difference between the exteriors and interiors of Urbino's so-called 'palaces'. Discreet grandeur was the rule outside, with doors and window-frames just a fraction deeper and more elaborate than those on the houses next to them, although there was sure to be a stone coat-of-arms telling you that so and so had performed such and such service for somebody or other very important (usually about six hundred years ago). Inside, though, you knew where you were damned quick: everything smacked of money. This place was no different. Mulberry silk lined the walls behind the gilt-framed portraits of previous ecclesiastical residents, and the huge door shut after Donna's entry with an expensively muffled *whoomph*, as if nervous about disturbing these plump, not altogether benign gents. Their critical gaze followed her as she was shown down the long corridor by a man who introduced himself as Monsignor Seguita's secretary, the same man who had phoned her last night to ask for a meeting in the apartments of Urbino's bishop.

A guest of the local bishop, Monsignor Seguita was waiting for her in a wood-panelled room at the end of the corridor. As she entered, Donna twitched her black dress further down over her knees. Men, especially Italian men (even priests, Donna knew from experience), usually followed a set game plan, clocking your eyes, then your mouth, tits, crotch, legs, and back to your eyes. Not this man. His large dark eyes never wavered from hers except to flick now and then to his notes on the big leather-topped desk. Though balding, his olive-brown head was shapely, the black stripes of his thick eyebrows and lashes as graphic as a military badge of office above the high, flat cheekbones. A wise General of the Church, with a commanding nose and precisely folded jawline. The kind of face you see on postage stamps.

'Will you take coffee and cakes?' he asked. His voice was a pleasant, husky tenor.

With a martyr's sense of voluptuous self-denial, Donna accepted only black coffee. The fine china cup with its gold insignia shook slightly in her hand, and she knew she'd made the right choice when she saw the bishop abstain from cream, sugar *and* cakes.

'I have heard, Signorina Ricco,' he said, after his secretary had removed the tray and closed the door, 'that you were at the forefront of Tuesday's events, close enough to observe what happened to the painting.'

'I guess . . . well, a couple feet away. I'm the presenter on this TV series, you know?'

'An important position, I imagine. Were you looking at the painting or at Count Malaspino when the woman attacked?'

'Well, sort of both . . . at the Count when he was talking, then the painting when he drew back the curtain, then back at the Count when that nut . . .'

'Did you notice any evidence of blood on the painting before she actually touched it?'

'No. Well . . . I don't think so, but . . .'

He tapped a pencil lightly on his notes. In his other hand was a small ivory-coloured object which he continually turned over and over between long slender fingers, sometimes cradling it in his palm and caressing it slowly with his thumb as if it were a pet mouse or a bird he was fondling.

Donna shivered with pleasure to watch. What *was* it? She couldn't see . . .

'You are such an astute observer, signorina, try to remember.' He leaned towards her, his face very earnest, his dark eyes holding hers. 'Your contribution could be of tremendous help to all of us.'

An astute observer! She felt he could see through her to all the untapped talent inside. She felt her soul being sucked into his, rinsed and spun and laid out to dry in the sun. 'Well, like, it sort of happened all in a rush, you know? I mean, like, one minute he's pulling back the curtain? Talking and smiling at the camera? So my eyes are going: painting, curtain, Count, painting, curtain – '

'Yes, I see.' Soothing, uncritical, Monsignor Seguita showed no sign of impatience. The ivory object rolled and slipped through his graceful fingers, turning and turning. Was it a chesspiece? Or one of those little Japanese ivory carving things? 'Now, try to summon up that precise moment when the curtain was pulled back, signorina . . . can you recall seeing any blood on the painting at that point?'

Donna closed her eyes and obediently tried to imagine that scene, but however much she tried, the only image she managed to evoke was Monsignor Seguita's severely beautiful face. She sighed and opened her eyes again. 'Sorry. I just can't seem to see it clearly. The Count's hand, you know, it was kinda in the way.'

'It is just possible, then, that the blood on Raphael's painting might have occurred *before* the woman struck it?'

'Yeah, well, I guess. I mean, like, I guess I couldn't say for sure the Count didn't do it himself.'

Monsignor Seguita's delicately feathered eyebrows contracted sharply. 'You are not saying that Count Malaspino might have been responsible?'

She almost swallowed her tongue in her effort to withdraw the suggestion. 'No! I mean, I thought you meant, you know, you were trying to establish absolute proof . . . It's probably Charlotte – Charlotte Penton, the restorer? She probably put the idea in my head. I mean, not that the Count did it, but, you know, some link between this loony cleaning lady and him, the War or something, I don't know.'

'Charlotte Penton believes that there is a war connection common to Count Malaspino and the mute woman who attacked the Raphael . . .' Donna, who had not been to confession in years, was ready to confess, even to other people's secrets, and the bishop's weary acceptance of her statement encouraged her to see Charlotte's suspicions as fact. She let the story come out in a rush, everything Charlotte had said or implied about the mute woman, including Muta's whereabouts, the flowers she left by the bullet-scarred church door at San Rocco, the family connections.

For most of her recitation the bishop removed his gaze from her face and kept it on his notes. Like a priest in a confessional he seemed barely aware of Donna's presence as an individual, not looking up until there was a snapping sound and she saw that the pencil had broken between his fingers. She stopped. He gave her his saddest smile. 'I'm sorry, signorina. One is always moved by such tragic stories. Please continue . . . you were saying . . . about the poor woman's connections to the tragedy at San Rocco?'

'Well, you know, like Charlotte said, the Count's place, this Villa Rosa? It's not so far from San Rocco, walking distance maybe . . . ' Happily Donna dredged up and elaborated on all the gossip she had gleaned over the past few days – from the palace staff, the police station, Paolo's friends. Not suffering from non-committal Charlotte's scepticism, she omitted her colleague's very English qualifiers. No 'quite' or 'possibly'. No 'it seems to me'. No 'perhaps . . . I do not know . . . I am not sure . . . after all this time . . . it may well be otherwise'; Charlotte's story, translated by Donna, was all certainties.

At the end of it, the bishop's eyes appeared even more heavily weighted. 'One final question before you go, signorina. It concerns Paolo, the young Italian restorer who is assistant to Signora Penton. Has he indicated to you that he might have prior knowledge of the woman who attacked the Raphael?'

'Paolo! No *way*!'

'No communication with her at all?' The little ivory figure rolled and rolled between his fingers. His faint smile encouraged her trust. 'I believe he is rather fond of you . . . he hasn't mentioned this woman?'

'No . . . but, like, how could he communicate with her? She's a mute, right? Like Helen Keller without the miracle-worker? Completely deaf and dumb, that's what the palace staff say and the guy who hired her. Can't even write her name – if she has one.'

Fabio was a block further down the street when Donna left, but this time she perceived him as part of the scenery, one more old statue in a town full of them. Her cheeks were burning. Even in her thin dress she wasn't cold. Leaning against the walls of the bishop's palace, she felt them radiating the warmth that their old stones had stored in the afternoon sun, stones warm as a living body, hot-blooded. Blood coursed through her as if she'd been running. She *wanted* to run out of sheer excitement.

Seguita's gentle inquisition had revived in her a native fearlessness dimmed by her experience with the Count and by her disastrous performance on the day of the Raphael attack. She took a deep breath of some night-scented flower that lingered heavily on the air, a potent reminder of tropical holidays. Further on, its sweetness dissolved into the honeyed smell of beeswax from the crowds in the arcaded market below Raphael's house. A fortune-teller was doing a brisk trade in futures, her cards spread out on an upturned olive barrel. Donna, passing her, heard the murmur of men's voices from above and looked up to see *La Muta*'s guards sitting on the worn stone seats in the second-storey window. They could have been players preparing lines for a street performance of *Romeo and Juliet*. Smoke from their cigarettes drifted up and wrote its inscrutable calligraphy in the night sky, a message smudged by the first light breeze.

Even with so little Italian, Donna could still appreciate the way people greeted each other in the street, the older men dipping their heads like courtiers. *Courtly*, that was the word. She thought of all the stuff Charlotte had spouted last night about Duke Federigo's court. Nothing ever stopped here, it just kept going round. Even the streets themselves had a life of their own. You couldn't believe they were ever *built*, they just fuckin' *grew* that way, out of the rocks and the sun. She had high hopes again, like the hokey song her mom used to sing: '*high* in the *sky* apple *pie* hopes' . . . And she wasn't sorry about having betrayed Charlotte's confidence. Not much. Anyway, it wasn't a real betrayal. Seguita was a bishop, after all, and if Donna had some qualms about her Church (like why was the Vatican so rich? or why didn't the Pope threaten the Italian Mafia and all Irish terrorists with excommunication, along with their families and anyone who helped them?), she still had faith in bishops. Catholic in the secular way some Jews were Jewish, by birth rather than application, she rarely went to church any more, never considered the implications of incense and the communal host. Yet they still remained part of her vocabulary.

One thing she knew: a priest never violated a confession, not from adulterers, rapists, not even from murderers.

In her room at the *pensione* Charlotte had uncorked the half-bottle of grappa bought earlier that week at the Bar Raffaello and she began flicking through thirty-odd channels, the majority devoted to offering amateurs the opportunity to display questionable talents, a few to selling furs modelled by busty near-naked models or to promoting uniquely useless kitchen implements.

She saw that a rogue wolf or wolf-pack in the mountainous borders between Umbria and the Marches had killed fifty sheep and sparked off a furious debate between Italian farmers and wildlife campaigners, the farmers wanting to launch a wolf hunt, the campaigners insisting that there must be room for wolves in the mountains. 'When hunting in packs wolves performed a useful service by controlling the unchecked breeding of wild boars,' said one conservation expert. 'The danger occurs when wolves hunt alone and choose defenceless prey.'

The issue of the Catholic's Church's links to the Mafia was said to be 'posed dramatically', with allegations of complicity being levelled against Bishop Salvatore Cassisa, who was called 'a close friend of Sicilian politician Salvo Lima, regarded as being the Christian Democrat Party's ambassador to the Mafia'. Charlotte vaguely remembered that Lima's murder by the Mafia the previous year had been attributed to the fact that the changing political climate prevented him from fulfilling his promises to them any longer.

A magistrate in Milan whose name Charlotte recognised as the owner of several Raphael cartoons had abruptly withdrawn on the grounds of ill health from presiding over the usual labyrinthian corruption case, this one involving two officials from the Nerruzzi food-products consortium, said to be one of Italy's richest companies.

A man, identified as a former employee of the same consortium, had been found whipped to death and left on a tip near Urbino's outskirts. 'Is it true that the dead man was the son of another Nerruzzi employee, Domenico Montagna, who died recently at their farm outside Urbino?' a blonde reporter asked Luigi Bernardini, the young policeman who had found the corpse, tipped off by an anonymous call. The blonde looked like a double for one of the models on the fur channel.

'I know nothing of all this,' responded Bernardini, whom Charlotte recognised as a friend of Paolo's.

'You didn't know that the dead man's father, Domenico Montagna, had an elder brother who committed suicide rather than appear on charges before the Clean Hands committee in Milan?'

'This is not my concern,' the young man insisted. From a close-up showing his face the camera panned to a weeping woman who was pushing aside the police, running to lift the flayed man's head and shoulders in her arms, an unsigned *pietà*, with mourners replaced by forensic investigators in latex gloves. When the camera zoomed past the mother to close in on the mutilated man's face Charlotte quickly pressed the remote control. She had always preferred to look away.

MIRACLE NUMBER 22

Restless Bones

In bed that night, Monsignor Seguita turned uneasily from his right side to his left and back to his right. Finally giving up on sleep, he switched on the television, to watch, with growing dismay, the same news bulletins as Charlotte had. In his long fingers he turned and turned a small, bone-coloured object. Like Charlotte, he too switched off the television at the camera's intrusion into a mother's grief. The horror lay in intimacy, thought Seguita, who liked the distance from intimacy granted him by his position in the Church. Even a Raphael, examined under a microscope, proved to be full of flaws, lesions, the pockmarks wreaked by insects or pollution, the lumpy accretions where centuries of discoloured varnish or paint loss had been retouched yet again in a cavalier fashion. Magnified, *La Muta*'s velvet skin looked like mortified flesh. How much more true was this of humanity? Yet pull back from the surface of the painting or the individual and its original beauty was once more revealed.

Replacing the bone in its reliquary (his souvenir of years spent classifying and cataloguing the Vatican's ossuary of relics), he caught sight of his own face in the darkened television screen and looked away quickly, then back again, switching the machine on. One can't confront horrors face to face, he thought. We are turned to stone if we do, like the story of Medusa. We have to examine horrors through a mirror – and television is that mirror we look in to see reflections of horror. This was his constant theme, the horror of man's conscience, which he was responsible for investigating. He believed –

prayed – that it was possible to be a good investigator or a good judge and yet to live in a way that contradicted the idea of being either. To avoid investigating one's own life. We live daily among such contradictions, he told himself; a good investigator did not necessarily investigate well, only tried to be a friend of truth . . . until the truth became too intimate, came too close.

MIRACLE NUMBER 23

An Underground Song

Charlotte woke early with a raging thirst, a reminder of the previous evening's grappa. Even more penetrating than her hangover were her misgivings about her promise to go with Donna to San Rocco. I would like to see the place again first before she does, Charlotte told herself, and in the back of her mind was the half-formed idea that it would be a good opportunity to clear up her misunderstanding with Procopio, whose 'disagreeable reputation' she assumed to be nothing more than a difference of political opinion with Count Malaspino. After all, hadn't the café owner gone out of his way to help her? And to warn me against talking about San Rocco, Charlotte couldn't avoid remembering. What on earth had led her to discuss the mute woman so openly with Donna? Was it the girl's own openness? Or the influence of Italy, of this place in particular, with all its whisperings in alleyways, the fluid intimacies of a town where everyone knew everyone else's secrets.

Whatever Charlotte's motives for revisiting San Rocco, she didn't examine them too closely. She salved her conscience by writing Donna a cryptic note postponing their visit. This she left in care of the *pensione*'s concierge and then set off for the Piazza Mercatale to catch a bus.

Already a large crowd of pilgrims had gathered by Raphael's house, many of whom, to judge by their sleeping bags and flasks, had maintained an overnight vigil. 'Una bella giornata, signora!' one of the regulars called to Charlotte. Simple Italian courtesy, she knew, yet it made her take notice. He was right, the day was indeed fine, the air saturated with all those tantalising, enigmatic Italian promises of a better life that smell of garlic and rosemary and spit-roasting pork from the mobile *porchetta* trucks. It was market day. 'Mandorle Tenerissime' she read on a wicker basket full of young almonds still on their branches. She manoeuvred her way round maternal women built like comfortable chairs. Well-padded, their springs long since gone, they billowed over stalls of chickpeas and chestnuts and tiny goat's and sheep's cheeses laid out on brown oak leaves, they squeezed pumpkins and closely examined cauliflowers to find the whitest, most densely packed, they sniffed a few knobbly white truffles and complained about the price. These were the women you saw lighting candles in the cathedral and talking about 'Our Lady' outside Raphael's house, while their husbands pursued a different faith by religiously watching football on the Sport Bar's TV. Their lives were too full of routines and rituals to allow for doubt. They were still tied to the seasons, to fresh broad beans for two weeks in late May, wild strawberries in early summer, root vegetables enriched by the pheasanty aroma of truffles in the winter months. Charlotte marvelled at how much time in Italy was devoted to eating. An activity she had always viewed as being essential yet uninteresting was transformed here into an inescapable form of communication.

On the bus she sat behind three women who complained for her entire journey that the month had been too dry for *porcini*. Hugely amused by the idea that anyone could talk for so long about something so prosaic as *funghi*, she disembarked, still in high spirits, at the track that would lead eventually to San Rocco and the Fattoria Procopio. From her bag she took an apple bought in the market and crunched into it as she walked, enjoying the spicy smell of autumn leaves in the air and the hills around her rolling up to pantiled farms and copses of open woods. The track she was following hugged the land's feminine contours as if it were a river rather than chalky earth. Charlotte could almost hear an antique voice humming with serpentine pleasure along the white road, whispering in and out of the dry-stone walls.

After fifteen minutes' walk, the valley steepened and narrowed to fold back on itself. The angle of the hills grew sharper, with fewer farmhouses, most of them abandoned. The road surface roughened, a stripe of weeds rose up down its centre, and encroaching hedges of rusty brambles and stinging nettles left trails of feverish white bumps across her arms. You could hardly blame anyone for deserting this land, Charlotte thought; maintaining such steep terraces must be murderous work. She came to a stretch where half the road had collapsed down the hill, carrying with it for a few feet a sign on which she read of danger during snow. Hunters had left bullet-holes in handwritten notices warning off trespassers and claiming rights to fungi and game.

The opposite side of the valley, the deep woods where she'd been lost a week earlier, remained in permanent shade. Why was this valley so oppressive? Was it the isolation, the perpendicular geography that for centuries had cut it off from the rest of Italy? The deserted farms? Was she letting the warnings from Procopio and the Count affect her judgement? She had an uncanny sense of the land here remembering all its bloody tragedies and keeping score. There were places like this in the Balkans and the Middle East and Africa, places where there had always been trouble and it felt as if there always would be.

Since the Raphael attack Charlotte had been conscious of her emotions slipping out of control, a sensation she didn't relish. But hadn't she come to Italy to lose control a little? She tried to concentrate on the Count's offer of a year in the Villa Rosa. She might take an even lengthier sabbatical. She might never go back!

Ahead of her a hot dry breeze scurried across the track, blowing a phantom of white dust into the air, sucking the breath out of her. Her trousers were ghosted white to the knees from this chalky dust, as if she were slowly disappearing from the feet up. If there were any people left here, they were people with calluses on their hands from hard labour, people with a knowledge of the seasons, people who would know how to sew up the gut on a hunting dog ripped open by a wild boar. Or a wolf.

At San Rocco, Charlotte stood for a few minutes staring at the old bullet-holes in the splintered church door. She was in two minds about turning back. What was the legend of Saint Rocco – a man who worked miracles on the plague-stricken while he himself was afflicted with the same judgement. Often depicted with a dog (as he was in the rather kitsch painting in Urbino's Ducal Palace) . . . or was it a wolf? A reference, anyway, to the creature who brought him bread while he himself was dying of plague in the forest. Restoration from an unlikely source.

On the ground by the pock-marked door another bouquet of flowers lay, already drooping, as wild flowers often do after being picked. From here Charlotte could clearly see the depression Procopio had referred to as Lucifer's Gate, a hollow of grassy coils that had sunk into the ground as if an enormous serpent had curled up to sleep there and left its impression on the land. Chilled by the image, she moved around to sit against the sunny side of the church wall, closing her eyes in the warmth.

At first the singing seemed to come from inside her head.

She opened her eyes drowsily, thinking it was some trick of the wind on that shuddering church bell. A tiny green lizard, inches from her face and immobile as an enamel brooch, blinked its bright ruby eye at her and chirruped shrilly. Was that what she'd heard? She listened carefully. Nothing. Then it came again, not the lizard's piping whistle . . . but what? A bird? A woman? Surely not! Where and what was this singer?

Charlotte stood up and moved towards the roofless farmhouse. The sounds were fainter now. Gone. Silence all around. Too silent. A listening silence. She climbed through the broken window into what must once have been the kitchen, now roofless, where a stone sink, full of leaves, stood marooned like a misplaced Dada sculpture.

She crouched down to wipe away a little dirt from the broken tiled floor. Someone else had done this same thing, quite recently. A wild animal scratching for grubs? Leaves blew across the tiles with the rustling sound of footsteps. She straightened up and glanced around her, feeling ridiculous, yet unable to rid herself of an obscure sense of dread. I have to get out of here, she decided, and marched off with the exaggerated stride of someone trying to prove to a sceptical inner jury that she is not afraid.

At her first sight of the four crucified bodies swaying in the fruit trees Charlotte stopped as if she'd run hard into a wall. Two men and two women with faces smothered in pillow-cases, their outstretched limbs blackened and stiffening. Victims of an execution. She shut her eyes, only to find that the mental image of those hanging figures was even more vivid. Her heartbeat was hammering at her ears. A rational woman, she opened her eyes again and saw the executed bodies for what they were.

'Spaventapasseri,' she whispered, calming herself with a definition. Scarecrows, just scarecrows, although she'd never seen any scarecrows like these. And what sorry birds would be tempted by this haggard orchard?

Closer inspection revealed the scarecrows' limbs to be branches thrust into the sleeves of old jackets, the bodies cobbled together with threadbare trousers and woollen skirts filled with weeds and twigs. The 'faces' and the sightless blank eyes that gave them their ghostly, Hallowe'en appearance were nothing more sinister than holes torn in dirty pillow-cases attached to the crowns of straw hats. The pillow-cases floated free at shoulder level so that the scarecrows resembled a quartet of executed Ku Klux Klanners.

Procopio's farmhouse felt almost like a refuge when she reached it twenty minutes later. Bright sunlight made it less grim, and its courtyard's rough neatness, which had originally led Charlotte to assume an absence of women, was explained today by a narrow old creature wielding a primitive twig broom. Shyly she invited Charlotte inside, indicating that she wait in a huge dark parlour lined with books. It smelled strongly of woodsmoke, garlic sausage and cigars. 'Moment',' said the woman, disappearing into the cavernous recesses of the house.

In the fifteen minutes she was left waiting, Charlotte had time to establish that apart from a few guidebooks to Urbino and a rather nice edition of Baldassare Castiglione's *The Book of the Courtier* (a surprising insight into Francesco Procopio, if he'd read it), all of the books here were cookbooks – hundreds of them; old, new, in English, French and Spanish as well as Italian. When Procopio finally appeared, he was wearing another of his immaculate double-cuffed white shirts, although his hair was wet. Had he been called from his pigs and felt the need to shower?

'What can I do for you, Signora Penton?' he asked very formally, and seated himself in a cracked leather chair as big as a throne, gesturing towards an equally gargantuan seat opposite him.

Sinking into it, Charlotte felt like Goldilocks in the bears' house. She struggled to find the right words to stretch across the empty twelve feet of cold tile floor, her first attempt at an explanation smothered by squeaks from the chair leather. She raised her voice a little. 'I've come to – ' and stopped mid-sentence as the old woman entered to lay a tray of coffee and biscuits on the table beside Procopio, then vanished again.

He poured them each a cup and offered the biscuits, square and solid as paving. 'Be careful of your teeth,' he warned. 'She gets them from her cousin in Sicily who is better at building walls than cakes.' Biting down noisily on one of these cobblestones, he waited for Charlotte to continue.

'I've come here to apologise,' she said.

'For what?' Loudly he bit off another chunk.

'For . . . for being so late yesterday . . .'

When Procopio didn't take up the thread, she struggled on. 'I had an appointment . . . It proved impossible to break . . .'

'You were forging important connections.'

'It was – '

'More important than mine.'

Crunch crunch crunch: her excuses were ground into gravel by his big white teeth. Someone in the restaurant must have reported back to Procopio. Well, it was none of his damned business what her appointment had been. More coolly she added, 'I felt, as well . . . I felt that I hadn't adequately expressed my gratitude for your kindness.'

'What kindness?'

The man had no *grace*, no sense of discretion. He was deliberately making this as difficult as possible! 'Your kindness in driving me home after I made such a fool of myself and . . . your kindness in . . . teaching me about ice-cream?' She tried a smile. He did not respond. To cover her embarrassment, she gingerly bit into one of the biscuits, an antique variety with the texture of mortar and a faint taste of aniseed. 'And for the jasmine,' she finished.

He crunched his way through more biscuit and washed it down with inky coffee. 'You thought I was being . . . *kind*?'

Why had she felt it was important to apologise? She wished herself anywhere but here in this room with its ticking clock and its family photographs yellowed from smoke. Despite the bear-sized furniture there was something intimate about it – too intimate, the muted beat of the old clock like a single pulse uniting her with this man. She stood. 'I . . . well. That's all I wanted to . . . I should be . . .'

He remained seated, taking a good long look at her, up and down. She held his ironic stare as levelly as possible. 'That's it, Signora Penton? You come all this way and leave without uncovering any of my secrets?'

'But . . . I . . . had no intention of . . .'

'No?' He leaned over to take a cigar from a box on the table. 'Didn't you?' He lit the cigar and blew smoke away from his face almost impatiently, as if he wanted to judge her reaction more clearly.

'No. *No!* I came to apologise, that's *all*!'

'That's all?'

She wanted to leave immediately, yet hated to let the wretched man think she had come here simply longing for him to continue his unfinished seduction. Honestly, what vanity! His inappropriate shirts should have warned her. She was close enough now to see the fine hand-stitching around each large cuff. Shirts that he wore like a uniform, made especially for him, clearly. A soldier's daughter, she was conscious of the distinction and anonymity conferred by uniforms. To what state was he claiming allegiance with these white flags?

He stretched to tap out the ash on his cigar and as he did, the heavy cuff of his shirt dropped back from his hand. Charlotte, expecting at the very least a rose tattoo or a gold bracelet, was shocked to see a white knotted rope of scar tissue twisting halfway round his wrist. She couldn't take her eyes away.

'Have you seen enough, signora?' he asked after a moment. 'Or you want to examine the other?' He pushed his left cuff back to reveal a matching scar.

'I'm so sorry . . . I didn't mean . . .' Was this what the Count had implied? 'Disagreeable' surely was an inadequate word to describe attempted suicide, and that's what Procopio's scars looked like. She sat down again abruptly, words tumbling clumsily out. 'You see . . . I was planning to visit San Rocco with Donna, the Canadian girl I work with . . . because she saw the mute woman – Raphael's attacker – in the street near his house, Raphael's house, two nights ago . . . and then . . . well, I wanted to apologise to you first, in private . . .'

'Is the beautiful Canadian waiting for you outside?' Procopio asked with mock innocence. 'Please tell her to come in, by all means.'

'No . . . she . . .' How could she possibly explain her motives? Charlotte started again. 'I was on my way here – alone – to apologise for being so late, when I stopped at San Rocco and . . . I heard *singing*, Signor Procopio!'

He barely skipped a beat. 'We are a great nation of opera lovers, you must know that. Even in the fields farmers have been known to burst spontaneously into song. Even butchers.'

He was making fun of her. 'Don't forget, signora, Rossini was born not far from here. Maybe his ghost . . . ?'

'It wasn't opera I heard. And I doubt it was a farmer. The song came from underground, I believe, which I know must seem a little . . . mad. But it sounded like a bird singing underground.'

He took the cigar from his mouth, examined it carefully for suspected flaws and slowly stubbed it out in the ashtray. 'Poor thing,' he said. 'She *is* fond of her little songbird.'

'*Who* is . . . the mute woman?'

With one hand he rubbed his opposite wrist, twisting it back and forth, the action of a prisoner manacled too tightly.

'If someone is living there, underground, signor, she needs help.'

'Why? She has lived like that for years. She is perfectly happy.'

'Perhaps she was happy once, but things have changed, you know they have. It wasn't a happy woman who attacked the Raphael.'

'What would you do, signora? Arrest her? Put her in jail? A hospital? Get the psychologists and the psychiatrists and all the other psychos after her? What good will that do her – or your precious Raphael?'

'She may be entering another phase, don't you see? If her mutism is symptomatic of psychosis – schizophrenia, perhaps . . .' His disgusted expression stopped her. 'I don't want her put in jail, Signor Procopio, really I don't. But . . . we may have frightened her the other night. Donna chased her. The poor woman may be hiding down there in a state of shock. She might starve down there, don't you see?'

'Not starve,' the big man said, shaking his head. 'Other things maybe, but not starvation. We don't let that happen in our valley. This isn't Rome or London, you know, where people die alone in the streets. Here we are loyal to our own.' He thought for a minute, then came to a decision. 'Look, I tell you what . . . You English pride yourselves on discretion, yes? Not like us poor noisy Italians. So . . . if I show you something at San Rocco to ease your mind about Muta, I can trust you to keep quiet?'

'As it happens, you're the second man to praise my discreet silence.' Perhaps Geoffrey is right, Charlotte thought; I should speak up more.

As they crossed the yard to the jeep the scar-faced dog appeared, the one that had frightened Charlotte the first day, unchained this time, but wagging his tail and pulling the good half of his face into something resembling a smile. Procopio stooped to greet him with a soft 'Baldassare!' and the hound sat back on his haunches and raised his front legs to place his paws gravely on his master's shoulders. After a moment of silent communion, Procopio said, '*Basta.*' The dog withdrew his paws and watched them walk away, his long tail drifting back and forth with the slow and graceful regularity of a pendulum on a grandfather clock.

'Baldassare seems an odd name for a hunting dog,' Charlotte said, getting into the jeep.

Procopio gave her a little smile. 'I named him after Baldassare Castiglione. Primo – you know him? The mayor? Years ago, when I joined the Communist party, he gave me a copy of Castiglione's *The Book of the Courtier*. I think he was making a joke at my expense, but it's a nice book.'

'Did you read it?'

'Not much. Enough to know that this dog of mine represents the ideal Renaissance gentleman.' His eyes teased her. 'Always dressed in sober colours and adept at what Castiglione called sprezzatura . . . you know this word? It means to make hard work look easy.'

MIRACLE NUMBER 24
The Ideal City

Procopio stopped his jeep on the crest of a hill above San Rocco, where the whole valley spread out ahead of them. 'Lucifer's Gate,' he said, pointing beyond San Rocco's bell tower to a crater visible only as a slight dip in the land filled with grass and brown, blown seed-heads. No serpent had lain there, Charlotte thought. She couldn't imagine where the image had come from that morning, or why she had felt so uneasy. From this distance the hamlet resembled the kind of ruin popular with eighteenth-century Romantics on their Grand Tours of Italy.

The big man beside her started up the jeep and drove down into San Rocco, parking close to the ruined church. 'That pig farm I showed you?' he said. 'Just this side of it there will soon be a development for farmers like me who are tired of farming. Golf course, swimming pool, conference centre. It will spread over that hill, where my house lies, missing San Rocco by half a mile, although I am told that its church will be restored to provide an attractive perspective for the conference centre, which will be presented as an ideal place for wedding receptions. Weddings are big business in Italy.' His brown eyes slewed towards her. 'For myself . . . well, pig-farming is not what it was. These days I prefer ice-cream.'

He lifted his chin at the bullet-holes on the church door. 'I wonder if they will keep those for local colour. I hear bloodstains from the War are popular to show off in French hotels.'

'What did San Rocco look like before?' she asked softly.

'Before what?'

'Before the War, before whatever happened here.'

'You are suggesting I am old enough to remember the War?' He was teasing her. 'Thank you for the compliment. I'm fifty-seven, born in 1936.'

'So you were not too young to remember San Rocco?'

'Too young to be interested in the architecture of old buildings, anyway. But . . . I believe it was very beautiful.' His face became heavier and she thought: this is something he cares about. 'My father,' he said, 'who was a man of action more than words, he used to say that San Rocco *stood* for something in this valley.'

'What did it stand for, Signor Procopio?'

'That was the problem – he never did say!' He grinned at her. 'I told you he was no man of words. But . . . I believe it was to do with the place itself. You know they found what were claimed to be Etruscan tumuli here? Yes! A young German archaeology student wrote of it before the War.' His ironic tone of voice had slipped for a moment and he reclaimed it like a man donning armour he does not truly believe will protect him. 'But *history* you can find in any museum. It wasn't *history* that made this place special, except in the sense of its history of hospitality . . . to strangers, to everyone. And its construction, that too was important: houses and barns and bakery all growing out of each other in a pleasing fashion, so you could not take one wall away without them all collapsing. *Simbiotico*, we say. There must be an English word, there is always an English word when it comes to property.'

'Symbiotic? It's not particularly to do with property.'

'So it is the same in English. I had forgotten. A good word in any language. Anyway, it was impossible to imagine not being welcomed at San Rocco, impossible to imagine a time when it had not existed – or would not exist. San Rocco, it seemed part of the rocks and cliffs and ravines of this valley, part of who these people are . . . or *were* . . . All gone now, even its graveyard destroyed.'

'What kind of people destroy a village graveyard?'

'People who want to wipe out history?'

She paused, the Count's warning in mind. 'Was there ever an investigation?'

'Of what?'

'Of . . . whatever happened here.'

'Start investigating all the bombs and disappearances in the War, that makes for a lot of investigations.'

'I mean later, after the War was over. Surely an entire hamlet could not simply be wiped out and no one ever look into it.'

'Do you know what it was like here after the War? The woods full of bodies, the fields full of ruins, each political party pulling a different direction.' He smiled slightly. 'And we have so many parties, the benefits of a democratic society. Anyway, the War was not over for twenty years. Maybe not even now. We still have Americans, English, Germans fighting for this land, although they want it for other purposes.'

He took two heavy torches from the glove compartment. 'We'll need these. Now I will show you Muta's secret . . . *our* secret.'

The bird, silent through their descent of the ladder, immediately trilled a dawn welcome when Procopio's torch shone into its rustic cage. Charlotte's first thought was: How cruel, to keep it down here in permanent darkness! Then: 'Strange, for a deaf-mute to keep a – '

'It is for the company, not the song,' Procopio said quickly. 'You like the cage? I made it, out of green willow.'

The little creature continued whistling its complex melody. 'What kind of bird is it?'

'Oh, some uccello canterino I found in a hedge. Its wing was damaged. See how the right one hangs, what do you say, "out of kinder"?'

'Out of kilter,' Charlotte corrected him, smiling. 'You make so few mistakes in English – where did you learn it?'

'Two years cooking fish and chips in Brighton. Take-away or eat in, madam? You want vinegar with your chips?'

She laughed. 'I'm amazed you speak it so well, then! In

London all the fish and chip shops are run by Chinese and Turkish immigrants.'

'Brighton too. Fortunately, this one was big enough to employ a waitress. English girl, art student . . . very pretty.'

'Ah, I see. You had an interpreter.'

'Yes, she interpreted many things for me, delightfully, until she left me for a Spanish sterco.' ('A Spanish turd', Charlotte translated to herself.) 'It made me realise how good is our joke about traitors and translators. You know what I mean?'

It was one of those plays on words that made translation so subtle an art. How often in Italian history, Charlotte wondered, had the translator, *il traduttore*, turned out to be a traitor, *il traditore*? A slip of two letters made all the difference.

Procopio lit an oil lamp and hung it on the low ceiling, illuminating a cellar made of words and pictures. Walls, ceiling, the interiors of cupboards were covered by month after month, year after year of newspapers layered with postcards of well-known paintings from museums all over Italy, their corners curling in the damp air. Why would someone who collected reproductions of art hate a painting enough to destroy it? Surely only madness or desperation would drive anyone to that, Charlotte thought.

The bright postcards pinned up over the grey tower blocks of text reminded her of stretches of clear hillside glimpsed through city walls, and her precise, analytical mind began to search for some meaning or pattern in the random juxtapositions of images and headlines: GUERRA, MASSACRATI (she thought of Raphael's *Massacre of the Innocents*), ASSASSINIO, OMICIDIO (then della Francesca's *Flagellation*), VIOLENZA CARNALE, VIOLENZA SU DONNA, CELEBRITÀ SCANDALOSE. Crucifixions, martyred saints, virgins, all mixed up with war, massacres, assassination, homicide, rape, a movie star's scandalous life story . . . the same old stories used to sell newsprint, religion and nationalism over the last fifty years, reduced here to wallpaper. Charlotte walked past one war to read of another and another and another. Italians sent to be killed with Franco during the Spanish Civil War, Italians frozen on the Russian front. 'These newspapers must date back thirty years or more . . . Was it Muta's family who had this cellar?'

He grinned at her. 'Who is this Muta you talk of? A gypsy, maybe. Some wanderer who lost her way and wound up at San Rocco looking for shelter. There were lots of those kind during and after the War.'

Charlotte tried a new tack. 'Perhaps she can read, if she keeps these?'

'No. My aunt leaves our newspapers by the church and sometimes postcards, but to her they are just patterns, insulation. They keep out the cold and damp, useful for lighting the fire.' He showed off the rough chimney and brick stove the mute woman had constructed for herself.

'So she cooks?' Charlotte asked. Gnawed bones would not have surprised her. A wild animal's life.

'Yes, of course. Can't you smell the fish?'

To Charlotte the cellar smelled like an animal's den. She was appalled at the evidence of this silent underground existence, empty of any people except these postcard reproductions.

'I've caught sight of her trapping and fishing in the hills from time to time, although she never lets me get close. But these are mine.' He pointed at a plate piled with sausages. 'I flavour them with orange rind and spices and my aunt leaves them with the newspapers. The mute probably imagines they are a gift from the gods.' He picked up a rough bar of soap. 'This I made with caustic soda and bay leaves, just like my mother used to do.' He smiled a little maliciously. 'And with all the unusable scraps from the pig slaughtering, that is essential. You have to be careful, though. One glance from someone like you during the soap-making is enough to ruin the entire batch.'

The lamplight threw an enlarged silhouette of his shaggy head against the wall, his tight curls clearly defined. Aware of him like some powerful bullish creature behind her in this labyrinth of words, Charlotte moved away from the descriptions of sausages and soap past walls lined with preserves. Many of the labels dated back to the War, while some unlabelled jars must be more recent, judging by the fresher nature of their contents: briny fungi, with pale gills reminiscent of sea creatures, thumb-length pieces of white fish looking more like asparagus. She played her torch further down the cellar, where the room, narrowing to corridor width, was almost blocked by a small landslide of earth and broken wooden planks.

'Don't go down there!'

Procopio's command stopped her from following the beam of light as, with surprising grace and speed, he moved forward to lay a hand on her shoulder. She felt immobilised by the weight of it, as if an enormous paw or hoof had staked a claim to those inches of her skin. Something heavy had been driven into her, rooting her there. 'That is almost below Lucifer's Gate, where the grenades were thrown,' he said. She smelled cigars and aniseed on his breath, a mixture she found oddly pleasant. 'The ceiling is held up by no more than worms and rabbit droppings.'

He started to pull her away from the rubble, but not soon enough to prevent Charlotte flicking her torch over the walls again. Roots from above crawled over torn newspapers. 'Look! What's that?'

'Come away, Charlotte! It's dangerous!'

'No, wait, I want to see.' Charlotte shifted from under his hand, barely noticing his use of her Christian name, and moved cautiously down the passage to where a yellowed piece of notepaper was stuck to the wall. She struggled to make out the crabbed, faded handwriting, 'Good Lord, it's in English! This must be . . . it must date from the War!'

1/ Any farm with young men walking about is safe; they are deserters either from the Army or from Germany and in as bad a spot as yourself.

2/ The poorer the house, the safer it is: rich houses are invariably Fascist.

3/ Never remain static; one night and day in a house is ample.
4/ Women working in the fields are usually safe. They probably have sons your age.
5/ If a farmer sees you hiding in his fields, he will pass by and pretend not to have seen you. Later he will come back and, if he is sympathetic, will ask if you are hungry. If he doesn't produce food, go away quickly.
6/ Once you have stayed at a house, you are safe; they won't tell the Germans as their house would be burned.

Rules left by an Englishman on the run, she thought. A warning to others. 'How extraordinary that it still exists.' She was starting to peel the note off the wall when Procopio pulled her gently away. 'Leave it,' he said. 'These walls are very unstable.'

Frustrated by her attempt to remove the note in one piece, Charlotte shook her head. All she had achieved was a short vertical strip of Haiku: *deserters yourself Fascist pretend one night*.

Looking back at it, Procopio said softly, 'Sometimes I wonder if she even knows the War is over.'

'But . . . why is it here at all?' And what other scraps could be found under these layers of words?

He shrugged. 'In farm kitchens round here you will still find placards the Germans put up offering Italians a choice between death for helping Allied prisoners or a reward of 1800 lire for denouncing them – about £750 at present-day rates.' He smiled. 'Not bad money. I have my own souvenir – a leaflet distributed clandestinely by the Badoglio Government, offering 5000 lire to any Italian who gave hospitality to the British or Americans. Very sensible. To make them worth more alive than dead.'

'In England one seldom hears about the Marches' war, always about Rome, Naples, Sicily.'

'You know those smooth hills to the north of Urbino? You still find the old, dead-straight German roads around here, as I told you the first time we met. They formed part of what the Germans originally called Hitler's Line, a name they changed to the Gothic Line when they discovered they were losing the War.' The smile he gave her did not quite reach his eyes. 'For what you *call* a thing is very important, isn't that right, Signora Penton? And I call them admirable, the German roads. Like the Romans, the Germans were very thorough . . .'

Again Charlotte thought of the Count's warning. Still, Procopio would have been too young to be either *traduttore* or *traditore*.

'As a boy I used to wonder if the Allies had managed to remove all the mines left by the retreating Nazis in Urbino's walls. Only a few of the mines exploded, but it is a miracle – and a lot of hard work by British bomb-disposal teams after the Liberation – that the city was not blasted to destruction. If it had gone up . . . well, that would have been a true falò delle Muse to bring out all the little octopodi.'

'A what?'

'A bonfire of the muses.'

What a curious mixture he was: one minute boorish, the next making literary allusions. 'Do you mean Savonarola, his bonfire of the vanities?'

'No, I speak of what happened on our coast at Ancona. The Theatre of the Muses went up in flames and the fire brought thousands of octopus to the surface. Then the Anconetani (great octopus eaters), they jumped into their boats and scooped up with their bare hands all the octopodi and cooked them with white wine and bietole, as they do down there. Me, I prefer them plain – olive oil and a squeeze of lemon. Now we should allow the rabbit to return to her burrow.'

At Charlotte's hesitation, he said, 'Come away, *now*!' His voice was rougher, and this time he grasped her hand firmly in his.

'So you see,' he said, when they had emerged again into the light, 'she's perfectly content. She has everything she needs- . . . Which reminds me . . .' From his pocket he produced two packets wrapped in newspaper and placed them by the church door. 'Cheese and chocolate – she likes my homemade chocolates – and two more sheets for her walls.'

But Charlotte was nagged by his earlier comment; was it possible that this woman might not know the War was over? As if someone in wartime London had retreated underground during the Blitz and never come up into the light again, had carried on living in fear of death while all around the rest of the world was returning to life. 'Something must be done . . . What if she isn't mute after all?' Charlotte said, so softly that she was amazed to find herself spun round by Procopio's big mitts.

'You promised me, if I show you this, you will keep it quiet!' he said.

'Yes, but . . . yes, I promised, *I promise*!'

He dropped his hands from her shoulders. 'This is very dangerous to meddle in. Muta is safe here. We look after her. But if anyone even *thinks* she can speak, she is a dead woman! Leave her alone!'

'Yes, I will, I promised,' Charlotte managed to stutter. 'But please, won't you explain? You obviously know something about who she is, what happened to her . . . You said this was dangerous . . . *What* is? *Who* is?'

Procopio made an explosive sound and strode off to the jeep. Charlotte followed more slowly and found him gripping the wheel so that veins stood out under the bristling black hairs on his hands. They sat for several minutes in silence, then Procopio thrust his scarred wrists under Charlotte's eyes. 'A sign of suicide, that is what you think, am I right, Signora Penton?' he asked. 'But you are wrong. What I tried to do, to talk about this, wasn't suicide, though some people would call it that. I was a young, too-zealous policeman whom they left to die. They strung me up like a scarecrow and left me to die.'

'*Who* did, Signor Procopio?'

MIRACLE NUMBER 25

Isis and Her Famous Black Madonna

Donna was hurt by the stiff little note handed over by the concierge at the Pensione Raffaello. Why couldn't Charlotte have phoned? Why did she have to leave this crappy letter, so formal and *English*? She stepped out into the narrow cobbled street and almost collided with Paolo, dismounting from his pistachio-green Lambretta. At his delighted smile Donna felt a rush of pleasure. 'Charlotte's not here,' she said. 'We were supposed to meet, but she stood me up.'

He kissed her once on each cheek, and then as she was drawing back he took her face lightly in his hands and held it and stared into her eyes. She was certain he was about to kiss her on the lips. When he didn't, she said, '*What?* What is it?'

He shook his head and continued to stare.

'What is it, Paolo?' She felt breathless, as if he were trying to force an admission from her.

He smiled suddenly. 'Three times we do in Italy,' he said, and kissed her again, but just on the cheek. Keeping his face close to hers, he whispered, 'Maybe our Charlotte has a lover!'

Donna couldn't see it, not Charlotte with her flat shoes and her flappy clothes. 'More likely she's working overtime to fix that painting of yours.'

'No, this is what I came to tell her. The Raphael has been spirited away to the Ducal Palace in the care of Monsignor Seguita, the investigating bishop from Rome.'

'Why? How?'

'It is quite a story . . .' Paolo lifted her hand up and kissed it lightly. 'Come for a coffee, a drink! Better still, marry me! Then I can tell you all my stories in comfort, not here in the street.'

'A coffee would be fine.'

He looked at his watch and quickly added, 'I have an appointment right now at the university that I cannot break, but in . . . one hour? We could meet at Procopio's Caffè?' He kissed her again and before she could protest or refuse he had remounted his Lambretta and revved it dramatically, leaving a trail of rubber as he disappeared down the street.

With nothing better to do, Donna decided to wander down and have a look at the small travelling circus and fairground that had been set up on one of the few level stretches of grass beyond the city walls. She saw that several rides must have been packed up fairly recently, because there remained squares, circles and rectangles of pale ghost grass, a shadow carnival, where the carousels and dodgems formerly had stood.

What was left had a wild, edgy feel to it, not like the huge commercial ventures Donna knew from Canada. Goats were tethered to some of the caravans and fierce-looking mongrels prowled the field for scraps of food. She heard one dog give a low rumbling growl as it passed a cage which turned out to hold a pacing tiger, so ancient and underfed that its striped coat hung loosely from its bones like badly fitting upholstery off a wooden sofa frame.

Among the fire-eaters, jugglers and fortune-tellers entertaining the fair's customers, Donna saw several who regularly worked the crowds of pilgrims outside Raphael's house. Evidently this site was their temporary residence, for she recognised one juggler sitting on the steps of his caravan and smoking a pipe, and, disappearing into a tent as Donna walked by, a wizened old woman in outlandish gypsy clothes, her face familiar from the Piazza delle Erbe, where she could often be found reading palms and cards.

The sign on her tent was hand-lettered in red and gold:

CHIROMANZIA: SIGNORA ISIS

E SUA FAMOSA MADONNA NERA

Shortly after that Donna spotted Paolo, behind the fortune-teller's tent with a man in a baggy pinstriped suit. At first she thought she was mistaken; it wasn't Paolo at all. With the collar of his black leather jacket turned up and a navy ski hat pulled down low over his eyes, he looked tougher, more feral than usual. But the little black goatee was a giveaway, as was the quick, determined way he moved his hands, and she was about to call out to her friend when she noticed what he was doing.

He was paying the other man a substantial amount of money.

She watched the man pocket a thick roll of cash. Something about the two men's demeanour made Donna turn away, hiding her face. She contemplated a chimpanzee in the cage beside her, then followed Paolo's example and pulled the collar of her jacket up, tucking her hair inside. This is dumb, she thought. I'm acting like a spy. Out of the corner of her eyes she saw the man in pinstripes walk past her without giving her a glance. It was the older of the two security guards who had been on duty the day of the Raphael attack.

What was Paolo up to?

Donna waited to see if he would notice her among the crowd of teenagers and mothers with young children who made up the fair's customers. She stared at the chimpanzee, her heart beating fast. The chimp, with the weary yellow eyes of a hard-drinking chain-smoker, stared morosely back, his leathery mitt half-heartedly playing with a slender lilac penis.

After a few minutes, Donna felt it was safe to turn around.

Paolo had disappeared. She strolled over to the fortune-teller's tent and cautiously parted the curtains, preparing an alibi if she found him inside.

A thousand versions of herself hesitated at the entrance and fractured into ten thousand Donnas as she moved forward into the entirely mirrored and candlelit world of Signora Isis. The Famous Black Madonna, an elaborately veiled porcelain doll, was sitting on a gilt throne next to the old gypsy and holding in its arms a wax baby. The gypsy fortune-teller herself was holding a powerfully garlicky sausage the size of her own arm and biting off chunks of it. She greeted her new arrival with a stream of Italian, indicating that Donna should be seated opposite, then laid the sausage down on the table, wiped her hands on the heavily fringed velvet cloth covering it and picked up a cigarette. Three apples closely resembling the old woman's face rested between the ashtray and the sausage. Donna couldn't decide if they were lunch or part of the act. Searching for her few words of Italian, she said, 'Sono Donna . . . um . . . a friend of Paolo, *amica di Paolo*,' and, holding up some money, let the old woman decide how much was appropriate.

'Si, si, sono amica di Paolo anch'io, amica con mi amico Paolo . . .' the gypsy murmured, pocketing 10,000 lira. 'Grazie lui, la mia donna è tornata.' She nodded and patted the doll's head, then lifted its heavy lace veil to reveal a dark queen underneath, burned and seared and sooty from years of candle smoke, with only its glass eyes clear, glittering fiercely. 'Guarda! La cortina di segretezza è sollevata! Isis lifta da veil. Ora la Madonna Nera dice solo la verità! Now she say only troot, pretty lady! She tell what you wanna know bout love wit Paolo, she tell you watch out dark stranger, long voyage over water come soon . . .'

All the usual mumbo jumbo, thought Donna. She didn't need to have a translation to guess what the old fraud would tell her next. Frustrated, she gazed around at the circular tent, which must date back to the 1930s, with full-length walls of Art Deco mirrors fitted around the circumference like plate armour. Some of the mirrors were so worn that what remained of the reflective surface had flaked away to islands within a sea of glass and gilt, reducing Donna to a head, a dark eye, a pair of hands, fingers impatiently tapping. Over the gypsy's banal predictions she heard the ageing tiger's roar. It was time to go. 'Thank you, *grazie*, I have to – ' Donna was saying as she turned back to face Signora Isis. She stopped mid-sentence at the sight of the blood-red tears rolling down the face of the Famous Black Madonna.

'Una meraviglia!' the old crone barked in delight. 'Is a miracle! La Madonna is OK now. No more sick!'

MIRACLE NUMBER 26

An Obscure Light

Paolo's wry expression acknowledged the café's outdated interior, its curlicued iron furniture, the ancient waiter's balding head and flat feet, the stout furred ladies eating their way slowly and steadily through pounds of frosted cream and egg-white in only twelve different flavours, not the obligatory thirty or forty of Urbino's other *gelaterias*. 'I wanted to bring you here to Procopio's because it is a special place for me since I was a boy,' he said to Donna. 'The owner is an old Marxist, a friend of my grandfather's.'

'A Commie!' It didn't look like a Commie sort of place.

'A Marxist.'

'There's a difference?'

He shrugged. 'Who cares! What I love is the way these people seem always to have been here, like a painting. And here we can be more private, away from the university crowd. It is very intimate, what you call chiaroscuro, no?'

'Kee-ar-oh *what*?'

'I am sorry, you don't say that in English?'

'Yeah, I guess.' He had touched her lightly, the springy hairs on his arm brushing against her skin. He kept finding excuses to touch her, as he had the other night in the Caffè Repubblica – the knuckles of one hand brushed across the pulse of her wrist, his forefinger tapped on her palm, this arm thing. Nothing she could pin down, tell him to stop. All the time her treacherous skin was saying *yes! more!* If she let him he'd spoon her up and swallow her whole and spit her out in a kitchen with an apron around her spreading waist. Then where would Paolo be? Out looking for the next girl, she'd bet! Or out behind a fairground tent, as she'd caught him an hour ago, paying for . . . what?

'Chiaroscuro,' Paolo was saying, 'it is a term to describe the dark, mysterious quality of certain paintings. In English it translates literally as "obscure light" – funny, yes? How can a light be obscure? Very *Italian.*'

Surprised by the mild contempt in his voice, as if to be Italian was no great shakes, she thought of her dad and how differently he described his Roman heritage. With Dad, you'd think Italy was all coliseum and no gladiators. Pointedly ignoring the thumb Paolo had run down the side of her palm, she asked, 'So, you were going to tell me how Monsignor Seguita got the painting out under the noses of the crowd . . .'

At her brisk, impersonal tone he leaned back and lit a cigarette, frowning slightly. His own voice was cooler, a match for hers: 'They cut it from its frame and smuggled it out. Maybe under Seguita's robes, who knows? The cops were angry, of course, as were the public prosecutor and Criminalpol, our esteemed equivalent of the FBI, but the Bishop of Urbino, having himself been a witness to the miraculous weeping, has been given permission by the Vatican to hold the painting until proof has been provided that its blood is a hoax.'

Donna noticed how Paolo's eyes narrowed to half-moons as he hid a smile. What else was he hiding? Maybe he wasn't quite the sweet Italian boy-next-door she had imagined.

'No doubt they would like to arrest our bishop,' he went on, 'but the bishop being a bishop, with this other bishop from the Vatican to support him, it is difficult.' Again that contained smile. 'So now there is a very *Italian* compromise, where it has been agreed that our bishop keeps the lovely lady locked up in a sealed cupboard in the palace cellars, allowing access for the moment only to Monsignor Seguita, the public prosecutor, Criminalpol – and to the police, who have agreed not to violate the Church's autonomy.'

'What's the connection? I mean, Raphael's painting isn't religious . . .'

'That's one of the aspects of the case Monsignor Seguita is exploring.'

'Monsignor Seguita . . .' Donna took a spoonful of the jasmine ice Paolo had insisted she try and found that the taste it left on her tongue was not as unpleasant as she'd first thought.

'It is good, yes?'

'Oh . . . yeah, I guess . . . different.' He must be watching her closely, looking for ways to please her, get under her skin. 'Monsignor Seguita *must* have spirited the painting away to get past all those pilgrims.'

'You saw them this morning, with their "Free Raphael" placards? Urbino's parishioners are protesting over the state's interference with their plans to have the painting on view for the Feast of Relics next week. Someone quickly put up money for a lawyer to appeal to the Court of Cessation in Rome for La Muta's release. If he succeeds, he can add to his reputation for being the only lawyer in history to set the Virgin free.' Briefly he described a celebrated case in which another icon had been 'liberated'.

'What are they doing about the blood on the picture, if it *is* blood?'

'Oh it is!' Paolo said. 'Most upsetting for Professor Serafini – he was on the radio this morning, furious because the Vatican, in the person of Monsignor Seguita, the investigating bishop from Rome, has stopped him working on the Raphael. But also, I'm sure, because after all he has claimed over the years about these weeping Madonnas having tears made of dye or fat, La Muta's turns out to be human blood!'

'Was the blood female?'

'Male. So of course the Church men are angry as well, for the blood ought to be from a *woman*, at the very least! The painting can't be released until the Vatican scientists complete their DNA tests. Even then I believe the Church will only be satisfied if these bloody tears are found to come from Jesus Christ himself!'

'Have they tested Count Malaspino yet to see if the blood is his?'

'They have – and today they want to take samples from all of us who have worked on the painting, even the women. Meanwhile the painting is to be left as is. But if Church and state agree to release her, we – Charlotte, me, Anna – we've been asked to do a temporary patch-up on the poor mutinous lady, so the tear does not become any worse.'

'Is that what your urgent appointment was about this afternoon?' Donna asked the question casually, as if she wasn't that interested, and Paolo's hesitation before replying made the back of her neck tingle.

'I . . . yes, I was at the university, trying to track down the kind of vacuum table we would need to line the canvas.'

She was a fraction removed from asking if the circus supplied such modern technology, but she kept the comment to herself and leaned close to him. 'After all the work you put in you must be worried, Paolo.' His fine black brows drew together. She was conscious of his eyes questioning her, trying to make sense of her behaviour, although Donna couldn't make sense of it herself. Why not come right out and say she'd seen him at the circus?

'Worried, yes,' he said after a moment. 'I am worried that for some reason Count Malaspino has withdrawn his support from the project. Fortunately, the city council has offered money, as have the sponsors of Santa Chiara – ISIA, you know it? Our institute for artistic industries. But to finish in time for the Feast of Relics is impossible. Even if it is released soon, to have the painting lined and patched safely we would have to work through the nights . . . and Charlotte will not be pleased in any case. She will say, I am sure, that haste may cause permanent damage, which is true.'

He moved his leg so that his bare ankle was in close contact with hers. 'And you, cara, what did you get up to this afternoon?'

Suddenly tired of all the bullshit, Donna said sharply, 'Me? I wandered down to that crummy little circus on the edge of town.'

She felt Paolo's ankle shift away from hers as he said quickly,

'Such a third-rate affair, I cannot imagine why you should be interested . . .'

'I thought I'd have my fortune told . . . by that gypsy what's-her-name, Signora Isis?'

Now was Paolo's chance to come clean. Instead he gave her his most charming boyish smile, 'So if you like magic and circus tricks, carissima Donna, I imagine you are going to this event at Santa Chiara . . .'

'What event?'

'There were posters everywhere this morning: Serafini is putting on a show in Santa Chiara, a former monastery. He is planning to demonstrate how similar effects to our Raphael's bloody tears might be achieved. With the Vatican's prohibition against him examining La Muta and her blood, it is all the little professore can do, I'm afraid.'

'You sound as if you know Serafini quite well.'

'Not really. After university I had the silly fantasy of trying to get work with him . . . but my degree in restoration was not serious enough for the Professor. Still, I am interested in what he has to show me.' He looked at his watch. 'I'm going to Santa Chiara very soon . . . Would you . . .'

MIRACLE NUMBER 27

The Transforming Powers of Cold

If not for the scarecrows, she might be safely back in Urbino. That is what Charlotte was thinking while she scrubbed her hands clean with a yellow, oily piece of soap as marbled with dirty cracks as the sink in the huge, dim lavatory of Procopio's house. Why hadn't she rejected his lunch invitation? Blame it on the scarecrows, yes. She'd been asking Procopio for the names of the men responsible for stringing him up and he'd said it didn't matter: 'Men employed by other men employed by still more men. The old guard. All of them old men now.'

'They were arrested, punished?'

'You want to put old men in jail? All the old men in the cafés? Think of their poor innocent widows, the bambini without grandfathers! The noise of it! The weeping and wailing!' His voice had a certain dry humour. 'What is the word you restorers use – *pentimento*? You know its other meaning is repentance, regret? So. What you find under my shirtcuffs is evidence of my own repentance.'

'I don't understand.'

'So I keep saying! Women, always talk talk talk, never listen! Shall I tell you the only kind of restoration I am interested in these days? Ice-cream. The mysterious, *transforming* pleasures of cold. You know that Dante made the worst part of his Inferno cold, not hot? Good at preserving things, cold – and I learned a lot about preservation when I was strung up in the Montefeltro grottoes: *self*-preservation! Some of these grottoes are very beautiful, Charlotte. You should see them one day . . . Like chilly underground cathedrals – spiralling stairways, vaulted arches . . . I had a lot of time to admire the beauty of their architecture – and to repent, oh yes, I repented, I pleaded and begged for mercy and repented everything.' He waved away her questions, as if the details were unimportant. 'You see, I was the first policeman ever in a long line of cooks and butchers, and looking back down that vanishing line I acquired a sense of perspective as good as Raffaello's. That is the pentimento you discovered.'

'How did you get out of the cave?'

'My aunt, the woman who keeps house for me, she remembered that Uncle Tito used to store . . . equipment in the caves. Between her and her mule of a son they know every nook and cranny in this valley.'

'And the men? Why didn't they come back when they realised you were still alive?'

'They *did* come back, but I'd learned my lesson by then.' He started the jeep. 'You will share lunch with me today?'

'Oh, no . . . thank you so much . . . you are terribly kind . . .'

An Englishman would have understood what she wanted. He kept driving. 'If you could just . . .' she said. *Turn the jeep around. Take me back to Urbino.* Why didn't she say it?

Then they had reached the orchard and it was too late.

On their way from his farm to San Rocco Procopio had been on the wrong side to notice the scarecrows, but now he brought the jeep to a sliding, skidding stop and without a word to Charlotte jumped out to stride over and stand beneath the raddled fruit trees, staring up for minute after minute at the grotesque figures in their branches. She watched him grab a withered trunk and shake it, clearly trying to knock the figures onto the ground. The rags of clothing only flapped and billowed as if they did indeed enclose the angry, restless souls of men who had died by some violence at their own hands or the hands of others.

His expression was grim when he returned.

'They are yours, the scarecrows?' Charlotte asked, and when he didn't respond she said nervously, 'Anything wrong?'

'No.'

'You seem – '

'Not my *scarecrows*, but my clothes. Mine and Angelino's and the old woman's.' He swore proficiently in Italian.

'What's wrong? What do they mean?'

'In the old days . . .'

'In the old days, what?'

'Forget it!'

'Tell me, *please*, Signor Procopio . . .'

'In the old days "scarecrow" used to be the valley people's password for . . . traitor, turncoat . . .'

'What do they mean now, these scarecrows?'

'Nothing of interest to you.'

'What do they mean?'

The jeep started with its usual rattling cough. 'Maybe somebody's reminding me of the penalty for opening my big trap.'

Charlotte watched Procopio splash wine from an unlabelled bottle into her tumbler. Why hadn't she said *yes*, she *did* want to return to Urbino? This time she couldn't put it down to fear of hurting his feelings, her natural restraint, the usual inability to express herself. Was it a desire to clear up the mystery? Is that why she was here? For if so, it looked as if her curiosity would remain unsatisfied.

'You watch much football?' he asked.

'Not really.'

'Yet you claim to have an interest in our culture! You don't know our next Prime Minister may get in because he is president of a football team?'

'Oh, I can't believe that's the only – '

'AC Milano – good team. So long as his team keeps on winning, the people don't care if their next PM has a brother and business associate under investigation in the Clean Hands procedures, doesn't make any difference his close ally is on permanent holiday in Tunisia after massive accusations of corruption. The voters don't see any irony in a Prime Minister owning newspapers able to promote his election campaign or having power over state TV his own television networks compete with . . . but I tell you one thing – I bet our PM is rejected if his team loses the World Cup, for all his "self-made man of the people" talk . . . Ham?'

Before she could answer he had carried her plate over to an enormous sideboard covered in crocheted doilies, on which reclined an entire pig's leg complete with a hoof as elegantly pointed as a ballet dancer's shoe. Everything in the house was as out of scale as Procopio. Charlotte pictured herself once again as Goldilocks, now dining compatibly with one of the three bears.

'Our own prosciutto,' he said, offering her some ruddy slices of ham enclosed in thick white fat. It smelled strongly of pig, a smell permeating the whole house, and Charlotte, who liked meat only in small quantities and cooked until there was no suggestion of pink, remembered the fatty smell and colour of the soap she'd used to wash her hands. Her wayward insides lurched and settled unwillingly like a rowboat threatening to capsize in heavy weather. She took a mouthful of ham, trying to chew as little as possible, but the thorough mastication it demanded released a smoky sweetish pungency, inescapably piggy.

'It's good, yes?' Procopio nodded at her plate.

She smiled weakly and continued to chew, managing to swallow only with the help of a large gulp of red wine.

A second slice of ham appeared on her plate, thicker and thus chewier than the first. Up and down, round and round she volleyed it from one side of her tongue to another, without noticeably decreasing its size.

'You want more?' asked Procopio.

She couldn't shake her head for fear of gagging. Fibrous strings of meat or fat caught in her teeth like the braces she had worn as a child. The bolus of muscle and gristle slick with saliva gathered up all the words she might ever speak. Nightmare visions flashed into her head of anatomical drawings that proved how close we are to inhaling what we chew each time we swallow, only a slender, not always efficient flange of skin preventing us from choking. A boy she'd known had died by inhaling the whistle from a toy flute, his last words disguised by a trilling squeak.

Under threat from the sinuous ham slice dangling off Procopio's serving fork she finally managed to swallow. 'No thank you,' she gasped.

The next trial on her plate was a crude slab of blackened bread drenched in olive oil and lavishly rubbed with garlic and fresh tomatoes to transform the innocent toast into a reddish meaty pulp. How different this lunch was from her experience with the Count! She had to make an effort not to flinch when the housekeeper appeared with an enormous, chipped soup tureen and a platter mounded with dark green lentils lustrous with oil or fat and in which branches of rosemary and whole heads of garlic were embedded like fossils in limestone.

'Pheasant?' Procopio asked, dipping a spoon into the tureen.

'I . . . oh, that's too much . . .'

'We hit it with the car, remember? We hit it, she cooked it,' he said, gesturing with his shoulder at the old woman, with whom he seemed to communicate through a series of half-formed grunts and gestures. If requests were made of her or granted, they were unintelligible.

The pheasant turned out less bad than Charlotte feared. It had been skinned and jointed into pieces too small to be recognisable as the bird she had last seen having its neck broken between Procopio's able hands, then stewed in a winey sauce with small onions and wild mushrooms. The flesh was melting, hardly like meat at all, a surprisingly refined dish, she had to admit, even with the powerful garlickiness of the lentils.

'They come from Umbria,' Procopio informed her, pointing his fork at the khaki pulses on her plate.

To finish she was served a spoonful of the housekeeper's own cherries pickled in grappa, a weather-beaten pear with a russet skin like fine sandpaper and a tiny, hard goat cheese wrapped in a myrtle leaf. Considering the various metaphysical trials of the meal, Charlotte felt remarkably well, more a tribute to the quantity of wine she had consumed. Even the ham, in retrospect, didn't seem so bad. Safe now, she sipped some wine and took in details of the room more carefully, studying the heavy framed photograph of an earlier generation of grim-faced Italians. Two rifles of antique provenance hung just below the ceiling, and the walls bristled with proof of the gun-owner's proficiency in killing things. Moth-eaten boar, foxes, porcupine, marmots and various birds caught more and less successfully in flight glowered down at her as crossly as did Procopio's framed relatives. Charlotte's eyes, straying from the gaze of one particularly fierce *cinghiale* with tusks curling back on themselves like nests of macaroni, dropped to meet Procopio's, who was smiling at her in a proprietory way that made her feel like one of his collection of trophies.

'Thank you,' she said firmly. 'That was very good.'

'Even the prosciutto?' His large bright chestnut-coloured eyes narrowed with amusement.

The *devil*! So he had known *exactly* how she would respond to that lunch! Charlotte struggled between anger and amusement, her sense of humour winning out. 'Well, the ham was a bit of a test . . .' Her voice sounded warmer than she meant it to, almost flirtatious. But before she could correct the impression, Procopio had risen to his feet.

'Now I show you something.' She saw him stagger slightly. He must have drunk more than she'd noticed.

He returned with a framed photograph in his hand and dropped it on the table with a thump. 'Look here, see if you recognise anybody.'

Inevitably, it was a hunting picture. Men, boys, guns, dogs, a bristly wild boar (perhaps one of this room's grisly residents?) stretched out at their feet, one man grinning and holding up a hare by its flaccid neck. All suggestion of blood and barbarity reduced to history by the sepia tones of the image. An old farmhouse in the background that might be this one, might be any place in Italy where the houses had wooden shutters and peeling plaster walls and pantiled rooves. 'Your fattoria?' she guessed, and Procopio nodded solemnly.

'Look! More closely!' He tapped with his big blunt forefinger on the face of a man carrying a very young boy on his shoulders.

Judging by the men's clothes and their elaborate moustaches, the photo might have been taken twenty years before the War or ten years after. Like the farmhouse, the faces appeared generic, not personal. Tribal masks instead of portraits, Charlotte judged them, meant to conceal human individuality, not highlight it. 'I'm sorry,' she said.

Procopio made an impatient noise. He tapped the young boy on the man's shoulders. 'This is me and my father, Teodoro Mazzini, and next to him my uncle Tito, both butchers, although Tito was a bad one, very clumsy with a knife. You'd think he was cutting cabbage, not pigs. 1943, autumn. Papa turned the cinghiale into good prosciutto for the old Count, who shot it. He liked killing things.' A tall, frowning autocrat standing beside a young man of perhaps twelve or thirteen were the old Count and his son. 'Your *influential* friend,' he said. 'Those two dark giants are the Montagna brothers – Domenico, the one on the right, died a few weeks back at the pig farm. And these two here are Enrico Balducci and his cousin Cesare from San Rocco, who served the Count as beaters from time to time. Another Balducci cousin of theirs was a priest, a Communist. A highly vocal *Communist* priest – now that is a *very* dangerous kind of priest. A man who looked after the people in this valley, answered to the people in this valley, not the Pope! You can see why such a man might not live too long under a man like Pius XII, who was so very good at keeping silent about the Nazis' plans.'

Charlotte tried to fit Procopio's words to Count Malaspino's, wishing that her knowledge of the War in Italy was less limited. She knew more about the Guelphs and Ghibellines than she did about twentieth-century Italian politics. 'What happened to the priest? Are you suggesting that – '

'He disappeared. No one heard from him after . . .' He

turned back to the photo. 'And this is Carlo Seguita, the old Count's foreman.'

It was a brutally handsome face, but not attractive to Charlotte. She had never been drawn to the kind of men who exuded bullish power at the expense of all else. *Seguita*, she thought. 'Any relation to – '

'Older brother of the Vatican's chief miracle-chaser. The bishop was not born when this picture was taken, but see how the same set of features, twisted round, can make such a difference? Carlo was as smart as he was greedy, but couldn't hold his liquor, Uncle Tito said, who wasn't so good at it himself. Very nasty when he was drunk, Carlo, but just as smart, unlike Uncle Tito.' He jerked a thumb towards the kitchen. 'The old woman, she's Tito's widow and the cretino you met the first day here, the mule-driver Angelino – he's their son. Went funny in the head when he – '

Procopio stopped speaking as the old woman entered the room again and laid on the table a pot of coffee and a battered silver plate piled with brightly coloured sweetmeats that might have come from an Ottoman feast, plump dried apricots and dates stuffed with green almond paste, citrus peel sparkling with crystallised sugar, ribbons of pastry tied into knots and bows and deep-fried, dark wedges of a dense, potent fruit cake, candied clementines glistening with syrup, and in the centre four small whole pears dipped in chocolate, complete with chocolate leaves.

'My aunt is doing you proud,' said Procopio.

'Really, I'm not sure I could manage – '

'You must try at least one. Normally she reserves such treats for Christmas.'

Charlotte helped herself to the smallest of stuffed apricots and some candied peel. Frowning at this, Procopio's aunt added a chocolate pear to the plate, along with a mound of pastry knots dusty with icing sugar. As if we are tying up a contract in some ancient dessert ceremony, Charlotte thought, uneasily aware of a growing sense of complicity.

The old woman scowled at the photograph next to Charlotte's plate and made as if to remove the second bottle of wine, still half full, an action Procopio prevented by wrapping his hand round the bottle neck and grinning up at her. 'She doesn't like it when I drink. I talk too much. Like Uncle Tito.' With another inarticulate sound, possibly disapproval, the woman left. Procopio tapped the photo. 'Carlo, he got fat later, fat like those pigs up the road.'

'Later?'

'In the sixties. He moved to England – banking, I think, maybe stock-broking. Turned himself into a real little Englander: keep the darkie immigrants out, that sort of thing. I saw pictures of him in the newspaper when I was there. Done well for hisself, old Carlo, three wives, lotta grandchildren.' The alcohol was making Procopio's speech and accent sloppier. 'Not like me.'

'You don't have a . . .'

'She died.' Very deliberately his huge mitt moved across to envelop her hand. She felt herself flush all over. Her breathing became quick and shallow. Gin on an empty stomach, she thought, I've been too long without physical affection; it acts like gin on an empty stomach. What a pity he is not a type of man that I could . . . I like him, but he's too fleshy, too big, too hairy. She had always been attracted to clever men from social classes above her own, men like John who stimulated her mind. And betrayed me, she thought. She looked down at her small, pale hand covered by Procopio's bear paw, its coarse bristles scratching her palm every time they shook hands. Under his nails that same dark stain of black remained.

Still breathing quickly, she counted to five in her head before gently releasing her fingers.

He didn't seem offended by her rejection. 'Le's get more comf'table – in th'other room. You can try some Alkermes, local speciality.'

Getting comfortable with Procopio was the last thing Charlotte believed she wanted, but she couldn't think of a polite way to extricate herself. Heavily gallant, Procopio waved his hand and attempted a small bow, suggesting she should precede him into the living-room. She half-expected a slap or pinch on the bottom, but instead he picked up the old photograph and followed her without incident. Slumping heavily into one of the huge chairs, he dropped the photo on a coffee table and poured them each a large glass of a violent pink liqueur. Charlotte took a sip. Another acquired taste, like the aniseed biscuits his housekeeper had served in the morning. Holding the sickly liquid close to her chest, she made bright conversation while strolling round the walls of cookbooks, nervously pretending an interest she didn't feel: 'Who would imagine there were so many recipes in the world?'

'Not only recipes,' he said.

'No, I'm sure you're right,' she responded insincerely.

'Cooking is an art as well as a science, you know!'

'Of course, I – '

'You don't believe me? I say to you: we know more about the inside of the moon than we do about the inside of a soufflé! Why should that be true?'

'Well, I suppose – '

'I tell you why: because men are fools. They don't know how to enjoy what is offered under their noses.' Charlotte wondered if that was how he saw her, and when he heaved himself up, she stepped back quickly. But he lurched past her and with surprising accuracy found a book he was looking for on the shelves. 'I want to read you something: Listen!' His slurred speech sharpened, '"Here is delicate cheese, placed in reed baskets to dry, and the blonde plums of autumn; and chestnuts and pleasantly rosy apples. The innocent Ceres, Amor and Bromius reign here. And still more, there are blood-red mulberries and grapes in tender clusters and the deep green cucumber hangs from a vine . . ." Poetry, yes? And this is from the ancient Roman, Vergiliana!'

'Roman? How – '

'You have culture, I have agriculture, that's what you think?'

'Not at all, I – '

'Well, my father could barely read, my mother not at all! But

I taught myself all this!' He gestured at the books. '*Grapes in tender clusters and pleasantly rosy apples*: you don't find this poetic?'

'No . . . I mean yes, I do . . . I *do* think it's poetic, as it happens.' A practical poetry. Which was more poetic, the words he'd read or the idea of this huge man (this butcher) searching for poetry in anything so mundane as food? A man like her soldier father, she thought: practical and strong yet possessing an attractive strangeness and an ache for something broader and richer than his own past. For no reason at all, for a reason she couldn't or wouldn't analyse, Charlotte felt moved by a sense of delight. She was surprised at how much she was enjoying herself. The fire shimmering across the glass on old photographs and framed maps, the rumble and bluster and staccato crick crack as the chestnut logs gradually slumped into ash, the sweet smell of the chestnut smoke mixed with garlic and rosemary and pig and game, the deepening shadows in the room as the sun passed beyond range of the deep windows – all of it, all of this sharply smoky fatty rich very *living* experience. All her senses wide awake, or reawakening. *Happy*, that was it. She'd almost forgotten the sensation. Then in one of those sudden shifts of viewpoint more frequent since her divorce, Charlotte saw herself as John would, as a lonely, middle-aged scholar pathetically responding to the most obvious, the most . . .

Uncomfortable, she moved away from Procopio's close scrutiny to sit primly on the arm of a chair, trying to give the impression that her visit was drawing to a close.

'I wonder,' she asked, picking up the old photograph he had shown her. 'I wonder . . . is he still alive, this Carlo Seguita?'

Procopio sat down again and poured them both another glass of the vile magenta drink, which Charlotte swallowed like medicine. He'd had four or five to her two. How was she going to get back if he continued to drink so much? There was no phone here, she remembered, no chance to call a taxi.

'Carlo? Oh, he comes back here fr' time to time . . . visits old friends . . . investments . . . that slaughterhouse up the road.'

He spoke with the slow deliberation of the drunk, pulling the words apart and holding them up like pieces of a complex jigsaw. 'Not that he gets involved with the butchery side any more. Keeps his hands clean these days. Ohhh yes, clean hands . . . verr' important!'

'Why did you show me this photograph, Francesco?' she asked. His Christian name slipped out accidentally and she saw his big features soften. He looked as happy with the familiarity as she was unhappy.

'Think you should know, tha's why,' he said. 'Worry you might try another *restoration* . . . of some of our other past unsightly errors.'

'You believe that Muta is connected to these men?'

He shrugged irritably. 'Who is this Muta? I told you I don't know her.'

'You don't remember any girls like her from when you were a boy? There are no girls in this picture – '

'At that age, who remembered girls?' He threw the remains of his drink down his throat. 'Anyway, you like this picture better than poetry, you keep it then, if it make you happy. Io non posso comprendere più.'

'It's not that I . . .' With dismay Charlotte watched Procopio's eyes flutter and close, then his big blunt chin hammered a few times onto his chest and remained there. So much for her worries about imminent seduction! She didn't know whether to feel relieved or insulted. How was she to get home? The thought of that walk in the dark was not appealing. *Why* had she accepted his invitation to lunch! She continued to study the photograph, hoping Procopio would wake, although the huff, rumble and growl of his breathing indicated how unlikely this was. Should she fetch the housekeeper? Before Charlotte could make up her mind, the old woman appeared and regarded the sleeping man for a few seconds. 'Stanco,' she said. 'Troppi massacrati, ora.' After this brutal description of her master's exhaustion during the pig-slaughtering season, she touched Charlotte on the shoulder and mumbled, 'Moment.'

A few minutes later she reappeared wearing a shapeless

overcoat which might once have been black. A huge ring of keys rattled in one hand and in the other was a plate of sausages, bulbous and pungent enough to be homemade. Charlotte understood that she was to follow, and was led around the back of the house to a rusted pick-up truck almost as venerable as the old woman. Two chickens nesting on the front seat flew up squawking. One of them left an egg behind, which the old woman gently placed on the back seat. Praying that the driver would not turn out to be the mule-driver or one of the butchers from Sunday, Charlotte discovered that the housekeeper herself was to be her chauffeur. The tiny old woman clambered into the driver's position with surprising agility, perching on three plastic cushions. Still she could barely see over the wheel. It seemed impossible to Charlotte that she would be able to drive an ox-cart, let alone a truck, but they managed well enough.

Between them not much more than ten words was spoken in the thirty minutes it took to reach Urbino's gate. Theirs was not a silent journey, however, not with the truck's roars, rattles and thuds providing a constant and percussive vocabulary to which the old woman, sensitive to its ancient dialect, responded by speeding up or slowing down with a terrible grinding of the gears. She had virtually to stand in order to reach the pedals. Passing the scarecrows, the old woman, a scarecrow herself, sucked in her lips and summoned a great gobbet of saliva to fire out the window. Once, when she lurched to a halt and climbed out to retrieve the egg from behind her and leave it with the plate of sausages by the jagged tooth of San Rocco's church, the housekeeper managed what might have been a brief sentence, something like 'Si, *mumble mumble* Balducci *mumble mumble*,' although its substance was drowned in the roar of the engine and her fine mist of spit.

This was in response to Charlotte's question, 'Is the food for Muta?'

At the main road they exchanged a few more words – left or right, Urbania or Urbino? That was about the extent of their stimulating discourse, hard to distinguish in the woman's toothless speech. Except for the name 'Balducci', Charlotte mused. Something Balducci, the woman had said, Balducci something . . . the words half-swallowed . . . not Muta, surely – perhaps Ella? Riella? *Gabriella?*

Gabriella Balducci: did such a person exist? Had she ever? Was it Gabriella or another wandering ghost haunting San Rocco?

MIRACLE NUMBER 28

A Buried Ham

Muta had seen the scarecrows too. On one of them she recognised a shoe she'd lost on the day the wolf came to San Rocco. *Mama's shoe.* She rested her head against the scabby trunk of a tree that no longer bore any but the most twisted and thick-skinned of pears, hard, resentful fruit only good for stewing.

The scarecrow trees, the priest saying, 'How art thou fallen from heaven, O Lucifer, son of the morning,' and then he said, 'Any man's death diminishes me because I am involved in mankind,' and then they broke the words, they blew up all the words and all the broken stories fell down around her in paper shreds like the peel of pears and apples from Mama's knife. Bombs fell for a long time afterwards. Was that here? She remembered a villa where a nice lady used to hand out food and clothing. The lady tried to make her speak but all Muta's words had vanished down the road those others had taken. Words, even opening her mouth, exhaling air, her breath, her soul, could allow penetration of her safe and private inner self, could kill the others. She had watched it happen.

Much later, when no one claimed her, Muta knew that she was just one more stone turned up by the plough of war and in that desert lost, of no more import than the broken cups and vessels in the shape of girls they found in their fields and the priest said were from times when counterfeit gods were worshipped ignorantly. The priest said Jesus was the Word made flesh and Mary was impregnated by the Word of God, and Muta wondered what was that word? She went unrecognised month after month, year after year, until all that was recognisable in her was a memory. Sometimes she was afraid of losing even that, the blood-red trees, the broken words, and she wondered if her connections to this place were imagined. Everywhere she'd gone there were bombs and death and cellars where hungry people hid or were hidden.

Was it *here* Muta remembered or another cellar she'd come across in the months of wandering?

But it was her cellar now, her wolf. Only when she was certain that San Rocco was clear of visitors did Muta return, where she checked what the wolf had left her. Although she had become used to such gifts as the egg and sausages, now she often came home to find laid on the trap-door to her cellar such prizes as a dead partridge or a half-eaten pheasant. These unasked-for offerings reminded Muta of the time – not long after the bombs fell, she thought it was – when she was so tired and hungry she was ready to push her head into the earth and go to sleep for good. She was rooting for potatoes and carrots and dug up a whole smoked ham, buried by a farmer so the Germans wouldn't find it, and still so pink and juicy, the bone-white fat so good, she forgot her knife and gnawed straight into it.

Today there was a hare, still warm, its neck broken but its throat barely pierced. The result of her changing relationship with the wolf, whose yellow eyes watched her closely from the shadows of the tower.

MIRACLE NUMBER 29

The Most Recently Recorded Date of the Liquefaction of the Blood of St Gennaro

A semi-circle of glass-fronted alcoves separated by slender wooden columns gave the effect of bookshelves in a private library, except that the alcoves in what had once been the Oratory of the Good Death, now used as a lecture and theatre space for ISIA, were not finished off with a classical cornice, but crenellated with human skulls, the books replaced by mummified corpses. Only the central mummy was clothed, in a floor-length white robe, whereas the yellow folds of old chamois leather in which the other mummies appeared to be draped – stiff and creased, as if used to polish many cars – was actually dried skin, crumpled in on itself with age. On the skulls all hair was gone, as were the eyes and fleshy parts of the nose, but a vestige of skin still clung to the jaws. Contracting over the centuries, it had stretched the gaping, lipless mouths back almost to their shrunken ears in grins or grimaces or perhaps silent howls. The mummies' crossed arms, clasped over their visible ribcages as if barely able to contain silent guffaws, seemed evidence of a post-mortal sense of humour, with one jovial skull resting on another mummy's leathery shoulder in helpless mirth: *Death, that old joke, it really creases you up . . .*

On a bench towards the front of the former oratory Donna was sitting next to Paolo, with Fabio and his friends to Paolo's left. They were part of an audience of several hundred that included everyone from the town's bishop to the mayor and his friend Franco from the Bar Raffaello. A further hundred-odd people were forced to stand at the back or to squeeze in around the sides. For an event arranged at such short notice, it was well organised, with pillows on the seats and headphones to provide a simultaneous translation for English-speakers.

'You'd think it was a meeting of international diplomats,' Paolo said.

The posters advertising the event had been equally professional, written in English as well as Italian. Donna had stopped to examine one on their way here and Paolo, moving close to her, could smell the perfume she used. Heavy, musky, not at all a young woman's scent. He could see into the neck of her shirt where her breasts lifted the fabric away from her collarbones, the lace of her bra just visible, and he thought about what he would do when they were finally alone, mentally tracing the angle of her jaw and running his hand down her long neck to slip inside her blouse.

'Tears From the Dead,' she read, her voice mocking, 'An open invitation to watch a demonstration by Italy's celebrated magician Alfredo Barrago, who will show how to conjure realistic tears of blood from the dead, with the assistance of Italy's foremost investigator of miracles, Professor Luigi Serafini of the University of Milan. The event will take place in Santa Chiara's former oratory, which boasts a unique collection of corpses removed from their burial places at the beginning of the nineteenth century and dried through a natural process caused by mould absorbing moisture from the bodies . . . Nice one, Paolo!'

'It should be quite . . . interesting . . . Don't you think?'

'Hell of a first date!'

Her provocative stare made him feel ridiculous and they finished the walk to Santa Chiara in silence, to be met by a group of Paolo's friends, none of whom looked pleased to see Donna. Fabio pulled Paolo aside and whispered in Italian, 'What'd you bring *her* for? She's the *last* person you should be hanging around! I told you last night on the phone what I saw.'

Paolo shrugged off his friend and took Donna's hand,

drawing her with him through the massive carved door of the former oratory.

'What was he saying about me?' she asked.

'Nothing. Just . . . it's nothing.' Paolo didn't want to spoil this time with her. To impress her, charm her, flirt with her, keep her beside him with any trick in the book: that's what he had in mind. To resolve one way or another the tension that had been building between them over the last week. He didn't give a damn about Donna's ignorance of art, Italy, history, politics – all the things his university friends mocked her for; he was tired of history, especially tired of Italian politics. Only the day before he'd heard of a scandal concerning the food consortium his father occasionally worked for. 'It might break any day soon,' his father admitted. 'You have to prepare yourself. Papa made a mistake, sent a cheque, not cash. To the wrong guy.'

First thing Papa taught him, years ago: you want to bribe somebody, don't write anything down. You can wash mud off, and words, they fly away in the wind like birds, but *carta canta*: paper sings! Well, Paolo had found his own way of making paper sing. Some day when they knew each other better, when he was sure of her, he would tell Donna all about it.

'Who's that?' she asked him, pointing to an old man several rows ahead who had turned to give the group of young people a long stare.

'Fabio's grandfather.'

'I thought there was something familiar about his face . . . Funny – night before last, in the café? I saw him, the old guy – at the table near ours. Fabio never said a word to him.'

'They don't speak. The old man's an unrepentant Fascist.'

'Oh yeah?'

The indifference in her voice told him that for her 'Fascist' was no more than a playground insult, a word you hurled at a college professor who shopped you for writing in library books. Not weighted with memory as it was here in Italy. He studied her profile, almost hidden by the fall of black hair. Except on girls in the South, he had never seen such hair, so dark that it absorbed the light. He willed her eyes, equally dark, to meet his, but they remained obstinately fixed on the flamboyant figure who had stepped up to a table in front of the mummies.

'The Great Barrago' sported a weighty, floor-length coat in stained-glass colours, possibly fashioned on one from a portrait of Suleiman the Magnificent, emperor of Constantinople. Trailing behind Barrago came an unprepossessing figure in a blue suit covered by a white lab-coat. 'Professor Luigi Serafini,' Barrago announced. 'Together we are going to see what miracles can be achieved using sleight of hand together with such things as lasers and holographs.'

Serafini approached the mike. 'A laser,' he said, his voice crackling too close to it, 'is light amplified to produce coherent radiation in the infrared, visible and ultraviolet regions of the electromagnetic spectrum.'

He said, 'Holography is a method of displaying a 3-D image, usually using coherent radiation from a laser combined with photographic plates.'

He said, 'A hologram results from a laser beam dividing and forming interference patterns on a photographic plate.'

He might as well have said, 'Abracadabra! Allakazam!' thought Paolo, glancing at the rapt faces around him. Most people here expected to see real miracles.

Instead of a wand, Barrago held a long rubber torch which he now pointed at the clothed mummy in the centre alcove, brandishing the torch like a choirmaster conducting a chorus of the dead: 'Prior Lorenzo Peccato, inventor of the necropolis.'

The electric lights dimmed in the chandeliers overhead and Donna drew her breath in with a sharp feeling of anticipation. Despite the cool welcome she'd received from Fabio and his friends, she was enjoying herself, aware of every slight movement of Paolo's thigh, his shoulder nudging hers when the woman next to Donna shifted them closer, the way his gold watch slid loose over his fine-boned brown wrist.

The oratory's cavernous interior, absolutely still, *dead* still, seemed to fill with silence. Then the shimmering ghost or spirit of Prior Peccato pulled itself from the mummified relic and briefly raised his transparent arms in blessing.

A woman in the front pew rose screaming to her feet, before crumpling into a dead faint. The spectral Prior gestured with one filmy hand towards a mummy purported to be that of a young lady who died whilst having a Caesarian. Seconds later, blood-red tears welled up in the empty sockets of her missing eyes.

The church erupted with women's cries, men's oaths, applause, exclamations of wonder, angry voices, impressed voices. This show (or outrage) was loudly contended to be either very progressive (or highly sacrilegious). Two members of the Brotherhood of the Good Death who had formerly run the oratory complained bitterly that a halt should be called to this spectacle before things went any further. It was suggested that things had already 'gone too far'.

Paolo, who understood perfectly well how the holographs and lasers had been used to produce the ghostly Prior and the mummies' tears, was thinking about whose ghost would be worth summoning. Raphael's, to guide their restoration? Or La Muta herself, to present her version of that concealed scar and plead the case for truth and reconciliation?

Serafini now stepped forward to uncover a collection of test tubes and calipers and a bunsen burner. 'The mayor of Urbino has asked me to provide a scientific explanation for various so-called "miracles" which have occurred recently,' he began, then had to wait for the audience's unhappy muttering to die down. 'Miracles like the congealed blood which last week liquefied in Urbania . . . and your own "miracle" of Raphael.'

His thin, nasal voice combined with the ironic quotation marks he put around any suggestion of a miracle made him sound as if he were complaining about a minor irritation: a fly in his soup, a pull in the lumpy cardigan which further disfigured his badly cut jacket. 'These follow in a long tradition – such as the liquefaction which occurs every August at a church in Amaseno near Naples, on the Feast of San Gennaro.'

He gestured at a rack of glass vials half-full of congealed matter in varying shades of tan, ginger and deep rusty brown, not dissimilar in colour to the luxuriant fur growing vigorously out from under his shirt cuffs and down in a thick pelt almost to his fingernails. The Professor's stiff, awkward movements and his furry hands, disproportionately large in comparison with the rest of his body, reminded Donna of a museum she'd been to in England, where stuffed animals had been dressed up in human clothes and arranged in stiff tableaux.

'You have seen Alfredo Barrago using the latest modern technology,' Serafini whined, his tone faintly accusing. 'But my experiments tonight will replicate techniques with which medieval artists could achieve unsophisticated but dramatic phase changes.'

'A phase change – what's he talking about?' Donna whispered to Paolo.

'A phase change is a change of matter from solid into liquid or liquid into gas,' he answered. 'Or living matter into dead and then back into living . . . which is, of course, impossible.'

Donna leaned closer and whispered, 'You *know* about this stuff, don't you? You're really *into* it.'

'What?' Their eyes and mouths were only inches apart, and her admiring tone distracted him. 'Oh . . . well . . . it interests me . . . but so far he's said nothing we – I – didn't know already.' He felt Fabio grip his arm.

'How do you know so much about it?' asked Donna.

He ignored Fabio's tightened grip. 'I did a few years' chemistry at university – but not enough to satisfy Serafini's high standards.' Every time she moved her head Paolo caught her perfume and a glimpse of pale neck through the curtain of hair. It made him think of the gap of white thigh at the top of women's stockings.

'Your dad wanted you to be a scientist?'

'Papa? Never! He was hoping I'd go into the family ceramics business, develop some new dishwasher-proof glazes for his rustic ashtrays and decorative olive oil jugs. That or – '

'*Basta*, Paolo!'

Stopped by Fabio's sharp retort, Paolo turned his attention back to the stage. Donna found herself admiring his profile, the slender frame, the big nose, the white teeth that could do with straightening. So different from the gymed-up, orthodentally perfect specimens of American TV she was used to. Then again, he wasn't what he seemed – he'd kept his visit to the circus a close secret, and she was sure that he and his friend Fabio were up to something . . . Did that make Paolo more or less interesting? With difficulty she concentrated again on Professor Serafini. Just visible behind the stretched-glass intestines and bladders of test tubes, beakers and microscopes, he was heating a pan of water with all the aplomb of an amateur television cook.

'My suspicion of miracles began with these claims of the liquefaction of saint's blood – always in the hottest months,' he said, holding up a vial. 'In this sealed container is the congealed saint's blood seen to liquefy in Urbania last week. The Brotherhood responsible for it have kindly allowed me to bring it here, though not to remove the seal. Now I want you to imagine that it is a very hot day in August when the temperature inside has risen to more than thirty degrees centigrade . . . So, I have heated the water to thirty degrees. Watch what happens to this normally solid material.'

Placing the vial for a few seconds into the water, he lifted it high enough to show the substance liquefied and glowing bright red.

'Che spettacolo!' Paolo murmured. 'You watch, Donna, when they see the truth they will not like it.'

'Now I plunge the vial in iced water,' said Serafini, 'and wait for its contents to resolidify, before bringing it back to thirty degrees. Again the contents congealed in the ice, then melted to red. 'Many relics consist of nothing more miraculous than this – thixotropy, the property of certain gels to liquefy when vibrated. But for proof, you would need to analyse the contents by extracting a tiny sample – '

'Do it, then, do it!' a man called. 'If you are so sure of yourself!'

Distractedly the professor ran both his hands through his hair, a gesture that left his orange pelt erect and waving with electricity. He exchanged a frustrated glance with Barrago. 'The Brotherhood who manage the Urbania Oratory have not given permission,' Serafini replied.

'A fraud! A fraud!' cried a man. 'You can prove nothing!'

'So many potential miracles!' Paolo said, shaking his head. 'I need Charlotte to give me the proper English . . . There is a murder of crows, yes? So a collection of miracles might be . . . a *chorus* of miracles? Perhaps . . . a *penance* of miracles?'

Serafini held up a communal wafer. With his outstretched hands and his halo of bristling orange hair floating above the white lab-coat he gave the appearance of a cultish religious figure in mid sermon. His voice too had a hectoring, evangelical flavour: 'Science can explain most mysteries involving blood. We begin with the "miracle" of the Mass of Bolsena celebrated in a fresco by Raphael!' Briefly he described the circumstances in which bloodstains had appeared on the communion host and sacramental linen at Bolsena in 1263. 'Since then there have been many similar "miracles" – all involving blood on starchy food, yet whenever these "miraculous" foods were tested, all proved negative for haemoglobin! We have always believed the answer might lie in the fungus Serratia marcescens, which can produce crimson stains on starchy food – '

An educated male voice from the front row interrupted him, 'You suggest that miracles which have been occurring since medieval times are the result of such elaborate tricks?'

'No, no! Those were probably done much more crudely. In emotionally charged occasions people see the truth they want to see . . . or are *told* to see.'

'Do you include *yourself* in this sweeping statement, Professor?' the voice pressed.

'I include sixty witnesses who testified to a theological commission that they saw bloody tears trickle from the Madonna at Civitavecchia, Monsignor! But I myself studied photos taken during this Madonna's weeping, and I can tell you the bloodstains did *not* change shape, despite the witnesses!'

'Is it your contention that some fanatical abbot perpetrated a deceit in order to dupe the masses?'

'If the Church has nothing to fear, Monsignor Seguita,' replied Serafini, 'why does the Vatican commission allow only theologians to investigate such miracles, never a chemist, a physician or any trained scientist?'

'But I *am* a trained scientist, Professor, as you well know.'

'You are the enemy of all good Catholics, Serafini!' shouted a woman.

'I was born and educated a Catholic, signora.' Reverting to his habitual irony, his last defence against a world where more people placed their faith in football and film stars than in scientific revelations, he added, 'One doesn't escape Catholicism, any more than one escapes Judaism. Religion is a form of tribal curse, a celebration of ignorance and misogyny!'

'People have to believe in something,' she called back.

Serafini's prehensile nose twitched agitatedly a few times as if to grab at this idea and shake it. 'If your faith can be destroyed by hearing the truth,' he said, 'then perhaps you need a new faith! What has forty-five years of a Christian Democrat party imprinted on us? A system of bribery and corruption where even the Vatican has ties with the Mafia!'

There was another roar from the audience, but before Serafini could add more fuel to their flaming disapproval, the lights came up and the elderly man who was evidently in charge rose and explained that the event was now concluded.

The audience started to rise and move towards the doors. Donna caught sight of James gesturing to several members of his film crew. 'Paolo, I've got to – ' He was talking to Fabio. She started squeezing past the wide-hipped woman dawdling in front of her. Paolo caught her hand and Donna flung a brilliant smile back at him and twisted her wrist out of his grip, calling back something he didn't catch.

'Your girl has bigger fish to fry,' said Fabio. 'And so do we.'

They made their way slowly out. Donna was thirty feet away talking to James, standing close to him and touching him, holding onto him at every opportunity. Paolo, turning his head away so he wouldn't have to watch, caught Fabio's thoughtful gaze. 'Don't go getting the urge to confess all your sins to la Belladonna, will you, Paolo?'

'I saw your beloved Fascist grandfather inside,' Paolo said deliberately. 'He looks very friendly with Bishop Seguita.'

'Look, Donna, I haven't got time for this right now!' James tried to pull away from her hand, his eyes on the cameraman.

'But I can do this piece, James! Just give me some idea what you want.'

'I told you, Donna, the presenter here has to think on his feet.' He called to the cameraman, 'Start rolling as soon as Serafini gets in range.'

'What about San Rocco, this thing I was telling you about?'

'Talk to Jillie, she'll fill me in.' He turned his back on Donna and one of his team raised a clipboard, forcing her to step back a pace. She looked around for Paolo, but he had disappeared. Jostled by the crowd, she watched Monsignor Seguita approaching, Serafini at his heels like a terrier nipping fruitlessly at a long-legged greyhound.

'I ask of you, Monsignor Seguita,' he barked, 'the question Erasmus of Rotterdam asked of the Romans under Pope Julius II: what disasters would befall if the supreme pontiffs, the Vicars of Christ, made the attempt to imitate His life of poverty and toil?'

His tall opponent continued walking, not deigning to reply.

'And I give you my annotation of Erasmus,' snapped the scientist. 'He said that if such an attempt were made by the Vatican City, thousands of scribes, sycophants and pimps would lose their employment! This is the *true* Renaissance man, the man we *should* be celebrating here – not a servant of pimps and popes like Raphael!'

Journalists were firing questions at Serafini: what would he do, did he have any suspicions? 'I'm going to get to the bottom of this miracle and the woman responsible!' he replied. 'And find the people who put her up to it!'

James called, 'Where are you off to, Professor? Back to Milan?'

'No such luck for Rome, signor! No such luck! I go to wake the dead! That's where I go: to wake the dead!'

MIRACLE NUMBER 30

Birth of a Second Republic

The name 'San Rocco' surfaced briefly in Urbino's pool of consciousness that evening. Bobbing up in the cafés and bars for a while, it released odorous bubbles of half-remembered gossip, then languidly sank again under the weight of news about the Clean Hands magistrates' ongoing war. All summer there had been bombs planted by the Mafia in the piazzas of Rome, Milan, Florence, proof that their influence extended far north of Sicily and Naples. The bombs were also seen as a protest against the January arrest of Sicily's mafioso godfather Totò Riina, after long years when he had supposedly been on the run.

'But as it happened,' said the mayor to Franco, 'the bastard had been living a tranquil existence in Palermo all along – even after his men murdered the magistrate Falcone! Turns out that a lot of the mafiosi we've been told were "fugitives from justice" who had "gone underground" have been discovered residing happily *above* ground and *above* the law in their home neighbourhoods, Franco! Quietly taking the passeggiata with their family, attending church, sending their kids to state schools like us normal citizens. All we can hope for is that now, finally, we are witnessing the death of Italy's first republic and the birth of a glorious second!'

'A messy business, birth,' said Franco gloomily.

MIRACLE NUMBER 31

A Feather from the Wing of the Archangel Gabriel

It was the kind of late October day to make the fortunes of those Urbino estate agents who dealt with foreign buyers. In this light even a squalid tenement with nothing to recommend it but hot- and cold-running cockroaches looked primed for a spread in *Architectural Digest*. Charlotte, gazing at photographs of local properties, tried to choose between a small farmhouse 'with views of the coastline' or a 'lavish' studio apartment in town. She could afford neither – so why not both? Filled with a sense of well-being, she viewed herself from on high – *Woman with an Invitation to the Perfect Italian Vineyard Lunch* – and smiled at her own giddy optimism. She took off her jacket, twisting her wrists around to feel the sun's warmth on her bare skin, a movement that brought back Procopio's story from yesterday. Walking away from this unpleasant image, she ducked into her favourite arcaded street, where the filtered light smoothed old people's lines and made young women's cheeks glow like alabaster fruit. A sculptor's light, not the harsh white photofinish of Italian high summer. Today I am going to forget Procopio and his gossip and accept the Count's offer, she decided. I am going to start my life over.

Charlotte had grown accustomed to taking the back routes from her *pensione*, avoiding the increasing numbers of pilgrims arriving by chartered buses from all over Europe. The old and the sick, the crippled in spirit as well as body, those who had had no relief from Fatima at Lourdes, from St Anthony at Padua – they were all here looking for miracles. Blind pilgrims picking their way with white sticks, oblivious to this city's beauty, next to *penitenti* from Spain, flogging their own backs with knotted ropes as they walked. Charlotte had seen people fall to the ground as soon as they left the bus and, kneeling, hobble painfully all the way up the Via Mazzini. Crossing this road now, she was forced to wait for the passing of a whole coach party of these kneeling pilgrims, whose bare knees left a long snail-trail of blood. In fact the cobbles' rusty colour was not from dirt or age, as Charlotte had supposed for days, it was an old stain from the dried blood of coachload after coachload of penitents.

In the Piazza Mercatale she found the minibus that had been sent to collect her and the TV crew, but she couldn't see Paolo or Donna. She joined James, who was watching another group of pilgrims depart in the direction of Raphael's house. 'Don't they realise the painting has been moved?' she asked.

'I don't think they care. It's gone beyond that.'

She was surprised to hear the TV crew congratulating James on his previous night's broadcast. 'Was Donna good?' she asked.

'Um . . . Donna didn't present the segment,' replied James. 'I did.'

'Isn't she well?' Charlotte had a pang of guilt at not having phoned the girl yet to apologise for standing her up.

'I think . . . ah . . . she's fine,' said James. 'Actually . . . ah . . . she wasn't actually invited. Actually . . . ah . . . it was the Countess who . . . ah specifically mentioned that Donna . . . was *not* to come . . . some unpleasant . . . incident with her at the Villa Rosa last week and, well . . .'

'Unpleasant? That doesn't sound like Donna,' Charlotte said. 'Perhaps it was a misunderstanding . . .'

'Ah . . . no, no, I got the impression it was more . . . ah . . . serious. An Etruscan statue she smashed . . . deliberately . . . family treasure.'

'But Donna doesn't know the first thing about the Etruscans!' Several people around Charlotte convulsed with laughter. 'What have I said that is so amusing?'

'I don't think it was the Etruscans . . . it was more personal . . .'

'I see . . . And Paolo?'

'He's meeting us at the Villa Rosa.'

Charlotte took a seat on the bus just behind the driver and turned her face towards the window. They drove out past the blocky outline of Urbino's modern university and she tried to ignore the Spanish-style haciendas and Swiss-style holiday chalets that were springing up here as everywhere in Italy, along with American-style billboards advertising sports centres and tourist complexes (in her opinion, complexity was the *last* thing most tourists wanted). She was pleased when they left the suburbs behind and turned in at a long double row of cypresses, arboreal exclamation marks that served in Italy as reminders of the approach to either an important building or a cemetery. Charlotte, remembering her previous visit to the Villa Rosa very well, failed to suppress a sense of anticipation as the bus swept up a steep white gravel road, tiger-striped by cypress shadows, towards the crest of a hill where a circle of towers like giant guards protected a small fortified hamlet. That time I was a paying customer, she thought happily, and this time I'm a guest of the owner himself.

Passing through the arched gateway, the bus parked on a large square with spectacular views over the countryside. Here the group disembarked, to be greeted by a suave young man in black, the Count's assistant. 'The Count and Countess are on their way,' he informed them, moving smoothly into a description of the Villa Rosa that interspersed the vacuous and inflated vocabulary of international PR with the bored gestures of an air hostess. His advertising patter was soon interrupted by the whine of Paolo's Lambretta, at which point James managed to ask if the group could explore the grounds. Paolo, following Charlotte, whispered, 'Looks like a pastiche from a book on gracious Italian living.'

She pulled him out of earshot of the others and together they strolled to the far side of the square. *Farmacia* read the carefully antiqued lettering on one shop, and glancing inside she was surprised to discover it empty except for a few dried leaves. Other immaculate façades turned out to conceal equally hollow shells, the edges blurred grey with cobwebs, where any distinction between rooms had collapsed into piles of bricks and mortar and splintered beams. In some cases even the exterior supporting walls had disintegrated into jagged fangs.

'I feel like I'm inside the skull of a dead giant,' Paolo said, 'peering out through his eye sockets or past the gaps in his teeth.'

'My set of rooms faces the Urbino view,' said a familiar woman's voice from behind them and Charlotte, hoping Paolo's comment had not been overheard, turned to see a graceful blonde who introduced herself as the Count's wife. 'As yours will be too, if you agree to stay, Signora Penton!' She lowered her voice to a conspiratorial whisper that made Charlotte feel part of an exclusive club where witty and talented people met to exchange important secrets. 'The view is only spoiled by these monstrous new apartment blocks and dreadful tourist hotels which are eating up the countryside around Urbino, spreading like melanoma.'

'Blame it on the peasants.' Paolo's dry comment froze their hostess's smile. 'They keep selling up their old houses to rich Swiss and Germans,' he went on, 'then the peasants can afford to build themselves modern flats nearer to town, complete with the latest in tiled floors and granite kitchen units. My father makes his living out of this monstrous melanoma.'

'This is my assistant – ' Charlotte said quickly, alarmed by Paolo's tactlessness. Donna's absence must have put him in a bad mood.

'Yes, we've met,' the Countess replied. 'Please excuse me, I see one of the staff requires my assistance.'

'She prefers the Disney version of Italy, d'you think?' Paolo remarked.

Charlotte frowned; she didn't want her high spirits dented. At least for one day she wanted to avoid looking too closely at the realities of Italian life outside the pleasant fiction of restoration. Relieved when the rest of the party caught them up, she moved away from Paolo and followed the Count out to a flat stretch of open hillside with a view clear to the Apennines in the north. Here a quadrangle of tables had been arranged, lavishly draped in pink linen that had been gathered in swags and rosettes of gilded leaves and nuts. At the centre stood a towering pyramid of pumpkins and gourds, plums and pears, walnuts, hazelnuts, grapes and sweet chestnuts, at least five feet high and twice that at its base. 'Entirely made of porcelain!' said the Countess. Napkins had been intricately folded into birds or flowers, each place-setting framed in garlands of vine leaves which on close inspection proved to be enamelled metal, while antique baskets woven of ceramic braids held rolls that were glazed so highly, Charlotte had to touch them to ensure that they too were not china. She felt she had stumbled into a banquet from Visconti's film of *The Leopard*, and wondered idly if the gods reclined on gilded couches overhead, gazing down with smiles inexorable as the autumn sky.

Seated between Paolo and Count Malaspino, Charlotte peered closely at the medley of nasturtium flowers, daisies and golden pansies mixed up with wild leaves and toasted pine nuts on her plate.

'Like eating Botticelli's meadow!' James said.

'I make the vinegar myself,' the Count explained with a modest smile. 'Every day I remain here I become more of a contadino.'

'One can't *become* a peasant, Dado,' his wife corrected him. 'It's not a vocation. One must be born into it.'

'A born-again peasant, then!' Gaily he went on to explain how his closest childhood friends had been 'genuine peasants' from a nearby valley, his story of those idyllic years before the War interrupted by a series of elaborate dishes, each containing several unlikely textures or ingredients. For no reason she could think of, Charlotte remembered Paolo's teasing suggestion that Count Malaspino had had a face-lift. If the allegation was true, then it must have been one of those expensive face-lifts ageing American women went in for, which if they were lucky made them look like composite photographs of several different but not quite matching beauties, and if they were unlucky left them resembling victims of a bad beating after a moderately effective reconstruction.

'Food for bored rich city people,' Paolo whispered to her, and she did find that after the fifth or sixth course her palate was weary of the relentless innovation. Whereas James and his assistant director were clearly in their element, happily discussing white truffles versus black with the Count, Charlotte was ill at ease, as she was in most social gatherings like this one. At Geoffrey's celebrated private views or at the dinner parties to which she was invited less and less frequently since her divorce, she felt utterly removed from conversations that drifted from stocks and shares to toilet training and family holidays abroad.

Once, staring out the window while a glass of white wine stole the warmth from her fingers and a London television executive lectured his rapt middle-aged audience on the need to have more arts programmes of appeal to the youth, Charlotte had watched as two teenagers smashed a car window, jump-started the motor and drove off. It had seemed too awkward a subject to raise with her hostess, at that moment enquiring brightly of another married guest, 'Tuscany or Umbria this year?' Occasionally one of the sensitive people at these events would remember the Martian in their midst and make an effort to include Poor Charlotte.

I am more in tune with those angry, outcast car thieves, she thought now, and nervously swallowed a sugared pansy, which tasted surprisingly nasty. With difficulty she managed to dislodge a petal from the roof of her mouth in time to respond to a comment from the Count. 'After lunch, if you like, Charlotte, I will show you where I find the herbs and flowers that went into this salad . . . Unless you would prefer a swim in the pool? I believe your colleagues have opted for that?' This question was addressed to the other guests, who greeted it with approval.

'The *new* pool,' said the Countess. 'Swimming in the *old* pool is ill advised.'

'No, no . . . I'd like . . . I'd prefer a walk,' said Charlotte softly.

The Count inclined his head towards her. 'And then you must see the paintings my wife and I hope you will agree to restore . . .'

A few minutes later he stood up and expressed the hope that his wife could convince them all to eat and drink more than was good for their figures. 'Now I hope you will excuse me while I show Signora Penton what James has so aptly christened our Botticelli meadow.'

Cicadas, unaware of summer's end, kept up a celebratory trilling as Charlotte and the Count strolled down the hill on a path mown through long, straw-coloured grass. She put out a hand and let the seedheads tickle her palm. Ahead was a dark copse of trees, beyond it the mountains shimmering in the afternoon heat, their lower slopes hidden in the mist. Each footstep stirred up the scent of hay, although not enough to override the muskier aromas of fermenting grapes and the familiar reek of silage. Beneath that, Charlotte caught another smell – heavier, less acceptable, slightly rotten.

Veering from the path before they reached the woods, the Count knelt down in a field. 'My mother was a real city woman,' he said. 'She told me that all her life she had looked at grass and seen nothing more than grass. Then one day after she moved to my father's estate here in Le Marche, she saw that a single square metre of grass held more than fifty other plants struggling to exist. A lesson about life as well as grass. It was a tragedy for both of us when we left this beautiful place. 1944. I was twelve. My father moved us to a palazzo Mama had inherited in Florence.'

'Because it was safer in Florence?'

'No. My father had sold our family home – the one you see in the distance.' He gestured towards the towers on the ridge where she had walked two weeks ago, where she'd had her own private 'vision'. 'Papa didn't warn us or explain his reasons. One day he simply handed me 50,000 lire and said: "Because I sold the house. Your share." A Fascist mentality: selling that house was for me like selling my childhood off.'

'I suppose you might buy it back . . .'

'No, it is lost for good, squeezed now between a pig farm and a battery chicken factory.' He smiled suddenly. 'But you don't want to hear such things.' From the grass he picked a dainty plant with rows of serrated button leaves like old-fashioned crewel work. 'Salad burnet – taste it! The mother of my childhood friends had a proverb: L'insalata non è bella se non c'è la salvastrella. It means "No salad is beautiful without salad burnet."'

'You sound as if you admired her.'

'Oh yes . . . loved her, even . . .'

His voice altered, he drew back a little. Charlotte was sure that he had been about to say more about the woman, then had changed his mind. 'Now the peasants are losing their knowledge. When the man who cares for my vines sees me picking wild chicory to boil and eat with cheese, he says, "I remember my grandmother doing that." He has broken from his past like a train from his engine. The demise of our old share-cropping system has done it.'

'The mezzadria, you mean? I know it used to be prevalent all over central Italy . . . but . . . it has always sounded rather . . . feudal . . .' Worried that her comment might offend him, she added, 'To me, that is.'

'Italians have never been good at democracy. Look at the mess we're in now! You know, when I was a boy, all I wanted was to be one of my father's peasants, who seemed rooted in this soil in a way my family could never be. I learned to think differently after the War. Our farmers abandoned the land as soon as they discovered more money could be made in the city. The city was like a mirage for them.'

'As the country was for you?'

'As the country was for me, dear Charlotte, until my wife's

family bought the Villa Rosa for us . . . It used to belong to my uncle.'

Stiffly he rose to his feet. Charlotte, feeling protective, was almost tempted to offer him her arm. She looked away so that he wouldn't see the pity in her eyes. In the copse of woods beyond where they stood she caught a flash of water. 'Is that the old pool?'

'My mother had it built in the twenties. It hasn't been used in years.'

'May I see it?'

'If you like.'

The reluctance she sensed in his reply was immediately understandable when they entered the copse of woods. Within an outer circle of beech were tall thin conifers jostling for space, their trunks too close to allow much light. The ground was red with their needles, and into the pool, stuccoed solid with green algae the colour of plastic bleach bottles, slipped an equally unhealthy-coloured stream from the rocky hillside, the origins of that underlying smell. Leakage from the stream had made the earth sticky and glutinous underfoot. Each time Charlotte lifted her foot there was a reluctant sucking noise around her shoe.

'A few kilometres up that hill is a battery pig farm,' said the Count.

Charlotte, noticing that the carpet of needles underfoot was alive with centipedes, suppressed a shudder.

'What is it, my dear? Are you cold?' He put his hand on her shoulder and squeezed gently. 'It's always rather chilly here. All these self-seeded trees have grown up since the War. That is why it is so dark.'

'It's just . . . Silly, I thought I heard . . . whispering, but I imagine it was only the . . .' She thought it rude to mention the centipedes: '. . . the stream.'

'Or the ghosts,' said the Count calmly. 'Sometimes I think I hear them, my mother and her friends. I have pictures of them from that time, seated around this pool in the sunshine . . . in Chanel swimming costumes, bobbed hair, all of them brown and sleek as seals. Oblivious to what was coming. If you concentrate on the pictures you can almost hear champagne bubbles pop.'

His gaze fell to the pool, a streamlined shape suitable for a 1930s ocean liner. 'My wife likes to emphasise the *new* pool because her brother's money paid for it and it was her willpower that impressed on me the need for a hotel of our standard to have one . . . I would be lost without her.' He looked up at the small ragged patches of sky visible through the pine needles. 'The sun never reaches this pool now . . .'

Charlotte noted how much the pool was in need of restoration. Most of the colour had fallen away from its Art Deco pattern and the blue dolphins leaping over gilded starfish were barely visible above the poisonous green surface. Count Malaspino bent to pick up a few stones and tossed them into the pool, where they landed on the algae with a wet slap slap slap. 'They didn't really understand, my mama and her pretty friends.' The stones remained visible for an instant, then their weight slowly broke through the algae and slid into the dark, silky water beneath the crust. 'Fascism had only just begun to make itself felt.'

He turned his deep-set eyes on Charlotte, a measuring look as if to weigh up the extent of their friendship. 'My father, though, he knew what was going on. Very much so . . .' he murmured.

She felt her lips twitch automatically into a social smile.

'Dear Charlotte,' he began, 'from the moment we met you seemed a woman I could trust, someone with whom any secret was safe . . .' His confessional tone made Charlotte uneasy, as if there were something just out of the frame that she didn't want to see. She kept getting forced close enough almost to identify it, but every time this *thing*, this shadowy *something*, slipped away round another corner and disappeared like a whisper. She tried to think of a way to deter the Count from any more intimacies that they might both regret.

'The Countess . . .' she started awkwardly, 'she . . . such a marvellous lunch . . . how did you meet her?'

'Meet her?'

'Yes . . . was it in Germany or . . .?'

'No, we met here, not Germany. Her older brother, Dieter, was my tutor for a few years before the War – and my greatest friend.'

'He introduced you . . . later?'

'No . . . no . . . he . . . died. He'd died, before Greta and I met.'

'So how . . . ?'

'He was . . . killed near here during the German retreat. Or so we heard. Greta came to Urbino in 1965 to see if she could find his grave. We met then, on one of my rare visits back here.'

'And did she . . . find his grave?'

Malaspino seemed quite taken aback by the question. 'I . . . no . . . no, he was never found . . . that is . . . the grave . . . there was no . . . it was never found.'

'Oh. I'm sorry if . . .'

Linking his arm through hers, he led them slowly back towards the villa. 'We have so many things to discuss, dear Charlotte. I do hope that when you see our collection you will agree to stay on.'

'Yes, I'm sure . . . and I suppose we really . . . the others will be . . . that is . . . you have been so kind to all of us . . .'

'We have an ulterior motive, you know. My wife hopes to persuade James not to broadcast so widely the attack on the Raphael, to indulge my city's reticence in showing this face to the world. It is, after all, a *celebration* he wants to produce?'

'Yes . . .' Charlotte tried to sound less doubtful of James's good intentions than she felt. 'Is this the chapel?' she asked, quickly changing the subject.

'Very modest,' said the Count, nodding at the serene little neo-classical building they were approaching, its proportions so perfect that it gave the appearance of a much grander cathedral viewed from further away. 'But rather beautiful inside, I hope you will agree.' He removed a large key from his pocket and unlocked the elaborately carved wooden door. Closing it behind them with a hollow sound, he flicked a light switch and the interior was illuminated by four baroque chandeliers as big as Volvos.

'Oh!' Charlotte gasped. One wall of the chapel was a fresco of Urbino, the epitome of her Camelot vision of the city, and in the painted cobalt sky overhead circled a riot of fat pink cherubs and solemn blonde angels engaged in blowing trumpets, playing harps and flutes, carrying olive branches and ceremonial banners. After the desolate atmosphere of the old pool, the fleshy celebration above her was an unexpected delight.

'Charming, isn't it?' said the Count. 'Not great art, of course, but pretty in its way . . .'

They paced slowly forward to join the painted procession of dignitaries who were leading a caravan of horses and mules weighed down with treasure. 'A visit to the Christ child,' said the Count. For each grave face he named a relative, long dead. 'The anonymous artist must have been asked to include as many of my ancestors as possible.'

Twelve rows of wooden benches, elaborately carved with more cherubs, were cushioned in red velvet. 'Is the chapel still used?' Charlotte asked.

'Oh yes. But I want you to see the real treasures. My personal collection.'

He unlocked another door into a private chapel or priest's room, a small, sweaty chamber where they descended from joyous sentiment to an altogether bleaker and bloodier vision. Framed against garnet-red walls were St Agatha with her breasts presented in a pewter bowl like scoops of Procopio's ice-cream, Doubting Thomas thrusting his finger into Christ's side as if he were tasting custard, a languidly camp San Rocco, muscular thighs askew to display a plague sore too close to his crotch, beside him a world-weary dog or wolf. San Sebastian appeared many times – Charlotte recognised one by Raphael's father, another by della Francesca, several that might be Giottos. All beautiful, all badly in need of restoration.

She felt the Count studying her reaction to each picture in

turn. 'They were my father's,' he said. 'No one has touched them since his death.'

'They're quite . . . *extraordinary*,' she said cautiously.

'You like the collection?'

'The painting is very fine . . .'

'And the subject matter, it doesn't worry you . . .'

'It's very . . . interesting . . .'

He nodded at a writhing St Sebastian. 'Tell me, do you ever worry about the morals of the artists you restore? After all, the painter of that work, Caravaggio, he was a murderer, so they say, as well as a corrupter of young men . . . Or is it all too long ago to matter?'

'I . . . I try not to confuse the art with the artist, Count.'

'Not to confuse the *image* with the imagination . . . Very wise. So . . . you would be happy . . . working on such things?'

'I . . .' Is this what it would cost, to stay here? 'I would love the opportunity . . .'

'The opportunity to . . .'

To work on any painting except *these*, she'd like to have told him. Casting around for a tactful way of expressing her distaste for the project, she finished desperately, 'To help in your restoration . . .' and was startled by the way the Count's hesitant expression changed instantly to one very close to excitement.

'*My* restoration . . . *yes*!' he breathed. Was it really so important to him that she restore this rather gruesome collection? There must be dozens of equally capable Italians.

'Do you know, my dear,' he said, 'I was sure that we had interests in common.'

'Yes, well . . .'

'Your face always struck me as having the resolute aspect of one of our medieval saints.'

Sister Charlotte: there it was again, the accusation of piousness. 'I suppose I look very . . . English.'

'Ah . . . the English vice,' he murmured, a comment she took for one of his rare mistakes in the language. She couldn't stifle the urge to glance at the time, and was surprised that it had only been thirty-five minutes since they'd left the others. The Count caught her wrist in both hands, covering the watch. 'Dear Charlotte, I won't keep you much longer from your colleagues! But first I want to show you something I believe you might appreciate even more than these pictures.' With that he crossed to a wooden confessional big enough to have held ten priests and disappeared inside. Charlotte heard drawers being opened, keys turning, doors creaking. She strolled round the chamber again. What was the Count doing? A sound made her turn.

He was naked to the waist but for huge white wings strapped to his arms and held in place by wide leather straps criss-crossing his hairless torso, very powerful for an older man's. One hand held a whip fringed with knots, of the kind penitents used. A costume, she told herself desperately. Some sort of theatrical costume, no more.

He raised his arms and the wings lifted heavily, with a dry rustling from the quills, each one almost a foot in length. Swan's? Eagle's? Charlotte felt a blush starting below her breasts.

He nodded amiably. 'You are excited, my dear? So am I.'

This is *impossible*! she thought. It can't be happening! Not to me! With his wife just a few hundred yards away! The others could come in at any moment . . . a servant . . . or is that part of the attraction?

He glanced down, drawing her reluctant eyes towards the modest erection swelling the ivory-coloured dancer's tights on his long thin legs. 'I was sure that we shared certain . . . *secrets*. You felt it too, I know. I suspected so, when we were discussing the *Flagellation* at lunch the other day.' He laughed softly. 'And when you hinted just now at the English vice . . . don't the French call it that?'

Swinging the fringed whip as gracefully as he had a fern in the Botticelli field, he moved towards her, and Charlotte, incapable of speech, took one step backward, to be brought up flat against the stone wall. She pressed her sweating palms there for comfort.

'This is your first time?' the Count asked, reaching for her hand. 'I remember my first – with my father, when I was young. The first time it hurt dreadfully, of course. Then when he saw that I had learned to enjoy it, he stopped. Later, I had to find other sources of inspiration.' His large, sad eyes left hers to roam over the collection of paintings. He fluttered his fingers in the direction of a particularly bloody flagellation. Charlotte felt him press the whip into her hand, warm and slightly damp from his own. Turning slowly, he presented to her a back embroidered with old white scars, arching it gracefully so that the immaculate wings rose with his shoulders and brushed against her legs. 'You may begin.'

It was her own fault. Something she'd said. She had let things Go Too Far, her mother's expression. To call a halt now would cause huge embarrassment to both of them. 'Does your wife . . . ' she began.

'Does my wife . . . what?'

'Know? Does she . . . '

'My wife makes her own arrangements.'

Charlotte was torn between a slightly hysterical desire to giggle and an almost equal desire to cry.

The Count turned his face towards her. 'I am ready. You may begin.' He paused. His features contorted slightly.

How offended would he be if she declined his offer? Then again, who was *she* to scorn another human being's private pursuits? Leadenly she raised the whip. He bowed his head. She brushed the wormy scars on his shoulders lightly with the black leather strips, letting the whip droop again. 'I'm terribly sorry, Count . . .'

'Harder, please,' he pressed, his face still turned away. He backed up a step so that she could smell his excitement.

She stammered another apology, 'I'm really *terribly* sorry, Count . . .'

'Please!'

'I don't . . .'

'I beg you . . .'

'I don't think I can go through with this.'

'Try.'

'No, really . . . I'm actually . . . I'm really quite sure.'

'This is enough playing!' His voice had risen. 'Now – *do it!*'

'I will not!'

'Please, I beg you!' He fell to his knees.

She thought: Oh dear, I'm going to laugh, I mustn't laugh, I *mustn't*! 'I'm not . . . It's not . . . I think there has been some . . . misunderstanding . . . You see . . . I really am sorry if I led . . . if some action of mine made you . . .'

The Count sighed. This time she did not hesitate to help him clamber to his feet, hampered as he was by the weight of those great white wings.

'I'm so awfully sorry, Count . . . I just . . . I can't.'

He turned and studied her face to assure himself that this hesitation was not part of a cruelly exciting game. 'No, no,' he said, 'it's no more than . . . a misinterpretation. So easy, isn't it, in a foreign language?'

Gently he retrieved his whip from her rigid hand. 'Strange,' he said, with a small deprecatory cough or laugh. 'It's the only way I've been able actually to *feel* anything for a very long time.'

'I'm so . . . sorry.' She couldn't bear to look at his blurred and beaten face. Was this where the disconnection in his features had come from? Was it simply the outward reflection of inner disharmony? An apple with a rotten core slowly wrinkling and caving in, that's what she saw.

'Will you wait while I change, my dear? I don't think the others would appreciate my . . . angelic costume . . .' He stroked with his right hand one of the massive wings. 'But they are lovely, aren't they? One of the few things rescued from the fires when the original Theatre of the Muses burned. It was said they were saved because one of the feathers came from the wing of the Archangel Gabriel.' He shrugged his shoulders, rustling the feathers. 'Despite these divine connections, it will only take a minute to divest myself of them.'

On their way back to the villa they discussed the weather.

Did the Count think it would stay fine for the grape harvest?
Did Charlotte find it cold at night?
How did rain affect the quality of his grapes?
What was the relative chill in England at this time of year?
How often did snow fall on Urbino?
Did London still suffer from terrible fogs?

'Did you know,' asked the Count with one of his curious changes of direction, 'Piero della Francesca's obsession with the mathematics of linear perspective drove him to the brink of insanity?'

'No, no, I didn't.'

'Yes. I've heard it offered as an explanation for the ambiguities in his *Flagellation*.' The Count's urbane manner was back in place. 'Strange that such a simple pictorial device should have so obsessed him . . . although it was, of course, the artistic sensation of the Renaissance.'

'Yes, quite.'

'I suppose it was because realistic perspective marked a fundamental rejection of medieval art, which dictated that a man's size on the canvas should reflect his importance in the world, rather than his actual stature.'

'Mmm.'

'Although a friend insists that the three figures in the foreground who are said to be ignoring the scourging of Christ in fact represent relatives of Urbino's Duke discussing the fate of the decadent Church. Then again, wasn't it you who told me that the leading English authority is adamant about the *Flagellation* representing the dream of St Jerome?'

'Possibly . . . I can't quite . . .' How much further was it to the pool?

'Yes, Jerome's dream of being flogged by fellow Catholics for reading the pagan Cicero, another explanation for the picture's discordance.'

A warning from della Francesca, Charlotte thought as the Count continued talking and talking. One had to accept the bitter fact of life outside the beauty of imposed perspective: our allies are seldom so virtuous as we hoped, nor our enemies so wicked. Despite the Count's perfect diplomacy, she knew that her dream of remaining here at the Villa Rosa was over, and she felt as if someone had led her hungry, thirsty, cold, out of the dark to stand in the doorway of a beautiful candle-lit room full of food and wine and happy guests, then at the last moment slammed the door in her face.

Before they arrived at the pool the Count stopped and asked politely that she not mention their little exploit. At her stammered promise to remain silent he smiled. 'I knew I could count on your discretion.'

'Of course! I wouldn't dream . . . I wouldn't – '

'No, no, of course you wouldn't.' He squeezed Charlotte's hand with a complicity that made her queasy.

Finally they reached the pool, where she saw with relief the varied shapes and sizes of sunburned flesh, another misguided drive to impose an idea of perfection.

MIRACLE NUMBER 32

The Dwarf's Riddle

'Un*fucking* believable! Charlotte told you that? About the wings? The whip? And she's usually such a tight ass.'

'I think she was still in shock. She needed someone to talk to.' Already Paolo felt guilty for betraying Charlotte's trust, a betrayal he justified by telling himself that it was to ease Donna's feelings at being excluded from the Count's lunch. She had sounded so hurt when he told her about the event – more hurt than surprised, in fact. She hadn't asked *why* she wasn't invited, and he didn't like to mention the allegations he'd heard from the crew at lunch. 'May I take you to dinner, cara? There's a nice – '

'I'm, like, pretty busy? Other work on the boil, you know . . .' She wanted to get off the phone before she started crying.

So here she was, three hours after Paolo's call, face to face with another blessed Virgin. Donna wired for sound, changing channels fast, faster, clickety-click, trying to keep up with the hot little diet pills shooting through her veins, telling her metabolism to keep rockin', don't stop rockin'. Can't get away from Madonnas and saints. One miracle after another: statues bought cheaply that started to weep, bleeding stigmata appearing on paintings, miraculous icons popping up (everything's a *miracle*!) all over the news. There's someone telling the story of the '*vera icona*', which in an Italian spin on the words had become the legend of Saint Veronica, the woman who gave Jesus a cloth to wipe his weary face on the hill of Calvary and, when it was returned, found on it a perfect likeness of Our Lord. There's Serafini, little guy practically in tears, shaking his head in despair: 'Too many miracles. Too many miracles.' Some other American station reporting that the blood on Raphael's *La Muta* had finally dried.

Donna could easily explain her own predicament (the pills, the wired paranoia). Two words: Count Malaspino. What a fuckhead! It wasn't enough the guy and his wife don't invite her to their fucking lunch, *oh* no! They have to spread nasty rumours! Not that Paolo would tell her *what* rumours, he's too sweet, in love with her. But she didn't need a decoding manual. The Count must've dropped ugly hints to James, maybe her credentials aren't all she claimed. And James, the creep, he's using it as an excuse to exclude her from any imminent shooting schedule. *His* word: 'You're not going to be needed in the *imminent* future, I think . . .' And by the way, Donna, he goes on, this real pissy tone in his voice, who *exactly* was that man you said you worked for at Cinecittà? When for once she was telling the truth. OK, maybe she never worked for him, not exactly, but he was a *real* producer, the guy who put her onto James in the first place, a connected guy who worked on big-budget movies at Cinecittà for a while. Or *said* he had. People said a lot of things to get into her pants.

She couldn't understand how her life could turn upside down so fast. One minute she's star of the show, courted by a Count, the next she's shit on everybody's shoes. Plus she's fat. Her jeans won't fit. So here she is, popping pills, flicking channels (Serafini in Italian, Serafini in broken English on CNN, a repeat of that shit James interviewing him for BBC World), feeling real bad, the Count's and James's treachery mixed up with other things Paolo told her, secrets heard from Charlotte about some foray she'd had with this Procopio guy, Donna thinking how Charlotte betrayed her (lied about going to San Rocco, found a tunnel or something, pictures) . . .

And suddenly, there he was, straight out of the screen into her eyes, Donna's eyes, speaking just to *her*.

She knew he was speaking to her because when she turned up

the sound, first thing she heard was his beautiful soft Italian, a voice you could trust with your life, and he was saying: 'Ma *Donna*,' something something she didn't understand, and then the English voice-over kicked in, nowhere near so seductive: 'We appeal to anyone who has any knowledge of these occurrences to come forward blah di blah di blah . . .'

Stoned Donna drinking him in. Someone she could talk to, confess her own and other people's sins and omissions. Confess everything right from the start: the broken statue and the money thrown at the Countess and all the things Donna had overheard or thought she'd overheard. Her own private restoration, only five minutes' walk away.

Outside in the streets of Urbino there were crowds sleeping, eating, drinking, protesting, celebrating, despite the best efforts of the police to move them on. Fireworks began to go off overhead, one by one and then all together – crack crack crack – and Donna heard an American girl say it was just like the fourth of July back home and an Englishman joke about the Blitz and then a quiet voice with a heavy accent say, no, it was like Beirut right now. There were fire-eaters, jugglers, doomsday preachers, riddling dwarves and town criers in medieval costumes, a madman claiming to be Lazarus. Fabio had a lot of competition, even outside the bishop's palace, usually pretty quiet. The spectators got in Donna's way, their faces starting to loom up too close, swirling and distorted, cartoons seen through a lava lamp. Like that painting by somebody or other. *The Scream*, that's it. Art run through an acid consciousness.

'Dado's out of control,' Lorenzi said, hearing of the Count's dreary escapades. 'We should make a call, I told you days ago.'

The eldest disagreed. 'Nothing is fixed yet. Things can be done. Precautions taken.'

The Chief of Police had also heard details of the Count's behaviour, but in his case it was from his son Fabio. They'd been having their regular fight concerning what the Chief called his son's 'gutless' lack of ambition, and Fabio, a little high, came out with the story of Malaspino and his wings. 'That's where *ambition* gets you, Papa!' he spat. 'A real high-flyer, yes?' Immediately Fabio regretted his indiscretion. Damn! He'd promised Paolo . . .

'That's rich coming from you!' said the Chief. 'Who could believe you would have no talent except for doing absolutely nothing! And expecting money for it! The best you can hope for is no one knows you even exist! With a father in my position!'

'With a father like *yours*, Papa, maybe it was better not to have any sons, did you ever consider?'

'Your grandfather is very fond of you, God alone knows why. He got you a real job that you – '

'I wouldn't work for that Fascist whore if he were – '

'Don't you use that language in my house, you little – '

'What language, Papa: work? or Fascist?'

The dwarf appeared out of nowhere, a dark laughing man in a satin tricorne hat who looked like the joker off an old pack of cards.

'How do we make change?' he asked Donna, running the riddle through at least seven languages, all of them heavy with a furred accent that might be Russian or Eastern European but certainly wasn't Italian. Even Donna could recognise that. She watched him toss his deck of cards high into the air and draw them back magically to his stumpy, agile hands in a waterfall of flashing colours. The cards disappeared and the dwarf twisted his hands together and raised them to catch the lamplight, casting a graceful shadow fish over the plaster surface of the wall opposite. Mesmerised, Donna saw the fish swim away to return with legs, then with a long iguana tail, the lizard's flame-shaped crest formed from three fingers of the dwarf's left hand. Next came a camel, an elephant, a swaying cobra with a forked tongue, and finally a shadow angel raised its wings and soared, disappearing into the night. Donna smiled and emptied her purse of a handful of mixed coins from all over Europe, piling them in the little man's outstretched hands. 'That's how we make one kind of change, signora,' he said, his saturnine features even more creased in amusement, 'but *why*? *Omnia mutantur, nihil interrit . . .*'

By midnight pilgrims had filled the Piazza Duca Federigo next to the palace entrance and overflowed down the adjoining Piazza Rinascimento and the Via Puccinotti. Most of them were aware by now that Raphael's painting had been transferred here, but some of those who had come from Eastern Europe were still confused and thought they were outside a prison where the living mute was being held. 'Not doing so bad, these decadent capitalists,' said one stout Croatian widow to her sister, 'if this is what their *jails* are like!'

When the lone security man guarding the painting in the chilly *sotterranei* was woken up from his short doze by the muffled stamp and rumble of hundreds of feet overhead, he thought at first it must be an earthquake and rushed to the surface to avoid being crushed. Seeing the constellations and galaxies of candleflames rippling over the piazza outside the gates, he cried out, '*Madonna!*' and, after crossing himself, phoned for reinforcements. In the dark, a shadow slipped past him and joined the less mobile shadows of the Cortile d'Onore, then down into the belly of the palace, where *La Muta* stood behind glass. By the time that police reinforcements had arrived (heavily armed and determined to prevent any pilgrims storming the palace gate), the painting was bleeding again.

The security guard, returning to his position in the underground vault, noticed a smudge of greenish-coloured grease on the glass and conscientiously cleaned it off with his handkerchief.

MIRACLE NUMBER 33

When the Theatre of the Muse Went Up in Flames

Muta was in the cellar preparing sausages and wild greens when they came for her. The fire wasn't lit yet because she wanted to enjoy the fresh, acidic smell of fennel seeds and dried orange peel before the smoke took over. She spooned some bacon dripping into the pan with chunks of windfall apple and saw a lump of earth fall next to the pan, then another. Pulling out the old fruit ladder, she stood on it to put her hand against the cellar roof. The vibration was powerful, more than one of them up there. Though her territory was marked out with wolf's spoor and urine, the trespassers disregarded this warning.

Shortly after the police had arrived at San Rocco, Charlotte pulled up in a taxi, directing the driver to park a few hundred metres from the two police cars. She couldn't decide what to do, whether to approach the police or not. What could she say? It wasn't the right place to explain all she surmised about this woman. They probably wouldn't listen. If she remained in the car as an observer, at least there would be a witness. This was how she justified her inaction. She was unaware of the arrival of James and a cameraman, who stopped on a hill above the ruined hamlet, a good vantage point from which to film without interference.

Charlotte had heard about the police's intended arrest that morning, while she and Anna were working under the bored eye of the Raphael's armed guard. The restoration team had been granted limited access to the painting since its secret removal to the palace cellar, where they had a large room off the former kitchen – the worst kind of atmosphere for a work of art, as Charlotte had protested, to no avail. The canvas, having been cut roughly from its frame by the bishop's men, was now enclosed in a shallow locked glass case. In the transfer from Raphael's house the blood on it had been smeared further across *La Muta*'s face and was still clearly wet. If it hadn't been for Charlotte's personal attachment to this work she certainly would have withdrawn from any further involvement in the restoration, despite the pleas from Geoffrey, who'd got the wrong end of the stick as usual. Delighted to hear his gallery's name mentioned several times on the BBC's World Service, he'd bubbled to Charlotte on the phone, 'and you are some kind of heroine, it appears!'

'Nonsense!' she'd said. 'It's all hype, that idiot James . . .'

Nevertheless, she had agreed to do what she could, which wasn't much. The Vatican's spokesman, Monsignor Seguita, had imposed stringent restrictions on her access to the painting. Although more pictures were needed of the damage, he had insisted that photographs be taken only through glass. And even if this man Paolo called 'the only lawyer in history to set the Virgin free' managed the same trick with *La Muta*, the restoration would still be enormous work. First there would be the removal of the blood and the delicate task of impregnating the Raphael with adhesive to secure what remained of its original colours, then the painting would have to be glued onto new fabric and the torn threads matched as closely as possible. For this work, she'd been offered full use of all the facilities and equipment available from the Accademia delle Belle Arte, as well as from the Free University. 'And should your team need any assistance,' said the director of the course in conservation, a man who had taught Paolo, 'feel free to ask for it from a member of my staff.' Already he had found her a piece of linen to match the Raphael's damaged canvas, on which the painting could eventually be glued for restretching.

This morning Charlotte's work had been interrupted by a furious Professor Serafini, to whom she explained, across the barrier of the guard's lowered machine-gun, that she would gladly share what information they had, 'When we *have* any, Professor! For the moment we are as much in the dark as you . . .'

'What did you tell him?' asked the guard, who spoke no English.

'She called you a cuckold and a fool!' shouted Serafini.

When Paolo burst into the room a little later, he too was stopped by the guard's gun across his chest. 'Oh let him in!' Charlotte said crossly. 'You know him, for God's sake!'

'The police are going to arrest the mute woman today at San Rocco,' Paolo announced. 'Luigi just told me.'

'Good!' said Anna. 'She is a very bad woman – and crazy too.'

'When are they going?' demanded Charlotte.

'Now, soon . . . He told me in the café – what are you doing, Charlotte?'

'I've got to stop . . .' She dragged her coat off the rack in the corner of the room.

'I'll take you,' said Paolo.

'No . . . You step in here, Paolo . . . there is so much to do . . . I . . . I'll be back later . . .'

Angelino came over the hill driving a stray mule and stopped abruptly at the sight of the police swarming through San Rocco. He didn't like men in uniform. They frightened him. One of them was peeing against Muta's kitchen wall while the others used a shovel to scrape away the moss and tiny ferns and wild flowers growing in the skin of soil that covered the cellar door.

Luigi was urinating because he was nervous. He hated his job. He felt stupid when the wooden door was dragged fully back on its hinges and the other police, all seven of them, drew their guns. What did they need guns for? Unwillingly he drew his own after his chief barked at him, 'She's maybe not alone!' Then, in a fine, commanding baritone, the Chief of Police ordered Muta to come out. When his order produced no visible or audible results, he fired a warning shot down the stairs.

'She's deaf – ' Luigi started to say and was abruptly silenced by a wiser colleague elbowing him in the ribs.

The Chief shouted to his posse to follow closely behind him, an order that proved impossible to obey, for the Chief was rather stout and the stairs rather narrow and steep, not much more than a ladder. It felt dangerous to the Chief, forced to descend with his generous backside exposed to an attack from below. Alarmed by the silent, murky cellar in which he found himself and by the lack of his comrades' support, the Chief fired off a few more gunshots, enough to worry some of the other members of his force into falling the last few feet of the steps.

Eventually, all eight men were assembled next to a wall of pickled fruit and vegetables. Luigi leaned over to admire the bottles. 'Damask plums,' he said appreciatively. 'My mum makes a good tart with – '

'Luigi!' shouted his superior. 'You're so relaxed, you go first!'

At the first hint of daylight from the cellar door being lifted, Muta had dropped what she was doing and run down the passageway to clamber over the pile of brick from a collapsing wall and into the narrow tunnel that had once led to a second exit from the cellar. While she had made many attempts over the years to clear the opening to that old exit, her efforts had never been successful, but her only thoughts now were to hide and keep quiet. Wriggling like a spider, she managed to wedge the long white roots of her legs into the rubble and to pull some of the bricks down on top of her, and with her cheek against the hard earth, she closed her eyes, letting herself fade into the bricks and mortar. She acceped the dust in her nostrils, she ignored the tickling trail of insects across her bare skin. Muta was the stone, she was the earth, she was all the words she had never spoken. *Close your eyes, if you must, block your ears, but keep silent. No screams, no cries, whatever you see. To save your life, keep silent.*

Passing San Rocco was Procopio's friend and neighbour Farmer Rossi, an old partisan, who stopped his tractor beside James to enquire what in the name of *Lucifero* was going on. When the director had managed with difficulty to decipher the old man's thick Italian he began to explain the situation, only to be interrupted almost immediately, 'Fascist pricks! Bastard sons of bastard whores!' For several minutes Farmer Rossi went on swearing furiously in this fashion (his archaic local dialect by now incomprehensible to James), then with elaborate politeness thanked the director and turned his tractor towards the Fattoria Procopio.

In the cellar the police had been brought up short when their torches revealed the pile of rubble and the collapsing wall. They were listening to their chief weigh up the advantages of tear gas over the risks of pressing on. 'She must have gone down that tunnel,' said the Chief.

His associates agreed to a man, waiting for his decision.

'But it's crazy!' he added. 'That wall could come down at any minute!'

'She *is* crazy, Boss,' said a young policeman.

'Maybe we should get reinforcements,' suggested another.

The Chief considered this option briefly and decided that it would gain him no kudos if it took more than eight healthy cops to arrest one old sick woman. 'No! What we do is go back on top and throw in the tear gas and order her to come – '

'She's a deaf mute, Boss,' Luigi pointed out.

His commander shrugged this off. 'Maybe, maybe. She could be faking.' The effects of tear gas had always impressed him when he'd seen it on television, and in the relative peace of Urbino he'd never had an opportunity to use it. 'This way, she gets a chance to give herself up without us using force. Then we go in with our gas masks on and drag her out if she doesn't take up the peaceful option.'

Two of his men, originally from Rome, had in the past inadvertently endured the 'peaceful' option of tear gas. They exchanged the cynical look of experienced centurions, but followed the commander up the stairs without expressing their own misgivings. Last to retreat from the cellar, Luigi heard the peeping and chirruping songbird, grabbed its tiny wooden cage and thrust it out into the open air ahead of him, provoking a burst of derisory laughter from his colleagues.

When the gas began rolling down the corridor Muta pulled her shirt over her head and writhed around like an eel to press her covered face against the brickwork, where a trickle of damp, earthy air was still available. The violent coughing and weeping fit which overcame her would have been far worse had she not been so far down the tunnel that the gas had greatly dispersed before it reached her, much of it sucked out by her chimney.

On a hill above San Rocco, Angelino watched, clasping his arms around himself and rocking back and forth desperately singing, '*Doo dah, doo dah, Camdarasetak dum dum dum, oh dah doo dah day.*'

The police were concentrating on the door of the cellar. They had not noticed the gas seeping from the hole in the ground thirty feet behind them, but their hearing was more astute than their eyesight. 'She's down there, Boss! I heard her cough!'

They waited a few minutes, hoping she would appear. The Chief told his men to put on their masks and have their guns ready. Half of them were already in the cellar before Procopio turned up in his jeep. He saw the tear gas billowing from the cellar and assumed they had started a fire to drive Muta out. Swearing, he ran towards the four policemen who remained above ground. A younger recruit, his vision hampered by the gas mask, failed to recognise Procopio and fired a shot at him which tore through the big man's jacket and carved a quarter-inch furrow across the top of his shoulder. Enraged by the pain,

Procopio threw himself at the cop who had fired and went down under the weight of the three others.

Charlotte saw one of the men punch Procopio in the side of the head twice. 'Oh God,' she said softly. 'Oh God.' She opened the taxi door and got out. 'Please,' she called out. 'Please stop.'

'You better get inside again, signora,' said the taxi-driver, taking her arm. 'This don' look so good. They goin' crazy now.'

One cop, who had never liked Procopio, got in a few hard punches to the café-owner's kidneys and again to the side of his head. This was better than fighting old women. A big guy, a real bull to wrestle. Something you could be proud of. They smashed his nose, they kicked him in the ribs, they hit him in the throat, they clubbed the side of his head, popping one ear. Then they cuffed him.

So many things that she should do, should say, thought Charlotte. She filled her lungs to shout, breathing hard, big deep breaths that surely must expel a roar of protest. But she felt the air hardening in her mouth, the words slippery cubes of ice that froze her tongue and paralysed her thoughts.

Behind them all a grey shadow in the scrub paced back and forth, head slunk well below bony shoulders. Occasionally driven by a force contrary to its own reclusive nature, it would creep forward whining, only to stop as if brought up by the limits of a cage.

Underground another battle was taking place. Having located the mute woman by the sounds of her choking and coughing, the police were having the devil of a time extracting her from her burrow. She lashed out with a boot and hit one of them in the groin and when they got firm hold of both her legs, dragging her out of the rubble, scraping her legs along the rough brick retaining wall of the tunnel, she managed to wedge an arm deeper into a crack that must once have been a doorway, and to grip something, rooting herself in the wall. Even with a policeman pulling hard on each of her legs and another one with his arm locked around her waist, it was impossible to extract her without dislocating her arm. The men's weight stretched her horizontally above the ground, a flag of rags and old yellow skin. Her rough skirt and jacket were almost entirely torn from her back, leaving her naked except for a few remnants – a waistband held by a leather belt, one sleeve on the arm she had worked into the wall, a man's heavy woollen vest. Her skin had been lacerated by the bricks as they hauled her out, and this, combined with her semi-nakedness, made her look like the victim of a sexual assault. The three young policemen, accustomed to their girlfriends' tears and cries in times of weakness, were unnerved by this old woman's silence. Oh, she kicked and punched and scratched with her free arm and managed to rip one of the men's face open from brow to chin with her nails, but her choking struggle for air was the only sound she let out.

One of the Romans was trying to get a firm grip around her neck. Her straggly black hair, coarse and wiry as an animal's pelt, wrapped itself around his hands and face with an electric, almost living energy of its own, getting in his mouth and distracting him while the old bitch manoeuvred her head close enough to the fleshy part of his lower arm to sink her teeth in. Snorting and snuffling because her nose was blocked by the tear gas, she pressed her whole face into his skin, drove her open jaw against his arm.

'Bitch!' he shouted, hitting the side of her head with his other fist, desperate to make her let go. The pain was terrible. His arm was going weak. He could feel her working her big blunt teeth, grinding them into his flesh until he thought they would meet. They went very deep. He pulled his arm away with a scream, felt a lump of himself tear off in her mouth. She spat this out and gasped for air.

The man with his arms around her waist shifted his position to try to loosen the arm that was embedded in the wall. Before he could do so she grabbed a brick from the floor with her free arm and began beating it against his masked face with a force that seemed incredible in an old woman. He felt the cartilage in his nose burst as the loose mask slipped sideways and slammed into it. Blood filled the mask and he let go and tried to pull the mask off to stop himself drowning in his own blood.

Furious at his men's inability to act on his command, the Chief stepped forward and gave the woman's locked arm a sharp blow with his gun butt. There was an audible crack and the arm immediately loosened and was yanked out, bringing with it a small avalanche of mortar and brick bloodied by the force with which she had driven her hand through it.

They were pulling her from her cellar of memory like a tree root from the ground and Muta knew what came next, the blood-red scarecrow trees and the burning roots and the words and bones falling down around her.

She let go suddenly and the three men gripping her tumbled on their backsides, a comic tug-of-war team whose living rope had gone slack, while she scrabbled with her one good hand to get a new grip on the newspapered wall, letters and words ruckling into shreds of nonsense under her sharp nails. Still she wouldn't give up, and with her broken arm flopping like a rag doll's from the shoulder, she managed to push past the stout Police Chief and run back towards the stairs.

Luigi, one of the unwounded policemen, younger and faster and unhindered by tear gas, got to his feet before his boss could move and ran after her. In the murky light of the cellar he staggered first into Muta's stove, knocking pots and pans and sausages to the floor, and then into the wall of ancient preserves, the power of his fall shifting the old shelves enough to bring down the War years with a crash of splintering glass bottles. Slipping on a sticky, lumpen wave of preserving alcohol and fruit syrup, plums and peaches, wild strawberries, blackberries, watermelon jam, mysterious, unindentified fungi, wild greens and small fish, opalescent with oil, he lunged forward to catch Muta by the legs just as she reached the top step, dragging her backwards kicking, her nails broken and black from scraping down the dirt wall. He pressed one side of his mask into her naked, skinny old buttocks, closed his eyes against the sight and against the horror of his job, and held on for dear life.

'*Doo dah, doo dah*,' whimpered Angelino, crouching on the hill.

Procopio was screaming abuse in all the languages acquired from years in a tourist town: 'Cretini! Fascisti! Bastards! Salauds! Cols! You fuckheads! Perdio! I kill you for this! She's old! You fucks!'

The policeman directly above her was deafened by Procopio's shouts and confused by his chief's bellows from underground. Turning towards Muta as she began to disappear, dragged down by Luigi, and assuming that the bloody woman was trying once more to escape, he grabbed her wrists and pulled hard. For a moment, with a policeman pulling on her legs from below and another dragging her skywards, it seemed that Muta would be torn in half. Not until Procopio, weeping, gave up struggling with the men still holding him down was one of them free to step forward. He shouted to the others below to let go and hit the woman on the head with his gun, knocking her out. Unfortunately Muta turned her face up towards the light at the moment the gun descended and the butt of it caught her across her right brow, missing her eye by only a fraction.

People in the valley (even Farmer Rossi, a man of limited imagination) would swear later to having heard a long hollow cry of sorrow at that moment, an inhuman howl that could have come from no dog's or fox's throat. Charlotte leaned against the taxi door and covered her face with her hands.

Tear gas was still seeping up through invisible holes in the ground. The wounded policemen who appeared from the cellar looked as if they were emerging from a volcano about to erupt. They half-carried, half-dragged the unconscious Muta – leaves and tree roots and strips of newspaper, whole sentences in her hair.

'Do you have all that?' James whispered to the cameraman.

Grim-faced, his Italian colleague nodded. 'But I think maybe we get out of here quick, yes? Before the Chief of Police realises he failed the John Wayne audition.'

A limp and unconscious Muta was wrapped in a blanket and carried to the police car, where the two Romans had to hold her upright between them. Procopio was warned that he was being arrested for aiding and abetting a criminal, obstructing police in the line of duty and resisting arrest and anything else the Chief could think of. Through his bloodied lips the big café-owner muttered something nonsensical about octopus. He was being marched to the second police car when Charlotte finally broke away from her protector and stumbled towards him, the driver trailing behind. 'I really must protest . . .' she began.

'Not another one!' said the Chief.

Procopio turned his bloody face away from Charlotte and said, 'Don't let that bitch near me.'

'Come on, lady,' said Charlotte's driver, 'I get you out of here.'

'No! Please . . . I . . .'

He took her arm and led her back to his car.

'Boss? What shall I do with the canary?'

'You fool, Luigi! Do whatever you bloody like with the damned thing!'

The bird in question, maybe killed by fear or escaping tear gas, lay prostrate and silent on the bottom of its willow cage. After a brief consideration, Luigi picked up the cage and brought it with him, holding it on his lap as the police cars sped away at high speed, sending a spray of stones and dust in their wake. He put his hand inside and stroked the little bird all the way back to Urbino, much to the amusement of his colleagues. 'You taking a dead canary back to the station, Luigi? Typical!'

By the time they had reached the station, the bird had revived enough to struggle in its captor's warm grasp.

'Another bloody miracle!' remarked the Chief.

'You ready to go now, signora?' asked Charlotte's driver.

She didn't answer. Poor lady, clearly speechless after what she'd witnessed, disturbed, as he was, a young man raised in a family of women. He gentled his voice, the way he did with his granny when she got disoriented. 'Maybe you be goin' back to

Urbino now, signora. Have a nice cuppa tea.' English tourists always liked to be reminded of tea, some kind of talisman for them. He opened the car door and with a courtier's flourish of one hand indicated that she should get in. 'Not'ing more you can do here, signora. Ever't'ing over.'

She got into the taxi like a robot.

'So, where you stay, signora? You wanna go there?' He was watching her in his rear-view mirror as he reversed the car and headed back down the road they'd come on. No reaction from her, she's just staring out the window.

Suddenly – *bam*! – there it is in front of the car!

'*Madonna*!' He wrenched the steering-wheel right, then left, and the sliding skid took over, leaving a serpentine trail of deep tracks in the road before he managed to get control again and stopped the car with a jolt that threw the woman forward and then back in her seat. Apologising even as he was winding down the window, he said, 'Sorry, lady, but you see dat? You see I nearly 'it 'im?' He stared back down the road, shaking his head. 'Is gone now.'

The woman behind him remained silent, still in a trance.

'Was a wolf! I swear it! Big grey old t'ing, all skinny and shaggy.' He took another look out the window. 'Ran off into dose woods. Plenty people t'ink it was a dog, but I swear . . . no mistaking dose yellow eyes. Lucky he see me first.'

With no instructions from the lady, not a word all the way back to Urbino, the driver took it on himself to drop her at the busy corner near the Piazza Repubblica where the buses turned. She must know somebody there, he figured, everybody knows *somebody* in the Piazza Repubblica. Still, he felt slightly guilty about leaving her, and flicking a glance back in the rear-view mirror as he pulled out into the traffic, he saw her looking around with those wide eyes, some kind of lost forest creature, or his grandmother on one of her bad days. Holding her handbag against her chest with both arms around it like it's a little baby, nothing better to hold, no wedding ring on her finger.

And then she's stepping out – *Madonna!* – she's stepping out

– *somebody stop her!* – and he was stamping on the brake – *Sweet Jesus!* – trying to turn, doing ten things at once, thinking ten things at once – *she's stepping out* – in front of this big delivery truck – PRODOTTI NERRUZZI plastered all over it, on its way most likely to the Caffè Repubblica – *she's stepping out* –

The car behind him smashed into the corner of his taxi and spun it around.

MIRACLE NUMBER 34

Clean Hands

'No, Charlotte!' Paolo was only a few feet from her and already running when she stepped off the pavement. 'Charlotte!' She didn't register her name, didn't see him.

'*Charlotte!*'

He watched her move out into the road, someone dipping a toe in a stream, testing the water. The truck just a few feet from her. Its driver – distracted by his long lunch, his girlfriend's great cooking, his girlfriend's beautiful breasts so generously offered – wasn't going fast up that cobbled hill into the piazza, aware as he was of the dozens of fresh eggs in the back of his truck, rows of white shells sticking up above their crates like the fragile bald skulls of elderly men.

Not fast, but fast enough.

'*Charlotte*!'

It doesn't take much for a truck to crush a woman's skull like an egg, like eggshell, broken shell: that's what Paolo was thinking as he watched it happen, seeing her first from the café near where he'd been seated when the taxi dropped her off, watching her step out while he dragged the chair back and knowing at once that it was impossible for him to reach her before the truck, he'd never forgive himself, it was his fault, he shouldn't have let her go alone to San Rocco. Luigi told him what had happened there, how upset she was, a gentle soul – the truck's brakes screaming as it swerved, scattering its freight across the road, an overtaking Vespa skidding on one wheel through the messy sunset of scrambled egg, pedestrians Jackson Pollocked with yolk and albumen and sticky shell –

and then he had her.

Paolo covered the last few metres as if he had wings and dragged her out of the way. Here she was, safe on the pavement, staring at him with incomprehension. Impossible! He wanted to hug her, shake her, he wanted to kiss every fine line on her bony English face. 'Where *were* you, cara? Some other world . . . I was calling and calling . . .'

'Me too!' cried the furious taxi-driver. 'An' looka my car!'

Paolo looked at smashed rear lights, crumpled mudguard and imagine Charlotte instead.

The truck-driver emerged and launched into a torrent of Italian.

'Sorry,' Paolo replied. 'She seems to be in shock. If you give me your names, I'll – '

'Don' be stupid!' The taxi-driver swore at the truck-driver, mentioning various people who might like to know why these eggs were being delivered so late and maybe some other kind of fragile eggs might get broken if he let a certain lady's husband know what she got up to with certain egg-scramblers. Then he held Charlotte's hand with both of his. 'Is justa car, lady. Long as you OK now, your frien' take you home.' He scowled at Paolo and gave the young man several Italian versions of what would happen to him and who he would answer to if he ever let his crazy English friend out on her own again. Then he left.

'Would you like some tea, Charlotte?' Paolo asked. 'Or would you prefer to lie down?'

She said nothing.

'It was San Rocco, wasn't it? The arrest? That's what's upset you? No need to . . . I heard . . . from Luigi. He had told James that the cops were going to make an arrest, so there's evidence on film of what happened. And Procopio's all right. He's been taken to the local jail, where he should only have a few days to wait for the . . . how do you say, the giudizio di convalida . . . the decision of confirmation by the GIP, the judge for preliminary investigation. That is unless . . .'

At Charlotte's expression, Paolo stopped. Best not to tell her about the alternative. If the Chief wanted to get really nasty,

Luigi had said, he could invoke the measure of *custodia cautelare*, preventative detention, by which Procopio could be kept in jail at the police's discretion for over three years without any charges being made. It was a system that had been mobilised usefully during Italy's years of terrorism in the seventies and eighties and now served more often as an instrument of intimidation. 'Responsible for locking up over half of our prison population,' Luigi pointed out. 'And also for containing some of the worst Mafia criminals. Very useful in those cases where witnesses and judges tend to turn up dead if they go to trial at all.'

Procopio had to watch himself, the young policeman added. 'Our chief is in a real mean mood. Work hasn't been going so good lately. Lots of pressure from the top – plus Fabio really pissed him off the other night. If the Chief wants to, he can drum up some handy evidence from the score of useful witnesses who want to turn repentant – and then Procopio won't even get a chance to plead his case before a judge.'

Repentance was a good card to play, Paolo knew. Another left-over from the terrorist emergency, *pentitismo* had been invoked in recent cases against the Mafia and at the 'Clean Hands' trials, where many of those who had participated in criminal acts had been persuaded to confess in return for reduced sentences (or no sentences at all), to become *pentiti* and turn state's evidence against the organisations that had formerly employed them. It was one way of breaking down the tradition of 'knowing silence' typical in Mafia and other high-profile cases against the Church or state, as these official repentants never had to appear in court; nor was there any visible evidence of the favours they received for their collaboration.

But this was certainly not the right time to discuss such matters with Charlotte. Paolo walked her like a blind woman back to her *pensione*. Asking the concierge to bring tea, then grappa, he sat beside his friend in her narrow attic room, patting her hand and listening to the daily battle of crows and doves outside.

An hour later she was still silent. 'Poverina,' said the

concierge, and poured herself some more grappa. Charlotte hadn't even touched the tea, which had cooled to a scummy grey beside her.

'What is it, Charlotte? Please tell me . . . You're safe now . . .' He was frightened by her silence. 'Nobody hurt *you*?'

Inside her head all the words, a carousel of words whirling and colliding . . . The *passeggiata* . . . I don't know what to do . . . All these mothers and babies . . . what about the *others*? Does no one care? Babies, babies, more babies . . . and all these *lost* people, the mute, the ones with*out* families, what about *them*, who looks after *them*? And now Procopio . . . and he *was* doing . . . something, at least . . . he was *trying* to help . . . while I . . . while I . . . Lumps of ice in her mouth, impossible to spit out, impossible to swallow.

'Speak to me, *cara*. What is it? What's wrong?'

Words words words . . . What was the point of talking? Nothing she could do, she'd done too much already . . . all too late.

'It's just San Rocco? That's why you're so upset? The mute's arrest? Nothing else? Don't think it's your fault . . . it was bound to get out, where she lived, sooner or later . . . Everything does in Urbino . . .' It was me, my fault, Paolo thought. I'm the one who told Donna and Fabio.

Absent-mindedly he continued to pat Charlotte's hand until suddenly she snatched it away, her mouth contorted. She looked savage, not his quiet, sweet English lady.

'Poverina,' said the concierge.

'We should've got rid of the bloody woman, like I've been telling you all along, not arrested her! Who encouraged my fool of a son to arrest her?' Lorenzi was furious. 'She's going to give us trouble, I warn you. What about your talented chum Benny – what's he here for, a holiday? Couldn't he have handled her?'

His friend looked chagrined, although he knew for a fact that Lorenzi had never suggested bumping the old broad. Then again, his memory, like his bladder, wasn't so reliable these days, a weakness he sure wasn't going to admit in present company.

'No,' said Grandpa thoughtfully. 'No, Lorenzi, it wasn't such a bad idea. Too many people were already interested in this woman. This way we keep the situation contained. She may be somebody, she may just be a crazy nobody who *thinks* she's somebody.'

'Like my idiot son, the big Police Chief!'

'Whoever she is, we find out what she knows, if she can talk or not – and maybe who she talked to, if she did.'

That night in the Oratorio di Santa Croce, the most ancient and venerable oratory in Urbino, fragments of a San Sebastian fresco painted by Raphael's father began to bleed. Blood seeped from the saint's nine arrow wounds and dripped onto the floor, nearly inducing a heart attack in the oratory's stout old cleaning woman, who, after crossing herself and vowing never to touch another of Procopio's almond cream pastries as long as she lived (hadn't her doctor warned her plenty already?), didn't take long to spread the story.

'Before Sebastian began to bleed, this oratory, dating back to 1334, was known chiefly for the Brotherhood of the Disciplined of the Holy Cross who would beat each other during secret ceremonies,' said James. *Sadistic old buggers*, he thought. It was later that night and he was giving the camera his full attention, attempting to be heard above the clamour of Italian reporters doing much the same thing. 'The oratory enjoyed special ecclesiastical protection due to the rigour with which the brothers submitted themselves. Its splendid structural condition also owes much to the family of Count Malaspino, whose father contributed to its restoration. Many people here in Urbino believe that the answer to such miracles as this bleeding Sebastian at Santa Croce may lie with the mysterious mute woman arrested earlier today. Her attack on Raphael's celebrated *La Muta* has been strongly linked to the portrait's continued bleeding. So far it has thwarted the best scientific efforts by Professor Serafini of CICAP, the Italian Committee for Investigation of Claims of the Paranormal, to prove the city's subsequent miracles fraudulent.'

By Tuesday night the doctors attending Muta were increasingly uneasy about her condition. While her broken arm had been set and she had regained consciousness, she was proving otherwise unresponsive. She would not walk and she had to be pulled into a sitting or standing position by the nurses, where she remained immobile as the scarecrow she resembled, urinating and defecating on that spot until physically moved again. She would not or could not eat or drink. She had to be fed on a drip. Brain scans to see if the blow to her head might be responsible for her state showed nothing unusual. She did not struggle or protest when her mouth was held open for an extensive examination of her peripheral speech organs, which proved to be intact. 'No observable motor impairment of the oropharyngeal and laryngeal musculature and no dysphagia,' said the examining doctor.

Early on Wednesday the mute woman was transferred to a different hospital, where she remained to all intents and purposes immune to the world. 'Shortly before noon we found her standing naked and pure as Santa Margherita of Cortona, clad only in the mat on which she had slept,' said her new doctor, a highly religious man.

His visitor allowed himself a small ironic smile, remembering that before she became a saint, Saint Margherita had been a beautiful unmarried mother, surely an indication that she was less than pure.

'Statueing,' said the doctor. 'That's the term I was explaining to Count Malaspino, although the technical term for such deliberate immobility is – '

'Malaspino? He was here?'

The doctor shook his head. 'Not here – we spoke on the phone.' He lowered his voice, the eminence of his latest visitor inspiring confidence. 'And although he doesn't wish it made public, I'm sure he wouldn't object to me telling someone like you: it was through his influence she was transferred here. You may not realise, but many of our former rectors were ancestors of the Count's.'

'Ah. I *thought* Santa Caterina was an unusual place for her to be sent.' The visitor smiled openly this time, while thinking, That *fool*! To choose *this* hospital, of all places! He couldn't have made his connection to the woman more obvious! The Spedale di Santa Caterina, a magnificently frescoed building constructed in the fifteenth century to sustain the abandoned children of Urbino, had slowly changed its function over time, so that now it accommodated only the most influential families (as everyone in the city was well aware). From their ranks all rectors of the hospital had originated – until recently, when, after centuries of conflict between religious and civil powers, Urbino's government had won the right to elect hospital rectors from outside that exclusive circle. In terms of patients, however, Santa Caterina's lofty frescoed rooms remained largely for the wealthy, the only drawback for them being the renegade tourists who from time to time traipsed through the hospital in search of its famous frescoes and lost their way, winding up in a private room confronted by an aristocratic former junkie, a rich alcoholic, or the anorexic daughter of a powerful local bank manager.

'Yes, the Count is taking a real interest in this poor mute woman's case,' said the doctor, as together the two men paced down a long corridor, its arching, midnight-blue ceiling frescoed with clouds and stars and various stern saints waving salutory texts. 'She seems to have captured the imagination of Urbino. If only she realised . . . '

The doctor's visitor nodded distantly. Anyone observing would have thought him more interested in the series of luminous frescoes along the corridor walls. 'I see you are beginning to restore the pilgrimage cycle,' he said. The fifteenth-century panels portrayed pilgrims and patients and the deeds of charity performed in their name by Santa Caterina's enormously fat rector. This was a place where the rich were always satisfyingly reminded of how much they were owed by the poor. There was no uncomfortable evidence here of the poor having anything to offer except their hunger. No kings inappropriately kneeling at the feet of humble carpenters, thought the visitor. No fishermen prophets.

The doctor stopped to scowl at a deep scratch in the frescoed plaster. 'You see this? The orderlies! They persist in ramming their trolleys and beds up against the walls . . . I suspect they feel this setting inappropriate for a modern hospital. Or they are simply oblivious to it. But why shouldn't the sick and the suffering benefit from such beauty?' He directed his eminent visitor to admire a panel in which the amputation of an arm was depicted in graphic detail.

'Indeed.' The visitor smiled almost imperceptibly as he studied the impressively realistic blood pouring copiously from a patient's open wound into a huge copper basin, and the hopeful dog waiting underneath the basin to catch any drips.

'It must be reassuring to be surrounded by these masterpieces, don't you think?' asked the doctor. 'Better than some insipid mountain view.'

His visitor noticed the open door they were approaching. 'Is it usual to leave the doors of such patients unlocked?' he asked.

'When you see this woman's condition I think you will agree there is little point in locking her up. She is catatonic, a state we might have prevented had the police been less determined she should testify – '

'They believe she *can* testify?'

'I am still trying to establish whether her mutism is hysterical or organic. The police do not seem to understand that such things cannot be achieved by force.' He gestured at the inert body on the bed. 'Only look where force has got them already.'

'Might not such . . . *force* have given her just the jolt she needed to speak?'

'Highly unlikely. Modern medical literature warns us that

where mutism reflects a deeply rooted problem, violent methods may result in a complete mental breakdown, for instance, as was the case with many soldiers during the First World War.'

'I see . . . and that would be tragic . . .'

'Even in less irregular cases it can be difficult to distinguish what we call *hysterical* or *functional* mutism from a real aphasic disorder, where a patient's mutism is caused by brain damage. Especially difficult if a patient has suffered an emotional shock or a head wound, as this one has.' He passed a ruler back and forth across her line of vision, to no effect. Her silver-grey eyes were cloudy mirrors, as if she were suffering from cataracts, blind as well as dumb. 'You see?'

'I have heard of mutism appearing after a dreadful experience . . . '

'Or a few days later, accompanied by functional deafness, even paralysis. One of the leaders in my field claimed that functional mutism, when accompanied by functional deafness, is pure defence. Having sustained an unbearable shock, the individual withdraws into a shell of silence from a world of horror, a world no longer trustworthy.'

'Can no one tell us how the original mutism occurred? This man the police arrested . . . Procopio, I think his name is? Didn't he know her?'

The doctor flipped through his case notes. 'All he has to say is that his housekeeper occasionally left food for the woman, whom he described as being unaccustomed to strangers, perhaps from an immigrant family.'

'An *immigrant*? So he's not claiming she was a local? But I've heard – ' The visitor checked himself. 'What difference would it make whether she was local or an immigrant?'

'Partial mutism can be caused, or at least increased, by the geographical isolation of immigrants who never mastered the language. But extra-familial mutism may be reinforced even in a local family, if they have always lived in a remote home, as this woman has – ' The doctor broke off to smile apologetically. 'And you know, even if she *were* to speak, the dialect of these more remote valleys is so antique that we might need a translator! We have also known mutism to be caused by a secret within a family, where the child has been advised or ordered not to talk to strangers.'

'And this childish tendency to be reticent with strangers ... it might be enhanced to virtual mutism by the parents' reminders to keep a secret?'

'Yes.'

'Can such cases be cured?'

'That depends. Some patients have conquered selective mutism by starting a new life away from familiar people, while with old acquaintances who knew them as mutes they remain silent.'

'So you are saying that a stranger might unlock the mute voice?'

The doctor cast his eyes once again over the still creature on the bed. 'It must also be said, Monsignor, that people who retreat into mutism as deeply as this woman has are more likely to be trapped in it indefinitely.'

'Can nothing be done?'

'It depends on the patient. Mutism remains fairly enigmatic to us. It is not "cured" easily.'

His visitor turned away from the mute woman to study the huge fresco dominating her room. Moon-marked by fallen plaster, it depicted a scene he recognised instantly as the biblical pool where animals were washed before being sacrificed.

'They say she likes animals,' said the doctor, earning a subtle smile.

'Have you considered the possibility that she might be happier remaining silent? Somewhere where there is less ... pressure, perhaps?'

'You mean an asylum? This woman's silence doesn't appear to have made her happy, not from what I have heard.'

'Forgive me, Doctor, but you must remember that those of us in religious orders consider silence a virtue. St Benedict himself imposed silence on his disciples, saying: "Whoso keepeth his mouth and his tongue keepeth his soul from troubles."' Raising his hand in a benediction (almost willing the deaf woman to take comfort, so the doctor believed), he recited in a melodious voice, 'God himself is silence. His perfection is infinite and above language.' He laid one hand on the woman's forehead, his long clean graceful fingers gripping her skull. 'Set watch, O Lord, before my mouth; keep the door of my lips.'

A quiver passed through the woman, who arched her back as if she had been subjected to an electric shock and then fell back motionless.

MIRACLE NUMBER 35

A Threat to Italian Football

Charlotte had gone to the palace with the intention of once more taking up her work with Paolo and Anna, but on entering the Courtyard of Honour she lost her courage and instead climbed the broad shallow steps to the palace's light-filled upper galleries. Here she spent an hour aimlessly criss-crossing from Bellini to della Francesca, Duccio to della Robbia, moving from one room to another, one floor to the next, up and round like that indigestible bolus of ham she had chewed and chewed at Procopio's lunch. This is where I should feel most at home, Charlotte thought. Yet today she found that every picture was an accusation. She felt as threadbare as the portrait she had tried to restore, no more than a thin layer of paint between her and a blank canvas.

Even *The Ideal City* failed to calm her; its aura of tranquillity was one more reminder of the silence she had betrayed. A righteous Christian mob in Uccello's *Miracle of the Profaned Host* beat down the door of a Jew and burned him and his family at the stake, and all Charlotte saw was her own failure to act while Muta was dragged out and broken by the police. She sat on one of the white plastic benches and stared at a thirteenth-century fresco of demons being exorcised from a woman, the exorcist literally hauling a host of black crabbed horny devils from the poor creature's mouth. Little black devils set free from her own mouth . . . *If I hadn't told . . . if I hadn't mentioned Muta and Procopio to the Count . . . Was it he who sent the police?*

She thought about her talent for restoration, a profession she could count on, her future secured. Things would always fall apart and require mending . . . the skill she lacked with people. Her years with John – so steady, so reliably safe – were proof enough. Somewhere along the road I lost my way, she thought. This isn't how it was supposed to be, this isn't who I am. *Pious Sister Charlotte.* I used to be different.

A red ball rolled across the museum floor and stopped at her feet. Charlotte scowled at the solemn small boy who appeared to claim it. He started to cry, and his pregnant mother, holding another child by the hand, caught the English woman's sour expression and called, 'Vieni, caro! Georgio, vieni! Non disturba la donna!' Charlotte was shocked by the rage she felt against this pretty young woman for so carelessly reproducing. Because *reproduction* was what it was all about, she thought bitterly. Not creativity – chips off the old block! Children were the promise of continuity, they re-produced a world of which she wanted little part, a world of more men who could do to old women what she had seen done today, more women to veil in the name of religion or strip bare for profit, more young men to serve as war fodder. Where did it come from, such thoughtless faith that people could change, *that people could learn to breathe and then to sing*?

For several more minutes she sat staring fixedly at the painting in front of her. A massacre of the innocents, with all the usual outrages perpetrated by all the usual suspects – men supported by their wives and mothers, Charlotte thought bitterly, men fed and nurtured and fucked by their women; murderers provided with sons and heirs. The gentle men, unless they were very smart or quick enough to get away, destroyed by the powerful. The children of one tribe murdered by the fathers of another whose wives and religious leaders, if they were not actual accomplices, were certainly compliant, complicit.

When Charlotte had had enough of the accusing images, she wandered out into the narrow alleys and arcades between the palace and the Via Mazzini and found herself outside the top entrance of the helicoidal ramp. I haven't been here in weeks, she thought, not since I first arrived in Urbino and wanted to see everything, explore everything. How far away that seemed! She entered the ramp and began walking slowly down the broad, shallow steps, only to be overwhelmed by a sense of grief. Her eyes filled with tears. A kind woman mortified Charlotte by asking if she was unwell, did she need any help? Mute with shame, Charlotte shook her head and turned her face away so no one else could see her cry. She pressed her hand against the pale pink bricks to steady herself and was aware of all the passing footsteps, the murmurs and chattering, the whistling and laughter, all the noise blurring into a single voice. Procopio's. What had he told her? To broaden her horizons beyond the picture frame. Perhaps that was the only secret.

The mayor was having trouble sleeping, which had to do with his current diet, which had to do with his wife. 'You should *do* something, Primo!' she'd said immediately when he told her about the mute woman's case.

The mayor adored his wife; she was his smart, fierce comrade in arms. But in this kind of mood she scared the pants off him, made him want to head straight back to the Bar Raffaello to top up his courage with enough grappa so he could ask, 'What, cara mia, *what* would you have me do?'

His failure to live up to his wife's expectations was evident in her scornful eyes and her even more scornful cooking. Garlic never appeared except burned to bitter blackness, pasta was always slimy with too much salt and either over- or under-cooked. She nagged him with bad cooking, she bullied him with silences, this woman to whom he was as close as paint on a wall, this woman he loved who had raised his children along with his dead brother's, who continued to care for his ailing, petulant mother with never a complaint, who joined him as a young Communist to carve her initials into the medieval bricks of the helicoidal ramp and then marched to ban the bomb and made love to him later with explosive enthusiasm.

Now, when it was his turn to show the stuff he was made of . . . But *Christ*! He was only one man, he couldn't take on the whole city!

'Start with one man, Primo,' she said. 'Find her an honest magistrate for this hearing they propose. One of the brave, intuitive, independent-minded ones that this sad country of ours still manages to produce against all odds. One of those with a talent for getting people like Francesco Procopio to unburden themselves of years of lies.'

He pleaded with her, 'Look at the roll-call of brave dead men who have spoken up about such things over the last couple of years, my love: Falcone, murdered last year with his wife and three of his bodyguards! Remember what he said only four days before those bastards blew his car up: "The enemy is always there, ready to strike!" And Ambrosoli (and he was appointed by the government, don't forget!) – murdered by the US Mafia at the bequest of Michele Sindona, the very man he was investigating! Sindona himself, with ties to the Vatican, for Christ's sake – and to Andreotti, twice Prime Minister! Yet Sindona, despite his connections, died of poison in prison! And where should I look for this honest magistrate, when the acting president of Milan's court is imprisoned for accepting bribes! I could go on, but – '

'You have already gone on . . . and from this recitation of the phone book I conclude you intend to do nothing to help the poor woman?'

'We don't even know who she is, my – '

'You are from that valley. Everyone from that valley can guess what happened at San Rocco!' Ignoring the wine he'd poured her, she slammed a plate of pasta down in front of him so hard it made the glass jump and splash its contents into the sauce, where it proceeded to curdle the cheese the way her disapproval curdled his stomach juices. Even without tasting the dinner Primo knew to expect the worst. The strands of tagliatelle coiled stiffly, patently uncooked and threatening in their leprous sauce.

'I suppose you are going to follow the official line and pretend the affair never happened!' she said.

'What can I do? The San Rocco files might be in Britain for all I know. Our government was not alone in wishing to keep the incident secret. No country wants to hear they were allied to people guilty of the same sort of atrocities as the Germans.'

'Lace underwear,' suggested Franco, to whom Primo took his arguments later. 'Get your wife some. Take her mind off San Rocco, make her happier . . . and you too, old friend!'

'You think she's right, Franco? You think I should speak up?'

'I dunno, Primo, I think – '

Speak up about San Rocco, the mayor reminded Franco, and waves of scandal could spread far beyond their own courtier's city on its double hills. They could splash mud on the spangled Versace of a talented record producer in Rome and over the polished brogues of one of London's most eminent merchant bankers, they could stain the apron of a charming mother of four innocent children, damage promising political careers in five of the ten major Italian political parties ('One of those parties supported by a solid majority of Mafia families *as well as* the Vatican Bank!' Primo emphasised), upset three bishops, two cardinals, a minor German aristocrat, a clutch of Italian Counts and two Popes. Not to mention the formerly Communist mayor of a small university town in the Marches heavily reliant on tourism (a mayor who *knows for a fact* that miracles don't happen, that Galileo's Law of Fall holds true for the innocent as well as the evil). Scandal could wash over the Alps into Germany, send ugly ripples across the Atlantic, interrupt the Italian car industry – *maybe even halt the next football match in Milan*!

That worried Franco.

'The point is,' said Primo, 'San Rocco's story is *over*, *forgotten*, nobody wants to *hear* about it any more! We have to think about Urbino's future, after all! How would such a story affect our city?'

His friend nodded. 'You think the mute woman could speak now, even to save her life, Primo?' Still worried about the possible decline of Milan football club, Franco crossed the bar to offer his other customer more wine. 'Is OK this wine for you?' he asked in broken English.

'Yes, thank you.'

'You wan' more bread, olive maybe?'

Graciously she declined his offer, smiling up at him. A proper English lady, not like some he got in here.

'But I wonder, signor . . . you wouldn't by any chance . . . know anything about a place called San Rocco, in a valley near here?'

'San Rocco?' He shook his head. 'Never hear of it. Sorry, lady.'

'Oh, I thought I heard you mention . . . '

'*Dan* Rocco you hear. Ol' frien'.'

His lie didn't surprise Charlotte. *All the old men in the cafés*: that's what Procopio had said. And after olives and bread and wine in various cafés around Urbino she had learned that just the mention of San Rocco was enough to silence people of a certain age. She could see the resonance in their faces, the name like a stone skipped across water, leaving a trail of interlocking ripples behind. Often people would respond eagerly, only to lead her on misleading tangents, as this bartender had. They were helped in this by the Italian language, which, having fewer of the hidden, unspoken consonants of English, gave its speakers the deceptive appearance of a transparency they did not possess. She tried ringing the state archives about San Rocco and was left hanging on the line for fifteen minutes, to be told eventually that there were no records for the hamlet predating the 1960s. She approached an elderly salesman in an academic bookshop and was offered a treatise on Saint Rocco himself, with charming woodblock illustrations of nineteenth-century peasants not remotely connected either to the place or to her question.

Paolo's act of atonement was more direct than Charlotte's. When she didn't show up to carry on with the Raphael restoration and didn't return any of his phone-calls, he went to see her at the Pensione Raffaello, only to be told by the concierge that the English lady was out and had left no messages for him. 'You have anything to tell her?'

'Just say I . . . no, no – tell her I hope to see her soon.'

The next morning he went to visit Procopio at the police station. It was possible that the café-owner, whom Paolo knew through his grandfather, might be able to explain more about what had happened to Charlotte.

The station's duty officer, a drinking pal of Luigi's, let them have a private room usually reserved for interrogations. It smelled of old disinfectant and of something else, difficult to remove with bleach. Overhead the lights buzzed with the sound of angry flies. To all this the big café-owner appeared oblivious. He was seated in a chair asleep, with his head resting heavily on one hand, barely hiding the dark bruises around his temples. Both eyes were puffy and his nose had plasters holding it in a passable stab at its former position. Paolo felt a surge of pity, surprising because he'd always thought of Procopio as a bit of a clown. A Marxist ice-cream maker: a bit like being an anarchist architect. Marxism was understandable in people of Paolo's grandfather's generation, but now it was completely discredited. Politics was a fool's game, Paolo thought, and especially so in Italy.

Procopio's heavy-lidded eyes opened reluctantly and he took in Paolo. The younger man watched him trying physically to pull himself together, each part of his body swearing allegiance to a separate flag, his arms and legs unwilling recruits. First his muscular neck straightened and pulled the battered head into line and he moved his hand away from the bruises to lay it with the other hand, one on each knee. When he had recovered sufficiently from the strain of this exertion, he flexed his fingers, the knuckles also badly bruised and swollen, and the action shot a grimace of pain across his face.

'You look as if you could do with this, Signor Procopio.' From a paper bag Paolo withdrew a bottle of wine, a large packet of Procopio's own prosciutto and a box of cakes only a little squashed by having been transported on the back of the Lambretta. 'Courtesy of your waiters.'

Procopio managed a thin smile and leaned forward to grasp the wine. 'How are they, the bastards – slacking off now the boss is locked up, I bet!' He examined the label and made a few scathing comments about the cruelty of his workmates in saving the best vintages for themselves.

Paolo tried to think how to phrase the questions he needed to ask. 'Luigi, one of the cops who arrested you – '

'The one who took the bird?'

'Useless cop – wanted to be an opera singer. A friend of mine from school. Anyway, he tells me that you've signed some paper to say you were drunk when you and the cops . . . nothing about trying to protect the mute woman. Why not?'

'Let's say I've been . . . advised. Certain quarters have let it be known that the less said about the subject the better.'

'Luigi told me they've threatened you with preventative detention.'

Procopio opened the box of cakes, not meeting Paolo's eyes. 'Your friend Luigi talks too much.'

'But what will happen to you now?'

'A fine, maybe a few months in jail, nothing more. Why you so interested in my fate?'

Paolo hesitated, then blurted out, 'It's Charlotte.' Before Procopio could express the emotion gathering in his face, Paolo said, 'It wasn't her fault, the arrest. That's why I've come, part of the reason. It wasn't Charlotte who told the police about the mute, it was me . . . I mean, not directly, but . . . it was probably because of something I said . . .' He lowered his gaze to the table and picked at the flaking surface with his paint-stained fingers.

'To the Canadian girl?'

Paolo looked up.

'Trying to impress her with how much you knew?' The

shadow of a smile crossed Procopio's face. 'Pretty girl . . . You keep trying to get her attention, she doesn't pay you any notice, am I right?'

'How – '

'I know the feeling. It's an old story. You'll get there, good-looking kid like you. Good education, good prospects.'

'Good, not great.'

'So you think this girl told the police about Muta?'

'Maybe Fabio . . .' The boy shrugged. 'I don't know. Someone told someone who told them . . . The point is . . . if it *was* her – and I don't believe it, not for a minute! But if it *was* her, she didn't mean to do any harm.'

Procopio's beaten features muscled up taut and wary. 'That's how a lot of harm gets done. For her own good, you tell her not to get any further involved. You too. Stay out of it.'

'Involved how?'

Luigi's face appeared at the window. 'Tell the girl to be careful, that's all,' said Procopio. 'Watch her mouth – and yours – in future.'

Luigi tapped on the reinforced glass and Paolo stood up. 'Anything else I can bring?'

'Nah,' Procopio said. Then, just before Paolo reached the door, he asked grudgingly, 'How is she, anyway?'

'The mute?'

'The English woman . . . Charlotte.'

'Pretty bad. Anything you want me to tell her?'

'Tell her . . . Tell her I . . . ' He shook his head. 'Forget it. One thing, Paolo – a favour. If I don't . . . if this doesn't go the way I expect, could you see that Baldassare goes to that bastard, Primo?'

'Your old hunting dog?' Even Paolo had heard how much Procopio liked that dog.

Procopio nodded. 'You know how Primo likes truffles and . . . well, Baldassare is too much for the old woman.'

There were many things Paolo wanted to ask Charlotte, to tell her, when she finally turned up for work at the palace, but he judged from her face and manner that she wasn't ready. Apart from offering him no explanation for her absence, she was more than usually quiet. Underneath the light suntan provided by weeks in Italy, her skin looked sallow, pinched around her mouth and soft blue eyes, the roses gone from her cheeks.

'It's good to have you back,' he said cautiously.

'I'll get you a cup of tea,' Anna said.

What Paolo did tell Charlotte while Anna was upstairs making tea was that she should go and see Francesco Procopio. 'He feels really bad about what he said to you.'

'How could I begin to . . .'

'You don't have to explain anything. I told him the arrest was my fault, because I . . . because I talked to . . . a friend . . . I never believed they would betray my confidence.'

Neither did I, thought Charlotte.

'Hey, this will cheer you up! You know Luigi rescued that songbird from the mute's cellar? He says it's chirping like a demon and driving everybody nuts at the police station, but nobody knows what to do about it. Nothing in the police rule book about canaries.'

His attempt at lightening her spirits failed to register. 'Procopio must have other friends, work associates who will visit him,' she said.

'Least said, soonest mended: isn't that what you say in England? This is the attitude towards the law of many Italians – not only of the older generation. We have a healthy wariness of getting near a jail. Never know what might rub off. However, if you want to visit Procopio – '

'I'll think about it, Paolo . . . But I have something else to do first.'

'It's just that . . . well, I didn't like to mention it earlier, but Procopio . . . well, if you're expecting him to testify to what happened when the mute was arrested, he isn't going to.'

'What do you mean? Why wouldn't he?'

'He isn't even going to contest the charges against him, except by claiming to be drunk, because if he does, they're threatening him with the custodia cautelare . . . preventative detention . . . which means they can hold him for at least three years without charging him.'

'But that's not possible! What about – '

'Didn't you know, Charlotte? Here in this Italy you love so much we have a legal code dating from Fascist days . . . none of this habeas corpus of yours: under Italian law there is no need to bring a detained prisoner before a judge or court. They have only to find a few witnesses to suggest that Procopio is suspected of terrorism and really they could lock him up and throw away the key. Even if it goes to trial, our legal system has three stages, each case an average length of three years – and a backlog of some three million cases.'

'Terrorism! But that's absurd! Procopio was only trying to protect – '

'Someone they don't want protected, evidently.'

MIRACLE NUMBER 36

A Starry Messenger

The woman on the bed had no more substance than a flake of fresco slipped from the wall. Her skin had been powdered a cheap orange tan, rosy over the sunken cheeks, and her mouth was a slash of cherry where a well-meaning nurse had attempted to make her look more cheerful, the lipstick cracking on the surface like enamel on the lips of a cheap souvenir saint. Charlotte heard her swallow painfully, but there were no tears from this saint, there were no tears.

'The tests at the previous hospital,' said the doctor quickly, 'they can leave the patient's throat dry . . .'

A faint aroma of urine drifted from the woman's bedside as the catheter bag slowly filled. 'Her face is very bruised,' said Charlotte, trying to ignore the smell. She was appalled. *What have I done?* Is this the same fierce *living* woman I saw being dragged from her cellar like a wild creature? Into what cavern of the mind has that other disappeared?

'The bruises are from the police. There was quite a struggle when – '

'I know what happened.' Staring into the mute's blank mask of a face, Charlotte struggled for a way to express her feelings of remorse, to convey comfort. What combination of words could possibly help? What could she say that the doctors hadn't?

'You've done your best,' said the doctor after he'd given his silent visitor a few more minutes of contemplating his equally silent patient. This woman confirmed his belief that the English as a race produced bad nurses. Their well-honed ability to tailor cloth and words and to say nothing politely made them hopeless at communicating real human sympathy. Give him one of the Africans any day.

'There must be . . . ' Charlotte said. 'I should have . . .'

'No, signora. Trust me, in cases like this, it can be the patient who is controlling us and not the reverse.' He was impatient to get back to work.

Charlotte remembered the picture she'd brought. 'I have . . . I don't know . . . perhaps it's not such a good . . .' Out of her pocket she drew the postcard of Raphael's mute, offering it to him for inspection. 'She kept a similar card in her . . .' The word 'den' sprang to mind. 'Her home.'

He held the card up in front of the mute woman on the bed, testing for a reaction. There was no flicker of interest. 'Well, I'm not sure it will have any effect, Signora Penton, but I don't see any harm. It's up to you.'

He gave it back to Charlotte, who leaned forward to tuck the pictures into the mute woman's limp hand, whispering, 'They saved your bird, did you know? Your songbird is safe.' Awkwardly she tried to mime a bird. 'Would you like me to see if the pol . . . if I can bring it here?' She swivelled towards the doctor and explained about the woman's pet. 'Would it help if I brought the bird?'

'Who knows? I'm willing to try anything at this point.'

'Would you like me to bring your songbird here . . . *Gabriella*?' she asked, the whispered name on her lips before she could question it. Charlotte was sure she saw some light in those mirrored eyes, a connection made between the interior and the exterior worlds. She needed to believe it.

Shortly after escorting Charlotte to the prisoners' interview room, the Chief of Police was honoured to receive another visitor. 'What a great privilege it is to meet you again!' he exclaimed. 'In my station, of all places!'

'How is your father? Still prospering, I hope?'

'Oh, very well, very well . . . These days he spends most of his time dozing in the sun with his friends at the Caffè Nazionale. Reliving the good old days . . . But tell me what I can do for you?'

The distinguished man opposite him explained that he had found himself increasingly concerned with the case of the mute woman arrested at San Rocco. 'My request is unusual, I know, but I wonder if you might have any details about her family background? I have promised her doctors to use my modest influence in assisting her recovery.'

Modest influence, *huh*! thought the Chief. 'I think I've given them everything . . .'

His visitor's eyebrows remained lifted in aloof but persistent inquiry, from which the Chief inferred that he wasn't going to get away with his usual excuses for avoiding work. Methodically he began sifting through the filing cabinet, passing over what slender pickings he could find.

'There seems to be nothing here about the place where she was arrested . . .' the visitor mused. 'San Rocco, is it?'

The Chief settled his bulk more comfortably into the expensive black leather chair. 'Classified war material. Even *I* can't access it.'

'What of the café-owner – Procopio? He must have previous connections with this poor mute . . . Any history of their association? I gather the man has a somewhat *disagreeable* past . . . would that be a criminal record?'

'Funny you should mention it, because the woman with him now asked me the same question. She seems entirely unaware of this man's reputation, and you'd never think to look at her, a real lady, she is, that she'd – '

'What woman?'

'The English restorer – Signora Penton.'

'She must be quite . . . *familiar* with this man, to visit him here . . .'

For the benefit of his visitor, the Chief happily elaborated on a relationship he knew little about, apart from the gossip spread by his wife's cousin, the concierge at the Pensione Raffaello.

'I wonder what two such . . . dissimilar people find to

discuss?' the visitor enquired, almost to himself. 'But . . . if I might bring you back to the question of the man's files, I presume you are suggesting that this English *art* restorer has never looked through them . . . ?'

'She couldn't see them, even if she had the authority.' The Chief explained that the files on Procopio's previous run-ins with the law had been lost in the move to these larger premises. 'Ten years ago – in my father's time. But of course everyone knows about Francesco's politics.'

Muta's songbird chose that moment to begin an elaborate and celebratory tune. 'How charming,' remarked the Chief's visitor, with barely a hint of irony. 'One never imagines a canary in a police station.'

'It's that fool Luigi! He rescued the thing from the mute woman's cellar at San Rocco.'

'Really? It was the deaf mute's, you say?'

'Now we're stuck with the damn bird. Technically, I suppose, it's the mute's property. We don't know what to do with it.'

'Perhaps you might let me offer a perfectly legal solution?'

Charlotte thought she had steeled herself for this meeting, but she was wrong. Her hands clenched and unclenched the grey wool of her skirt and under the unforgiving neon lights she noticed, *really* noticed for the first time, how crêpey the skin on the back of her hands had become. She preferred to think about ageing, about anything else, rather than meet the eyes of the man in front of her.

There was no sense of the centaur about him this time. He was a marionette flung carelessly onto a chair in a tangle of invisible strings, the puppeteer otherwise engaged. His greying auburn hair was greasy, he had shaved badly, or been shaved, and the grey patches of beard and scraped bruised skin aged him. He wore the same clothes in which he'd been arrested, the blue workshirt splashed with dark stains, his own blood this time. Charlotte had thought of him as too big a man ever to be contained and diminished by such a place, and yet he had been, and she was responsible, whatever excuses Paolo made for her.

'I'm sorry,' she whispered. The words, so inadequate, didn't begin to express her feelings. 'It's my fault. If I hadn't . . . if . . .'

'Paolo told me it wasn't you who sent the cops.'

'But if I hadn't spoken to – '

Procopio made an inarticulate sound and his bruised hand curled into a fist. 'No good going on about it.'

'What can I do? . . . Please . . . I – '

'Nothing.' The bloodshot eyes swept over her face. 'Still, it's nice to see you, Charlotte. Prettier than my regular guardians . . . almost as pretty as that scamp Paolo!'

She fumbled in her bag and brought out a box of hazelnut meringues sent by his staff at the café.

He took a meringue and bit into it. 'Not bad. You tried one? Not as good as mine, but my assistant's definitely improving.'

'Paolo says . . . you aren't going to tell what happened to you and the mute woman at San Rocco.'

He started on a second meringue. 'Nun's farts, that's what we call these, did you know?'

'Is there nothing I can do?'

'OK, sure. You have a piece of paper, a pencil?'

Charlotte waited patiently while he scribbled for several minutes. 'There,' he said, returning the notebook she'd offered him. 'Give it to Cosimo and he'll know who needs to see it.'

She examined several pages of surprisingly good drawings and annotations in Procopio's meticulous handwriting. 'What is this?' she asked. 'I don't understand.'

Procopio smiled. 'Very important, highly secret.'

'But what is it?'

'Plans for my café's annual contribution to the agricultural show.'

'The agricultural show!'

He started to explain the sketch he'd made and she listened carefully at first because she thought there must be some code, a hidden message he wanted to convey. When she realised that the only code was for quantities of ground almonds to sugar, she felt a surprising anger, and with the anger came even more surprisingly a sense of gratitude that she could still feel anger instead of the dull, mute resentment that had filled her for so long. Anger is a lively, noisy force, she thought, even creative. If I can feel anger I am not old yet, whatever tricks nature plays on me with these crêpey hands and grey hairs.

So for once she didn't suppress her anger. She wanted Procopio to wake up and face the situation – Muta's, if not his own. 'I suppose Paolo told you that pressure is being put on Muta's doctors to transfer her to a secure hospital for the mentally unsound?'

His eyes narrowed at her tone. 'Isn't that what you wanted?'

'No, no . . . I . . .' Her bubble of anger deflated. 'It's only . . . I expect no one has told you the worst . . .' Slowly, punishing herself with every word, Charlotte described the mute woman's vegetative state.

'Bastards!' Procopio stood up and turned his back on her, pressing his face into his bruised hands.

'You're right, they *are* bastards. And you are the only voice Muta has now. You have to tell someone the story, whatever it is, Francesco!' His name slipped out. 'Make the police understand why Muta fought so hard.'

'*No!*' He slapped his open hand down on the table, the force of it making Charlotte and the box of meringues jump. 'I *cannot* speak to anyone about this! I have told you before, this would help no one – *no one*, you understand! Because, my dear, sweet, naive English lady, if I speak – BOOM! It is not only this custodia cautelare they hold over my head, it is as if the Allies never defused those German mines in Urbino's foundations. If I speak, I am a dead man . . . and Muta too is probably dead.' He lifted his hands, let them drop again. 'If I was rich or influential – even *then* I would be at risk. Long time ago they told me, "Keep your big trap shut, Francesco, old boy, and maybe you live to see another day." So Francesco Mazzini shut up for good. Everything he was, everything he did – buried. I changed my life, I changed my name.'

'If it was the Mafia who told you this, if – '

'The Mafia, the Mafia! All you English think of is the Mafia! It's nothing to do with the Mafia! Not in the sense you mean. Don't you know that Italy is a country where the moral costs are very low of this spregiudicatezza I explained to you? This broad-minded lack of scruples? Until the Mani Pulite trials in Milan began, people in public life who perceived themselves as utmost foes of bribery and corruption would think nothing of receiving a limousine or free "loan" from their business friends. Why should they? Exposure of such practices brought neither legal sanctions nor social disgrace. "A canny fellow!" says the Italian public. "One of us!" They show him no prejudice. Like me – you think people would ever stop eating my ice-cream because of my morals? Listen, I have been a braggart, a drunk, a gambler, a womaniser, I took bribes – *yes*! That's stopped you, hasn't it! I got into debt with some very important people and neglected to pay back the favours I owed. But I thought I was a clever fellow, thought I could get out of it by proving what bad people they had been in the War . . . as if anyone cares, with half Europe run by ex-Fascists! In the end, I was lucky. They agreed to accept my father's farm as payment. I was lucky, yes – but it *killed* my father. That farm – to own his own land: that meant everything to him.'

'Count Malaspino . . .' Charlotte began. She couldn't help herself. 'He told me that San Rocco may have been destroyed by partisans for collaborating with the Germans.'

Procopio sat down as if the puppeteer had once again removed his hands from the strings supporting the marionette's legs. 'The Count told you they were collaborators, did he? OK, collaborators they were!'

Leaving the station, Charlotte stopped to ask Luigi if she might take the songbird.

'Sorry, Signora Penton, the bird is gone.'

'Gone? But I heard it singing when I arrived an hour ago.'

'Maybe the boss get sick of it, I dunno.'

'Could you ask him where he took it, Luigi?'

'Boss stepped out for a few minutes, signora.' Much as Luigi hated the man, he didn't dare tell the nice English lady that at this time in the afternoon his superior's absences were not unheard of, except by the Chief's wife, a woman with a face like a cell door. Nor was the Chief's *presence* unheard of in the bedroom of a slope-heeled little number in one of Urbino's less salubrious suburbs, to whom he was no doubt taking the bird at this very moment. 'I'll ask when he gets back.'

'Donna?' Paolo said to the silent girl opposite. They hadn't spoken since he'd phoned her after the Count's lunch. 'Donna, are you – '

'Well, you can't blame the cops. I mean, that old mute woman sure looked crazy that day at the palace.'

'To lock her away, though . . . that's what they're threatening.' He gave her a moment to consider the consequences of such an action, then asked, 'Will you come with me to see her?'

'I hate hospitals. They smell of piss and pickles.'

This hospital was very beautiful, Paolo told her; more like a museum, with frescoes on the walls that many people travelled miles to see.

'People travel miles to see the incorruptible tongue of Saint Anthony of Padua,' Donna said, 'and when you get close it's just a shrivelled-up black thing surrounded by a lot of gold. Looks pretty corrupt to me.'

She had spent the last three days in bed, watching TV, drifting in and out of sleep. Not sick, but ailing from an unspecified condition, lethargic, her limbs aching as if she had flu. James had refused to return any of her phone calls and she'd had a strange talk from his assistant yesterday, something about contracts, fine print. No *way* Donna was letting James get away with it. She'd phoned the producer in Rome, but he was off at some obscure film festival in an unpronounceable part of Eastern Europe. She'd phoned her dad to see if he understood the legal stuff, but he was fishing, and her mom was at a permanent PTA meeting, no doubt bragging about her Daughter Who Made it Big in Television. Washed up at twenty-one. Donna didn't want to think about it.

Paolo spoke so gently, he was very persuasive. He described how he had hated hospitals too, ever since his grandmother took a long time dying in one, he told Donna that he needed her moral support, he needed someone strong, he wanted to see her, talk to her, he missed her. At last she said, 'Yeah, OK, OK. I'll go with you . . . but if I get there and it seems too much . . . all I'm saying is I'm not promising anything.'

Donna needn't have worried. The hospital was now closed except to clergy and other authorised visitors, and she and Paolo were confronted by a massed crowd waving blurred, hand-coloured postcards of the living Muta. Professor Serafini was outside the front door hectoring the crowd, trying to convince them that 'La Muta' (as they were calling the living mute now) was no saint, no more than a poor sick woman. He also mentioned Galileo and his *Sidereus Nuncius*, of which no one had heard apart from Paolo and a few of the more learned doctors who had gathered on the hospital steps, amused by the gingery little man's ferocious defence of science over superstition.

'You may mount an opposition to lunar mountains,' Serafini shouted, 'just as the Jesuits did with Galileo, but you cannot prove I'm wrong, any more than they could disprove Galileo's telescope, his starry messenger!'

'Now he's Galileo!' joked a postcard vendor who was making a tidy profit out of the mute. 'Quick! Put the professor under house arrest!'

'*Eppur si muove! Eppure si muove!*' shouted Serafini in response. 'If there are to be miracles, why here in Urbino?'

'Why Bethlehem?' called a woman in the crowd.

'What's he on about?' Donna asked Paolo.

'Pretty obscure. Galileo published a pamphlet called "Sidereus Nuncius", "The Starry Messenger", about the earth moving around the stars and not vice versa.'

'But what's that "aypoor see mwohvay" business he keeps repeating?'

'It's what Galileo was rumoured to have said when he was leaving the Inquisition court after recanting all his theories. "Eppur si muove": Nevertheless, it – the earth – does move.' Paolo grinned. 'Although I'm not sure what connection there is to this particular case.'

Donna's memories of Galileo were limited to what a high-school teacher used to describe as the 'Galileo Syndrome', referring to those students who had skipped class the day he taught that the world did not revolve around them. She was thinking of this while Paolo pushed his way through the crowd to enquire about the hospital's closure. On his return he explained that an enterprising photographer had managed to get past security the previous night. Alone in the room with the mute, he had spread her hair across the pillow, pulled back her sheet to remove the sling from her arm and crossed both arms over her breast, a single lily in her hands. His two rolls of film he took to a backstreet printer who retouched the scar on Muta's face caused by the gun wound, thus exaggerating a previously non-existent resemblance to Raphael's mute. 'Nostra Donna da San Rocco' he had added above Muta's head, the gilt letters pushing the price up to 5000 lire a card. Different versions were on sale, because the mute woman's arms, lacking any muscular will to hold such an iconic posture, had been slipping all through the photo shoot, so that by the last frame her hands floated loosely out to the side, palms up, supported on a current of rumpled bedsheet like Millais' drowned Ophelia, a fluid death-slide into madness.

'Five thousand lire!' said Donna. 'Jesus! That's almost five dollars! For a postcard!'

Paolo bought two of these iconic postcards from the vendor, who also offered him a balloon, printed with an image of Raphael's Mute, which many foreign pilgrims had bought in the mistaken belief that it represented the living mute before she had been struck down.

Muta's next authorised visitor had no trouble entering the hospital – discreetly, through a back door not yet discovered by the pilgrims. The nursing sister gestured at the gift he'd brought. 'How thoughtful! But you know she won't hear the little thing's song?'

Muta opened her eyes to find him sitting a few feet away. Immediately the bird began to sing, and in spite of herself, Muta smiled.

'Ah, you like that, do you?' her visitor asked. 'Now, I wonder if you hear it or only sense its song . . .' It made him angry, the way she cowered away from him as he withdrew the bird from its willow cage and stroked it with his thumb, allowing just the beak to poke out. He could feel it struggling impotently in the prison of his hand. 'Such a fragile creature,' he said. He began explaining the fragility of life, how easily bones could be broken or lives ruined by the wrong words. Good people could fall in with the devil, he said, the devil was always looking for converts. Open your mouth and the devilish recruiters could rush in and close forever the path to Righteousness.

She watched his lips moving over his white teeth, the mouth opening and shutting, hissing and whispering.

He pointed to the fresco behind her, to the animals being bathed before sacrifice, and spoke of sacrifices to be made.

The little bird's struggles grew weaker.

He hadn't meant to go so far. The intimacy of death was as much a horror to him as the intimacy of life. When he realised what had happened, he slipped from the room as quietly as he had entered. In the corridor was the sister he'd spoken to earlier. 'There has been an unfortunate accident,' he said. 'I take responsibility for allowing the patient to . . .'

They entered the room together and the sister gasped to see the limp thing lying next to Muta's equally limp hand. Blood on its beak, the neck twisted awkwardly. 'Oh, you wicked, wicked creature!' she cried to Muta. 'To take such a helpless life! Now I will have to call the doctor.'

Muta's visitor left as discreetly as he'd come. The nursing sister picked up the dead bird and carried it into the lane behind the hospital. Poor thing! Too soft-hearted to dispose of it in one of the rubbish bins, the sister was about to bury it under a sprouting hedge of weeds by the back door when she caught sight of a flickering shadow rising above her on the wall. Enormous, it was, and strangely familiar, the silhouette from a grimmer fairy tale. A superstitious woman would have gone inside then and locked the door. But the nursing sister wasn't superstitious. Turning around to see what peculiar combination of wind and weeds and light had played such a trick, she caught sight of the scarred grey animal and opened her mouth wide to scream as the wolf moved its black-rimmed yellow eyes to fix them on her. With an inarticulate half-sound, she dropped the bird on the ground and ran. She was discovered later, sitting in the park at the top of the Via Raffaello, almost speechless with shock.

The nursing sister who took over the post was puzzled by the empty birdcage, which she removed to the lost property office to leave among the piles of one-eyed teddy bears, lost rubber balls, toy cars, umbrellas and dog-eared crime novels. And there, in all the commotion of her busy afternoon, she promptly forgot it.

MIRACLE NUMBER 37

Cracking the Bell

Paolo parked his Lambretta in the Piazza Repubblica and switched off the engine. He was reluctant to move while he could feel the girl's head pressed against his shoulder. She hadn't said a word since they'd left the hospital. 'Would you like a drink?' he asked softly.

Donna swung a long leg off the bike and stood up.

'Donna?'

'Well, you know, it kinda hit me, that postcard of her, the way she was lying all flattened, like she was already dead. The cops didn't have to use so much force. I mean, did they really need the whole entire *weight* of modern police technology, tear gas and all, just to bring down this one old lady? Seems like they could've done a tad more negotiating.' She lifted her face up to the sky so the tears couldn't escape, an actress's trick to stop her mascara from running.

He could see where the black salt trails of earlier tears had dried on her cheeks and they made him want to lick his finger and rub them away. He offered her his handkerchief and she took it and blew her nose hard. 'Come for a drink, Donna. I'm meeting Charlotte before – '

'No . . . I think I'll go for a walk or something.' That's *all* she needed, another sackload of guilt from Sister Charlotte! 'Think stuff over . . .'

Her hair fluttered out against Paolo's cheek as she turned to leave and he raised his hand quickly and let the black strands run through his fingers. He loved the texture and flow of her, but she was always escaping him. 'Donna! Hey, Donna!' he called, just to say her name. 'Meet you around six, in the Repubblica, OK?'

Without looking back at him she raised one hand in acknowledgement and walked away.

Charlotte, seated in the Caffè Repubblica with Paolo, listened to the city bells chiming or tolling six, each one a few seconds out of sync. It was one of the times when youngsters began mysteriously to gather here like sparrows. 'How do you decide on the best café?' she asked Paolo and his friends. 'Location? Clientele? The quality of coffee?'

'This is a very profound question, cara,' replied Paolo, his eyes sparkling. He seemed excited, expectant. 'One of the most profound you have ever asked!' He turned to the girl next to him. 'Maddalena, we must give this serious thought, no?'

The girl, a physics student from the university, smiled back at him, ready for any play he proposed. 'Claro! And we must first eliminate ourselves, of course, knowing that a thing cannot examine itself.'

'Let us take my papa, then.'

'Well, your papa is so much a fan of football, Paolo, that of course he spends all his free time in the Sport Bar, ever since my uncle Pietro installed that large screen.'

For several minutes they tossed the names of relatives and friends into the ether and batted them back and forth as lightly as shuttlecocks, the names matched to certain cafés and allied with quarters of the city, particular football clubs. They talked of their parents' and grandparents' political affiliations, and of other more tenuous connections. They discussed the favoured cafés of the editors of the local newspapers, *Pesaro* and *Corriere Adriatico*, and whether the papers were left wing or right wing or simply indifferent. 'With no wings at all,' said Paolo. It was a question of *campanilismo*, they explained. Loyalty to one's own set of bells.

The game of conversational badminton changed direction with the breeze of departures and arrivals:

Maddalena left, Anna arrived.

Anna left, Fabio arrived.

Then, as if in response to some frequency Charlotte wasn't tuned to, all the young people began to drift away and she was left alone with Paolo, who slouched in the chair beside her, his expression less elated than it had been earlier. Several times he had looked at his watch, but without making a move to leave. 'Are you waiting for someone?' she asked.

'No . . . not really . . .'

His thoughts were clearly not on the spangled, multi-coloured spectacle of the *passeggiata* any more than hers were. He ignored the passing girls who flirted with him – audaciously and silently, or giggling, darting meaningful glances at him while pretending to chatter to their girlfriends. For all the notice he took, they might have been pigeons.

Charlotte laid her hand on his arm. 'Paolo . . .'

'Si, cara?'

'If I wanted to trace some local families who disappeared in the War, where would I start?'

'Why?'

'I think . . . I think perhaps there is a sort of . . . well . . . a cover-up, if that's the right word – about the families from San Rocco.' She smiled. 'Our field of expertise, in other words. Wherever I ask about San Rocco I encounter layer after layer of obfuscation.'

'And I am the expert on removing old varnish, is that it? But what are you trying to find out, cara?'

'I'm not entirely sure – anything to help this mute woman . . . and Procopio, I suppose, in case things go badly for him. The case may not be as clear cut as he imagines, and if he will do nothing to help himself, well . . .'

Paolo had been nodding in agreement, his face thoughtful. 'Maybe in the genealogy department of the university we might look – '

'Oh no, I don't want you involved, Paolo!'

He ignored her protests and continued. 'When I was restoring that portrait last year, the one where the face had been so badly damaged – you remember, I showed the restored version to you? So . . . I tracked down all the living relatives through this office, and also some of the dead ones – there were old photographs, as well. I decided that as there were no other paintings of my subject I would make her look just a little like one of her twentieth-century descendants – '

'Very naughty, Paolo.'

Immediately he assumed an expression of false piety. 'Yes, I know, as you have since taught me. "Subjectivity is one of the worst sins of the old kind of restorer," no?'

She laughed at his solemn mimicry of her early advice to him. 'What about war records, Paolo? . . .'

'Mio nonno, my grandpapa, he is very interested in Urbino's war . . . very *boring* on the subject, to be honest, cara! Personally, it makes me grateful that he refused to move from our former dark and dank old apartment to the shiny new house Papa found in that monstrous melanoma beyond the city walls.'

So the Countess's comment still rankled. 'Could I meet him?'

'He would love it! Come for a drink later – ' He checked his watch again. 'Or now, I suppose, before dinner. Then we have an excuse to leave before he embroils us too much in the past. But be warned: if you ask him a question that takes one second to answer, mio nonno will give you a whole day's worth of answer. Also, his new false teeth are bothering him and between them and his accent, which is very strong, I may have to act as translator.'

Paolo's grandfather lived in a tiny apartment off one of the lanes squeezed up against the city walls behind the Mercatale square, so steep that the road itself had been terraced in shallow cobbled steps, worn over the centuries to a patina as smooth and slick as boiled sweets, like the window seats at the Casa Raffaello. Outside Paolo's grandfather's building a three-wheeled Piaggio truck full of leeks and cauliflowers was parked, taking up most of the narrow passageway, and a skeletal cat shot out from under the truck as Charlotte and Paolo approached. 'Nonno has three tiny rooms on the top floor,' Paolo warned her. 'I stay here when we work late or I drink too much . . . if I have the energy for this climb!' He pulled out an old-fashioned key. 'Can you wait for me outside in the hallway for a minute while I explain to him why you've come? That way we don't waste as much time.'

The 'hallway', with a single shuttered window, was barely large enough to accommodate the two of them. Charlotte had to press herself against the dark stone wall to allow Paolo room to open his grandfather's door. The sound of the key in an old, reluctant lock echoed loudly and she had the feeling of being in the tunnel entrance to a cave rather than an apartment. Even after Paolo entered his grandfather's living-room, half-shutting the door behind him, she could hear everything quite clearly, the old man's querulous voice starting up immediately, his accent rich and thick as potato soup and spiked with many dialect words she didn't understand. 'Who is this Serafini fellow and why is he asking me all these questions about you?'

'Shhh, Nonno, no need to shout,' said Paolo. 'Serafini – he was here?'

'I'm not shouting!' the old man roared. 'And of course he was here! What have I been telling you?'

To give them some semblance of privacy, Charlotte opened the hall's small window and leaned her head out. Two stone gargoyles glowered down at her from the corners of the tall building. The voices inside were still quite audible.

'What did you tell him, Grandfather?'

'Nothing! I told him nothing!' the old man squawked. 'Stranger like him – you think I tell him anything? What business is it of his, the paintbrushes and gesso and other things I am not supposed to mention even to my capitalist of a son, that you keep here and how much time you spend . . . And then all these dates . . . What is he on about with all these dates of miracles and does my apartment back onto the Oratory?

. . . Well, naturally it does, I told him. This used to be the curator's house . . . and am I not the one who sells tickets to the Oratory on Tuesdays?'

'You didn't mention Fabio, Nonno?'

Charlotte leaned further out the window, trying not to hear the exchange between Paolo and his grandfather.

'You think I am going senile? Of course not! Why should I tell this man who sleeps here and who doesn't and which nights and was it before or after these miracles I do not believe in? I don't know this man! He is no friend of mine, to be asking such questions and expecting answers.'

The dormer window was tucked right up underneath the roof adjoining the Oratory of St John the Baptist, San Giovanni Battista. From here Charlotte could have reached out and touched its pantiles. This was the Oratory where the first instance of painted wounds beginning to bleed had been reported weeks ago – on the fresco of San Sebastian. She leaned out further to catch a glimpse of the steep patch of greenery rising on the hill beyond the Oratory. A stretch of adjoining wall marked the edge of the public park dedicated to the Resistance. A slim, fit person could easily climb out this window and into the Oratory's, or stroll along the rooftops and from there to the city walls. Each feature seemed to grow out of another organically, one supporting the next in a symbiotic relationship not attributable to architects or builders. Just as Procopio had described San Rocco.

'The Parco della Resistenza.' Paolo's voice startled Charlotte and she pulled her head back inside like a snail withdrawing into its shell.

'That's why Nonno won't leave this dump. Because he was in the Resistance, as he will not fail to tell you in detail, I'm afraid.'

The old man, his dry walnut of a face half hidden behind a striped wool scarf, was waiting impatiently for them in a tiny room where he fitted as snugly as a doll in a glass display case. On the table next to him was a bottle of the violent pink liqueur Charlotte had drunk with Procopio. With forced enthusiasm she accepted a glass, as she did the old man's lengthy discourse on its benefits to her health. She saw it as the price she had to pay for making withdrawals from his bank of memories.

An album of treasured war photos appeared, and for the next half-hour Charlotte nodded and smiled her way through postcards from the old man's comrades who had emigrated to America, Canada, Britain. She admired autographed beer mats from a pub in Edinburgh, she read the football results of a team in Chicago run by a former Urbino Communist.

'The brother of Franco at the Bar Raffaello, you know him?' shouted the old man.

Charlotte nodded, 'Franco, yes, I know him, in a way.'

'Different, the football they play in America – did you know *that*, signora?'

'My esteemed English colleague has a *very important meeting*, Nonno!' Paolo said impatiently. 'She hasn't come here to spend the night with your dead comrades!'

Progress was slow, even with Paolo hurrying the stories along. His grandfather cackled merrily at the suggestion that Charlotte might have anything better to do, while he continued to open album after album. He had been an ardent Communist, he told her. Still was, a claim that bastard mayor Primo couldn't make! At this point she was treated to a long segue into recent Urbino politics, before Paolo led his grandfather onto the subject of San Rocco. 'San Rocco is a long way from here!' the old man said warily. 'This lady told me she was interested in the War in Urbino.'

'She is, Nonno, but . . .'

Paolo cocked a black eyebrow at Charlotte. She explained that her interests also concerned a San Rocco woman who had worked at the Ducal Palace. 'At least, she *might* be from San Rocco, she's lived there for many years.'

'You mean Muta, this madwoman our idiot Police Chief has arrested?'

Even Paolo looked surprised. 'You know her, Nonno?'

'Everyone knows of her!'

'*Of* her, yes . . . But did you know her personally – when she was young, I mean?' asked Charlotte. 'Her family?' Could it be this easy?

'Her, no. But everyone is saying she has a connection with the Balducci family and their cousins, the families from San Rocco, yes?'

'The Balducci family, yes,' repeated Charlotte.

'One week they were here in town selling their products, the next they weren't, and never came again. People went to San Rocco and found all that mess.'

'And have you any idea what happened to them? Were they killed?'

'Many ideas, signora,' he said, ignoring half her question. 'You know there was strong resistance to Fascism in that valley?' Many of the people in the San Rocco valley were anarchists, dissidents, Communists, he told her, although their politics would not have been approved by old Stalin, for their idea of Communism was not to shoot or be shot at, it was connected with sharing their lettuces and beans and drinking homemade wine and playing music with friends.

'Why that valley in particular?' asked Charlotte.

'Not in particular – this was true all over Italy. In those days when we were less mobile, when there were not so many cars, it was not unusual to have pockets of Fascism over here and pockets of anarchists and Communist partisans over there. Our landscape lends itself to the isolation of ideals in this way.'

'Skip the ideals, Nonno.' Paolo's tone was affectionate, and the old man's reply was no more than a good-humoured scowl.

'Were Enrico and Cesare Balducci Communist partisans?' Charlotte asked.

'Not Communists. This I know because I tried to recruit them! But partisans . . . well, I would call them dissenters, more. They stood out, they joined no man's group. They used to come in here selling their cheeses and Teodoro Mazzini's hams – '

'Mazzini . . . any relation to Francesco Procopio? Isn't he a Mazzini?'

'His father. Sheep and goats and pigs were all their land was good for. Terrible wine, sour as that communion swill, but very good cheeses Balducci made, and Mazzini's hams were famous . . . but then he was from Norcia, and the Norcini are famous for the skills with the knife.'

'So I've heard,' said Charlotte. 'Did they bring their families?'

'Of course! Without sons, there would be no one to carry the hams.'

'No daughters?'

Who remembered daughters, unless they were pretty?

She tried a different thread. 'Paolo tells me you were one of the leading lights in the Federaterra, the rural trade union . . .'

He smiled proudly. 'Yes! Sure! We built it up! We – the Communists!' He slapped his chest with an open palm. 'Built it from bases we established during the Resistance. Always the history books talk about the French, but we resisted too!' For a moment the old man looked less defenceless, more capable of resistance. 'We used to go from farmhouse to farmhouse organising meetings.' Subverting *La Veglia*, he said, using it as a cover. His eyes filled with tears. 'Poor Enrico! He was one of those who never learned that men can be right and good and still be beaten. He wanted to bring down all the palaces . . .'

'Then there would be nothing but ruins,' responded Paolo. 'All the better for restorers like me!'

'We were not afraid of ruins, not us! We who had always lived in slums and holes in the wall, we could manage, because we were going to inherit the earth, we carried a new world in our hearts!' Paolo rolled his eyes, but the old man didn't notice; he was young again. 'We are the ones who built these palaces brick by brick – we could have built them again or new ones to take their place! That is what Durrutti said!'

For a few minutes he muttered incomprehensibly to himself before his grandson brought him back to the present with a sharp, 'Nonno!'

'Maybe it is better Enrico disappeared,' the old man continued, 'because in the end, all that work he and I did to get back the land, it was all for nothing! Look at poor Francesco

Mazzini, Teodoro's son! Calls himself Procopio now. Same land as Enrico's and good only for pigs! Maybe the old Count knew all along, that's why he gave in to their demands . . .'

'The old Count?'

'Malaspino's father – a Fascist bastard, canny as a Tuscan! Look how he became such a big ally with the Brits and Yanks after the War! Doing their dirty work, helping rebuild Europe without the Communists.'

'I'm not quite clear, signor. What has the old Count got to do with Enrico Balducci and the Mazzinis? What demands did he grant?'

'He owned the land they cropped, of course! What else have I been telling you! That is what we were fighting! All this land – the Marches, Umbria, Tuscany,' he said, sweeping his arm in a gesture that transcended his own walls and tumbled the palaces and oratorios and cathedrals of Urbino so she could have a clear view. 'All this land was share-cropped.'

Barely taking in his words, Charlotte said, 'So . . . the Balduccis were fighting against the old Count's interests.'

'But the land was no good, I tell you! Too hard, too steep.' Again his parchment-yellow eyes filled with tears. 'When I think of how we fought to get the land – and then the younger generation are not prepared to work it. My own son, he had to start this painted pottery business.'

'That must be where Paolo got his artistic skills, signor.'

'Now we have no jobs for men, we are here to serve the tourists only.'

He used a dialect word Charlotte didn't understand. She looked to Paolo, who whispered that it was a local vulgarity. 'He means something like Italians are tame bulls servicing the tourist cow.'

'What's that?' the old man shouted. 'What are you saying, boy?'

'Translating your obscenity, Nonno.' Paolo rolled his eyes and tapped his watch. 'Is that the best you can do, Nonno? No murder and intrigue?'

His grandfather wasn't listening. 'All the young men went to the cities and the old men were left in charge of the rocks and the dirt.'

'About Francesco Procopio, Nonno: he's been arrested because he helped this mute woman and he will say nothing to defend himself – '

'Poor Francesco. He was a good comrade once, but he has given up, he has lost the battle.' Paolo's grandfather shrugged and thrust his tiny, wrinkled face towards Charlotte. 'For this will be the last great battle, signora, make no mistake! The battle between those of us who believe – '

'Don't start,' said Paolo.

'I speak of those who have faith that the world can be made a better place and those who do not, like you!'

'The signora is a big fan of mine, Nonno!'

A reluctant smile lifted his grandfather's mouth. 'But he is so cynical, signora – about *everything*! Like the rest of his generation.'

'Surely at his age, signor, you too were cynical . . . '

'At least we voted! We had faith things could be changed! This one . . . ' He gave Paolo a fond but reasonably hard shove. 'He believes in *nothing*!'

'Did you get anything out of that history lesson, Charlotte?'

'A confirmation of one name . . . and perhaps a reason to talk to Count Malaspino again . . . although I don't see . . . It might be helpful if you could . . . ' She hesitated, worried about involving him further. Worried, as well, for herself. She'd certainly had enough warnings against interfering. Yet there was a stubborn side to her that resisted the attempts that had been made to keep this story – whatever it was – a secret, to hide this mute woman away and stop her from offending the tourists, the rich-and-smug, the happily-married-with-two-children. My tough little soldier-father's side, Charlotte thought. Usually she limited her stubbornness to her work, not giving up until a restoration was as complete as she could make it, regardless of time or economic constraints. It is true what

Procopio said about me, she thought, I am an incurable restorer.

'Tell me, Charlotte! You are looking so mysterious!'

'Could you get your grandfather to write down all the names he remembers from the group that included Enrico Balducci and Teodoro Mazzini? If he doesn't remember, perhaps he has friends who do. And I will go to the university to see if there are any records of the families who lived in San Rocco at the time it was destroyed.'

'You want me to ask around the cafés, see what I can find out, who's still alive from that time? The old men are more likely to talk to me than they are to you. The old Commies, at least. Because of my grandfather.'

'Would you? But . . . be discreet. Don't ask anything that . . . can get you or . . . Procopio into trouble . . . *more* trouble.'

MIRACLE NUMBER 38

A Recipe for Victoria Sandwich

To compile a record of Urbino's war Charlotte went first to the university geneaology department and then to the public archives. Sifting through photos of handsome men and women who had betrayed their closest friends and of others who had died to save perfect strangers, she began to wonder what betrayal looked like. How would you paint it? Is it written on a face?

She came across many photos and news stories relating to Count Malaspino's father, a man whose creamy, unsmiling visage made her think of her lunch at the Villa Rosa, the buildings and food designed to look like anything except what they were. 'The old Count' had always been a chameleon, it seemed, a man who changed colours to fit the political environment. As a minor politico in the Marches throughout the fifties and sixties he had been quoted regularly in the local papers, but the language of politics he and other Italian politicians spoke, like that of the Catholic Church from which it largely derived, was a coded form of communication designed for translation largely by fellow practitioners. To break through the infinity of escape clauses and trap-doors built into this impenetrable jargon required a code-book missing from the files. The British and Americans bleated about their desire for political clarity, for truth and reconciliation, but clarification was just a method of generating even more confusion, Charlotte found. Real agreements made by the Allies (immunity in exchange for information from Fascists like the old Count) were often unstated, unrecorded. Even so, she managed to piece together enough to feel a great sense of disillusionment. While somewhere in the back of her mind she *must* have known that Britain's and America's objectives in the immediate aftermath of World War II had not been to eradicate Fascists from Italy, but rather to prevent another revolution by red shirts in the wake of black, the extent to which this had been true was still a shock. As was the extent to which she had ignored Italy's present for so long and kept her head buried firmly in the sand of Italian art and culture from four hundred years ago.

'La carta canta,' said Paolo when she showed him the photocopies of her meagre pickings.

'Paper sings?' Charlotte wasn't convinced. The only concrete evidence she'd found was a note to the effect that the man recommended by the Allies to investigate the 'incident' at San Rocco had been the old Count himself.

'Something my papa told me years ago. Malaspino's father should have made sure he left no traces.'

'He left very little. Nothing to indicate there was anything dishonourable about his investigation.' She regarded her colleague's bright face with interest. There was something different about him, more alive. 'Paolo, what is it? Have you had any more luck than I?'

Drifting dreams, cobwebs of the past in the corners of Nonno's cluttered mind: that's how Paolo had always viewed the war stories he had half-listened to for years. They were no more Paolo's than were the paintings and statues he restored – until he began searching for a key to unlock San Rocco's mystery. Escorting Nonno from one café full of veterans to another, hearing other voices speaking the roles his grandfather had created, Paolo found that the theatre of war in Italy acquired substance for the first time, its characters gained weight and volume and colour. Thin, moustachioed old men describing their lovers, the young women who wore ankle socks because there was no money for stockings, and carried guns over their shoulders instead of handbags. No need to diet in those days – most of them were hungry, if not actually starving.

'Food was short because of the ammassi, the state granaries,' one man explained. 'We were forced to give away our grain.'

'There was little enough. The Germans left our fields full of mines.'

'Yet the harvest had to be brought in if we weren't to starve.'

'We did what we could, but men in power saw to it that there was barely enough for us, let alone for the wanderers.'

'The wanderers?' Paolo asked. A word here, a phrase there, he was collecting traces of the original picture.

'She might have been one of them, this mute,' said a man who had not yet spoken. The wanderers, he explained to Paolo, were what they'd called the gypsies, hawkers and beggars, the rag-and-bone men and fleeing Jews, those Italian men who refused the Fascist call-up of 8 September 1944 – as well as the 70,000 POWs at large in Italy, nearly half of whom escaped with the help of men and women like these friends of Nonno's. All those to whom the share-croppers gave a bed in their hayloft, some bread, oil. 'In return for the news, the *real* news,' said a man in the Bar Raffaello. 'When politicians and bankers and advertising men control the news, who hears the truth?'

'She might have been the child of casanolenti like our mayor,' said a man in the Sport Bar. 'They had no land, no house, unlike us mezzadri.'

The old men gave Paolo not only a sense of his own history, but the gift of their rich antique dialect, untempered even now by television. Often his grandfather had to translate for him: the blood-thinning wind from the Apennines that shivered San Rocco's bells they knew as *bora*, *buriana*, *barburana*, not *tramontana*, as Paolo did. Some of them, great-grandfathers from the Urbino region, dropped the vowels at the end of words, twisting their language into something more like French or Spanish. Secrets were inherent in the language, it retained archaic meanings, double meanings, so that at first when Paolo heard someone say, 'He was no villain, the one who did for San Rocco!' he thought the speaker approved of whatever had happened. But no. By *el vilèn* ('*il villano*', translated Nonno) the man meant 'villain' in the old way – peasant, countryman, rustic.

He was no *peasant*, the man who did for San Rocco.

'It's not enough,' Charlotte said. 'The hearing is the day after tomorrow.'

'We could spend tomorrow talking to – '

'What could we do in a day, Paolo? By the end of this day's work all we have accomplished is to narrow down the list of San Rocco's inhabitants – and no Gabriella . . .'

'Which proves nothing. Many people in those remote valleys didn't bother to register births. I still want to question the mayor again. His uncle worked on a farm near San Rocco.'

'You believe the mayor knows anything about what happened?'

'I think so, but nothing he'll admit. He's very loyal to Urbino. Doesn't want its reputation tarnished.'

'So we have reached a dead end.'

Charlotte gave up on sleep, and pulling on the pair of thick wool socks she wore instead of slippers, she wrapped herself in her quilted dressing-gown to sit at her desk with a cup of chamomile tea, trying to concentrate on Paolo's detailed photographs of the damaged Raphael.

La Muta's scar was clearly visible again. Their work to conceal the pentimento had been torn away, ripped apart, the damage worse now than it had been before they started. In places there was nothing left of the canvas, let alone the portrait. If the picture was released for restoration and she did what the city council wanted, there would be nothing left of Raphael, nothing left of the truth, just one layer of Charlotte's own brushstrokes after another, one lie after another. Better simply to leave the painting and seal it behind glass, all the wounds visible. Now *I'm* guilty of the same superstitious nonsense as Anna, she thought irritably. This place is turning me into the worst sort of romantic fool.

She began to write: 'These days, with the wide availablility of such godsends as computers, photography, spectrum technology and synthetic thermoplastic adhesives, we like to think that the "science" of contemporary restoration is above suspicion. Science offers the ultimate truth, we believe; the practice of Renaissance "creative" intervention is beneath us. Yet in restoring this Raphael I have continued in a deception . . .'

She stopped. Her wooden shutters were open and the moon, rising like a great bubble above the tiled roof outside, had thrown a wedge of silver across the postcard of the living mute Paolo had given her. She forced her eyes away, crumpled up what she had written and began a new page: 'The most one can hope for from "conservation" is to protect a work of art from further decay. "Restoration" is a misleading term implying the return to an imagined "perfect" condition. No such perfection is possible, of course, yet there must be a certain honesty before . . .'

Again she stopped and her eyes drifted towards the postcard of Muta posed like a sacrificial victim. We have come so close, Charlotte thought. All I want is for someone to tell me the truth, tell me what really happened at San Rocco. I need to hear it admitted out loud. Why Muta hated the Count or the Raphael enough to perpetrate this savage act against a work of art. I want to hear from the Count if he knows his father was responsible for investigating the San Rocco incident. And if he does, how much *more* does he know . . . and why would he tell me? A thought flicked across the recesses of her mind: *Because I have something on him*. Of course she would never dream of making the story public! But the little devil whispered, *You wouldn't have to . . .*

One more phone-call, she thought. Tomorrow I will make one more call and then it's finished. Picking up her pen again she wrote: 'There can be no reconciliation, no restoration, without first revealing the truth. Otherwise we are no better than dishonest morticians painting smiles on dead faces.'

'Some English,' Paolo's mother said, passing him the phone later that night. 'Must be crazy, ringing at this time. *Sounds* crazy.' She shrugged and rolled her eyes. 'Now my son is hanging around with crazy women. It's not enough he has to be best friends with some fellow can't even get a job, has to *beg*, oh excuse me, *work* as a living statue, what's the difference between that and begging is what I want to know, but nobody tells me, your father, does he tell me? Nobody tells me anything, my own son, who I raised . . .' She stalked off down the corridor, still talking.

It wasn't like Charlotte to call him at home, especially not after midnight. She must have changed her mind, or something had gone very wrong. 'Sorry, my mother doesn't speak much English . . . Hello? What's – '

The voice, slightly hysterical, cut him off. 'The thing is, I know all you guys think it's like somehow *my* fault, like maybe I told somebody, blabbed the *Big Fucking Secret*, but it's not like that, it's not anyone I told or – '

'Donna –'

' . . . because the only person I . . . anyway, nobody I told would be interested in, like, *arresting* this mute woman and I'm *sorry* – '

'Donna – '

' . . . I'm really *sorry*, she looked awful and I would never, I didn't mean to and I'm going to make it up to you, I've got an idea and – '

'Donna, it's all right, no one thinks any of this is your fault.'

'Oh yeah, *sure*! You're telling me Sister Charlotte hasn't, like, dropped a few fucking *hints* that – '

'No, Charlotte said nothing about you.' He could hear the girl breathing hard and the hesitations as tears threatened to take over. 'Donna . . . please . . . Let me come over.'

'Yeah, well, I don't know.'

'I'm coming right away.'

'You look tired, Paolo,' his grandfather said the next morning. They were on their way to the Bar Raffaello to talk once more to the bartender, an old friend from the War. 'Tired and – '

'Happy,' said Paolo, forestalling a lecture. 'I'm happy to be out with you on such a beautiful morning.'

The old man made a derisive noise, rightly guessing that the cause of his grandson's good humour lay elsewhere.

Donna woke smiling. She eased onto her belly to occupy the place in her bed only recently vacated by Paolo. So *warm*! She pressed her pelvis into the sheet, rolling her hips lazily and breathing in the smell of him on the pillow. His smell permeating her skin as well. Not wanting to let go of the night, she opened her eyes reluctantly and read a note on the chair next to her: '6 p.m. tonight. Remember your promise!' To meet Charlotte: Donna regretted it already. What could she possibly say to the woman? Everything had seemed much simpler with Paolo stroking her hair and calling her his *bella bambina*, his *angelina*, his brave, beautiful girl. Donna smiled again at some of the other surprising new vocabulary she had learned in the night, along with all the stories they'd exchanged. She knew now why Paolo had been paying off that man at the circus. Confessions offered: you tell me this, I'll tell you that. Paolo already knew things about her that she couldn't believe. 'How do you know I talked to Seguita?'

'Fabio saw you.'

'Where? What do you mean?'

'In and out of the bishop's palace . . . Fabio's always around, you know. People get so used to seeing him they forget he's not a real statue.'

Paolo forgiving her everything, *anything*. He'd promised that Charlotte too would forgive, but Donna was less convinced. Charlotte had a steely English side to her. There must be *something* I can do to set things straight, Donna thought. She wanted to prove to Paolo that his faith in her was justified. She wanted his eyes to widen at her daring. She wanted him to kiss her again and call her his brave, courageous girl. A week, even a few days ago, she would have been thinking of her career, of impressing her parents or James. *James* . . . Had James told anyone outside the crew that he was letting her go? If not, she had a better weapon than Paolo's or Charlotte's. Who was to know that James had fired her or, if they *did* know, that she wouldn't take the story elsewhere, to a newspaper or radio station where it could do equal damage?

'You worry yourself about nothing,' said the old military man. 'What does he have to go on, this so-called "honest" magistrate the mayor has found? How many magistrates have you known that you couldn't turn?'

'That was the old days, Lorenzi,' said Grandfather with a sigh of nostalgia. 'Times are changing.'

'So who are these witnesses, then? One of them, if she *is* one of them, hasn't spoken in fifty years. One is a half-wit. Two know they are dead meat if they speak.'

'And one of them,' finished the eldest, 'one of them can't shut up to save her life. If she has talked so freely to Monsignor Seguita, who else will she talk to? What else does she know?'

Paolo didn't appear at the palace until just after four. Worn out but pleased with himself, he marched past the guard and Anna directly to Charlotte. 'Read this!' he said. 'It's not much, but it's a start, something to make the magistrate listen.'

Charlotte scanned his brief notes and the photocopies of old newspaper articles. 'How did you find out about this?'

The boy shrugged, his eyes evasive. 'Professor Serafini. We made a deal. I traded him some information he wanted for some information I wanted. Franco put me onto him – Franco, at the

Bar Raffaello. They're distantly related. Both families are from Carpegna and Franco told me they had something to do with the San Rocco people during the War.'

'Does Serafini know anything about Muta, who she is?'

'No, but if she is from San Rocco, then you can see how there might be a connection between her and the Raphael.' He took the clippings back.

'It's pretty tenuous, Paolo.'

'But it's something! Maybe we can turn the tables on whoever is putting pressure on Procopio to keep quiet. Maybe we can get Procopio as one of the penitenti instead of whoever the cops have got. I'd like to show it to Procopio, give him another chance to tell us what he knows.'

'Let me.'

Paolo performed a melodramatic double take. 'Let *you*, signora? Let *you*?' At Charlotte's deep blush, he added softly, 'You like him, don't you?'

'It has nothing to do with liking him, Paolo, I – '

'No, I'm sure, nothing at all.' He patted her on the shoulder and handed her the clippings again. 'Good luck, cara. But you know what my sister says about Italian men? My older sister who married the American and lives now somewhere unpronounceable like Tallahassee? She tells her girlfriends: Italian men are very charming, they love women. Do whatever you like with Italian men – and she means *everything*, *cara*! Whatever you like . . . except marry one.' At Charlotte's protests his grin widened and he nodded agreeably, not believing her for an instant.

'Give me some good news, Charlotte!' said Procopio, pushing Paolo's notes away from him with barely a glance. 'Not this old stuff.'

'You knew about the story already?'

He shrugged, his big fleshy face registering disinterest. 'What difference does it make?'

'But . . . it could explain all those postcards Muta kept.'

He grabbed the pages and slapped them on the prison table

for emphasis. 'If you imagine this is the sum of her story, you are dangerously mistaken. How did Malaspino take it when you mentioned it to him on the phone?'

'He was . . . non-committal.'

Procopio laughed. 'Me too, I'm non-committal. A good, safe way to be. Keep your head down, work hard, eat well.'

'But you might as well be an animal if that's all – '

'It's the kind of animal I am, Charlotte.'

She didn't believe him. Those antique cookbooks he'd collected, surely they were evidence of a longing for something beyond the merely physical. After all, who could possibly need a thousand recipes for pasta, a food designed to level everyone to a childlike state of playful mess?

'A good life is the best revenge, that's my motto these days,' Procopio went on, as if deliberately refuting her internal argument. 'It's fine for you to take up this crusade for a while. When the hearing is over you can go home to whatever life you have back in London, full of art and books and . . . whatever you big-city people do to fill your days. But I will still be here. This is my place, my country, my history. I can't walk away.'

'You're wrong!' she burst out. 'I can't walk away from here unchanged, not after what I've seen. You can't know what I feel . . .' She faltered, not sure where the sentence was leading.

'*What*, Charlotte, *what* do you feel?'

'I feel . . .' She felt that for years, ever since accepting the first of John's 'little flings', she had been shutting off her feelings, biting her tongue to avoid expressing what she really thought, extinguishing her *self*, the smiling, open self she could see in old photos. Not much left of that Charlotte, no more than a slight impression in the sand, a process of fossilisation that should have been completed by Muta's arrest. Instead she felt peeled and raw. Yet however painful it was to have her feelings so close to the surface again, she couldn't face returning to London, reversing the process.

'I don't know if it's you who's been pulling strings, Charlotte, but if so, then you must be determined to get me killed.'

'Oh no, I – '

'I've got the cops pulling me one way, insisting on silence, and now this magistrate Primo's found is pulling the other. Thanks to him and that *maledetto* video your friend James took, it looks like I'm gonna get called into this hearing with Muta after all, forced to make a statement about how crazy I think she is.'

'But she's not crazy, is she? Or she wasn't until I . . .'

'Give me some good news, Charlotte,' said Procopio softly, letting her off the hook. 'I need some good news. Tell me what Cosimo said about my plans for the agricultural show. He liked them?'

She sighed, both relieved and disturbed by his change of subject. 'He worries that the cake base won't hold the weight of the edible bridge you planned . . . Actually, I think he's right. Sponge cake hasn't the correct density. If you must have an edible bridge, perhaps an almond-based – '

'You know about cakes, Charlotte?'

'Not really . . . Well, yes, I suppose I used to be quite a dab hand, although . . . I haven't had much opportunity lately.' Curiously, it was one of the things she missed most about her marriage, having someone to bake for. 'My mother was a countrywoman from the Yorkshire Dales who thought it important for every girl to know how to make a good pie crust and a proper Victoria sandwich.'

'A Victoria sandwich! Very regal.'

Charlotted smiled. 'Not really, just a butter sponge layered with jam.'

'What did you love so much about baking, Charlotte?'

'The precision, I suppose, the rhythm and the measuring, knowing there was a right and wrong way to do it.'

'Like your work.'

'Oh no! Much more ephemeral. Cakes get eaten, after all, but pictures endure, with a little care.'

'So do the people you fed the cakes.'

'I suppose so, I've never thought of it in that way.' She laughed. What a strange conversation to be having! Paolo was right, though, she liked this man. She liked his earthy humour and his solid red-brown bulk, also grounded in the earth, so different from John's city whiteness. Procopio seemed secure, like a brick farmhouse with reliable foundations.

'Me too, I like the precision,' he said. 'What about the smell of baking? Good, yes?'

'Oh yes – the smells of baking biscuits and cakes are lovely!'

He studied her. 'You have a nice face, Charlotte. Not pretty, exactly, but a good clean face with all the honest bones showing.'

'Oh . . .' She blushed. 'Thank you . . . well . . .' She looked at her watch and started to gather up Paolo's notes. Procopio moved his hands to enclose hers and she noticed how white the old scars circling his wrists stood out against the recent bruises. 'You have cold fingers,' he said. 'Good for pastry, not bread.' A surge of emotion filled her. The warmth of his big hands made her want to lower her head onto the table and give in. She understood, not for the first time, what it meant for a heart to feel heavy, although in this case her heart was not weighted with loss, as it had been after John left her; this time it was heavy with the arrival of some bittersweet presence, something new.

'I'm sorry, Charlotte. If you came here looking for a hero, I'm not it. I'd like to be a hero, but no one can get aurum in stercore . . . no gold from shit.' He squeezed her hands once more between his and then stood up. 'In bocca al lupo, cara, in bocca al lupo.' *In the mouth of the wolf*. The old expression was as close as he dared get to wishing her luck.

MIRACLE NUMBER 39

A Book of Hours

'Tell me again what exactly you are threatening to do with this so-called "evidence", Signorina Ricco?'

On her elegant ringed fingers the German woman counted off Donna's list of accusations: 'You've told me about the destruction of a village that may have been investigated by my husband's father. You've told me the people of that village were share-croppers of his and may have been Communists, partisans, agitators – common enough at the time, I assure you. Has it occurred to you that perhaps they were simply deserters, men who refused to fight for their country? In which case, all my husband's father had to do was to report them and they would have been arrested. And as for this . . . what was it you said? Something about villains "doing" for San Rocco? Excuse me, *not* villains, isn't that it? I think your Italian is not really up to coping with the local dialect.'

Thrown by the Countess's steely composure, Donna decided that her own memory for lines had obviously misled her – or Paolo had. This case was not as strong as it had seemed last night in bed. 'There must be some reason the mute attacked the Count!' she burst out.

The Countess raised her shoulders in a gesture of indifference. 'Even granting that it was my husband she attacked and not the Raphael, as everyone else claims, how does this reflect on Dado?'

'So you don't care if James broadcasts the stuff about the old Count, then?' said Donna desperately.

'I have little respect for the television networks,' the

Countess replied in a level voice, 'but enough to know that James wouldn't risk a lawsuit by making any accusations founded on mere conjecture.'

Count Malaspino appeared in the doorway. With a small apologetic laugh his wife filled him in on the reason for this surprise visit. 'My *dear* Donna,' he said, looking genuinely concerned, 'I do understand that you were hurt by our . . . encounter . . . but this isn't the way to resolve it.'

'Fuck you!' she said. 'It isn't about that!' Although it was, of course, and for all her bravado, she was close to tears. In her mind, the scene had played quite differently: she had presented Paolo's information, the Countess had turned as white as she had that first night, the Count had blurted out his guilty secret (whatever it was) and – hey presto! – Donna got her self-respect back. She saw now that she had come here under-rehearsed and failed the audition once again.

The final humiliation was having the Countess bring her a cup of tea. 'One of my husband's special herbal tisanes. Very soothing.'

'I'll get my driver – ' the Count began.

Donna slammed the cup down on their glass table. 'Don't bother! I came in a taxi, I can leave in it. He's waiting outside.'

'You OK, signorina?' asked the driver as they swung away between the dark prison stripes of cypress.

'I'm fine,' Donna said. She could just *hear* the Count on the phone to James the instant she'd left. What a dope she'd look! *More* of a dope! I *can't* go back and face Charlotte, she thought, I just *can't*! 'There's supposed to be a ruined village with a church called San Rocco – d'you know where it is? In a valley somewhere near here?'

The driver nodded. 'Sure, I know it. A few miles offa road to Urbania.'

'Can you take me there?'

'Bad road, Signorina, white road, all gravel and dust. I don' like takin' my car.'

Donna reached in her handbag and drew out a wad of cash. 'I'll pay you . . . double?'

The Count watched his wife, to whom he had years ago confessed a highly edited version of his part in the San Rocco incident. 'You were right, my darling. James wouldn't dream of repeating her allegations.'

His wife lit a cigarette and crossed her arms tightly over her breasts as if to prevent any feminine sympathy escaping. 'Not on *television*.'

'Then . . . what's wrong, my dear?'

'First Charlotte Penton on the phone and now this little tart – '

'I told you I dealt with Signora Penton perfectly satisfactorily, Greta. I misjudged the situation with her originally, but now – '

'There have been too many slips like that recently, Dado.'

'I know, my dear, I'm sorry. I'm . . . weak. But Charlotte Penton would never dream of – '

'Perhaps not – or not as you imagine – but *this* one? This little tart of yours strikes me as one who could and *will* go too far, regardless of the consequences. We have had already some evidence of this, no? Whatever her morals, she is very tough, she has courage – and a very deep anger.'

'I don't think – '

'You haven't told me *everything* about that night at San Rocco, have you, Dado?'

'Almost everything, my dear. You must leave me a few secrets.'

She blew a curl of smoke into the air. 'No, Dado, I think you'd better finish the story.'

He placed his hands against her cheeks and stared into the cool blue eyes he admired. They stared back at him, unmoved. 'You used to say it was better not to know too much, Greta . . . about your father, I believe . . .'

'That's who I'm thinking of – or my family, at least. My brothers and I have worked hard to erase the past. They have a lot of investors – and *investments*, as you should know.'

'I am well aware that it is your brothers' money which has kept me going until – '

'My brothers and their German associates wouldn't like to be made to look as if they had been condoning anything to do with war crimes . . . or any other kind of crimes – especially more recent ones.'

'No, no, of course not. Business must at least give the *appearance* of having the purest of intentions.' With an effort he tried to suppress the irony in his voice. 'However, it's unlikely that this story will – '

'I come from a small town in Germany, Dado. Never underestimate the power of gossip in a small town. Have you seen this?' From her pocket she withdrew a piece of paper and unfolded it to show him the words printed there. 'Copies were to be found all over Urbino when I went into town this morning – in Italian as well. Rumour has it that the mayor's wife and her Communist friends are responsible, with the translation efforts of our friend Charlotte Penton.'

Her husband took the cheaply printed notice and read:

- We, women of Urbino, pledge not to turn blind eyes to current malpractices, lending them consent simply because *cosi fan tutte* – 'that's how the world is'.
- We pledge to renounce any privileges which could derive from contacts and help of a clientelistic or mafioso type.
- We pledge to recognise justice for all as a value superior to our own individual interests.
- We pledge not to forget the people of San Rocco and all those who have suffered for us in the fight against injustice, and to remember them as if they were members of our own families who died for us.

The Count's eyes met his wife's. 'But this is no more than a second-rate version of the pledge made by those mourners at the funeral of Falcone and his bodyguards in Palermo last year. Except in Palermo the pledge read "not to forget Giovanni

Falcone and all those who have died in the fight against the Mafia". This is nothing, Greta. I have nothing to do with the Mafia – '

'This is not nothing, Dado!' she cut him off. 'There were forty thousand mourners at that funeral in Palermo. How many will there be here? People are joining forces. This is not nothing, it's the continuation of a situation you should have faced up to years ago. Now tell me exactly what it is we are fighting.'

He hesitated. She was not just the holder of the purse-strings, his arbitrator of taste, she was the one who had given him back whatever slender reason he had to live. Without her he was nothing. She was his guiding star, he thought, observing how her eyes retained their chilly brilliance almost undimmed all through the tragedy he proceeded to relate. Sometimes he spoke in Italian, occasionally in German. He still couldn't bring himself to tell her everything, but he made references to Dante's *Inferno*, literary allusions standing in for truth, because for him it was not possible to speak directly or completely of that incident. He felt separate from it, as if the whole thing had happened to another person and he had been no more than a witness. Guilt had eaten its way out of him over the years like a fat worm in a bag of grain.

'That's all?' she asked when he finished. 'That's the last of it?'

Not all, he thought, but enough.

'It's going to come out, one way or another, Dado.'

'Procopio won't talk . . . you heard what that girl – '

'Someone will. Things have gone too far.'

'We could go away again, Greta.' But even as he made the suggestion he read a negative in her eyes. 'I could speak to the magistrate, ring him up now. He might believe – '

'No, Dado. It would look as if I had known all along, as if I had condoned your actions and your father's. My brothers went through enough with Papa. This is one war atrocity that is *not* going to be blamed on the Germans. It has to be public, your confession.'

She lit another cigarette, considered the options. 'Better you repent now and admit it, before the press force you. Look at what has been happening in Milan – at least those who confess willingly can get it over with. No, when you go to this mute woman's hearing tomorrow, you must explain everything, just as you did to me . . . and then there's a chance people will forgive. You were a boy, after all . . .' Her mouth twisted bitterly. 'They've forgiven worse.'

And condemned less, he thought, remembering parts of the story he could not bear to speak of or even to think about. It wasn't just a question of reputations. He knew too well what had happened when the story threatened to come out in the past. Procopio got off easily. Others hadn't. He didn't like to think about them either.

'And if I won't testify?'

She stubbed out her cigarette. 'Then I will.'

'You'll back me, though? You'll stick with me through this?'

'If you make it clear that my family and I didn't know the true story.'

Despite the brilliant sunshine, the taxi-driver was reluctant to leave Donna alone. The light only served to illuminate each bullet-hole in the church doors, an implication of old violence that made him nervous. 'How you get back, signorina?'

'I can walk. And there's a bus.'

'The bus goes along the Urbania road, signorina, five- or six-kilometre walk from here. It don' come up this kinda road.' Walking was for poor people like his father and grandfather, not for North Americans. Only the crazy English and Germans liked to walk for pleasure. 'You sure you don' wan' I should wait?' His conscience tweaked. 'I only charge you half . . .' She was already paying him four times what any Italian would.

'I'll be fine.' Donna pulled a small torch out of her bag, her mind on what might remain in Muta's cellar. There must be *something* here she could find. 'Thanks.'

Unhappily the driver started up his taxi. If she were *his*

daughter . . . but she wasn't, and these modern American girls were strong, healthy specimens who always made you feel they could take care of themselves. He preferred his women to show some vulnerability. A vulnerable woman made a man feel strong.

'*Doo dah, doo dah,*' mourned Angelino from a hiding-place in the woods. His animals grazed, the soft clang of their bells failing to comfort him today. He was watching the angel below. Angelino knew about angels, his mother had told him about angels, how they lost their wings and fell.

The driver of the grey car had trailed Donna patiently from Urbino to the Villa Rosa turn-off and then to this valley, where he had parked his car behind a copse of trees to wait until the taxi disappeared. Inside the car a second man regarded the living picture stretched out before them: a girl (subject, artist's model, victim) walking through a sunlit valley towards an uncertain fate, fields shorn to stubble on either side. He thought it might serve to illustrate the parable in a medieval fresco or Book of Hours. 'Faith in Human Endeavour,' he murmured, then corrected himself, 'perhaps "The Punishment for Ignoring History" '. The light had the bright yet subaqueous illumination of a lunar eclipse, the kind of light radiating from angels bringing visions of the Apocalypse.

He didn't bother expressing this idea to the grey-eyed driver, a grey man altogether who would have no idea what he was talking about. Instead he spoke to the unseen artist responsible for the work of art, asking: where does this apocalyptic light come from, Lord? And answering his own question: from *us*, it's coming from *us*. He felt himself to be a good man at heart, yet by the end of this day his moral convergence with those other men would no longer be illusory. That's why they had phoned him this morning, insisting on his presence here. To establish an even greater complicity. For he *knew* the story, he had known for years. If not his brother's keeper, he was the keeper of his brother's secrets. The white gravel road to San Rocco was a chalk mark drawn to intersect another, invisible path at a single point in time, an illusory 'vanishing point' into which his life disappeared. He was being taught a lesson in perspective. The straight, true road was lost to sight . . .

So much of his life had been spent looking over his shoulder that he had come to see himself as one of Dante's sorcerers, strangely twisted so that his face must always turn towards his own backside and backwards must he creep, all power of looking forward denied as if by some paralytic fit. When he'd asked his callers this morning what would happen if someone saw him here at San Rocco, they had laughed. 'There are any number of men we know who, if you need them to, will happily swear to your presence in confession or visiting a hospital, a nursing home – any suitably holy or worthy location other than San Rocco.'

I am only here as a witness, he told himself. And it is possible that my presence may prevent the worst of it.

The slate-eyed driver released his clutch and let the vehicle slide silently down the hill towards San Rocco.

Gingerly Donna lowered first one foot and then the other, descending to the cellar floor to feel glass crunch underfoot. There she stopped in a brilliant square of sunlight from the open door above her, like an unrehearsed actress in the spotlight waiting for her prompt.

The cellar reeked of smoke and scorched pans and decomposing food. Donna felt no inclination to move away from the sun's security into those stinking shadows and, playing her torch over the chaos, she saw the smashed bottles, their contents no longer preserved, and the walls lined with newspapers – some shredded, others blackened by years of cooking smoke and fat. Reluctantly she made her way through the mess, edging around the fallen shelves. She heard the somnolent buzzing of flies on the corpse of a pickled fish and stumbled over a basket, spilling its contents of ragged clothing and odd shoes. With her toe she pushed aside the debris to expose a small leather glove embroidered with dainty flowers. Leaning to pick it up, she found that it concealed a handful of bullets and yellowed teeth and dropped it quickly, shuddering.

When the noise came from behind her Donna whirled around, a child of the TV era and the drive-in who knew that every cellar hides its obligatory serial killer. All she saw was a rat's tail, pink and scaly, disappearing behind the makeshift stove, but it made her anxious to breathe fresh air again and she retreated back the way she had come. Awkwardly she clambered through the wreckage and up the steps until she was level with the turf, where her eyes were attracted to something white and round a few feet from her, buried in a patch of weeds. Anyone standing on the grass would have missed it. She balanced on the cellar's top step and stretched forward to pick it up, a small ivory-white bone no bigger than a curled-up harvest mouse, its surface worn creamy by constant handling. Or *fondling*, Donna remembered, in her mind's eye the picture of his long slender fingers cradling it in his palm and stroking it slowly with his thumb as if it were a pet bird he was caressing. She did the same, and this action, combined with San Rocco's strange graveyard stillness, brought back her first conversation with Count Malaspino. How had he described this place? A giant cemetery, a bony landscape where scarred white stones pushed up like kneecaps or ribcages through the skin of grass. Donna felt again the brittle clay of the statue she had smashed.

Around her the buzz of insects and birds dimmed. Her breathing became shallow, the ruined village shimmering, enfolding her. For the space of five or six minutes she lived another life and forgot her own. With the little bone threading in and out of her fingers Donna was remembering overheard names from that disastrous afternoon at the Villa Rosa, names that held meaning for her now. Carlo *Seguita* (the brother of her Monsignor). Lorenzi. A consortium of pig-farmers.

Thinking about all the lost voices, she sat staring across the valley to the deeply shaded woods on the other side, until a sound or movement behind her made her turn. She saw him then, standing well back, disassociating himself from what was to come. Then a heavy weight came down on her skull and she was falling sideways into the cellar, literally grasping at straws as she fell and bringing down stones and clumps of vegetation, her head flooded with the smell of earth and peppery autumn leaves as she dropped past all the words – MASSACRATI, ASSASSINIO, OMICIDIO, VIOLENZA CARNALE, VIOLENZA SU DONNA. She felt her ankle snap easily as it caught in the steps, then her torso and her head slammed into the hard beaten earth and the broken glass like a side of beef landing on a butcher's block. The last thing she was aware of was the sound of bells and thunder, thundering hooves, heartbeats . . . She was being swallowed up, sinking, drowning. And all the while that brilliant, apocalyptic light lit her fall.

MIRACLE NUMBER 40

In the Mouth of the Wolf

A dense grey cloud had drifted down from the Apennines overnight to shroud Urbino. Out of it, part of it, the wolf materialised, slipping through the streets unseen by Charlotte, for whom every lamp glowed through the mist like an animal's eyes picked up by car headlights at night. Already on her cautious progress towards the magistrate's court she could have sworn to leaping dolphins, cobwebbed ships in full sail, angels, mermaids, sirens. Edging through lakes of cloud in the piazzas, she kept one hand against the walls and buildings, glad to feel the reptilian scales of lichen under her fingers, while crossing the voids of alleys and roads required a trusting leap into the unknown. The dreamy, isolating effect of the mist, the cobbles underfoot, slick and greasy with condensation, gave her the sense of climbing a stony mountain island rather than a city street.

Watching her pass, the thin grey man turned up the collar on his jacket and wished he were in Rome. Mist curdled around him, erasing his edges to make him as chalky and indeterminate as a graphite sketch, and he moved off in Charlotte's wake with fog unravelling behind him like threads from his mohair suit.

'Guillotined by a weather pattern,' said the mayor to his wife, as he left the house and saw how the low cloud had severed the head of the living statue of Raphael. 'Ciao, Fabio!' he called out, but the statue didn't hear him: sounds as well as colours were muted, distorted. The wasping complaints from mopeds and three-wheeled Piaggio trucks bounced back in their drivers' faces and footsteps appeared to be nearer than they were, echoing off the mist. 'As if the entire population of Urbino were treading on hollow ground,' the mayor muttered to himself.

The white tide ebbed and flowed around the courthouse. Twice Charlotte had passed it before its doorway was revealed in a brief transparency. There was the sound of a moped and she jumped back just in time to avoid a Lambretta whining past, all but the driver's black loafers and the lower half of his vehicle's wheels obliterated in a waterspout of mist. His vision equally impaired, Paolo cursed a woman's flat shoes (unrecognised as Charlotte's) and a navy-blue suit cut off at the waist. His mind was not on his driving. Last night he'd waited almost three hours for Donna. One *passeggiata* had finished and the second one had begun before he left the café where they'd arranged to meet. The receptionist at Donna's hotel claimed not to have seen her that evening, but he'd only just come on duty in the last hour. Sure, he'd pass on Paolo's message. 'If the girl phones,' the man said. His flat voice made it clear how unlikely he thought that was.

At midnight, having drunk his way round every café in Urbino, Paolo returned to the hotel. This time the receptionist offered him no more than a patronising look, a look that had been betrayed by uglier women than Donna. Paolo did the round of cafés again and then went home very late to spend a sleepless few hours, one side of him arguing in Donna's favour, while the devil's advocate (sounding remarkably like Fabio) suggested more likely possibilities: *Not the first time that's happened, is it?* But this is different! *A richer man? A better offer in a bigger film?*

This morning he had been up before his mother, 'For the first time since you were six months old! These miracles are reaching even my own house, Paolo!' He'd driven first to Donna's hotel, where a different receptionist asked his name and Donna's three times between phone-calls. Yes, she decided finally, there might have been a phone call from l'americana, 'Maybe from Rome?'

'Rome!'

Maybe not. 'Possibly a different American.' The receptionist's glossy fingernails required immediate attention.

So far as Paolo knew, the only connection Donna had in Rome was the producer who'd got her this job with James, so Paolo rang James and caused a scene, failing to establish either the producer's name or his number. James told him to grow up, the girl was probably shagging Antonio the cameraman at this very . . . Paolo slammed the phone down and set off on his Lambretta, determined to make a nuisance of himself at every hotel and *pensione* in and around Urbino.

Whistler and Turner had painted this obfuscating mist, never Raphael, whose skies were always jewel clear, thought Charlotte, watching witnesses and other spectators slowly washing up on the courtroom steps, blinking and hesitant, like pilgrims arriving at the pier of a mysterious fog-bound port. They cast no shadows in the flat white light and seemed as insubstantial to her as Dante's boatload of lost souls.

Even more intangible was the slate-eyed grey-suited man who took up a position in a café facing the courthouse, where he paid the extra for a table and sat down patiently with a Rome newspaper to wait next to the payphone.

Inside the court, Charlotte discovered that the hearing was to be held in a room so small that few people beyond those who had witnessed the Raphael attack could find seats. Paolo had explained to Charlotte that usually during such an *udienza preliminare* no witnesses would be present and only the people directly involved – the arrested person, the police and the victim – would be questioned by the magistrate. However, given that the victim was a painting and the aggressor a half-crazy deaf mute now rendered even more uncommunicative by the police action, the usual procedure had been altered to take into account the circumstances.

With the exception of the mute woman, her nurse and the

Countess, Charlotte was surrounded by men in suits. The power of uniformity, Charlotte thought, observing this effective camouflage of slate grey and navy blue. A solidification of the fog outside. 'More than my job's worth, old boy,' she imagined the featureless suits saying when asked to stand up for any threadbare principles not removed in the last dry-cleaning.

She was aware of Fabio's grandfather, Lorenzi, passing her to stroll towards the front row, where the Count and his wife were seated. 'Dado, you don't mind me joining you and Greta?' he asked pleasantly, a comment that only served to intensify the Count's look of strain.

'To give you the support of an old family friend,' added Lorenzi.

'No . . . I . . . please do, Dottore.' The Count's face grew more ashen than ever, as if Lorenzi's comment were a threat rather than an offer of solidarity, Charlotte decided. She was thinking about Paolo, who was late as usual, and about the absence of Donna, a primary witness. Still, no one expected this preliminary hearing to be anything more than a formality, proof on paper that justice had been served. No security measures had been taken to protect the witnesses, who were expected to give their seal of approval to an almost foregone conclusion: the mute woman's attack was an act of paranoia, her mutism the result of isolation or dementia.

Muta's arrival was in keeping with the predicted verdict. The doctor had brought Muta to the court in a wheelchair in which she sat like a graven idol. Her silence opaque, unbreachable, she might have been manufactured from wax or china, a painted effigy dressed up in real clothes and wheeled out for ceremonial occasions.

Professor Serafini was almost the last to arrive, pushing inside just as the duty officer was closing the courtroom door.

Informed of Donna Ricco's absence, the magistrate checked his notes and decided to proceed anyway. He avoided meeting anyone's eyes while he explained how 'through special dispensation' the proceedings today would differ from the usual hearing. Then a deposition was read to him about the attack on Raphael's painting, with written statements from a long list of minor witnesses, including Charlotte, who had not been asked to testify. The Chief of Police explained at length his own courageous role in the wild woman's arrest, with no protests from Procopio, who stared fixedly at Muta throughout the statements.

At this rate, thought the magistrate, they should be able to break early for lunch. A pleasant image came into his mind of a restaurant he remembered from his last visit here, an old-fashioned place whose cook had never heard of cholesterol, and as Count Malaspino stood to make his statement the magistrate's head was filled by a happy vision of wild boar larded heavily with prosciutto fat and truffles. 'Do you wish to alter any of the comments you made earlier to the police, Count?' he asked, his voice silky with the anticipated *lardo*. What should he drink to balance the pheasanty aroma of the truffles? No fan of the thin local wines, the magistrate imagined something bold and red from Piemonte. He might even stretch to a Barolo, an antidote to the milky clouds obscuring his view from the court windows.

At the Count's continued silence, the magistrate dragged his mind reluctantly from lunch. 'Did you hear me, Count Malaspino?'

'Yes, I . . . That is . . . yes, perhaps I can . . . I can imagine a reason for this woman to attack me.'

'Attack *you*? Surely the police have ruled out that possibility?'

'They are not in possession of all the facts. My father made sure of that.'

'How can your father have anything to do with this case, Count Malaspino?' Sons were bad enough, the magistrate thought; if once we begin on fathers (and dead fathers at that), where will it all end!

The Count hesitated again, glancing quickly at Lorenzi this time. There had been a phone-call last night, assurances: 'You have only to keep your head, Dado.' Wrestling with the story, he searched for scraps that he could throw towards the hungry magistrate. 'I believe she – this mute woman – she may have attacked me because of an . . . incident at San Rocco during the War.'

Alerted by some warning note in the Count's voice, the magistrate sighed deeply and asked, 'What manner of *incident*, Count?'

'I . . . it's possible that this mute woman might . . . might have been hiding at San Rocco and may have heard . . .'

'May have *heard*? She is a deaf mute, is she not?'

'May have seen . . .'

Frowning with the effort not to shout *Will you come to the point!* the magistrate said crisply, 'May have seen *what*?'

The Count steadied himself. His gaze dropped to his hands, gripped together so tightly that his knuckles had whitened, and forcibly he opened them to spread the fingers out like two starfish clinging by suckers to the rock of his dark suit. 'I was ten . . . ' he began slowly, 'when . . . when I first began to act as an interpreter for the German and Italian officials my parents entertained. Neither of my parents spoke any German, but I'd had a German tutor for six years before the War – Dieter, my wife's older brother.' And closer to me than any brother, he thought, catching his wife's smile. 'The German officers who were billeted at our house for a while, they liked to hear the songs Dieter had taught me. In those days I had a lovely singing voice.'

The magistrate felt as if the mist outside had managed to penetrate the room and tangle grey wool around the speaker's tongue. 'Yes, yes, go on, Count . . . I trust your singing voice will soon become relevant.'

'I . . . you see, I was friends – *close* friends – with some of my father's tenants at San Rocco. I don't remember when I discovered that most of them were deserters, or had never enlisted. They trusted me completely not to give them away, for I had known them for years . . . secretly . . . My father . . . he didn't know about this friendship . . . until one night . . .' Observing the magistrate's expression, the Count began to stammer badly, 'One night . . . one night . . . I was twelve . . . one night . . .'

'*Really*, Count Malaspino, I can't keep this court in suspense for – '

'One night my father found out about my association with these deserters at San Rocco and got . . . very angry . . .' Catching a frown from Lorenzi, the Count lost control of his hands again; they took on a winged life of their own, fluttering towards his wife and then settling uneasily against his sides. 'So I told him.' He regained control, lacing his hands tightly together, and apart from a faint tremor around his left eye, his face betrayed no emotion.

'Told him what?'

'Everything, anything I could think of . . .' *Anything to make him stop*. 'When he realised how much information I had passed on – '

'His associates would hardly have allowed a *child* to translate anything important, whatever you remember, Count.'

'Oh, but these were people whom they considered to be traitors! It was for that reason that my father went . . . he went with friends to San Rocco.' A fly landed on the Count's cheek and began strolling towards his eye.

'To look for deserters? To make arrests?'

'No . . . I . . . Yes, arrests, that's it. Yes.'

'They arrested the deserters and you think this is what the mute woman may have seen?' the magistrate pressed. Charlotte was fascinated by the fly, now resting below the Count's nose like a small clipped moustache.

'Yes . . . Well . . . there was more . . . I . . . they threw grenades . . . bombs . . . into San Rocco . . . to set an example.' He felt Lorenzi's careful scrutiny and quickly added, 'The women were away . . . another veglia . . .' He pressed a finger against his eyelid as the tremor spread out seismically across his face, dislodging the fly.

'It was wartime, Count Malaspino, a war in which there were many such tragic incidents. I'm sorry, but you have not yet convinced me that this leads to a mute woman's *personal* attack on you fifty years later.'

'I was there . . . my father insisted I come with him to watch . . .'

'There were other people there as well,' the magistrate said, his voice again silky, this time with suspicion. 'Surely some of your father's associates are still alive? Has this mute attacked any of *them*?'

'No, but you see . . . I was a friend of San Rocco . . . I – '

'Why don't you take me through the names of those who went with your father?'

From where she sat Charlotte could see the tremor around the Count's eyes start up again. 'I don't remember any names.'

'Not one?'

'No.'

'Even these men you described as your father's friends?'

'No. They are . . . all dead now . . .'

'You know they are dead, but you don't know their names. I see.' The magistrate pursed his lips. 'Well, it is clear that you want to unburden your conscience of *something*, but frankly I find it hard to credit any connection – yes, what is it? You have something to add, Professor Serafini?'

The gingery little professor stood up. 'I believe I may be able to shed some light on why the conjunction of Count Malaspino and the Raphael could have sparked a violent memory in this deaf mute. My family came from Carpegna, north of here, which was used during the War to hide artwork – paintings, sculpture – from all over Italy. When the Germans began their retreat a friend of my father's discovered that Carpegna was going to be used as the SS base. He therefore arranged for all the artwork to be conveyed back to Urbino by way of various safe houses. Possibly San Rocco was – '

'Including the Raphael portrait?'

'I don't know. At any rate, the Balducci farm may have – '

The magistrate's feeling of resentment at missing his leisurely lunch finally broke through: 'May have, possibly, might! I need something definite if we are to proceed!' He swung his angry eyes towards the duty clerk. 'What is that infernal racket outside?'

The clerk approached the magistrate, who said crossly, 'An urgent message? Concerning this case? Because if it has no bearing on – '

'She insists it does, sir.'

'Very well, show her in.' He had been asked to give the witnesses leeway, but really, this hearing was turning into a circus!

Procopio's aunt came through the door with her son, Angelino. Casting a wary eye at Procopio, who at her appearance had thrown himself back against his chair with a soft oath, the old woman approached the magistrate and mumbled something almost inaudible to the court. *Sepolti vivi* were the only words Charlotte heard. 'The buried alive.' This, she remembered, was the name Italians had given to a sect of perpetually cloistered nuns, but also to those Jews and partisans and escaped prisoners of war who had been hidden away in cellars and attics.

Angelino had begun murmuring, 'Mama says we can't keep the angel, she says we have to bring the angel back or people will think, people will think, Mama says – '

'Hush, hush!' Procopio's aunt said, and laid one hand on her son's shoulder, her head barely reaching his chest. 'Later, Angelino, you tell them later.'

MIRACLE NUMBER 41

The Incorruptible Tongue

Had the magistrate been cross-examined before this hearing, he might have quoted Galileo, who had said that it is in human nature to take up causes whereby a man may oppress his neighbour, no matter how unjustly. The magistrate, veteran of a host of corruption cases that had never reached the public eye, would have sworn that he was too old, too fat and too tired to be angry or surprised at men any more. Men had all kinds of minor sins and perversions they wished to conceal, while they clung tenaciously to major sins that bothered them not one whit.

An oblique hint from his old friend Primo having indicated that this particular case was no different, the magistrate had been prepared for the various discreet offers and veiled threats made to him over the past few days, all of which he had successfully managed to divert or ignore. So far. He had no family, fortunately. No wife, no children, no relations he loved on whom they could put pressure.

'A poofter!' Lorenzi had snarled to his friends at the Caffè Nazionale, but no boys either could be found to use against the magistrate. What could you do with a man like that? And then there was the unnatural speed with which this hearing had been arranged. While officially a preliminary hearing was supposed to take place two to three days after arrest, in complicated cases like this one you generally could count on months passing before anything came before a judge, by which time many things could be arranged.

Lorenzi felt more confident, however, at the conclusion of

the old woman's brief whispering statement (rendered almost but not entirely incomprehensible to the magistrate by her arcane dialect). He'd heard almost nothing of what she'd said, but studying the magistrate's body language, he concluded that a more reasonable man might soon be arranged to adjudicate.

The mayor's chosen man had removed his glasses, closed his eyes to shut out the court and was now gripping his large nose firmly between thumb and forefinger as if he were trying to block out a bad smell. He was filled with a vast weariness and a deep desire for a cigar. I never claimed to be a brave man, he thought. I'm not Falcone, to lose my life for the sake of sending a few mafiosi to prison. I would be perfectly justified in dismissing this woman and her gibbering son and passing the case on to someone else. It has gone far beyond what I was asked to do.

For several moments the magistrate considered his options, until his own inner trial was disturbed by a hum, a see-saw noise that Charlotte too thought she could hear. Nonsense words, louder this time, that seemed to come out of nowhere:

'Doo dah, doo dah.'

Angelino knew about angels, he was named after angels. His mother had told him how the people at San Rocco went away all but one, then they were angels and now they were coming back one by one. He knew angels when he saw them and devils; he knew when an angel had fallen to earth and he brought his mules down from the hills like thunder upon the two devils, the grey devil and the priest devil, the two hell-hounds flying from the bells. He was going to find her, dig her out. His own angel, light as feathers when he picked her up, and floppy as a dead pup. He carried her home. Angels, he said, and his mother was glad to have another one and she laid this one out and then they went in the truck with the eggs. He liked the truck. He didn't like the hospital and he didn't like this room either. The people in it reminded him of something that made him sway back and forth to the tune he remembered singing when the devils came.

'Doo dah, doo dah.'

Before the magistrate could call a halt, Muta had laid her good hand on the armrest of her wheelchair and pushed herself into a standing position. The entire courtroom, even Angelino, fell into a long breathless wordless pause in which the slightest sound was exaggerated.

With an expression of pain the mute woman opened her mouth and formed inaudible words. Charlotte heard Procopio swallow hard. The courtroom grew not simply quiet but actively noiseless, heavy with expectancy, every atom humming. But it was Procopio's aunt's rough scraped voice that finally broke through the hush: *'Set thee not down in that deep well whose grasp holds Judas and Lucifer fast!'*

'What does your aunt mean, Signor Procopio?' boomed the magistrate. '"Set thee not down in that deep well"? What does she mean?'

Procopio, his eyes still fixed on Muta, slowly stood up. 'My aunt is Sicilian,' he said, as if that were explanation enough. His battered shaggy head moved heavily around to face the magistrate. 'Although she came to San Rocco when she was young, she still eats Sicilian, speaks Sicilian, thinks Sicilian . . . All she learned of Italian is our valley dialect and the language of a priest she used to know.'

'But you understand her.'

'Some words I understand, but *her*? No, never.'

'Ask her about this mute woman's connection to San Rocco.'

Muta could feel the words, the words were almost ready, she rolled them like seeds across her tongue.

Procopio barked a few indecipherable phrases at his aunt, to which she responded with a hard shake of her head and a thorny hedge of farming metaphors woven through the San Rocco dialect, baroque strands of Latin tangled up with flowering tendrils from Dante and mistranslations into modern Italian.

'Could you translate what she just said, Signor Procopio?'

Charlotte watched the tension in Procopio's face and massive shoulders increase. 'Roughly translated, she told me she has nothing left to lose.' He paused. 'But I promise you that what she knows about San Rocco is not relevant to – '

'*The Chocolate Man . . .*' said Angelino.

Most of the audience was straining, half-standing to catch sight of the muleteer, but Charlotte pressed her shoulders back into her chair like someone in a car bracing for a crash. Charlotte, who for days had been intent on bringing the truth to light, felt a sudden deep desire *not* to know, not to hear anything more. She told herself that Procopio had been too young to have anything to do with what happened at San Rocco. Since then, though, what had he done since then? She felt cold and powerless to prevent the collision.

Procopio apologised, 'My own cousin, but I have to say, a half-wit.'

His aunt shouted back a stream of words only halted by the magistrate's interjection: 'I believe she is insisting her son has as much a right as anyone to be here because he too . . . he too . . . *has been to the very gates where Lucifer fell*?'

'Lucifer's Gate . . .' said Procopio. 'It's what the people in our locality call the hole at San Rocco where the grenades or bombs were thrown . . . But if you want to know whether she and her son know the names of the men responsible for . . . the arrests at San Rocco, they *don't*!'

'Arrests?' the old woman shouted. 'No one was arrested!'

Muta audibly cleared her throat. Once again a paralysed silence gripped the court and in this stifling pause the fly sounded like a warning buzzer. It landed near Lorenzi, who caught it with surprising accuracy and then squeezed it between thumb and index finger with a slight 'click'.

There was a liquid noise bubbling and gurgling in her ears, the sound of rivers, streams, springs. She was underwater rushing up towards the light.

She raised her hands like someone conducting a choir:

That night the prisoners were above ground for la Veglia.

She watched the rusty voice pass her as if it were the shadow of a lost soul returned. Even as a small child she had been quiet, she was always among the listeners. So many secrets to keep, the less she said, the fuller she felt. Now her old head was a wandering maze of borrowed words from books read aloud by the priest who loved her and taught her and phrases collected from newspaper stories on her walls that she had picked out sentence by sentence over the years and used to explain what she had witnessed, repetitious stories that in her circling *passeggiata* through them took on the patina of a path eroded with overuse. *La Veglia*, the watches of the night. Oh, she had watched all right, observed the peace of those winter nights altering, the stories changing, stories of unions and resistance carried from one farmhouse to the next. Until that final night.

'La veglia funebre.'

Muta felt the letters hanging in the air, visible to all.

But it wasn't Muta who had spoken, Muta remained silent; it was Procopio and his aunt, although the mute woman's lips had moved in unison with theirs. These were her words, spoken in their voices. *La veglia funebre*: the last wakening, the last watch. Even today she could smell the medlars, chocolatey with rot. 'Not that we had chocolate . . . not until the American came with his bubble gum and chocolate and cigarettes. We'd never seen anyone so dark. Dark like chocolate.'

'The Chocolate Man,' Angelino murmured again, and Charlotte felt a great relief. Not Francesco, she thought. It wasn't Francesco.

'"Holy *smoke*!" the prisoner said the first time he saw the white pillow-cases with holes for eyes. "Figgered it was Klanners come to git me." The Englishman translated and made us laugh. We had three that night: Dieter, the German – him we knew already from before the War . . .' Few people in the court heard the Countess's sharp intake of breath, muted anyway by the two voices, Procopio's and his aunt's, now speaking almost as one. The big man seemed to be reciting a story heard so many times, rehearsed so many times, that it had become his own. 'Then there was a quiet Englishman and an American, a very noisy, very funny man. Hard to keep such a noisy American hidden for so long. Most of the escaped prisoners of war stayed in the cellar only for one night before moving on, but the Englishman and the American were sick when they arrived, skinny, and the German's leg was broken. The English one, he always wanted to go fishing, it was what he liked to do most. The American used to play the Balduccis' violin, which they called by a different name where he came from.' Procopio's aunt said it in English, 'feedle'. 'He was teaching us that foolish song Angelino sings . . . *Camtan races dum dum dum, doo dah, doo dah, Camtan races dum dum dum, oh doo dah day.*

'At the veglia that night there were the six San Rocco families and some visitors I didn't know, as well as the priest and the three prisoners. I was helping Muta's mother cook frascarelli, a flour polenta seasoned with her own tomatoes bottled in the summer and bittersweet with added grape must. The men were gambling and telling stories and drinking up Balducci's powerful vino cotto brewed with quinces and he was grumbling that there would be none left for his own family, what with the Englishman's and German's hard heads and the American's passion for what he called "moonshine". Muta kept slipping away from the kitchen, probably to check if Dado had arrived yet. She used to follow him round like a shadow. She was always a quiet, plain little thing.'

'Quiet?' repeated the magistrate. 'Doesn't she mean mute, Signor Procopio?'

Procopio turned his head very deliberately to find Charlotte.

'Signor Procopio?' said the magistrate again.

Still Francesco held Charlotte's eyes. He searched her face carefully, as if she were a country, a safe place he was leaving, and in those few moments of silence he made her see exactly what she was losing. A different kind of poetry. The pungent flavours, smells and textures of his life. *Take this route*, she understood at last, *and there will be reprisals*. If not now, then tomorrow. If not tomorrow, then the next day, next month, next year. She wanted to tell him to stop, save yourself, save *us*, but before she could find the words, Procopio had faced the magistrate again: 'She was never mute . . . or deaf.'

That night, Muta was the first to see the firefly light of torches bobbing in the woods above their farm. She thought it must be hunters because they were so silent, or maybe partisans. Uneasy, she ran back to the barn to tell her father and brothers, who would know what to do. But she couldn't get their attention because they were practising on the American's fiddle, laughing and trying to sing along to the chorus:

'*Doo dah doo dah . . .*'

She ran to the kitchen, but it was several turns of the spoon in the tomato sauce before her mother followed her outside to see the torchlights, closer now. Then all the torches were extinguished and there were only the silhouettes of guns black against the sky.

Signora Balducci clapped one hand over her mouth and one on her bosom, the bosom of a ship's figurehead, Dado used to say, and like a ship she sailed towards the people in the barn, sweeping Muta along in her wake. When she stopped in the doorway she cried out: '*Scarecrows coming!*' Their private code for 'turncoats' silenced all singers except Angelino. Her mother didn't wait but, gripping Muta tightly, ran with her towards the cellar and, with a countrywoman's instinct for preservation (something put by for a rainy day), pushed her only daughter down the stairs. *Close your eyes, block your ears, but keep silent, Gabriella. To save your life. No screams, no cries, whatever you see, whatever you hear.*

The trap-door at the back of the cellar never had shut properly, and through its finger-breadth opening Muta could clearly see the old Count and his men approach her father, who answered them with a greeting that was fitting and courteous. The old Count waited for him to finish speaking and then he shot him. Muta heard the shot and watched her father fall, slowly as a heavy tree. Events speeded up and over the screams of Muta's mother Dieter began to explain that it was a mistake, the people of San Rocco didn't know they were sheltering prisoners. 'Don't you remember me, Count Malaspino? Dieter, Dado's tutor!' He protested even more as they took hold of the Englishman.

'Take me.' The big American had stepped forward. 'The English guy's sick. Take me!'

'Take the negro first,' said the old Count.

Tito had always liked killing. He had good hunting dogs, he was good at finding boar, Muta's brothers said, but never a good butcher like Francesco's father and her own. Tito, he was better at gelding. He strung the chocolate man up on a tree next to the pig they had butchered that day and called him a big black boar and used a knife on him, and all the men called out, 'Evviva il coltello!'

There was so much blood, Muta thought she was going to cry out and they would come for her too, so she stopped her ears and thought about how the American played his fiddle. A funny way, happy and quick, not like they did in her valley. But he died very slow, very noisy. The Englishman, though, the fisherman, he died quietly, the way he did everything. They gutted him like a fish and quiet as a fish he just slipped away.

'Doo dah, doo day, oh duh doo dah day . . .'

All through the killing Angelino kept up the senseless chorus, while from the narrow perspective of her cellar Muta heard the priest, who was Dado's friend as well as hers, praying, 'How art thou fallen from heaven, O Lucifer son of the morning,' and she saw the blaze of shots being fired. After that they took Dieter, a tall blond man with blue eyes like his sister's. They made him climb the church tower and they called him a traitor to his country and their own cause and they threw him off together with a skinny little mountain woman from further up the valley who was neither Communist nor partisan. No more nor less than a good cheesemaker. 'To see who falls fastest,' said Carlo, an educated man.

'Tito went to live in Urbino after a few years.' Procopio finished the translation of his aunt's testimony. 'Got a big lump in his jaw, made his whole face rot off. In the end he couldn't speak, just bark like a dog. They say it was from cigars but we knew differently, may he rot in hell. Tito didn't know that his wife and Angelino were at San Rocco for la Veglia that night until they rounded everybody up. They let the two of them off because they were Tito's. My aunt says of Tito that if she had known what "un fior del diavolo" he was, "a flower of the devil's", she would never have married him. Tito, my father's brother. But my father didn't speak to him again, not after we heard what she told us, what little she would tell us.'

'So you and your family have known about this . . . *incident* for years.'

Evviva il coltello, Charlotte thought. *Evviva il coltello.*

'One thing we knew!' Procopio's big face had been swelling and reddening under the magistrate's interrogation and now he burst out, '*Ask Malaspino who killed the priest and Dieter! Ask who killed his good friend, his tutor, the man who was a brother to him!*' He took a step towards the Count, and Lorenzi leaned sharply forward, attached to Procopio by an invisible line.

The Countess began to weep, a rough sound to come out of such a smooth woman. Her husband reached for her hand, but she snatched it away. 'One of one of one of . . .' the Count stammered. 'One of . . . the men . . . who has since . . . who has . . . died.'

'That's a lie! *You* shot the priest! Tito boasted to my father, how Carlo held your hand while you just stood there and then together you took Dieter to the top of the tower . . .'

'Yes,' said the Count finally. 'Yes, it's true. You see, I hated my father, really hated him. All my life he'd called me a weakling, a coward, because I did not enjoy shooting things as he did. He used to . . . taunt me. On the night of San Rocco, it went too far. I told him how all his peasants hated him too, how everyone at San Rocco was saying the War was nearly over and when it was over men like him would get what was coming to them. Then Papa said I was no son of his, "I'll make a man of you," he said and beat me harder than he had ever done and I wanted it to stop, I thought I was going to die. Then we went to San Rocco and Dieter fell.'

In her mind Charlotte heard Paolo, He was no *peasant*, the man who did for San Rocco.

'Carlo?' asked the magistrate, as if he hadn't been listening to Malaspino. 'Who is this Carlo?'

The Count took a moment and then replied, 'Carlo Seguita, my father's foreman. A banker now, in London. I spoke to him recently. Carlo Seguita of the Banca Internationale . . . Did I tell you that before the War Dieter was my best friend?' The Count's voice was higher, younger. 'We were fond of archaeology. I was thinking about that when Carlo stood the priest and Dieter up against the church door and put the gun into my hands. So we would all be implicated, he said. "Choose," he said. When we . . . when I . . . pulled the trigger, my father said . . . Papa said . . . He said, "*Now* you are a man" . . . Then they killed Dieter anyway, of course, and everyone else, the women and children as well.'

'And other acts worse than killing they performed,' said the aunt, 'with Dado's help. All those foul acts of which men are capable when God turns his face away from mankind. Things I will not speak of for the shame. Angelino wasn't right in the head after that.'

'Unspeakable acts,' confirmed the Count in his sweet boy's voice. 'Unimaginable. Then Papa had us pile up the dead and throw in the grenades.' So that even the bones could not bear witness. The earth alone could testify and the statue, thrown up by the bombs miraculously whole. He took it with him, something of Dieter, his friend. 'So far as I was aware until now, there were no living witnesses from San Rocco itself.'

'A few other children were hidden away,' said the aunt.

During the final part of the aunt's testimony the mayor had crossed and re-crossed his arms over his chest. *He had not heard, not seen, he was too young, too far away, he would recognise no one, he could swear to nothing.* 'Little ones,' the aunt went on, and the mayor's hands' grip on his upper arms tightened. 'I don't know who they were or where they went after that. I hope they got away. So small and downy they might have drifted away into the night like feathers.'

'I don't even remember seeing this woman and her son,' the Count was murmuring. 'It was all smoke . . . They finished all the killing, you see, then they searched everywhere . . . except the cellar . . .'

And the tower. The mayor closed his eyes and as quickly opened them wide again, avoiding his old nightmare of a tower with bullets rattling against the doors, a tower where bodies fell and were seen to fall evenly, big or small, heavy or light. Galileo's law.

'Why didn't your father and his associates look in the cellar, Count?'

'I didn't tell them. And they were all very excited by then.'

'He was only twelve years old! A child!' It was the Countess, on her feet. 'His father used to beat him! The old Count was a sadist! You want proof? You have to see the actual scars? What do you people expect of us? How long must this process of recrimination continue?'

Her husband's hand fluttered up in appeasement. 'It's all right, Greta. You see, I hoped . . . someone might still be alive down there.'

The magistrate, watching the guilt-ridden man falling apart in front of his eyes, tried for kindness, but in the light of Malaspino's many denials he found it difficult. 'What motive did your father have for this act of savagery?'

'Motive?' repeated the Count. He sounded detached, almost removed from the proceedings, a priest discussing a dead parishioner. 'I believe that he destroyed San Rocco simply to prove that his was the only way, there could be no dissident voices. And he was right, wasn't he? No one was brave enough to speak out against him, not after San Rocco. He died in his bed in the 1960s, a celebrated European politician, cultivated by the British and the Americans. I believe he was known to have a very fine cellar, for which he was much admired by the English.'

The mayor, for whom 'San Rocco' had been a curse and a nightmare all his life, could feel around him the silent demands from those who wanted names. But not Grandpa's or dear Uncle Claudio's, he was sure of that. No one imagined returning the profits earned from Cousin Enrico's little deal with the Nazis. No family wanted to hear the details of saintly Aunt Bella's unfortunate marriage, any more than they wanted to check for the dirt of corruption under their own nails. We prefer to lay the blame on our political and business leaders, Primo thought, and for the first time since he was a boy he prayed, *Please God in heaven, for the sake of my city which I love, for all our sakes, let it end here.*

After a lengthy pause to allow for miraculous interventions, the Count spoke up again: 'Domenico Montagna, the man murdered at the Nerruzzi consortium's pig farm several weeks ago,' he said quietly. 'He was one of those responsible for San Rocco. It had started to prey on him, I think. And his son, the man who was found beaten to death last week, was the nephew of two others. The judge trying the case against the Nerruzzi consortium – he was forced into withdrawing.'

The magistrate became aware of church bells tolling the hour, each church a little out of sync. It was three o'clock, well past time for lunch. Thank God, he thought. I had enough courage to do my job – *more* than my job. With a clear conscience he –

'There were others, but before I . . .' the Count said. 'I would like to ask . . . in case I don't get . . .'

He turned to face Muta for the first time and stood waiting silently, arms loose at his sides. Narrow and upright in his dark suit, he reminded Charlotte of the cypress trees along the road to the Villa Rosa, or that image of the priest facing his firing squad. She wanted to believe that the Count was asking forgiveness for all of them, for everyone in this ideal city whose silence over the incident at San Rocco had said to the mute woman: you are not our family, not our tribe, you are on your own.

Muta swung her eyes over each witness in turn. She took a deep breath, and the anticipation in the courtroom thickened. But no words came, although the corners of her mouth trembled with the effort. In the silence she could hear Mama screaming, see Mama, a big woman with breadmaker's fists, beating at them and screaming, and she closed her eyes, blocked her ears, *whatever you see, whatever you hear, say nothing.* They had broken all the words Muta remembered, all the words from the cellar walls flew up into the air with the bones and the gloves and the shoes and the stones, the earth, the scarecrow trees. All San Rocco's stories torn apart while she waited – for someone to get her out. She was there in the cellar while the smell drifting in from outside got worse, she was frightened, she trusted no one and so one day she left the cellar and lost herself.

When she returned, the other mute was gone. Someone had come to the cellar and taken her away and Muta didn't see her again until she went to work in the palace and recognised on the walls, in the postcard shop, all those painted faces who had passed through San Rocco years ago.

Yes, Dado, this old flesh, it forgives, but inside, inside . . .

She looked back at the Count. Reading his judgement in her eyes, he staggered and would have fallen if Procopio and the Countess had not moved to take his arms. The magistrate announced gruffly that as it was long past time for a recess, they would adjourn this hearing until the next morning at ten.

MIRACLE NUMBER 42

How to Wake a Dead Man

Paolo had arrived at the courtroom just after they'd closed the doors and left again when he'd been told by the duty clerk that no, Signorina Ricco was *not* inside. About thirty minutes after Procopio's aunt entered, Paolo returned to the court, but the uniformed guard outside, advised by the magistrate to allow no more interruptions, had denied him entrance. 'All I want to know is if Donna Ricco has arrived yet,' Paolo had said. He was jumpy, his mobile face strained with anxiety. At the guard's uncomprehending look he added, 'The TV girl: tall, dark-haired, beautiful.'

In fact, the guard didn't need a description. He knew the girl perfectly well, having seen Paolo parading around town with this *americana* as if he were driving the latest model Cadillac, and he was delighted now to be in a position where he could exert his own dominance over the young man. Without answering Paolo he flicked an imaginary dustmote off one starched cuff.

'Come on, you little prick!' the young restorer said. 'You must be able to tell me that! It can't be classified!'

Arrogant little *cazzo* yourself! thought the other man, minutely adjusting the position of his tie.

Paolo stormed out of the courthouse and caught sight of Fabio's disembodied features floating through the fog. 'Fabio! Did you see Donna go inside this morning?'

Fabio shrugged. 'I didn't get here until ten minutes ago.' His face disappeared into the clouds again. Unsure what to do next, Paolo had taken a table in a café opposite the courtroom and sat down to wait. He noticed a man at the next table, only because he was reading the obituaries in a Roman paper: either this fellow was the type who always read the obits first, or he was scraping the bottom of the barrel, maybe waiting for someone in the court as well. 'Been here long?' Paolo asked.

The man looked up but didn't respond.

'You haven't seen a tall dark girl go into the court?'

'A tall dark girl.'

'Very pretty, long legs – you couldn't miss her.'

The slate-grey eyes narrowed slightly in what might have been private amusement. 'I couldn't miss her. No . . . I suppose I didn't.'

Paolo frowned. 'You didn't see her?'

But the man's eyes were on the obituaries again.

Finishing his coffee, Paolo went to the shop next door to get a newspaper for himself. When he returned to the café, the man was gone. Paolo barely noticed. He had difficulty focusing on the news. Every time footsteps passed through the square he looked up, hoping for Donna. Where *was* she?

After a while he noticed a crowd gathering by the courtroom door. Scrappy patches of blue sky were tearing open in the grey sky overhead and what remained of the cloud had settled in a thick quilt of white across the piazza. Paolo had to jostle to get to the front of the gathered spectators as people began to emerge from the courtroom a few at a time. Out of the low-lying mist their figures rose into the sunlight like visions of saints or warriors from the smoke of a great battle.

First came Lorenzi and the Chief of Police with several of his men, behind them the bewildered Angelino and his mother, then the Count, supported between his wife and Procopio, with Charlotte close by. A low hiss came from the crowd as the Count moved forward, but at Muta's appearance everyone fell silent for a moment. Walking slowly between her nurse and the doctor, she put up her hand to shield her eyes against the lightning flare of a hundred cameras and the microphones thrust at her by journalists who, seeing her on her feet, jumped to the wrong conclusion and assumed there had been another miracle, as did the spectators, many of whom were in search of Urbino's answer to Fatima. The same questions were put to her over and over, 'How do you feel? What do you want?'

'After fifty years' silence – how do you feel?'

Sixty voices: *Feel feel feel think feel want feel do feel feel feel.*

She stared blankly, a speechless oracle. As it became clear that there were no prophecies to be gained from her, the baying pack of journalists swept towards the Count. Even Muta's doctor and nurse turned their attention away to hear what Malaspino would say outside the court. Would he reveal the remaining names on his roll-call of murderers?

Townspeople recruited by the mayor's wife had their ammunition ready and two of her friends were carrying a long hand-painted banner that read in Italian:

WE KNOW, BUT WE DON'T HAVE THE PROOF

In one hand the mayor's wife held a peeled egg. But she hesitated to throw it when she saw how heavily the Count was leaning for support on his own wife, who clung to him tightly enough that when the first tomato hit him and exploded in red against his tailored chest, the Countess staggered too and nearly fell under his weight. The cameras were ready to catch the Count's expression as the second tomato hit his forehead, leaving him bloodied, although few cameras caught the third and the fourth tomatoes, misdirected, which hit the Countess with such force that her elegant head was spun sideways. And so, like the gathered police and journalists, doctors, nurses and lawyers, the Countess did not notice the first shot. It missed her, as it did her husband, pulled abruptly sideways by her arm.

Procopio looked down with comical surprise at the red streak across his arm nearest the Count. He put his hand to the mark and it came away wet with blood. 'My God!' Paolo saw the big man mouth, and then Procopio was turning to shout at the Count – or making the motions of shouting. There was so much noise, so much going on, that for Paolo it was as if

Procopio were part of a silent film or one of those nightmares where you scream for help but no sound emerges.

A man in a pale grey suit almost the same colour as the fog stood in the shadow of a statue, his arm resting on its supporting plinth, while the angry crowd helped themselves to ammunition from a vegetable cart deliberately parked in front of him, its vendor nowhere to be found then or later. With a pile of tomatoes as cover, the grey-eyed, grey-suited man took aim again, only to feel his hand knocked aside as a boy in the crowd darted in close to grab one of the tomatoes and fire his vegetable missile with deadly accuracy. The tomato hit the Count in his chest, a blow he seemed not to feel until a few moments later when he slumped against his wife and began to sag at the knees.

'Stand up, Dado!' she whispered, trying unsuccessfully to brace him. 'You must stand up and face them!' She wanted him to have dignity, at least. She couldn't understand what was happening. She thought he'd been hit by another tomato, even after the blood from him began to leak onto her supporting arm and she cried out, almost blowing the headset off the RAI sound man. He cursed and dropped his microphone, thereby missing the Count's mumbled comment, 'It's all right, my dear, it doesn't hurt . . .' He felt himself sinking into the numbing chill of the old pool, his legs very light, floating to the surface. *Can't touch bottom wid a ten-foot pole, Oh! doo dah day*. He whispered, 'Hush, hush, cara,' and other words only shared with a solitary woman who couldn't hear him any more. The weight of his wings was dragging him down. Over his face came an expression of relief, as if he'd been searching for an old friend in the crowd, someone he hadn't seen for years and had just found again.

Using the panic around the Count and Countess for cover, the grey man stepped forward out of the shadow of Raphael to get a clear shot at his next target. His only witness was positioned artfully on the plinth left behind when a statue in the piazza had been removed for restoration. Failed artist, amateur footballer, grandson of a Fascist, Fabio did not stop to consider the risk as he launched himself in a goalie's tackle from his pedestal, a farcical, operatic display that delighted the tourists and other spectators who had been unaware of his existence until then. They laughed and applauded. All part of the act! All part of the great Italian melodrama! Aiming for the grey man's firing arm, the living bronze Raphael managed – yes! – effectively to knock the shot off its intended trajectory so that the bullet's graphic pencil line traversing the piazza failed to make its mark, never made it that far, instead ploughed an uneven furrow up through the goalie's own belly, past his heart and right through and out of an artery in his neck, pulling the blood with it in increasingly irregular jets from the green-painted body and onto the piazza's white stone cobbles as Fabio's heart beat and beat and slowed and finally stopped.

Lorenzi had reached him by then and with his strong clean old man's hands he raised his grandson's head from the bloodied cobbles.

'Get away from my son, you devil! Get away from him!' the Chief of Police shouted at his father. Pushing his way desperately through the crowd, he elbowed Lorenzi aside. 'You did this! Leave him alone! He hated you!'

Muta didn't see Charlotte reach for Procopio's good hand and clasp it tightly. She wasn't aware of everyone's attention on Raphael's first live performance in almost five hundred years, a work of art in patriotic red, white and green being performed right here! right now! in the central piazza (the mayor shaking his head, 'Commedia, commedia, commedia'), because in the instant that Fabio launched himself in a football tackle at the grey man and knocked him to the ground, Muta had slipped away from her nurse and lost herself in the stately carousel of Urbino's first *passeggiata* of the evening, up and down through all the coils of the city and round the helicoidal ramp past the carved names of forgotten heroes and villains and out into the broad Piazza Mercatale where the buses waited, disgorging the latest crop of pilgrims. A solitary figure, walking, then running. When she reached the woods beyond the paved road, the wolf was waiting, and for a few paces they ran side by side, until to anyone watching it would have seemed that the two lean figures, more spectral than ever, had merged into one long grey shadow racing through the valley maze of San Rocco, up the steep hill, gone for good.

MIRACLE NUMBER 43

A Penance of Miracles

'Of course, Monsignor Seguita denies everything,' said the mayor to Franco, when the bartender returned from his year-long honeymoon with Signora Tommaso's widowed sister. They'd been to visit Franco's brother Beppo in Chicago, with a view to settling there. But Franco missed home too much to contemplate becoming an American. Primo had the postcards of various anonymous skyscrapers to prove it:

> *Very windy here. No truffles. No homemade grappa to speak of.*
>
> *Franco (and Mona)*

'They don't have any proof against him, do they, Primo?' Franco wouldn't like to be the one to break the news to Mona, even more religious than his first wife, despite the black silk stockings.

'Against his brother, plenty, but no concrete proof against the bishop, so *far*,' grumbled the mayor. 'He disappeared back to Rome on the day of the hearing. But after they found the Monsignor's brother they had plenty of questions. You heard about Carlo?'

'Sure, Primo, what you think? Even in America people have heard of Carlo Seguita. Plus, the way he died . . . it's not your typical international businessman's suicide, to be found hanging under a bridge . . .'

'Especially with his hands tied behind his back,' said Primo drily. 'Some suicide. And his brother the bishop – '

'Behind his back? You know that for a fact about Carlo?'

The mayor shrugged. 'Anyway, the *bishop* . . . they approached him unofficially at first, but when he wouldn't cooperate – '

'Who would do such a thing?'

'Prosecutors, members of our Finance Guards Unit . . . *Anyway*, as I was saying, they served him a warrant to search his home in Rome – '

'A *warrant*! They warranted a *bishop*!' His wife wouldn't like it.

'*Sure* a bishop, why not a bishop?' Impatiently the mayor rushed to finish his story before Franco could interrupt again. 'Monsignor Seguita promptly threatened a diplomatic incident and claimed that his residence, being an office of the papacy, enjoyed diplomatic immunity and extra-territorial status – maybe even extra-*terrestrial* status for all I know. So for the time being there's a stalemate, until the government and the Pope sort it out. Could take years. Look at that Fascist Licio Gelli – charged with being involved in the drugs and arms trade, fraud, blackmail.' Primo ticked the charges off on his fingers. 'Jailed in Switzerland, escaped, currently living the good life here despite all the charges filed!'

Franco poured them both some more grappa. 'And the girl, Primo, what happened to the girl?'

'After she got out of hospital she swore on a stack of bibles she knew nothing, saw nothing except that one man, the guy they clocked as Malaspino's shooter, had no idea why he attacked her. Can't be budged. She's back in Canada. Her parents came and took her home again soon as the doctors would let them.'

'My wife worries about her.'

'Paolo she should worry about. Walking around like a dead soul, waiting for her to come back. It's enough to make a stone weep.'

'He loved her, didn't he, Primo? You could see it that day he came in here after Fabio died.'

Both men blinked vigorously and swallowed their grappa.

'No more miracles after Fabio died, isn't that right?' said Franco.

'After Fabio died and Paolo retired from miracle-working.'

'Serafini ever file charges?'

The mayor shook his head.

'And the painting?'

'The blood stopped. It dried. But between the Vatican and the police nobody can decide what to do. The Vatican authorities maintain their usual ban on speaking out. They do what they always do with a scandal, like what they've done for years with reports of paedophile priests. They refuse all requests for information, they refuse to open their files to outside bodies, they live their lives behind closed doors and insist that any ugly rumours can be attributed to those wicked souls who listen, like Luther, to the Devil whispering in their ears.'

For months after Donna returned to Toronto the letters continued to arrive from Urbino. She didn't open them or glance at their return addresses, not wanting to return to Italy, even on paper. Along with her bones, her mind needed time to heal: that's what her parents reasoned.

When Donna's time was no longer occupied with physical therapy and speech therapy (the fall into the cellar having caused temporary motor impairment of her larynx), she went back to school. She took courses. French and Italian. Modern History. Renaissance Art. Television production. Eventually she got a small job in local TV which led, a few years later, to a better job on a cable arts channel, which led her back to Europe and, inescapably, to Italy.

Speaking to the camera with authority this time, and in her own words, Donna discussed the della Francescas in Arezzo and the Raphaels in the Vatican Museum. Head thrown back to stare up at the Sistine Chapel (which in 1993 had offered her nothing more than a stiff neck), she was able to appreciate for herself Michelangelo's expression of muscular, passionate humanity. After seven years, Donna didn't need a teacher to point out the sharp contrast between the Florentine's work and that of Piero della Francesca, whose obsession with light and the source of light gave all his figures a grave, marble stillness.

'Della Francesca's most humble figures remain aloof from the onlooker, as if engaged in a scene of cosmic significance,' she said to the camera, 'whereas even the angels are sensuous and tactile in the paintings of Michelangelo and Raphael; they share a continuous space with us; they are as much part of our world as we are of theirs.'

These were Charlotte's words from years ago, or close enough, Donna realised, and recalled the example Charlotte had given – one of Raphael's later works, a final Transfiguration left unfinished at his death, in which the nominal religious subject was placed at the back, and in the foreground was a disturbed and passionate scene with a significance not immediately clear. A boy being cured of possession by demons: that was it. Hadn't the young Count Malaspino been possessed by those older men just as surely? The memory brought back other, more painful memories for Donna, and she began to see that the picture in which she herself had seemed to sit centre frame had been the portrait of someone else entirely. She had been a minor figure in the background, important for the spiralling dynamics of the composition as a whole, no more.

'That's a wrap,' said the producer. 'Donna, you OK with that? You ready to go back to the hotel or you wanna retake?'

'Yes,' Donna said, answering a different question entirely. 'I mean no, I think that take was fine.' And yes, I am ready now to go back. What was it that Charlotte had said about how she conceived Raphael's genius? Something about him insisting on the worth of *human* emotion and suffering, showing us that while we were a small part of a broader canvas, we were still integral to it.

When Donna did, finally, return to Urbino, she avoided the easy solution of renting a car in Rome and instead took the long slow pilgrim's journey north; first by train to Arezzo, travelling second class in a non-smoking carriage dense with the cigarette smoke from two dapper soldiers, their sister and their bulky, black-clad mother, whose own brother, the sister explained in broken English, had recently been killed while restoring the famous cathedral at Assisi, a tragedy that had not inhibited the family's appetite. Between cigarettes, they ate and drank constantly – stony red wine from an unlabelled flask, handfuls of wizened black olives, crusty bread cut with a big saw-bladed knife against his chest by one of the soldiers and then rubbed with raw garlic by his mother, hard, dry, blackish garlic sausage, plump, pink-flushed tomatoes the size of small cabbages – all of which they insisted Donna share, despite her protests. Gradually the smell of garlic and pork filled every corner of the carriage, so that when Donna left the train in Arezzo her clothes were as impregnated as the walls of a charcuterie smokehouse, a ripe aroma that could only have endeared her to the occupants of the bus she took from Arezzo to the mournful little town of Sansepolcro and on, almost seasick from the switchback mountain road, over the Alpe della Luna (*the Alps of the Moon*, she whispered to herself), past half-deserted villages and lime-washed ochre farmhouses standing alone and lonely in the rough landscape like child's drawings in their foursquare simplicity.

Finally, in the late afternoon, she reached Urbino on its double hills.

The university had spread a bit further over the western hills and there were a few more Swiss-style chalets and neo-brutalist conference hotels around the edges, but Urbino, the core of it at least, had remained intact in a way that her own had not.

She was surprised by how well she remembered the city layout, impossibly complex to that younger Donna. Perhaps because the street names – Garibaldi, Rinascimento, Mazzini, Matteotti – had gained resonance and meaning over the years, her feet now found their way almost without a conscious decision on her part. Guided by an interior map of their own, they led her through streets smelling of woodsmoke and rosemary to a narrow passage off the Via Raffaello (where a window display of cakes and pastries in the old café was even more splendidly baroque than she remembered it seven years ago), and then around the corner to the door of the Casa Raffaello itself.

Uncertain what to do next, Donna stood for a moment outside the building, trying to decipher the Latin in which the memorial plaque on the wall was inscribed.

'It is the house of Raphael, a museum now.' The voice, in lightly accented English, came from a pretty Italian woman perhaps a few years younger than Donna. 'Very nice inside. Very . . . simpatica. You can visit.'

'Yes,' said Donna, 'I know. I worked here for a short time years ago.'

The girl's dark eyes widened. 'But . . . I *know* you! You are Donna Ricco, no? A great hero – heroine – of this place! I have seen all the old newspaper stories. My colleague keeps them. She will want to meet you!'

'Your colleague?'

'She is working with the Accademia Raffaello and I have the privilege of staying with her and studying with her because my grandmother was the sister of the father of Francesco.'

Donna smiled. Her first day back in Urbino and already the *passeggiata* of obscure connections was beginning again. 'Oh, I'm not sure – your colleague? – I'm not sure that your – '

'Charlotte will never never forgive if I let you escape! Come in, come in! I am Nina, her assistant.'

Charlotte. 'Has she been here long . . . your colleague?'

'Since before the miracle happened, what we are calling for a long time the Miracle of San Rocco, those of us who believe.' The girl's voice dropped. 'Don't tell Charlotte I say it! She doesn't like such talk. She is very . . . *scientific*, you know? Very good friends with the mayor and Professor Serafini and all that bunch.'

Had they passed each other in the street, would Donna have recognised the smiling woman who came forward to greet her? What was different? Charlotte must be in her mid to late fifties now, less bony, not so faded. Working in Italy had softened and brightened her face, warmed her all over like a lick of fresh paint. To Donna, whose career in television had done the reverse, it seemed impossible. She thought: I must be romanticising the effect of this place.

Then Charlotte grasped her shoulders and kissed her on each cheek. What a very unCharlotte thing to do! 'Donna, how lovely to see you again after all these years! Let me ring Francesco and tell him you are here and then – '

'Francesco . . . ?'

'Francesco Procopio, my husband. I'm sorry, I am so used to everyone knowing everyone else's business that I forget what it is like outside our small world. But Francesco will want to see you. You must come for drinks – dinner.'

'Oh, I'm not sure if . . . that is, I can't stay long . . .'

'Nonsense! It would be unthinkable not to feed you while you are here. You are much too thin . . .' Charlotte stopped herself, laughing. 'I am sorry – again! I am sounding like any other Italian mama! But truly, we would like so much to hear about what you have been doing since you left . . . and there is so much for us to tell you, as well.' She laid her hand on Donna's arm. 'Please stay.'

'What is that delicious smell?' asked Donna, climbing from a door on the Via Raffaello to the apartment Charlotte shared with Procopio.

'It rises up from Francesco's kitchens,' Charlotte answered. 'The café entrance is off the other street. Very dangerous for la bella figura – I am instantly hungry every time I step through this door.'

Their apartment wasn't large, although its proportions made it seem so. Full of light, with high ceilings, enormous windows and creaking wooden floors of narrow, molasses-coloured planks, the room's furnishings were spare apart from its walls, covered with fine pencil drawings of architecture and sculpture. 'They are Charlotte's,' whispered Nina. 'She is on the committee of restoration for Urbino's monuments.'

'Your drawings are wonderful,' said Donna quickly and tactfully – although tact wasn't necessary; the drawings were indeed wonderful. 'I recognise some of the buildings.'

'But not the cakes, I think!' Charlotte laughed, easily, as if laughter were never far off. 'Some of those sketches are of the cake displays I design for Francesco's windows and his annual events. You can hear of my current artistic exploits from Nina while I make us some coffee.'

Nina waited until the sound and smell of coffee being ground came from the kitchen, then said, 'Three times a year Charlotte takes over from Francesco and creates these amazing marzipan and cake landscapes of Urbino for the windows of his café. Every building so precise, it is impossible to believe they are not real buildings seen from far away. Charlotte speaks through her fingers – that's what Francesco says about her, and it's true that when it comes to pastry, she's a real artist.'

'Your English is very good – did she teach you?'

'No, but thanks to Charlotte I studied in America for a year. And she is very good for the accent, of course.'

'I interrupted – you were telling me about these sugar landscapes of hers . . .'

'The only help she has is from her friend Paolo, a professor of conservation at the Free University.' Nina grinned. 'Very handsome! His female students, you can tell they're all in love with him, they invent excuses to walk by Procopio's while Paolo and Charlotte spend a whole day crawling around like two Gullivers in charge of a sugar Lilliput.'

'Paolo . . . didn't he work with her on the Raphael restoration?'

The girl put her hand against her mouth in dismay. 'I'm so sorry, signora, I forgot about . . .'

'That's all right, Nina. It was a long time ago.' Donna summoned up the smile she used to encourage reluctant interviewees. 'Tell me, how is Paolo – did he ever marry?'

'Oh yes,' the girl continued eagerly, 'although he waited two whole years for you to change your mind! This is very romantic, no? Then he gave up and married Flavia. At least, that's what Charlotte told me, on Christmas Eve five years ago when I came from Sicily to stay with her here. One night we were in the kitchen making this tagliatelle she does with cinnamon and ground nuts and bitter chocolate – it dates from the Renaissance, a recipe she found in one of Francesco's old books – '

'And it led her to tell you about . . .' Gently Donna brought the girl back on to the subject.

'Oh yes . . . I suppose I asked in a roundabout fashion how she got here from there, how a woman like her came to be married to my uncle Francesco – who may be good at ice-cream, but we must face it, yes? He isn't exactly the brightest bulb in the chandelier . . .' Nina stopped, perhaps remembering the loyalty she owed her host, and then the story bubbled up in her again. 'Anyway, maybe you remember how sometimes Charlotte can go for a whole day without saying much? But that night, when I asked how they got together . . . well, once she started, she couldn't seem to stop. She would roll and stretch and turn that sheet of yellow pasta, and with each roll and turn and stretch she would add a little flour and the pasta would get longer and wider and thinner and more elastic and so would her story. All the time she never stop rolling out the pasta and slicing it with her big knife into long parchment-yellow ribbons like sentences.'

The girl smiled at Donna. 'That's how I came to hear everything, you see . . . about you and Paolo and the mute woman and all the rest. And you won't guess what Charlotte said at the end, because it is very unlike her to be even a little bit superstitious – '

Charlotte had appeared in the doorway, a tray with coffee and cakes in her hands. 'What fantasies is Nina telling you?'

The girl grinned and finished her sentence. 'The painting was a witness, Charlotte said, the only one to see the change coming (or the Renaissance, the revolution, the tragedy – call it whatever you like), although each of them was given fair warning.'

In the end, Donna stayed to see the improvements Procopio had made in the café and to admire Charlotte's cake designs for this year's agricultural fair. She stayed for drinks and for dinner, during which simple yet lengthy meal she caught Procopio quite often looking at his wife with a little smile around the eyes as if he couldn't believe his luck – and when Charlotte looked back her whole face lit up.

So maybe he adds more watts to the chandelier than is immediately evident, thought Donna.

After Procopio went to bed ('Tomorrow we make a very laborious Sicilian pastry with many layers, so I have an early start!'), Donna stayed to hear Charlotte's story, which began on the crest of a hill overlooking the Villa Rosa, the spine of a decision. Before and after, either-or.

'What should I have done differently?' Charlotte asked. 'If I had not chosen the easy solution and turned away when the hunters vanished over that hill, could I have stopped or changed what happened? Would I be here now, with Francesco? Would Count Malaspino still be alive? Would Paolo . . .' She stopped. 'But I have been talking too much. What about you, Donna? Tell me about your career – is it going well?'

'Would Paolo what? Go on, Charlotte: what were you going to say?'

'It's just that . . .' Again she stopped, then finished, with a trace of her old shyness, 'He was so very much in love with you.'

The bitterness Donna had held inside for seven years pressed against her ribs, giving her a headache. 'Not so much in love that he came to see me in the hospital!' There, it was out.

Charlotte's eyes widened. 'But he did! We all did! Tried to. Your parents – your father – wouldn't let us see you, and the doctors backed him up. They said it wasn't in your best interests.'

'They let the police in fast enough.'

'There was no choice about that.'

Donna shook her head, denying Charlotte's excuses. She couldn't let herself hear them. The past seven years had been built on a powerful belief that Paolo had abandoned her when she needed him most, a pain she'd worried away at like a terrier with a snapping rat.

'And then he wrote to you,' Charlotte went on. 'We both did, but Paolo wrote letter after letter.'

'I never read them.' She thought she'd let them all down. 'I thought . . .'

'What?'

'You blamed me . . .'

'For what, Donna?'

'For betraying Muta . . . and then later you might have thought I was lying . . . to save my own skin . . . but the story I told the police . . . well, that's how I saw it. What I saw. At the time.'

'You only described one of your attackers to the police,' said Charlotte, reading Donna's mind, 'the man they later identified as Benny the Shooter, who killed Count Malaspino. *Was* he alone, Donna?'

'That was the man who hit me at San Rocco.'

'But there was someone else there with him, they think. Angelino, in his muddled way, indicated that he saw another figure at San Rocco. He called him the fallen angel.'

'I couldn't see. He was a long way from me. Watching. Not involved. He wouldn't hurt . . . He didn't . . . hurt me. He just . . . watched. He said nothing. And then, you see, I was falling too . . . the mules were coming . . . there was dust . . . How could I be sure what . . . ?' Donna felt Charlotte's hands take hold of hers. 'The . . . other man . . . just being there, he probably saved my life . . .'

'Angelino saved your life. He dug you out and then he and his mother took you to the hospital. Paolo had been looking for you since you missed your date with him. He was up all night, crazy with worry. He missed the trial because he was trying to find you.'

'I should . . . phone him . . . See him . . .'

'I think it's better if you . . .'

'What?'

'Don't.'

'Don't speak to him? See him?'

'He's happy now.'

Donna tried to stop her own hands from clenching into fists under the constraint of Charlotte's. This was more like the old Charlotte. Don't complain, don't make a fuss. 'With Flavia,' she said finally.

'They have two sons. Sweet boys. He has a busy job at the university, yet still finds time to help out both me and Professor Serafini.'

When Donna didn't respond, Charlotte added, 'You remember Serafini?'

After another long pause Donna said, 'Still, I don't blame Monsignor Seguita, although I did then, when I still believed in the omnipotence of priests. He probably wasn't told what . . . Benny? What Benny was planning. Monsignor Seguita probably had his reasons for . . . He probably stopped Benny from . . .'

'Seguita's brother was one of the leading figures in the Nerruzzi consortium, who had donated millions to the Vatican. The police suspect your Monsignor kept the secret of San Rocco for years.'

'Suspect?'

'He suffered a fatal heart attack, not long after Carlo Seguita was found hanging under the bridge.'

The full moon was shining a soft blue spotlight through the window onto Charlotte, revealing every fine line in her face like craquelure in porcelain. A kind face, thought Donna, a hard-won happiness. She noticed that behind Charlotte on the wall was a framed photoprint of Raphael's *La Muta*, strangely out of focus, a double exposure, perhaps. Charlotte must be able to obtain a better reproduction than this – why keep it? Perhaps the lack of focus was due to the moonlight. No, when Donna got up to examine the picture more closely, she saw that it looked as if the camera had moved just as the shutter went off. The photograph could have been taken in an earthquake, so blurred was the image, and all over its surface was a tracery of small dots.

'It's a copy made by Monsignor Seguita of an infra-red spectrogram he did of La Muta,' Charlotte explained. 'He sent it to me shortly before he died. The only explanation was a note on which he'd written, "Religion, particularly Catholicism, exists to offer certainties. Concede that priests are guilty of human sin and you risk destroying a greater cause." I suppose he thought I might like a record of . . . Well, since the Vatican impounded the painting, all we have of La Muta is that image, my sketches and the photos Paolo took of our work in progress.'

Donna touched the dots.

'Those dots are where the powdered charcoal markings from the original drawing have transferred onto the canvas,' said Charlotte. 'You can see how he changed the position of the hand and head.'

'It looks . . .'

'Like a portrait of two different women, yes.' The moon had slipped below the pantiled roof opposite. Charlotte, framed by the window, was now in deep shadow, two-dimensional. *Chiaroscuro*, Donna thought.

The silence and shadows stretched around them.

'Don't you worry, Charlotte? After Francesco proved how much he knew, how much he could reveal, didn't you worry that the men responsible for San Rocco might come back?'

'Come back? They never left! They're always here. We see them every time we go for a coffee in the Piazza Repubblica. But we never buy their brand of coffee or polenta or wine.'

Donna couldn't help smiling. 'Your own private embargo.' So typical of Charlotte.

Leaving Urbino early the next morning, Donna deliberately chose a less direct route, walking to her bus stop along the serene arcades of the Corso Garibaldi under the palace walls, where she had onced chased Muta's shadow. Reaching the entrance to the helicoidal ramp, she noticed that there was now the option of an automatic lift. Those wishing to avoid the effort of climbing could pay a tiny sum to ascend or descend. Donna, her mind still occupied with Charlotte's story from the night before, chose the ramp. She was alone except for the caretaker, the same glowering old man from seven years ago, who trailed closely behind her. Ignoring his muttered comments, she ran her hands over the words scratched into the surface of the narrow pink bricks, searching for a particular name. 'Some people tell you it has been there for years,' Charlotte had said, 'and some tell you it didn't appear until after the trial. The custodian complains that a vandal did it – carved it into the bricks, he doesn't know when. Whatever the truth of the matter, there the name is, about halfway down the ramp, three bricks from the bottom.'

Gabriella Balducci, 1932–

Having found it, Donna couldn't think what more there was to do, and she wound her way out of the city down the sweeping auricular steps of the ramp and into the sunshine, leaving her own story of Urbino to uncoil behind her with all the others. As she got on the bus she was thinking of what Nina had said last night: 'Three times a year Charlotte does the windows, that's all. Once for the Feast of Relics on the fourth Sunday in October, once for Christmas, once on Good Friday – but not for Christ, as you'd imagine. Charlotte insists it's for Raphael, to celebrate his birth and his death. Raphael, Urbino's most famous son, who died on Good Friday in 1520, precisely thirty-seven years *to the day* after he was born, and whose faith in humanity, so Charlotte claims, is the one sure miracle she can vouch for.'

ACKNOWLEDGEMENTS

To the people of Urbino and The Marches, my apologies for having invented the valley of San Rocco, along with various monuments that suited my fiction. The *Mani Pulite* 'Clean Hands' investigations are real, as are the Italian Committee for Investigation of Claims of the Paranormal, Raphael's house in Urbino and his painting *La Muta*, but there is no Professor Serafini and no hidden scar on Raphael's portrait, nor any scar on Urbino's reputation, although its walls were indeed mined by retreating Germans during World War II and its paintings stored for protection outside the city.

Special thanks to Stefania Ramelli and Renata Whurr for their advice on Italian legal procedure and selective mutism respectively, and to Renata for giving me two fine books on communication disorders, Clive Baldwin's *Selective Mutism in Children* and R. Lesser's *Linguistic Investigations of Aphasia*. Other useful books for me were: Iris Origo's magnificent diary of 1943–4, *War in Val d'Orcia*, Dino Tiberi's *Le Marche, I Proverbi e le Stagioni*, Richard Lamb's *War in Italy 1943–1945*, Paul Ginsborg's *A History of Contemporary Italy*, and Patrick McCarthy's *The Crisis of the Italian State* and *Italy and its Discontents*.